The Mo

Pra

'The writing is subtle, poignant and tremendously skilful. She brings great tenderness and insight to bear on a story of surviving the pain of everyday life. And within that context, she is not afraid to take on big themes: life, love, death, illness and the inescapable influence of families. Her characters are complex and thoughtful, especially self-deluding Adrian and Irene, who is not 'poor Irene' at all when she discovers her husband's deception but marvellously, shamingly furious. As in *Things We Knew Were True*, there is a 'secret ending', in this case a shocking revelation which throws not just certain scenes but the entire novel into a tragic new light. It sent me back to the beginning, trying, like Irene, to make sense of the past, rereading conversations which were already highly emotionally charged but which take on a heartbreaking new meaning when you know at last quite how much she has lost.' *Observer*

'I have never before read an example of this genre that so accurately portrays the disintegration and ultimate death of self caused by the discovery that all your past existence was a lie and the future you were moving towards is no longer possible.' *Guardian*

'Truthful and wise . . . this is a fine anti-romance.' *Daily Mail*

'In this unpretentious and page-turning account of a marital breakdown, Gerrard writes tenderly about marriage, children and the comforts of domesticity. Transformation is the reward of every good heroine, and Gerrard sorts out Irene's mess much better than any marriage counsellor.' *Independent*

'Acutely observed, this is modern relationship territory with a twist.' *Elle*

'Insightfully and beautifully written.' *Eve*

'Nicci Gerrard writes of ordinary people and gets under their skins – and she'll get under yours too. *Solace* is about more than just motherhood and

marriage on the brink. It's a story about real love and its consequences.'
In Style

'An intoxicating, bittersweet breath of fresh air.' *Daily Record*

'A heartening story of a woman betrayed by her husband who slowly realizes she has her own passions and dreams to follow.' *Good Housekeeping*

Praise for *Things We Knew Were True*:

'A very clever book ... about female desire ... a book with a secret ending.' *Sunday Telegraph*

'Beguiling, poignant, wonderful.' *Sunday Express*

'... A quietly impressive novel that isn't afraid to take on big themes of life, love and the inescapable influences of families.' *Guardian*

'A skilfully observed book about grief, sibling relations and first love.' *Company*

'Gerrard brings tenderness and insight to a story of surviving everyday life.' *Harpers and Queen*

'Love and married life are explored with candour and affection ... Gerrard proves she is a skilled observer.' *Daily Mail*

'A thoughtful tale of love, sibling rivalry and family secrets.' *Vogue*

'Well observed, touching, thoughtful, sensitive ... sure to strike a chord.' *Eve*

'Such beguiling candour and clarity ... poignant and all too true to life.' Helen Dunmore

'In Nicci Gerrard's novel *Things We Knew Were True*, the past is not a sunshine destination, but a treacherous place freighted with emotional danger and damage ... [It] describes the way time erodes even the most precious of memories.' *Observer*

'This tale about middle-aged angst is quietly compelling.' *Daily Mirror*

'A moving and perceptive insight into deception and renewal.' *Sunday Mirror*

'Poignant and true to life.' *Daily Express*

The Moment You Were Gone

NICCI GERRARD

PENGUIN BOOKS

PENGUIN BOOKS

Published by the Penguin Group
Penguin Books Ltd, 80 Strand, London WC2R ORL, England ·
Penguin Group (USA) Inc., 375 Hudson Street, New York, New York 10014, USA
Penguin Group (Canada), 90 Eglinton Avenue East, Suite 700, Toronto, Ontario, Canada M4P 2Y3
(a division of Pearson Penguin Canada Inc.)
Penguin Ireland, 25 St Stephen's Green, Dublin 2, Ireland
(a division of Penguin Books Ltd)
Penguin Group (Australia), 250 Camberwell Road, Camberwell, Victoria 3124, Australia
(a division of Pearson Australia Group Pty Ltd)
Penguin Books India Pvt Ltd, 11 Community Centre, Panchsheel Park, New Delhi – 110 017, India
Penguin Group (NZ), 67 Apollo Drive, Rosedale, North Shore 0632, New Zealand
(a division of Pearson New Zealand Ltd)
Penguin Books (South Africa) (Pty) Ltd, 24 Sturdee Avenue, Rosebank, Johannesburg 2196, South Africa

Penguin Books Ltd, Registered Offices: 80 Strand, London WC2R ORL, England

www.penguin.com

First published 2007

6

'First Day of My Life', Lyrics by Conor Oberst, © Bedrooms, Bedrooms and
Spiders/Sony/ATV Songs LLC. All rights reserved

'You're Just in Love', Words & Music by Irving Berlin, © 1950 Irving Berlin Music Corp.
All rights administered by Warner/Chappell Music Ltd, London W6 8BS. Reproduced by permission.

Set in 12.5/14.75 pt Monotype Garamond
Typeset by Rowland Phototypesetting Ltd, Bury St Edmunds, Suffolk
Printed in England by Clays Ltd, St Ives plc

ISBN: 978–0–141–02406–6

To my parents

Prologue

Someone, somewhere, was calling her name, but Gaby could not move. Not up, into the thinning branches that were straining and creaking in the wind; not down, to the far-off safety of the unattainable ground. She could only stay exactly where she now was, hugging the trunk of the beech tree, her cheek pressed against its rough bark. Her left hand was stretched above her body, gripping a stump; her right hand was twisted awkwardly into a small hollow and her wrist throbbed with the pressure. She was quite sure that if she took away either hand, she would fall; she could already imagine her body crashing through the twigs and leaves on to the hard earth beneath. She shifted her weight fractionally and felt the branch on which she stood move. It was going to break under her weight, she thought. Or her hand, sweaty with fear, was going to slide off.

Gaby looked up. Through the leaves, which were still sticky with newness and rippled queasily in the sunlight, she saw the blue slab of the sky. White clouds hurtled past. The tree was tipping towards her. She pressed herself closer against the trunk, feeling she must fall backwards at any minute.

She looked down, at where she had come from. Her heart gave a wild lurch. The branches were like hundreds of quivering veins; the leaves, ruffled by the wind, were in continuous green motion. Beneath them she could see ground, which no longer seemed solid, but churned uneasily like a sluggish brown river. A tiny whimper escaped her. Her heart chugged in her chest; her breath rasped painfully; her calves burnt, her palms stung and her wrist ached. A little trickle of blood ran down her cheek, irritating as a fly that she couldn't swat. She put out her tongue and caught its ferrous taste on the tip. Soon, she thought, she would let go because she couldn't wait any longer to fall. She might as well get it over with.

'Gaby – you mustn't look down,' said a voice.

'I'm stuck.'

'There's a branch just under where you're standing. If you move your left foot down and a bit to the left you'll feel it. It's quite thick.'

'I can't.'

'Course you can. It's not hard, really.'

Gaby lowered her foot gingerly, feeling about with her toes. Her throat was thick with fear; her mouth was chalky.

'A bit more down, just a witchy bit. There. Now your right hand. There's a branch by your waist.'

'But I can't let go.'

'Well, you have to let go some time, don't you? You can't just stay there. Shall I get help?'

'No! Don't leave me.'

'OK, then. Just move your hand a little bit. There – that was OK, wasn't it? So now you can move your left hand down. That's it. And then your other foot.'

As Gaby stepped on to the lower branch, she felt a hand close round her ankle, just above her trainers. It was dry and warm, and it made her feel slightly safer.

'See? I'm standing on the big fork so you're just about there.'

'How far?'

'One more big step, but I think you can reach it OK. You'll have to move your right hand down again, but there's a branch in front of you.'

Gaby stretched her right foot down and lowered herself after it. Her left knee was almost under her chin and her arms quivered from the effort of hanging from the branches. She looked down and saw a face peering up at her through the kaleidoscope of leaves, the firm jaw and turquoise eyes. A hand stretched up towards her.

'Take my hand,' her friend said. 'And jump.'

Gaby jumped. Her feet hit the wooden platform of the tree-house and she stumbled, then collapsed in a heap beside Nancy. Her legs were trembling badly so she wrapped her arms round them and put her chin on her knees. She waited for her heart to stop thudding and the world to stop tipping. Above her the leaves rustled in the breeze and the sun shone down from a calm blue sky.

Nancy, looking at her, saw that her cheeks were stained with blood, mud, moss and tears and her lower lip was still wobbling. She rummaged in their knapsack, taking longer than she needed to pull out a paper napkin.

'Your face is all mucky.'

'Thanks,' said Gaby, gruffly. She was grateful for her friend's tactful silence, the way she wasn't fussing about it, which would have made her feel even more stupid and undignified than she already did. She dabbed at the graze on her cheek. 'Is that all right?'

'There's some here.' Nancy touched her own face to show her. 'And here. Shall I do it for you?'

'OK, then.'

Nancy moistened the paper napkin with the tip of her tongue, in a curiously motherly gesture, and wiped Gaby's face gently, frowning in concentration. 'There. All gone.'

They sat in silence for a bit, Gaby leaning her back against the tree-trunk. If she craned her neck, she could see the kitchen window and her mother standing at the sink, probably washing dishes and listening to the radio. She closed her eyes and listened to the birdsong and the whispering of the breeze, which no longer sounded threatening but merry.

They had built this tree-house two years ago, shortly after they had met and become friends. Gaby's brothers, Antony, Max and Stefan, had helped them with the structure, but they had painted it themselves. It was getting shabby now: birds' mess spattered the boards and some of the slats had come loose. The bell that they had hung there had disappeared, and all that was left was a piece of frayed rope. That first summer, they had made a table out of two planks balanced on bricks, and had rigged up a screen so that they could hide from the rest of the world. Almost every day they had clambered up Stefan's rope-ladder, to spend hours talking, reading, eating the picnic they had prepared in Gaby's kitchen.

Now they came up here less. After all, Nancy was thirteen and Gaby nearly so. Their bodies were rounding out; they had shallow breasts, hair between their legs and under their arms, adolescent spots under their skin. Nancy had started having periods. They looked at boys in a

4

different way, and at their own reflections in the mirror with a new seriousness and anxiety. They painted their nails and experimented with makeup and hair styles – though Nancy's hair was too short to do much with, and Gaby's was so long and curly and full of impossible knots that she would howl as Nancy forced a comb through it, tears springing to her eyes. They were both half conscious that their childhood was ending, and when they came up to their tree-house they did so in a spirit of sentimental nostalgia for the flat-chested, spindly-limbed girls they had been when they first knew each other.

'I was scared,' Gaby said, once her heart was calm and her limbs had stopped trembling.

'I told you not to go that high.'

'Well, you were right. I knew you were right, anyway, before I did it. I just had to.'

'Why?'

'Oh,' said Gaby, vaguely, 'I don't know. As soon as I thought of it I knew I was going to do it, even though I didn't want to. It was like a kind of – bubble in my chest.'

'Like one of your dares?'

'Yeah. So I can't say no. Don't you ever get that feeling?'

'No.'

'Never?'

'Never. I don't want to get hurt.'

'Nor do I,' said Gaby.

'And I don't like to be noticed.'

'Oh!' said Gaby, wincing. 'You think I show off.'

'I *know* you show off. But only in a nice way,' Nancy

added hastily, seeing Gaby's expression. 'Not to make yourself look good or important. It's like an actor or something, playing different parts.'

'But I don't need to play parts with you.'

'No.'

'Maybe you saved my life today.'

'Don't be daft. If you'd been really stuck I could have called your mum.'

'I was really stuck. I couldn't move an inch. I thought the tree was falling on top of me.'

'What sandwich do you want? Mashed banana or peanut butter. They look rather like each other. Beige.'

'Banana.'

'Here.'

They sat and ate their sandwiches in silence. The sun rose higher in the sky, filtering through the leaves; it laid its dappled patterns round them and warmed their faces and the napes of their necks. Nancy removed her jersey and folded it into a cushion for her back; Gaby undid the laces of her trainers and pulled them off, wriggling her toes. She looked across at her friend. Nancy sat cross-legged and straight-backed. She was slim and neat and clean. Her hair was brushed back behind her ears, which were newly pierced and still slightly red and swollen. On her thirteenth birthday, Gaby had passed a rather large needle through a flame to sterilize it, then plunged the blackened point through the fleshy tissue of both Nancy's ear-lobes and into half a raw potato pressed against the other side. The ears had become badly infected, and the holes were visibly asymmetrical, an odd effect in the impeccable evenness of Nancy's face. Beside her, Gaby felt grubby: her jeans were ripped; the heels of both socks were bald; there was dirt under her nails and grit on her neck. Her hair fell into her eyes. Her clothes scratched her. She sighed and looked up into the boughs of the tree, letting herself remember how it had felt to be up there, knowing that she must fall.

'I wonder which one of us will die first,' she said dreamily.

'Die!'

'It'll probably be me, falling out of a tree or something.'

'No, you've got nine lives.'

'I'd like to be put in a burning boat, like the Vikings were, and I'd float out to sea all in flames.'

'I want to be buried in a cardboard box, vertical. I read about it in a book. That way I get eaten up by bugs quicker.'

'That's disgusting!'

'It's not. It's only Nature's way. Everyone gets eaten in the end.'

'Not if they're burnt on a boat, they don't.'

'You'll get married first, anyway.'

'Will I?'

'Yeah – anyway, I'm not going to get married at all. I'm going to live by myself with a cat for company and do whatever I want.'

'Can't I live with you?'

'You can until you get married.'

'Don't you want children?'

'I don't know. Mum always says children are too hard – all pain and no gain, she says.'

'She only had you.'

'Right.'

Gaby stared at her for a moment, then looked away. 'I want children,' she said determinedly, 'four, and if I can choose – which of course I know I can't so don't make that face at me as if I'm a baby who doesn't know the facts of life – two boys, called Oliver and Jack, and two girls called Rosie and Poppy. And a cat and a dog and hens and a hamster.'

'You don't want hamsters when you're grown-up!'

'Why not?'

'You just don't.'

'Oh,' said Gaby, nonplussed. She squinted up into the sunlight. 'Sometimes I don't want to grow up. It's too complicated, too messy. I want to stay right where we are now. In this tree-house eating banana sandwiches and making plans but not having to do anything about them.'

'Mmm,' murmured Nancy. She yawned, and Gaby saw her tonsils quivering at the back of her pink mouth.

'You don't know what's going to happen to you when you grow up. It's a strange feeling. Everything ahead seems in a kind of blur.'

'Have a chocolate Bourbon.'

'I know one thing, though – we'll always be friends, won't we?'

'Yes, of course we will.'

'Until we're ninety.'

'If we're still alive.'

'Shall we make a promise?'

'What? To be alive?'

'To be friends until we die.'

'OK.' Nancy let herself become solemn, to match her

friend's mood, though she remained slightly awkward and self-conscious. 'I promise we'll be friends until we die.' She paused. 'So help me God,' she added, for extra weight.

'You said you didn't believe in God!'

'I don't. It just sounded better.'

'Not to me. Not when I know you don't mean it.'

'I do mean it – about being friends, at least. Anyway, it's your turn now.'

'Right.' Gaby reached out and took Nancy's hands in hers. She saw that her friend's nails were bitten and there were rings of eczema round both wrists. For some reason the sight made her feel sad and grown-up. She looked into Nancy's pale turquoise eyes. 'I faithfully promise to be your friend,' she said, with a shy intensity. Suddenly there were tears in her eyes again and her heart was pounding against her ribs. 'And nothing and nobody will get in the way. Not ever. Now give me that chocolate Bourbon before it melts.'

One

'How did we meet?' asked Gaby, smiling into the young face in front of her. 'Ah, well, it was all a bit dramatic. We met by an accident.'

'By accident?'

'By *an* accident. I remember it as clearly as if it happened yesterday.'

Every couple has the story of how they met: they tell it to each other and then they repeat it, with improvised additions and interruptions, to family and friends. Their own story was wild, vivid, streaked through with someone else's tragedy, and when they told it they would look across at each other and remember the sunken lane and the dark velvet of the night and they would seem to each other and themselves like figures in a Gothic painting. For they did not meet at school or college, or in an office or at a party; not through a friend, an evening class or a dating agency; not on a train or a plane or a beach; not even eyes meeting, breath thickening and the world slowing. They met because of a car crash. Their worlds were entirely separate and would have remained so had it not been for three drunk students driving an old and uninsured Rover too fast round a sharp corner and into the ancient horse-chestnut tree, whose massive trunk was barely marked. The car crumpled on impact like cardboard, folding up on itself in a screech of tearing metal and shattering glass, and someone's short cry that sounded from a distance like an owl's shriek. Three people's stories ended that night – the two passengers' almost at once, under the boughs of the tree, and the driver's on the way to hospital, calling for his mates – and their story began.

Over the years, Gaby had lost track of the difference between their two accounts. Connor's memories of their meeting came to seem like her own; her memories belonged to him too. It was an uncanny sensation, like a bright and feverish dream in which she saw herself through Connor's eyes, and felt Connor's emotions inside her skull. Was this love, she would wonder, when you cannot separate the self from the other? The thought scared her, for she wasn't sure that she should let herself disappear like that, be so dissolved by intimacy. She sometimes wanted her distinct story back, the one with clear lines and a single point of view. She needed edges or she felt she might fall apart. The night they met, Connor had found her and she – euphorically, unequivocally – had lost herself. As she listened to him tell their story, she felt herself plummet into the past and a kind of vertigo overwhelm her. Was this how it had happened?

Connor was driving back to Oxford from a visit to his parents, just outside Birmingham. His father, a machine operator and a lifetime smoker, had been diagnosed with lung cancer. His mother, who had always felt that life had let her down, had taken to drinking in the daytime with the ferocity she applied to cleaning the house, banging on the rugs with a broom to scatter dust in the backyard. Connor had been thinking about his parents as he drove: his father had been surprisingly cheery about the diagnosis, almost sprightly, with a malicious gleam in his eye as he took his regular swipes at Connor's politics and his convict's blunt-scissored haircut, while his mother seemed more wretchedly fleshless than ever and her eyes had turned a marbled yellow. He could still feel her fingers on his upper arms where she'd gripped him when they'd said goodbye. Although she was only fifty, she had seemed to him like a leering witch out of a fairy-tale, dragging him back into the stifling, dimly lit hovel of his childhood. 'Come again soon,' she'd hissed, cheap red wine and brandy on her breath, and he'd had to make an enormous effort not to pull away in revulsion.

As he drove, he tried not to think too deeply but, rather, to let fragments and images drift in loose formations across his sore mind. The book he'd been reading about tropical medicine. The words of a song, what was it?, lying in a burnt-out basement, something-something, hoping for – hoping for what? He couldn't remember; the words flickered across the corner of his memory and, as he tried to catch hold of them, out of sight. The meal he'd had with his parents, shepherd's pie with tepid potato forked into crests and tinned carrots. His body felt itchy and unclean, his limbs heavy with all the driving. He would go on a run tomorrow morning, before he went to the hospital – he would get up at six thirty, before it was properly light, and run along the canal as the sun rose in the sky. He glanced at the clock on the dashboard and saw that it was past midnight; only a few miles to go

13

and already there was the faint orange luminescence of the city on the skyline. He'd never been in absolute darkness, and perhaps it would scare him but he thought he would like it. He found darkness quite welcoming; it was harsh light he disliked. Bare lightbulbs; deserts; wastes of dazzling snow.

Sally would probably have gone to bed by now; he pictured her dark hair spread across the pillow and her calm face. Outside his room there was mess, noise, the chaos of a shared household, but inside it was neat. Things were in their proper place. The cupboard doors were shut and his textbooks were stacked on the table where he worked. Sally often stayed over but she was careful not to disturb the order. There would be a tumbler of water on the table beside her, a dial of pills and probably a novel or a medical textbook, its bookmark in place. Her clothes would be folded neatly on the chair by the door. She wore a tiny enigmatic smile while sleeping, but occasionally she opened her eyes so that only the whites would show, and Connor, unnerved, would lightly press his thumbs on the lids to close them again, feeling like an undertaker with a corpse.

He was finding it hard to stay awake although his journey was nearly over and he only had to last another twenty minutes or so. He knew that he should get out of the car for a few minutes, yet he continued sluggishly to drive. The heating wasn't working properly, so the air that blew out of the right vent was icy, while the one on the left was too warm. His eyelids were heavy and the road wavered in the glare of his headlights. He strained his pebble-eyes wider and stretched his face in an exaggerated, rubbery grimace, trying to focus. He sat up stiff and straight, then took the last square of milk chocolate that was lying in its wrapper on the seat beside him and sucked it slowly, to make it last. Sweetness dribbled down his throat; for a brief moment he felt alert and the road lay blessedly clear before him. But how strange, when you know that to sleep is to die, that it can be so impossible to stay awake. He chewed his lip, then pinched his cheek for a second, hard enough to cause him pain. He tightened his grip on the steering-wheel. If the radio worked, he could find a station, sing along loudly, but all he could get was an unpleasant hissing crackle, with occasional isolated words bursting through the static. He opened his windows to the sharp slap of autumn air and, although he had sworn to himself he would give up smoking, pressed in the car lighter. When it sprang out again, he lit a cigarette. Its tip glowed red as he sucked on it and his lungs ached. He thought of his father's scorched lungs, he thought about dying, and still sleep pressed down on him. Somewhere ahead he thought he heard a sound, a thunderclap or the shot of a gun, even, then the shriek of an owl. He rubbed his eyes feverishly as the road lurched and trees tipped giddily towards him.

A figure burst out of the hedgerow and plunged towards his car. At first – even as he pressed his foot on the brake and swerved violently, tyres screaming, and a toxic burst of adrenaline – he thought it was a shadow, a trick of the darkness and of his fatigue. He couldn't even tell which direction it was coming from; perhaps it was a large bird flying close overhead. But then the figure resolved itself. He saw that it was shouting, waving its arms as it wove in front of the car, into and out of the glare of his headlights. He saw, then lost again, a white patch of face with a darkly open mouth and holes where eyes must be, a flying stream of hair, a long skirt knotted up.

'What the fuck?'

Fists pounded on his window. He pulled on the handbrake and pushed the door open. She half fell in on him, in a yabber of incomprehensible sounds. He caught the smell of tobacco and perfume, a clatter of beads round her neck.

'Oh-God-help-a-car-bodies-help-I-think-they're-dead-so-young-ambulance-Jesus . . .'

'Slow down,' he said sharply, fully awake now. 'Tell me what you know.'

'Car crash,' she said, making a visible effort. 'Just round the corner. They ploughed into a tree. I don't know if anyone's alive. The car's all – it's mashed up, and I looked in but, oh, Jesus Christ . . .' and she came to a juddering halt.

Gaby herself could not remember what she had said to him. She could not even remember speaking; nor did she have any idea then of whom she was speaking to – man or woman, young or old. All she knew was that she was leaning into a car that smelt of leather, smoke and chocolate, while behind her lay blood and carnage.

'Let me see.' Connor was out of the car, his legs steady under him; his heartbeat was regular. He felt strangely calm and his voice was authoritative. But everything was happening at a distance. Even as he spoke and acted he was conscious of the figure he cut, the doctor taking charge in a crisis. He felt simultaneously noble yet absurd, a fraud. But the woman in front of him seemed to believe him. She visibly calmed as he spoke.

Had she? She didn't remember that, either. But it was true that the man who stood before her possessed an air of authority and she had immediately trusted him to take over. She was no longer alone in the wild night with dead people.

'Show me,' he said firmly.

'No! Listen! You've got to go to someone's house and call an ambulance. I've only got a bike and I think the chain broke when I stopped.'

'I'm a doctor,' he said – one day he would be, anyway, and saying the words gave him authority, permission to take charge. 'You should go and call the emergency services, and I'll stay and see if there's anything I can do here. Can you drive?'

'Kind of,' she said. 'I mean – yes. Yes!'

'Take my car, then. Turn round here. There's a group of houses about three or four miles away.'

'Try to save them.' She flung herself into the driver's seat, pulling the door shut on her striped skirt so it fluttered against the sill in a frippery of colour, and reversed up against the bank in a spray of mud. Shot forward, narrowly missing the ditch; wrenched the wheel round again. The engine roared and the wheels spun into a rut, then took hold. The car bucked. She was leaning right forward in the seat, her face almost above the steering-wheel. Connor saw it, her glittering eyes, her Medusa hair, and felt a twinge of alarm. She was driving the car as if she was trying to break in an unruly stallion: one would win and the other lose. Then he turned his back on her and ran along the road the way she had come.

Now that he was alone, the confidence leaked rapidly away. He dreaded what he would see when he rounded the corner, and he had no idea what he would do.

'So you were scared too?' Gaby had said, when they first rehearsed their story, picking out details, remembering things that might or might not be true, but that over time became real in their minds. 'Yes, I was scared,' he replied. 'Terrified.'

In the event, there was little he could do. It was at the darkest time of night and only the light from the half-moon, low in the sky, and the few pinprick stars lit the scene that lay in front of him. He stopped and drew a deep breath, feeling sweat clammy on his forehead. The car, wrapped round the tree, was barely recognizable. Its entire front was crushed in on itself, and it was impossible to believe that someone might be alive in there. He had to check, though: he couldn't just stand and look on like a useless spectator. He forced himself forward a few steps, peering at the wreckage through squinting, unwilling eyes. He could see a hand dangling limply out of the back window like a motionless wave for help, but otherwise he could not make out anything. The car had closed up on its occupants like a tin can stamped on by a hobnail boot.

'Hello,' he said, as he reached it. He was glad to hear his voice come out firm and calm. 'Can anyone hear me in there? The ambulance is on its way. Soon, very soon.'

The silence all around him was thick, terrible, and he held his own breath so as not to break it. Nothing.

Just the rustle and scrape of a leaf as it fell from the tree above him.

'I'm here to help,' he said, and tried to wrench open the dented back door. It didn't budge. He picked up the dangling hand and felt for a pulse while trying to make out the body it was attached to, somewhere inside the carnage of the car. He could smell blood, metallic and sweet, and shit: it caught in his nostrils. Was this the smell of death? He'd cut up corpses in his first year, but they'd reeked of formaldehyde. Pickled and discoloured, they'd barely resembled people.

'Hold on,' he whispered uselessly. No pulse throbbed under his thumb. He laid the hand back and pushed his head into the car, trying to avoid the jagged spikes of glass that still crusted the window frame. He pushed his hand in, feeling for a body. He touched a shoulder in a denim jacket, an ear, then soft, tufty hair that he imagined as brown although, of course, he couldn't know; jerked back instinctively as his fingers found the face, slick with blood. He leant into the darkness, listening for a breath, a moan. Nothing. Squinting, he tried to make out the shapes heaped and tangled there and saw the paleness of flesh. He forced himself further in and touched an arm but it was quite cold and rubbery. How quickly a body loses its warmth, he thought. He could hear his uneven breath; only his breath, no one else's.

Then he heard a sound, so tiny that it might have been the faint creak of a branch. It was coming from outside the car, and he struggled upright and listened intently. There it was again, just ahead of him, beyond the remnants of the bonnet. If only he had a torch. He scrabbled in the pocket of his coat and fished out his lighter, flicked it on and held it at arm's length. Its blue light wavered and, for an instant, he saw a face pressed against the car's splintered front window, its open eyes glassily upon him. He looked away.

'Where are you?' he called softly, walking forward.

The young man was lying up the bank, a few yards from the tree. His leg was twisted at an impossible angle, and his torso was dark with blood. But he was alive. Connor could hear the faint shuddering gasps he made. He let his lighter go out and squatted down beside him, in the damp grass and among the nettles, putting a hand on his forehead. 'An ambulance will be here soon,' he said. 'Just hold on.'

He didn't know what to do next. The young man – hardly more than a boy, he could see now – was breathing. He didn't need mouth-to-mouth resuscitation or cardiac stimulation. Connor took off his coat and rolled it into a pillow, which he eased under the youth's head, noticing how thick and dark his hair was and how he had a plaster on his jaw where presumably he'd cut himself shaving. The plaster seemed horribly sad to Connor. His shirt was sodden with blood.

'My mates?'

'Don't worry about that now.'

'Gary? Dan?'

'Hold on.'

'Don't leave me here in the dark.'

'I'm not going to. I'll be with you until the ambulance arrives.'

Now he could hear the high whine of a car being

driven fast, in too low a gear, then a sudden screech of brakes and a thump. He didn't move, but leant over the body in front of him.

'Where are you?' he heard her call, but didn't reply. He didn't want to shout or make a loud noise.

Then she slid beside him, and as she did so the moon rose above the trees, illuminating the scene in its ghostly light.

'It'll be here any minute,' she whispered. As if it were the most natural thing in the world, she leant forward and kissed the young man on his forehead, then wriggled out of her own coat – a Regency-style frock-coat, ripped at the armpit – and laid it over him. She picked up his hand in both of hers and held it firmly. The necklace she wore swung above his head like a metronome; her hair fell round him.

Oh, but she did remember that. The face that stared up at her, pale in the moonlight with huge, terrified eyes, as though she alone could rescue him. She remembered how he smelt, fear giving off its own dank and lonely odour, and how clammy, icily sticky his skin was to her touch. She had been filled with such agonizing tenderness for him, as if she was his mother, his sister, his lover, his friend all in one, and at that moment she would have done anything to save him.

'I'm Gaby,' she said, not to Connor but to the figure lying on the bank, his eyes gradually closing. 'You're going to be all right now. They're on their way.'

'Keep your eyes open,' Connor said insistently, less because of what he'd learnt as a medic than from seeing films where the cop bends over his fatally wounded buddy and urges him to stay awake a little longer. The phrase 'bleeding out' came into his mind.

'My fault,' whimpered the youth.

'No,' said Gaby. 'No, it's not your fault. Don't think that.' She wiped his forehead with the hem of her skirt, which Connor could see was made of some thin, shimmering material, but was now streaked heavily with oil and blood.

A bubble of blood escaped from the young man's mouth and Connor took the tissue from his pocket and dabbed it away. The man jerked and Connor laid a hand on his shoulder. 'Lie still,' he said.

'Hold on,' said Gaby. 'Please hold on, sweetheart. Please.'

Together they leant over the dying man, speaking to him in turn, telling him he was going to be all right, assuring him they were with him. Nonsense words in the dark. Connor felt intensely moved by the intimacy of the scene, and at the same time oddly tranquil, although he knew that the young man was dying in front of them and behind them two more people lay dead. Then the sound of a siren cut through the silence and blue lights came round the bend. All was now bustle and purpose. Several vehicles lined the road. Orders were shouted urgently. Bright lights shone on the scene, lighting it up as if it were a film set, and figures carrying stretchers ran forward.

'Stand back, please,' a man said, and Gaby and Connor got to their feet and watched as the injured man was slid on to a stretcher and taken away. For a moment, they said nothing.

Then Gaby, asked, 'Will he be all right?'

'I don't know. Perhaps.' Connor looked at her carefully in the gloom. Her pale face glimmered and her eyes were enormous. 'Are you all right, though?'

'Me?'

'You did beautifully.' Connor bent down and retrieved his coat from the ground. It didn't seem right to put it back on, though the night was cold. He glanced across at Gaby. She had on slouchy boots under her long skirt, but only a black camisole top. 'You must be freezing,' he said.

'I suppose I am.' She sounded dazed.

'Do you want to have my coat?'

'No!' She wrapped her arms round herself and shivered violently. 'In the car, those bodies,' she said, then stopped. 'Well, I've never seen a dead person before.'

'Nor have I – not like that, anyway. I've only seen corpses.' He was going to say that it was like seeing chicken breasts shrink-wrapped in a supermarket, then coming across a slaughtered bird hanging by its legs in a butcher's shop, but stopped himself. It would have sounded heartless.

'But I thought you were a doctor?'

'I'm not really a doctor. I'm only a medical student.'

'You acted like a doctor,' she said.

'I didn't do anything.'

Two men wearing yellow jackets and helmets, carrying giant metal cutters, came towards the car.

'I don't want to watch this,' she said.

'No,' said Connor, although he couldn't look away. 'We should probably go. We can't do anything here.'

'Don't we have to give our names to the police or something?'

'Probably,' he said. 'I don't know what the procedure is. But you're right. We should wait a bit, I guess. Do you want a cigarette?'

'Yes,' she said. 'But first I want to be hugged.'

So he put his arms round her and she laid her head on his shoulder. Her hair tickled his cheek and he felt her full, soft breasts squash against him. His T-shirt was damp and he understood that she must be crying, and then he realized that he was too. Tears trickled down his cheek and into his mouth and he made no effort to wipe them away. He couldn't remember the last time he had wept, and he didn't know why he was weeping now.

Gaby felt his thin body pressed against her, his strong arms holding her, the scrape of his stubble on her cheeks. She felt his tears; a stranger sobbing in her arms while she sobbed in his. Perhaps it was then that something untied in her; she was falling and knew there was no stopping herself now; she didn't want to stop herself and she didn't want to step out of the circle of his embrace into the cold night where three young men had just been snuffed out. They should stay like this, holding each other, and never let go.

'I was at a party kind of thing,' said Gaby, into Connor's shoulder, her voice muffled. 'I didn't really want to go – I was a bit tired and behind with work and besides, I knew that this boy would be there who I didn't want to meet. But, actually, it didn't really matter as much as I thought it would. I suddenly realized I didn't care about him after all, and it was like a weight being lifted off me. The party was fun. There were some nice people there. This weird guy was doing magic tricks in the kitchen. He kept pulling aces off the top of the pack. I couldn't work out how he did it. I keep thinking I should learn to do tricks like that, but I never do. And I danced. I love dancing. Don't you?'

Her fingers found the tears on his cheek and wiped them away as she spoke. 'Anyway, when I was biking back, I was feeling happy. It was dark, and there was a moon, and I was all on my own, between two places, just freewheeling down the hill with the wind and the trees and nothing else, and I felt that everything was OK. Then I saw that car. That's how quickly everything can end. It sounds really stupid, a cliché, but they've just stopped. That's it. They were driving along and probably talking and laughing, not paying attention, then everything was over for them. All their plans. Wiped out. It's hard to believe. And, one by one, their parents and friends and lovers will find out and everything will be changed for them. Maybe right now there's a phone ringing in a bedroom. They'll jerk awake, and when they see that it's still the middle of the night, do you think they'll know at once that something's happened to their son? My mother always says that once you've got a child, you always carry them around in your head and worry when you don't know exactly where they are, even when they're fully grown-up. And we'll just go on our way. We don't know anything about them. Except I'm always going to remember this – I hope I do, anyway. It's almost like a responsibility, being the last witness.'

'Do you always talk so much?' He breathed in the softness of her hair, not wanting her to stop. Her words were like ribbons and scraps of silk that she was weaving round him, protecting him from what was happening beyond.

'Maybe it's the shock. Have they finished getting them out of the car yet?'

'Yes. They've taken them away.'

She gave a sigh, then stepped out of his arms. 'Let's have that cigarette.'

He shook two out of the packet and handed her one, then flicked the wheel of his lighter. In its flare, he saw her face differently – splotches of freckles, a full mouth, thick brows, a faint smudge of mascara beneath eyes that seemed almost black, a mole on her neck, sharp collarbone and the swell of her breasts.

And she saw him: sharp angles and planes, thin lips, exhausted eyes. 'I don't even know your name.'

'Connor.'

'Connor,' she said, and took a deep drag, the smoke curling round her head. 'What an odd way to meet.'

'Here he comes.'

A police officer was making his way towards them. As Gaby gave a statement to him, he watched her. Her name was Gabriella Graham and she was twenty years old, a student at the university. She lived at 22 Jerome Street with four other students. She lifted her arms as she talked, leant towards the officer, pointed, pushed her hair behind her ears impatiently. The car had overtaken her at speed and crashed into the tree shortly after. No one else had been involved. She knew that two of them – the two in the car – were called Gary and Dan because the third man had called for them while he lay on the bank, but she didn't know the name of the other. She thought –

she turned to Connor for confirmation – that he had probably been the driver because he'd claimed it was his fault, but she didn't know for sure.

'Would you like a lift back to the city?' the officer asked, when she'd finished. The ambulances were gone now; two men in luminous yellow coats were arranging cones round the wreckage.

'It's OK. I've got my car,' said Connor. 'I can drive us both.'

'If you're sure you're in a fit state.'

'My bike's here,' said Gaby. 'And about your car –'

'You can't ride home. We can shove it in the back somehow,' said Connor. 'Or just put it in the boot and leave it open. It's only a few miles.'

'It's up to you,' said the officer.

'I parked your car in a bit of a hurry,' said Gaby. She gave a nervous cough. 'Um, it might be a bit tricky to reverse out.'

'Where are the keys?'

'I think I left them in there. I can't remember, it's all a blur, but I haven't got them on me, so . . .'

'Let's go and see.'

'The thing is, I might have put them into my coat pocket, and I laid that over the top of him, remember, and it was still on top of him when they took him away, wasn't it? So your keys might be on the way to the hospital.'

'Right,' said Connor, watching the police car leave.

But he found he didn't mind. For once in his life he wasn't thinking about consequences, schedules, the controlled execution of careful plans. He didn't care what happened tomorrow, for the night had the quality of a dream, dislocated from the before-and-after, with its own internal logic. Indeed, he would have been almost disappointed to find that the keys were in the ignition, had it not been that the car was tilted at a steep angle, deep in the nettle-filled ditch.

'Sorry,' said Gaby. 'I was in a bit of a flap when I parked.'

'Parked?' He raised his eyebrows at her sardonically, feeling inexplicably cheerful all of a sudden. 'How did you ever pass your test?'

'Well, about that – when I said I could drive, I wasn't being completely honest. I mean, I *can* drive, but I haven't passed my test as such.'

'As such?'

'I've failed four times, so far.'

'Maybe you should have got a lift with the police officer after all.'

'Too late for that.'

'You'd better take your bike.'

'I want to help you.'

'Help?'

'You keep echoing me. It makes me nervous.'

'Nervous?'

She stared at his deadpan expression for a few seconds, then laughed. 'We'll just have to walk,' she said. 'I'll push my bike. It's only a few miles.'

'Probably about seven or something.'

'Two hours,' she said. 'I walk fast and I bet you do. You look the type.'

'What type is that?'

'Driven. Terse. You probably sleep about five hours every night, get up at dawn to row or run or swim before going off to work for ten hours with only a cup of black coffee to keep you going. Am I right?'

'Maybe.'

'Whereas I'm a slob. I need at least ten hours' sleep. I can sleep anywhere, any time. And I do. Once I went to sleep in the airport bus on the way to the plane, standing up.'

'Like a horse.'

'Did you know that horses' knees lock into position while they sleep?'

'I can't say I did.'

'I have a friend who's got a big car – well, it used to be a hearse. I don't know why he gets such a kick out of driving around in a hearse – he thinks it's *ironic*, though I don't get the irony myself. Anyway I'm sure he can come out and tow you out of the ditch tomorrow.'

'I can do it,' he said. Connor felt clumsy, anxious, inarticulate, older than her. He thought he knew the kind of background she came from – middle class and probably a bit Bohemian; loving parents who had always given her lots of praise, several siblings, lots of grandparents and godparents and cousins; a big, untidy, ramshackle old house; noise, laughter. She was careless, expansive, uncensored, light-footed; she didn't mind spouting nonsense or fear that she was making a fool of herself. She'd always been herself, had never had to invent the woman she was to become. She belonged to a different world, one that had always been out of his reach, and he felt a spasm of familiar, sour resentment. But then it struck him that she was, through her kookiness, actually and deliberately taking care of him. She was trying to draw him out, and her words were like a trail she was scattering in her wake, hoping he'd want to follow. And he did want to; he did.

He wished that he could go on walking with her for the rest of the night, and deliberately slowed his pace. He pushed her bike, and when she shivered, he insisted on draping his coat round her shoulders, buttoning it up into a cape, carefully pushing her hair out of the way as he did so. He wanted her to feel safe with him, and he wished that she would stumble so that he could support her, or that she would cry again so that he could hold her in his arms to comfort her. There was a half-moon; there was corn stubble in the fields on either side of the hedges, and bales standing in massed shapes on the horizon. It was like a landscape in his mind and he knew he would remember it later. He matched his footsteps to hers, heard their joint rhythm pulsing behind their conversation, stored away her words. He knew he would bring them out when he was alone; that he would return to the image of her glowing face as it turned towards him. She said she had three brothers and she was the baby of the family. She mentioned someone called Stefan, but he ignored it. Stefan and Sally didn't belong to this night. He knew very well that his heightened feelings were caused by the particular circumstances – his father was dying, his mother was drinking, he was tired and had been working too hard, there had been a car crash. Gaby had come to him like a figure out of a dream. Like a dream, she would fade with morning and his old life would resume.

'What are you studying?' he asked, as they walked.

'Physics and philosophy.' His expression must have altered because she looked at him shrewdly. 'What? You thought I was doing, let's see – psychology. Or maybe English and art.'

'No!'

'Yes, you did. Scatty girl.'

'I didn't mean –'

'Never mind. Do you always pull on your ear-lobe like that?'

'Yes.'

'And you never talk much?'

'I don't know. Probably not.'

'Is that because you don't want to?'

'Well,' he said, then stopped.

'I mean, are there things you want to say but don't know how to, or do you want to keep your thoughts private inside yourself? Or maybe there are a select few people you confide in.'

'What I hate,' he said, 'is saying something that seems important and feeling that the person you're saying it to isn't really hearing it. Not hearing it the way you want it to be heard, if you see what I mean. That makes me feel – well, I hate it. I'd prefer to remain silent.'

'I see,' said Gaby. Then, after a pause: 'Listen, Connor, I lied to you – I'm not studying physics and philosophy, I only said that to impress you. English literature, after all.'

'You never needed to try to impress me,' said Connor. He felt intoxicated by sudden happiness.

'And the car swerved to avoid me,' said Gaby.

'You mean –'

'It swerved to avoid me. I was in the middle of the road, going down the hill. It swerved, skidded and went out of control round the bend. And I didn't even say that to the policeman.'

'Are you sure?'

'It's my fault.'

'It's not your fault,' said Connor. 'He was probably drunk, and –'

'Don't try to comfort me. I know. If it hadn't been for me on my bloody bike, they would still be alive.'

Connor didn't reply. He took one hand off the bike, reached out for Gaby's, and put it under his on the handlebar. He knew that she was crying again, although he didn't look at her but ahead, at the road that wound like a ribbon through the cornfields. They walked in time, and in silence. He could hear the thud as their feet slapped against the earth. At what they estimated to be the half-way point, they stopped to have another cigarette. They sat on the side of the road, their backs against a tree; Gaby drew her legs up under her and wrapped the coat more tightly round her against the cold. The tips of their cigarettes glowed.

'I told myself I wouldn't smoke again,' said Connor. 'My father's got lung cancer.' He had the sensation of being slightly drunk, although he hadn't touched a drop of alcohol, and painfully awake, though he had not slept for over twenty hours. His skin tingled and his throat ached.

Gaby turned towards him, tented by the coat, her face half hidden by her hair. She was barely more than a shape, splashed with moonlight. Connor forced himself to think of Sally, lying trustingly in his bed and waiting for him to come home. He'd ease himself in beside her and she'd open her arms and hug his chilly, tired body and murmur into his ear. He knew how lucky he was to be with Sally. He didn't deserve her. He was twisted and thorny and full of deceit; he didn't deserve anyone.

'That's where I was coming from,' he said. 'When I saw you.'

Gaby let her cigarette fall on to the ground and put the heel of her boot on to its red eye. Say nothing else, he told himself. Stand up and start walking. Now, before it's too late. But he didn't move.

'I thought I was dreaming you,' he said. 'Maybe I'm still dreaming you.'

He, too, let drop his cigarette, watched it glimmer and die. He could hear himself breathing raggedly as she sat motionless and half invisible beside him, and he imagined what must happen next: he would push his hand into the tangle of her hair and hold her face away from his, drown in the darkness of her eyes. For a moment they would stare blindly at each other, then he would pull her urgently towards him and they would kiss each other behind the protective curtain of her hair. Her arms would be round him, under the thin shirt, and his hands would be on her breasts. And then – he half shut his eyes . . . He put out a hand and with one finger traced the shape of her mouth. He felt her lips open and the pattern of her breathing changed. He touched her cheek, which was still damp from tears. 'Jesus,' he whispered, 'but you're lovely.'

A shaft of light fell on them, almost dazzling them. For an instant, Connor saw Gaby's face clearly in the headlights, like a hallucination. Then the car roared past, sending up a shower of grit, a horn blared twice, and it was gone, tail-lights disappearing round the bend.

Connor sat up straight and blinked.

'Wake-up call,' said Gaby, lightly brushing the grass and dirt from his back. He shivered at her touch but pulled away.

'Yes, sorry. We should go.'

'We don't need to, you know.'

'It's late.'

'It was always late.'

'I mean to say,' he replied, very formally, 'that I'm involved with someone.'

'Oh.'

'Gaby –'

'You're right. We should go.' She stood up in one easy, fluid movement and held out her hand, hauling him to his feet.

'Thanks.'

'Still miles to go before we sleep,' she said. 'It'll be dawn before we get there. Come on.'

He didn't come. Day after day, Gaby waited for him. She would wake each morning thinking, Perhaps it will be today. She would dress with care and stare anxiously at herself in the mirror, to see the face that he would see. She would pretend indifference, pretend not to start every time someone knocked at the door or the telephone rang. She would go out and steel herself not to look for him in

34

every face she passed. Gradually the certainty she had held wavered, became a dim hope, almost died. She tried to tell herself it didn't matter – who was he, after all? Just a stern young man who was going to be a doctor. But he'd wept in her arms and she could still feel his tears on her skin. And he'd looked at her so attentively, as if he recognized her; she had felt beautiful under his rapt gaze. He'd grazed his thumb along her lower lip, half closing his eyes, and told her she was lovely. And he'd nearly kissed her, so very nearly. Just one tantalizing second more – and how she wished now she could turn back the clock and be there again with nothing to stop them this time. She could see his serious face coming towards her, his lips parted, his eyes looking into hers, and she could feel the way she had melted, ready for him; the way she melted still, just thinking of him. In her dreams she drew him into her and wouldn't let him go.

Several times she made up her mind to track him down. Several times she stopped herself because she heard his voice in her head, telling her quite calmly that he was involved with another woman. There was nothing he could say that would change that.

In the end, Gaby phoned her friend Nancy, waking her in the early hours of the morning, to pour everything out. It sounded so paltry when she said it out loud, so insignificant; she was almost embarrassed to hear herself speak. Nothing had happened between them: they had witnessed a crash together, then walked home through the night; they had hardly touched, and had not-quite kissed; he had told her he was not free and he had left her at dawn without saying anything except 'Goodbye'.

So why did she feel so jittery, so sick with desire when she remembered him, so hollow and sad when he didn't call? Nancy listened without interrupting; Gaby could imagine her at the other end of the line, sitting up straight in bed in her stripy pyjamas, neat and calm even though it was the small hours and she'd just been woken up.

Gaby stopped talking. For a few seconds the silence buzzed between them.

'You've fallen in love,' said Nancy.

'I have,' said Gaby, half giggling but feeling the tears gather. 'Isn't it ridiculous? But it hurts so much that I don't know what to do with myself.'

'There's probably nothing, really,' said Nancy. 'No way round except through.'

'I do wish you weren't so far away,' said Gaby. 'You're the only one I could possibly say this to without feeling an utter fool, and you don't try to cheer me up by saying things like "Time heals everything."'

'Which it kind of does.'

'And "There are plenty more . . ."'

'There are.'

'Don't spoil it.'

'Are you feeling really down?'

'I guess I am. Down and blue. I know it's stupid.'

'I tell you what, shall I come and visit? I could, you know. How about tomorrow?'

'No, don't even think of it.'

'I've already thought of it.'

'I know it will pass.'

'But I'd like to come. I miss you. I can get there by early evening, is that OK?'

'What would I do without you?'

'You'd do the same for me.'

'Any time.'

Ten days after the crash, Connor stood outside 22 Jerome Street. He had been there since eight o'clock in the morning and it was now nearly eleven. The sky was low and grey; there was a persistent drizzle that had soaked through his clothes and made his hair stick to his skull. He was damp and hungry and hugely embarrassed by himself. He kept thinking that he should go, then giving himself ten more minutes, then another ten. At half past nine a young man had slouched out of the house, long blond hair pulled back in a ponytail. At just gone ten a woman of about Gaby's age, but tall and slim, with hair cut short and wearing ripped black jeans and a leather jacket, had emerged. No sign of Gaby. Upstairs, all the curtains remained closed. He paced up the street, then back again. If someone was looking at him, they'd think he was casing the joint. No, they'd think he was a stalker – and he was a kind of stalker, a risible figure, skulking in this narrow street, waiting for someone who'd probably not given him a moment's thought since they'd parted in the darkness, on the outskirts of the city, as the first faint band of light appeared on the horizon. He shifted irritably from foot to foot, feeling trickles of water escape down his neck. Of course, he should simply knock at the door and ask for her. But he couldn't bear the thought of being ushered into the house like a guest, to her pitying surprise, or being turned away politely with the news that she wasn't there or, worse, was still in bed with whoever she had chosen to go to bed with the night before.

He'd give himself till a quarter past. Then he'd forget about her. End of story.

He'd give himself till half past. Not a minute after.

At twenty to twelve the door of 22 Jerome Street opened and Gaby stepped into the street. He'd been tormented by her image, day and night, and there she was – a bit smaller than he remembered, her face a little thinner, her hair the colour of golden syrup, her eyes dark. She was stuffing a croissant into her mouth and laughing, while little flakes of pastry scattered round her. There was a man behind her, tall and broad and – Fuck him, thought Connor. Fuck him and fuck everyone who looked like that, so easy and happy and nice, inheriting the earth and not even noticing, while he, Connor, was skinny and serious and gripped with such cramps of longing for Gaby that he thought he'd die of it. For a second, as he stood there, he understood that while he had spent the past week and a half rearranging his entire life, Gaby had gone about her business as usual, scarcely casting a backward glance at the night in which they'd met. Of course she hadn't, because there she was in front of him, in a calf-length purple dress with dozens of tiny buttons, and black wellington boots, her hair tamed into plaits and a cloth cap on her head and, following her, a man. She was smiling over her shoulder at him, teasing him. There! She'd put her arm through his proprietorially as they reached the pavement and popped the last piece of croissant into his mouth.

Connor told himself to hurry away; she wouldn't even

notice he was there, a scrawny, damp rat in the gutter. But even as he was thinking this he had stepped forward and was standing before her.

'Connor!' she said. 'I thought –' she stopped. She wasn't smiling, just looking at him.

Connor stared into her face, into her large dark eyes, trying not to see the handsome, smiling face of her companion, or the third person who'd now emerged from the house. 'The man died,' he said. 'I thought you'd want to know.'

'I do know. He died on the way to the hospital. His name was Ethan and he was studying engineering. He was an only child. I met his mother.'

'He was well over the limit,' said Connor.

'I know. I talked to the police. I went to see them,' she added.

'So you know that that was why he crashed.'

'Maybe.'

'It was,' he insisted.

'You're very kind,' she said formally.

'Well, then –'

'Well, then,' she replied. She didn't move and neither did he. Drops of rain trickled down his cheek.

'And I'm no longer involved with anyone,' he said, grinding out the futile words in spite of the man at Gaby's side. 'I wanted to tell you that as well.'

'I see,' said Gaby.

'I shouldn't have bothered you. It was ridiculous. Ludicrous!' he added, with self-loathing.

'We were just going to the laundrette,' said Gaby, and Connor noticed the man beside her was carrying two large plastic bags, which, he could see now, were stuffed with sheets. Dirty sheets. He felt bile in his throat. 'Do you want to come with us?'

'No, thank you.' He almost spat the words at her. 'I don't think I will.'

'This is Stefan, by the way,' said Gaby. 'Stefan, Connor.'

Stefan. Of course. Connor nodded brusquely, trying to snarl his lips in an approximation of a smile, although he knew he was fooling no one.

'Stefan's my youngest brother,' said Gaby. 'Well, he's older than me, but he's the youngest of my older brothers. He's staying for the weekend.'

'Your brother,' said Connor. 'Oh!'

'Hello,' said Stefan, shyly, putting the plastic bags on the pavement and holding out a large hand. Connor was suffused with a warm affection for him. He shook Stefan's hand vigorously, for too long.

'And this,' Gaby added, as a young woman joined them on the pavement, 'this is my dearest friend Nancy. She's here with Stefan. Or, rather, Stefan is here with her.'

'Nancy,' said Connor. 'Stefan and Nancy.' He beamed at them both, his cheeks flushed with foolishness and joy, and they smiled kindly back at him, Stefan's arm draped loosely round Nancy's shoulders. 'Gaby?' Connor said, turning back to her.

'Yes?'

'Can I come to the laundrette after all?'

'I don't see why not. But you're wet through – how long have you been out here?'

Connor opened his mouth to say he'd been passing

and happened to see her, then swallowed the words. He was sick of the subterfuge and the self-control of his life. He wanted to bare his soul before her, begin afresh. 'Three and a half hours,' he said.

'Three and a half hours?'

Connor felt utterly exhausted with desire, and could barely stand upright. His flesh ached and his heart was a violent bruise. All he wanted was to hold her and be held. Nothing else mattered any more.

'A woman could fall in love with you,' said Gaby. 'Here, carry this bag.'

'Gaby, I have to tell you that –'

'Later. Tell me later.' For one tormenting moment, she laid a hand softly against his hectic cheek and smiled at him at last. 'We have lots of time.'

Two

She found the A4, spiral-bound, lined notebook inside a sequined pink bag that Sonia had loved many years ago when she was little. It was pushed to the back of the wardrobe, along with neatly paired shoes, a coiled-up belt with an ornate buckle that she couldn't remember having seen before, a sewing-box, a dress that had slipped from its hanger, a box of old school books and GCSE course-work, a couple of paperbacks (*Tess of the D'Urbervilles* and a dog-eared Agatha Christie omnibus) and a black bin bag packed with clothes Sonia had grown out of but couldn't bear to throw or give away. It was clearly hidden, not meant to be found, let alone read. She was an honest woman; she prided herself on being trustworthy and even felt a bit guilty when she snuck a glance at postcards friends had left lying around on their kitchen table. Never-theless, she found herself pulling the notebook out of the bag. Knowing that she shouldn't, she opened it. The writing, in blue ink, was round, neat, familiar. The date was at the top – 1 September 2005 – and underlined.

It's three in the morning, muggy and warm, and I'm writing this to you although I don't even know who you are. I don't know what to call you because you don't have a face or a name. You could be anyone at all, and for as long as I can remember that has scared me. Really scared me – not like the kind of nervousness I get before exams, when I have to take deep breaths to clear the tightness in my chest. More like the fear I feel in nightmares, black waves coiling over me, and even after I have lurched awake and know it was all a dream, it takes time for the fear to lift. Ominous, that's the word. I can feel it all day, like a great black monster on my back. I mean, what if you turn out to be – oh, I don't know – weird in some way? What if something's wrong with you? What if I hate you or you hate me? There's a thought experiment we all did once, when we had to try to make ourselves not think of something and of course we couldn't. If you try not to think of something, that's what you're thinking of. I'm trying not to think about you. I think about you all the time. I'm always looking around me and wondering, Is that you? The one in that coat, the one with the dog, the small one with a shuffling walk, the old one, the rich one, the poor one, the beggar in the town centre whose buttons are all undone and whose hand is outstretched and whose red face is a mixture of humility and hatred, the unhinged one who's shouting at the whole world and nobody wants to look at because it's as if they'll be cursed; the one who meets my eye and smiles, or doesn't smile, who looks away . . . Even writing this, my mouth goes dry and my heart beats a bit faster.

And I don't even know why I'm writing to you. Well, I guess I talk to you often enough in my head. Other people talk to their cat or their hamster or something. My friend Goldie talks to her fish, for goodness' sake, I've seen her do it. She presses her face against the bowl, so her eyes go goggly, and mutters things. Mad. I have a dog – he's a golden retriever, George, and I've had him since I was six so he's pretty old now; he lies in the porch and farts a lot, and whenever I go near him, even if his eyes are closed, he thumps his tail on the floor – and I have been known to talk to him when I've felt that no one else in the world understands me. But mostly I talk to you. I have to warn you, what I say isn't always very loving. Lots of times, I've told you I hate you. Can you hate someone you don't know?

We had this teacher in year eleven, who took us for life skills. Mrs Sadler. She was short and dumpy and always wore skirts just below her knees, and cardigans; she left last term because she had cancer and I don't know if she's going to be all right or not. She did all the required stuff – you know, about sex and taking proper precautions and about being in a caring relationship and about being able to say no and having self-esteem; or about drugs and how smoking's the most dangerous drug of all and how you don't need to follow the group. Blah-blah. And after all that, or alongside it, I guess, we had these discussions in class. I don't know why it happened, but people really talked about what they felt about things in a way I'd never heard them do before. Even ones I thought I knew quite well, or boys who thought that talking about emotions was sissy. You know, it was quite touching – the boys with their number-one haircuts and their tattoos and their swagger, or the girls with sideways ponytails and fake nails and bottles of vodka in their schoolbags who call you 'boffin' and 'sad' if you read anything except stupid magazines, or anyone who'd been having sex since they were thirteen – and you realized they were quite like you, after all, not just hard and indifferent but worried about things, with troubles at home and trying to cover it all up.

So there was this one week – we were probably discussing peer-group pressure or something – when we were talking about the need to know who you are and to be strong and confident in that. It started off with Mrs Sadler saying it was dangerous to try to impress people by pretending to be someone you weren't, and it didn't work anyway. It was better to be yourself, and people would respect that in the end. But Theresa suddenly said, 'What if you hate who you are?' Everyone knew she'd been cutting herself with the blade of her pencil-sharpener. Then clever-clogs Alex butted in and said that he didn't think there was a real 'you' – you were just made up of everything that had happened to you in your life, and you could decide who you wanted to be – and Lee said no, he thought you were born the way you were and you couldn't change that. You were stuck with yourself and that was that. It sounds a bit obvious when I write it down, but it didn't feel like that at the time.

I remember I started to feel all strange and agitated. I put up my hand to say something, and everyone turned towards me. And I burst into tears. It wasn't silent, graceful tears, the way they have in soppy films, that trickle down your cheeks and don't change the way you look – oh, no. Great, gulpy, snotty, noisy, ugly crying. I knew my eyes were swollen, my nose was red, my skin was all blotchy. I felt as if my chest was trying to come up my throat and my whole body was shaking. It was like I was turning inside out, all the raw, pulpy bits of myself I keep hidden coming to the surface. But I couldn't stop. I cried for ages. Mrs Sadler told Goldie to take me to the medical room where I lay down on the bed and sobbed even more while people fussed round me and someone said I was probably on my period. I think I was as well. No one knew what to say to me afterwards. I don't think I'd ever cried at school before, even though I've been there since I was eleven. I'm just not like that. (I'm the boffin, remember.) Afterwards,

I felt completely drained. I could hardly move. And I didn't know where it had come from, all that grief.

Anyway, so the point is that next week is my birthday: 6 September. Perhaps that's why I'm writing this down rather than saying it in my head. I'm going to be eighteen. Eighteen years old. Officially an adult, though I don't feel it. Then I can drink (I already drink). Go to any film (I already do that as well). Get married without my parents' permission (I'm not about to do that, I promise; I don't see any reason why I should ever marry). Get into debt. Gamble. Vote (the Green Party, I think, though I'll have to wait and see). I'm already old enough to join the army and kill someone. But on the day I turn eighteen, I'll start school again for my final year. That doesn't seem so exciting, does it?

But Mum and Dad are throwing a party for me in the hall down the road at the weekend. They insisted, and kept going on about what a big day it is and how I deserve it to be properly marked, and I don't dare tell them I'm kind of dreading it. I'm not very good at big parties anyway, and at my own I'll feel responsible for everyone and worry if it's going OK, and what if lots of gatecrashers come and throw bottles around? I would have preferred to go out with a few friends, something more intimate. Or just with Alex for a meal.

They're right, it is a big day. Not in the way that they mean, though – or maybe that is what they mean, deep down, but they can't bring themselves to say it out loud. We don't talk about it. We talk about everything else instead, so many words to cover up what's not being said. Sometimes I think one of us is going to mention it – my heart starts thudding away in my chest and my mouth gets all parched – and then the moment passes.

Mrs Sadler would say I should talk about it and I know she's right. She would say that things are less scary when you talk about them and I know that's right too. I don't know if it counts, writing this letter to you. It's more like a diary, anyway. I'm kind of talking to myself by talking to someone else.

If I tell you all about me, so you know me, maybe that'll mean I know myself. Whatever Alex says about the self not really existing at all.

It's starting to rain at last, so heavy it's like someone's throwing gravel against the windows. It's dry here, the earth all cracked after the summer and the grass yellow, but in the morning everything will feel fresher. I wonder what it's like where you are. I wonder where you live. I've always loved being inside, in the dark, and listening to the rain. When I was nine, Dad took me camping, just the two of us and George, and just for one night. I'd been pestering him for ages and finally he gave in. We cooked sausages on the little throwaway barbecue and played cards by torchlight. I was cold and wore my socks to bed and my jersey over my pyjamas. There were mosquitoes buzzing about and when I lay in my sleeping-bag I could hear them whining next to my ear. That night it rained and rained and rained. I remember lying in the tent, with Dad snoring by my side and George snoring at my feet, and listening to the drops falling on the canvas over my head and feeling completely safe. 'Safe and sound,' as Mum would say.

Mum also says that it's better to regret the things you do than to regret the things you don't do (although I'm not sure if she believes it: she's pretty cautious herself). I'm not going to send this letter. It's not really written to you anyway. How can you write a letter to someone who's a complete blank, an absence? This is probably a kind of diary, a diary that's pretending not to be. I always promised I wouldn't write a diary, full of all those stupid, embarrassing, nobody-knows-who-I-really-am thoughts. It's four in the morning now, and outside it's dark and windy and wet. It's easy to imagine that not a single person is awake except me. Real diary-writing time, real nobody-knows-who-I-am time.

But I'm going to try to get in touch. I've decided.

I don't really know how to sign off. In Keats's last letter, which he wrote to Fanny's mother not to Fanny herself, because it made him too upset to write to her, he said, 'I've always made an awkward bow.' Isn't that incredibly sad? I'll just put my name.

Sonia

The last four lines were at the top of a page, under which there was a blank space. The woman hesitated, then turned it over. The writing was not as neat. It looked as if it had been written in a hurry, or in distress. Words were crossed out violently.

12 September 2005

I've done it. I took the day off school (the very first time I've ever truanted, and I only missed physics and maths because I had lots of free periods – that's what I'm like: I do a life-changing thing, but I make sure I only do it on the one day I don't miss many lessons). I was surprised by how easy it turned out to be. Ridiculously easy, after all these years. So now I know who you are. And in a few days you'll know who I am, or my name, anyway. One day I will see you. I feel like I've stepped over some crack, and as soon as I did, it opened up into a great abyss behind me, so now I can't go back to where

I was before. All of that's over. My childhood is over, I suppose, and all of a sudden I want it back, more than I've ever wanted anything in my life. I can't believe what I've done. It's as if I've committed a terrible crime. I feel bad, really, really sick and yucky, and just want to curl up in a little ball. I don't want to know. I don't want to know. I don't want to know.

The woman sat for a few minutes on the bed, looking at the sentences before her. Her face was expressionless. Then she shut the book and carefully replaced it in the sequined pink bag. She pushed the bag to the back of the wardrobe, exactly where it had been before, and closed the wardrobe door. She patted out the indentation in the bedclothes, where she'd been sitting, then left the room.

Three

She would have behaved differently on any other day. This was a date that Gaby had dreaded for months. She and Ethan had left late – they always left late, each as bad as the other – and as the door of the house slammed, she patted her pockets, rummaged in her capacious bag, among the cheque books, lipsticks, tissues, pens, scraps of paper, tampons, perfume, notebook, comb, the jangle of loose change and foreign currency, and realized that the house keys must still be inside. In fact, she thought she could remember tossing them on to the kitchen table, among the debris of their breakfast, when she was doing her last-minute look-round.

'Oh well,' she shrugged, 'never mind that now. I've got the car key.' She brandished it.

'How will you get back in?'

'I'll think about that later. I'm sure I've left a window open round the back or something. I guess I ought to keep my house and car keys together, but since I always lose them, I figure it's better to be without one set and not both. If you see what I mean.'

'Not really. It sounds a bit counter-intuitive to me,' said Ethan. 'Wallet, glasses, phone and keys – I'm sure there's some Freudian explanation. Forgetting vital parts of yourself wherever you go.'

'At least all your stuff's already in the car.'

'Yup.'

'Let's be on our way.'

Ethan hitched his backpack over his shoulder and opened the car door.

'But doesn't this feel strange?' said Gaby, walking round to the driver's side. 'We should do something ritualistic, don't you think?'

'No.'

'It seems such a very short while ago that –'

'Oh, no, you don't, Mum!'

'Sorry! You're quite right. Anyway, a term's only ten weeks or something ridiculously brief. Do you really need all of this? It looks like you're emigrating. What's that thing there, anyway?'

'A fan heater.'

'Why on earth are you taking that? Where did you find it, anyway? Hey! And that's Dad's favourite frying-pan you've got. What else have you squirrelled away?'

'Mum, we're late and we're getting later –'

'Sorry.' She turned the key in the ignition and they jerked away from the kerb. Several books flew off the piled-up possessions and tumbled to the floor. Ethan sighed, put on his dark glasses, leant back and closed his eyes. They were in for a bumpy ride.

They drove through London in the hot haze of exhaust fumes. Everything was limp and dirty, for the summer was at its end. Gaby sat in her familiar posture, crouched over the steering-wheel as if it was getting dark outside and she was straining to see. She muttered curses at neighbouring cars and occasionally swerved into other lanes. She was wearing a long skirt that was slightly too large for her, held up by a canvas belt, and had taken off her sandals so her feet were bare, the toenails painted orange. Her hair was tied back loosely with what looked like a shoelace, and long earrings jangled from her lobes. Ethan gave a sly grin: she had never dressed like most other mothers he knew, and when he was young her flamboyant appearance had embarrassed and sometimes enraged him. Children like their parents to be unremark- able, invisible.

He vividly remembered an occasion – he must have been eleven or twelve – when he'd confronted her after she'd turned up for a parents' evening at his secondary school in a long red velvet coat she'd unearthed from the wardrobe and that smelt of mothballs. 'You don't know what it's like to be a child,' he'd shouted tearfully. She'd bent down towards him and replied, 'You don't know what it's like to be a mother.' The softness of her voice and the steeliness of her gaze had stopped him dead in his tracks; his anger had turned to a vague dread. He hadn't properly understood what she meant, and he hadn't wanted to. These days, however, he liked the way she looked. He approved of her bold carelessness, her random stylishness – although maybe she worked hard at her gypsy appearance, standing in front of the long, mottled mirror in the bedroom and trying on the clothes that were strewn round her, turning to examine her reflection.

'What?' she said, feeling his eyes on her.

'Nothing.'

'You were staring at me. What is it?'

'Really, nothing.'

'My buttons are done up wrong.'

'No, honestly, you look fine. Did you mind having children?'

'What?'

'I said, did you –'

'I know what you said. That was quite obviously just a yelp, not a question. Anyway, not children, *child*,' she corrected him. 'Singular. You.' She glanced across. 'Very singular, as it turned out.'

'OK. Did you ever mind having a child?'

'You do choose your moments, Ethan! Get me on to the M25, then I'll answer.'

'Just pretend you're going to the ice rink, you must know that road, and then I'll instruct you. Where's the atlas? We should have worked out our route before we left. Dad would have done. In fact,' he added, grinning fondly, 'I'm surprised he didn't think of it before he left on Thursday – he thought of practically everything else. He gave me a list of things I had to remember.'

'He gave me one too, but I lost it. Poor Connor, to be stuck with two people like us. The atlas is under the seat.'

'OK. Here. Take the next turning. That's right. Then it's the A10 all the way to the motorway.'

'So, did I mind having you? No, I can honestly say there was never a fragment of a second when I regretted it, even when I was at my lowest.'

'I didn't mean *me* – that's something different,' said Ethan. 'It wasn't meant to be a personal question like that. More a philosophical kind of one. You gave up things. I don't mean career opportunities or money or time or all the obvious stuff they write about every week in the Sunday supplements. I mean –' He remembered again the sharp tug of anxiety he'd felt when she'd looked him in the eye as if he were her enemy, and said, *You don't know what it's like to be a mother.* 'I mean, bits of yourself.'

'My self,' she mused. 'What's that, then?'

'You know what I mean. Remember to go anticlockwise on to the M25. Towards the M40 and M1.'

'Maybe I found it harder than some people do – look at Maggie, for instance. She's got five children. Five children, for God's sake! And she's got a proper job, not like me. And she still manages to bake and take them swimming at weekends, and keep the house clean and beautiful. And she's always so cheerful, and looks great. It seems to come naturally to her – though maybe I'm not doing her credit, and she finds it incredibly tiring but doesn't show it.'

'Doesn't it irritate you?'

'Irritate? It makes me want to howl at the moon.'

'She's probably on drugs.'

'Anyway, what I think is that you always lose things when you gain things.'

'Very Zen,' Ethan said drily.

'No, really. I chose to be a mother. If I'd chosen not to be a mother, I would have lost different things.'

'Like what?'

'A whole new world of feelings. And you – I'd have lost you, my darling.'

'Or whoever I would have been if I hadn't, by some random one-in-a-billionth chance, turned out to be me.'

She ignored him. 'Of course, I would never have

known I was losing you, since I would never have had you in the first place. That's the thing. When you don't have children, you don't know exactly what it is you're losing. But you have to say goodbye to something.'

'Or someone.'

'Or someone.'

'That makes it sound a bit sad.'

'Does it? More exciting than sad.'

'So why did you only have me?'

'Did you mind – being the only one?'

'I dunno. I used to think it would be nice to have a brother or sister. There can be something a bit lonely about being the only one. But you haven't answered my question. Why just me?'

'It was the way it worked out,' said Gaby. 'First of all, I was – well, a bit ill after you were born.' She frowned and her hands tightened on the steering-wheel. Briefly she was assaulted by memories from the past, of grey days and long nights and a sense of dull despair. She shook her head, as if to scatter the thoughts. 'We tried, you know.'

'You mean, you couldn't get pregnant?'

'I had a couple of miscarriages. And then, well, after a bit it seemed we'd gone past the moment. You were older, it would have been a big gap, like starting again.'

'Were you upset?'

'We both were. It was oddly shocking. You can't help yourself, you have all this hope and love invested. But when it happens, what are you mourning? Not a person. I guess you're mourning lost hope, lost possibility, a version of the future that won't happen now. It's hard to describe.'

Ethan watched her for a few seconds, then said: 'If you take someone like Stefan –'

'Stefan would have been a completely besotted father, if he'd got that far. He's much more selfless than me. He probably wouldn't even have understood your question about losing things when you become a parent. As it was –' She stopped.

'As it was?'

'Nothing.'

'Mum?'

'Things don't turn out the way you think they will. That's all.' She hesitated. 'Have I ever told you about Nancy?'

'My godmother, or non-godmother, Nancy, whom I don't think I've ever met?'

'That's the one.'

'Not really. I know the bare bones, of course: that she was your childhood friend who went out with Stefan for ages, then left him. I don't know the details. You've always been a bit cagey about her and I didn't want to pry.'

'She was my best friend. That sounds childish, doesn't it? But she really was my very best friend, from the age of eleven until shortly after you were born. I've never had another friend like her.'

'So what happened?'

'As you say, she went out with Stefan for ages. Everyone thought they'd stay together; that was the way it seemed. Then one day she up and left and never came back. Just disappeared out of all our lives. Sometimes I think Stefan's never got over it.'

'And you haven't either?'

She glanced at him, then back at the road. 'I guess I haven't, not really. Weeks go by when I don't think about her, but then something triggers a recollection and it's as fresh and sore as ever. Perhaps I'm thinking about it now because it's one of those days – you leaving home brings everything back. It was so long ago, but it's funny how near it all seems. When we were young together, Nancy and me, so full of hopes and dreams for our lives, we were going to know each other until we died. We were going to have such fun together.'

'I never knew.'

'Well, it was all over before you were old enough to speak.'

'What else haven't you told me?'

'It wasn't a secret or anything. Just a raw patch.'

'It sounds heartbreaking.'

'Oh,' said Gaby, 'I don't know. Perhaps it's just today that it feels like that. I've never been good at saying goodbye.'

Ethan laid a hand lightly on her shoulder. 'It's not really goodbye, Mum. It's more like, see you in a bit.'

'I know. Sorry.' She frowned. 'This car feels a bit funny. Can you smell burning?'

'A bit. Is the handbrake on or something?'

'Of course not,' she replied, checking surreptitiously to make sure.

'It's probably coming from outside,' he said. He pulled a pile of CDs out of his backpack, selected one and slid it into the player, turned up the volume, then lay back and watched through his dark glasses as the fields rolled emptily by, golden and green under the heavy sky, the blur of high hedges, the swift string of houses, the sudden trees that cast a bar of shade over the hot car, then slid into the distance. Cows, stubble, swallows lining up on telegraph wires. I'm leaving home, he thought. The words throbbed inside his head like a refrain. His body was heavy in the warmth. His hands, folded loosely in his lap, felt as if they belonged to someone else. He could feel his eyelids growing heavier, until at last he let them close . . .

Gaby let her gaze rest briefly on his profile as he slept. Such a beautiful face, she thought. A wing of tawny hair over his forehead, thick straight eyebrows above eyes so deep brown they were almost black, like sloes, cheeks still pale and smooth, although he shaved every day now, a dimple in his chin like the one in hers, a small mole under his left ear. He was half man and half lean, beautiful boy; there was still that freshness about him, a physical sweetness that made her want to reach out and put her hand on his thin shoulder, stroke the soft flop of his hair.

She let herself remember him as he was in the photograph that stood on the piano at home: four years old, in red shorts, blue T-shirt and sandals, outside his grandparents' greenhouse holding a cardboard basket of tomatoes, and on his face a look of frightened uncertainty, as if he didn't know where on earth he was or to whom he should turn for help. A tiny boy who used to stand with his soft hand in hers, shifting fretfully from foot to foot; who was scared of heights, enclosed spaces, beetles and flies, cows, waves, cracks in pavements, older boys, crowds, clowns, balloons, fireworks, the dark, being left alone. She used to sit by his bed at night, and he'd wind his fingers through her hair while she sang lullabies and half-remembered songs from her own childhood. He wouldn't go to sleep without her there, watching over him like a sentinel until his hand slipped back on to the pillow, the fist uncurling, his eyes dragged shut, his breathing deepened, and then she would creep from the room. Now he towered over her. Now he shut his door on her, locked it. He lectured Connor on politics, told them surreal jokes and giggled with friends over musical trivia or the worst film titles. He played the piano when he thought no one was listening, sitting upright on the piano stool, his long fingers rippling over the keys, staring into the distance as though he could see a whole different landscape out there. He went out at night with condoms in the pockets of his ripped jeans, smelt of cigarette smoke and beer and sweat and secrets, gazed at her with an inscrutable expression on his young, romantic face, or was kind to her and Connor in a way that made her feel how he was leaving them, how he'd left. But, still, she sometimes remembered the early years, and wondered what had happened to that solemn, scared child. Had he simply vanished, melted away, or was he still lurking, waiting to unsettle them all again? Even now there were times when she woke in the middle of the night and had to steal into his room to make sure he was there, dreamy and beautiful on the pillow. But she was supposed to trust him and believe him to be safe. That was their pact. She couldn't voice her fears. And today she and Connor were letting him go. He was on his own at last. For a minute, her eyes pricked with tears and she blinked them furiously away.

'Stop it!' Ethan's eyes snapped open.

'What?'

'You know.'

Yesterday his girlfriend Rosie, with whom he had spent the past five months travelling round South America, had told him they should separate, not start their university life feeling tied to each other. And today Gaby was taking him to university for the first time. The back seat, laid flat to make space, was piled high with books on modern history and Western philosophy, the frying-pan, a clatter of cutlery, mugs and assorted plates, a coffee-grinder, the fan heater, a tennis racket, a bin bag of sheets and duvet, two suitcases with his clothes, a neat laptop in its black carrying case stuffed between the front and back seats, a desk lamp, a small CD-player with separate speakers lying on top of it and splitting plastic bag of CDs, many of which he'd borrowed from Stefan and never got round to returning, a cardboard box packed with tea-bags and coffee beans, several packets of stem-ginger biscuits, a few tins of tuna, a jar of Marmite and another of honey, a bottle of lime cordial, plastic pots of vitamins, a bag of sugar. A couple of jackets – including the lovely thick grey one they'd given him for his birthday a couple of months ago – and a dark blue towel were laid across the top of the shifting pile. At his feet was his bulging back-pack, full of odds and ends (an iPod, a book of twentieth-century poetry, a notebook already half filled with his illegible, spidery writing, an address book, his phone, wallet, the documents he would need when he arrived, an ancient pencil case with a broken zip, playing cards, a portable chess set). And on the back of the car, its thin wheels spinning slowly, was his bicycle.

'Are you nervous?'

Really, she wanted to ask him if he was all right, but she knew he wouldn't answer that – you couldn't draw confidences out of Ethan: he gave them abruptly, unexpectedly. Yesterday he had returned from meeting Rosie with a set expression on his face, as if someone had taken a cloth to it and wiped away any sign of life, told Gaby the news in a curt tone that forbade her to respond, and gone to his room. She had heard the door close firmly and the key turn in the lock. Later that night, she woke and lay there, listening to the piano being played. Just a simple melody over and over again; the notes seemed to hang shining in the close darkness around her. She waited until the music stopped, then rolled out of bed, pulled on a dressing-gown, pushed her feet into slippers and stumbled downstairs into the kitchen. Ethan was there, in jeans but bare-chested. He sat at the table, looking down at his fingers, a leather band round the bony wrist.

'I'll make us tea, shall I?' asked Gaby.

'I might have known you'd find me. Cocoa would be more comforting. I couldn't sleep – I don't think I'm going to now. You don't look very awake, you know – are you sure you don't want to go back to bed?'

They'd sat together drinking cocoa in the brightly lit kitchen while all the rooms around them lay in creaking darkness, and the starless night pressed against the windows. Ethan had got out his cigarettes and offered one to Gaby. She took it casually as though it hadn't been about twenty years since she'd last smoked. Exactly twenty years, in fact – she'd given up when she was pregnant with Ethan. He lit them both with a shared match, took a deep drag on his, and said, with a half-smile, 'I never thought we'd get *married* or anything. To tell you the truth, I didn't want to be together any more either. It hadn't felt right for months. The magic had gone out of it somehow – so of course it's better like this. It should be a relief. And she did it before I'd plucked up the courage, so I don't even need to feel guilty. I just have to get used to it.' Then he added, abruptly, holding her gaze with his own dark, glinting one: 'All the same, it's odd how it *hurts*.'

'Yes,' Gaby had muttered, pulling the smoke into her lungs, feeling a little rush of dizziness hit her and, with it, the sudden memory of being a teenager herself, leaning forward towards the match in a cupped hand, the first acrid inhalation. There wasn't really anything else to say. If she leant across and hugged him he'd probably pat her on the shoulder, as if he was consoling her. Instead, they'd played racing demon (he'd won, he always did), and later, as grey dawn seeped across the sky, she'd cooked bacon and eggs – conscious of the ridiculous, last-gasp domesticity of it all. That was what you did with a son who was about to leave home: you turned into a picture-book version of a mother. You gave him a cooked breakfast (even though she punctured the yolk and singed the bacon), made a fresh pot of coffee, ran him a bath; then you checked his room after he had vacated it and gazed at the blank surfaces, bare shelves, stripped bed, half-empty wardrobe, the whiter patches on walls where he'd taken down pictures, the abandoned belongings of childhood.

'Am I nervous?' he repeated now. 'Of course.'

He leant forward and turned on the radio, still keeping his eyes on the road. He turned the dial through the static hiss until he found a music station he liked. He wound the window down several inches and lit a cigarette.

'There's *definitely* a smell of burning now.'

'It's my cigarette.'

'No. Burning. It can't be from outside. Can't you smell it? Oh, my God, look at that!'

Thick plumes of smoke were curling from the bonnet.

'Pull over!'

They steamed to a halt on the hard shoulder and Gaby killed the engine. Smoke still billowed from the front of the car, which rocked as pantechnicons thundered past.

'Oh dear,' said Ethan, after a pause.

'Shall I open the bonnet to have a look?'

'What will we be looking for? Neither of us knows a radiator or a – a *sump*,' he said wildly, plucking the word out of the recesses of his brain, 'from a dead badger.'

'No. You're right. I'll call the AA.'

'That's a better idea.'

'Should we get out in case we burst into flames?'

'OK, but mind the cars. Get out of the passenger door.'

After Gaby had spoken to the rescue service on her mobile, and someone had promised to be along as soon as possible, she turned to Ethan and said, in a small voice, 'I've got a confession to make.'

'What?'

'I think I know what's wrong with the car. Or, at least, *why* what's wrong with it is wrong. I was driving it in the wrong gear.'

'It's an automatic. It doesn't have gears.'

'It has an extra gear for when you're pulling a heavy load up a hill.'

'And you were in that?'

'I must have been. Yes. I saw when I stopped.'

'Ah,' said Ethan. 'That'll be it, then. Shall we have our picnic?'

'If you want. We may as well. You're being very nice about this.'

'It's OK. There's nothing we can do about it. And I'll get there in the end. I hope the car doesn't explode, though. All my wordly possessions are in it.'

They scrambled up the bank and sat at the top, with scrubby, blackened bushes snared with litter behind them and the rumbling flow of cars beneath. Gaby brought out squidgy packages of sandwiches.

'Nice view,' said Ethan.

'What if they can't fix it?'

'Well,' he shrugged, 'they'll have to tow us.'

And he leant back against the grimy grass.

Gaby could tell that Ethan wanted her to go. They had carried all his belongings, in several stages, into his room. The AA man had helped them, before departing with the car. The room was square, small, and newly painted in a neutral ivory. There was a bathroom opposite and a small kitchen a few doors down at the end of the corridor, which was full of new students and their anxious-looking parents. Gaby smiled energetically, catching people's eyes, and said, 'Hello,' to anyone who smiled back. She nudged Ethan a couple of times to indicate promising faces, but he ignored her.

Now he had wandered off to make tea for them, and while he was gone, Gaby rang up for train times from Exeter to London. Then she squatted among the boxes and bin bags, unzipped his larger suitcase and lifted out a pile of creased T-shirts.

'Here we are. It's a bit milky. What are you doing?'

'Unpacking.'

'Why?'

'I don't know. I was being motherly, I suppose.'

'I prefer it when you're not, you know. It unnerves me. I can do all of that later.'

'Of course you can.' She grinned at Ethan ruefully. 'Sorry. I'll drink this and be on my way.'

'Have you got plans for the evening?'

'Apart from breaking into the house, you mean? I don't think so. Maybe I'll go to a film or something. I'll see if anyone's free.' She sipped her tea. 'What'll you do?'

'No idea.'

'There are lots of things laid on for you if you want, aren't there?' She gestured at the leaflets that had been waiting for him.

'I guess.'

This was just the idling talk before leaving. She took a large gulp of tepid tea and put down her mug purposefully. 'Will you call me soon, let me know how you're getting on?'

'Sure. Um – about what we were saying earlier . . .'

'What were we saying earlier?'

'You know, about being a mother and whether you ever regretted it.'

'Oh, OK. Yes?'

'Did you think of having me aborted?'

'No!' Of course they had. It wasn't what they'd planned; it wasn't what *she*'d planned. She'd wanted to work, to travel, to cast around for who she really was, to choose who she wanted to be. That was how it had always felt to her and still did in a way. She didn't want to be responsible for someone else and lose the carefree, reckless twenties to sleepless nights, nappies and selflessness. Yet, like a perfect little clock, the growing life ticked away inside her.

'I don't mind, you know. I put it wrongly – of course, it wasn't me you would have been aborting, just a cluster of cells the size of a pea. Lots of people think that a foetus doesn't become a baby until it's born.' He got up and looked out of the window, his hands thrust deep into his pockets. 'Rosie had an abortion.'

'Did she?' So that was what all the questioning had been about. Gaby tried to keep her voice neutral in spite of the sharp pity that ripped through her. 'When?'

'A month or two ago.'

'Is that why –?'

'Why she ended it? Or why I couldn't end it, even though I wanted to? Maybe. I don't know. Maybe she couldn't bear to have me around after that and I couldn't bring myself to leave. Not while she might need me.'

'What did you feel about it?'

Ethan rubbed his eyes. Suddenly he seemed very

66

young. 'I would have been really disturbed if she'd said she wanted to keep it. Christ, I didn't want to have a baby. It would have been insane. It was obvious she'd have an abortion. And it was her decision, anyway. Not really anything to do with me. Except it felt so weird, knowing it was growing inside her even though it was totally invisible, and if she did nothing it would – Well, it's confusing, isn't it? You think, My life could change, just like that. Except, of course, it was never going to. I'm rambling.'

'It doesn't matter. I'm glad you're telling me this.'

He could have been a father, she thought. My little boy. Then she thought, And I could have been a grandmother. Absurd.

'Anyway, it made me think. Not about abortions – I still *think* what I always did about that. It just made me think. Everything was going the way it was meant to go, you know – the right grades at fucking A level, a gap year, a bit of travelling to "broaden my mind", a steady girlfriend, all that kind of middle-class crap.'

'And then this.'

'I know it's not much, really.'

'It's enough,' she said, remembering her miscarriage when Ethan was a toddler and her sense of precariousness, of a blithely planned future crumbling in front of her.

'Well, I've not got terminal cancer or walked across a continent to find a safe haven or lost my parents in a fire or anything dramatic. It's nothing historic, just the same little things that happen to everyone. If they're lucky, that is. But I was thinking last night how unfamiliar everything looked now, like when you drive at night and you have to really concentrate because you don't know what's round the corner any more. Everything looks different. You can't think about much else. Wow, I'm really tired, you know.'

He pulled up the sash window and the sounds of the campus poured into the room. He lit another cigarette and drew on it deeply; she saw the hollows sucked into his cheeks. Then he smiled at Gaby through the blue smoke. 'It's OK,' he said. 'I'll be fine. And you've got to go now.'

'I can stay as long as you want. We could have a walk and get a bite to eat . . .'

'Nah. I kind of want to get on with things.'

'But –'

'Come on, Mum. Goodbye time. I'll be back before you know it anyway – you'll hardly have time to clean my room, if that's what you were planning to do, before I come and mess it up again.'

'Are you all right for money?'

'We've been through this.'

'OK. But if you need anything . . .'

'Yeah, yeah.'

'And, Ethan . . .'

'What?'

'I don't know what I was going to say.'

'I do, though. You were going to say, "Take care, and don't worry, and time heals, and work hard but not too hard, and ring home often but not so often that you'll start worrying I'm wretched, and eat healthy food sometimes, and make new friends, and don't smoke so much or take too many drugs, or any drugs, and be careful on your bike."'

68

'You forgot "And I love you very much. And I'm very proud of you." I was going to end on that. Unironically.'

He stubbed out his cigarette on the windowsill and chucked it outside. 'It's been a nice childhood,' he said. 'Don't cry.'

'I'm not sad, just emotional. Anyway, you're crying too.'

'Of course I am.' He put his arms round her and lifted her up so that her feet dangled above the ground and one shoe slipped and hung from her toe. Then he lowered her and let her go. 'See you,' he said.

Gaby walked through Exeter in the drizzle, not sure where she was headed. The streets were full of young students, jostling and laughing, moving in clotted groups, and among them she felt muted, like a charcoal figure among all the vivid oil-painted ones. She had the sense that nobody could see her, and that if she opened her mouth to speak, nobody would hear the words. Her body was heavy and slow; her sinuses ached with unshed tears and her throat hurt. She wished she could speak to Connor. She wanted to hear his voice as a reminder of the world she was returning to.

The station was a few minutes away, and when she looked at her watch she saw that if she hurried she could still get the 15.01 express to London. But she didn't want to hurry – or, at least, she couldn't seem to make herself do anything more than dawdle along the crowded weekend streets. Each step seemed to take a long time; she heard her feet slap against the damp pavement, and she moved as in a dream past shops and cafés. Sometimes she glimpsed her reflection, among all the other reflected figures, and was surprised how upright, energetic, full of purpose she looked.

Without knowing that she was going to, she turned up an alley and entered a dark little café. The humid warmth embraced her, the hiss of the espresso machine and the melodic chink of cups. She ordered a cappuccino and an almond pastry and sat at a table near the window, easing off her jacket and settling back. She almost felt that she could go to sleep right now – put her arms on the table, rest her face on them, close her eyes. She drank some frothy coffee, licking the foam off her lips; took a bite of the pastry and chewed it slowly. She wondered what Ethan was doing right now. She saw his face as he'd told her about Rosie, and wanted to race back and hug him tight and tell him she would make everything all right, knowing that those days were years in the past. He had said it had been a good childhood, but had it really? Had she been a good enough mother? She'd been chaotic, forgetful, volatile, haphazard. She remembered all those moments of fatigue and irritation, and the way she had longed for time to herself; she had that now but no longer wanted it. His present-day face – impatient and beautiful – was replaced in her mind by a younger one, red-eyed and beseeching. His hands used to be dimpled at the knuckles. His belly used to be plump, his body like a sack of flour, changing shape in her arms.

She drank more cappuccino to steady herself, took another bite of the pastry. People poured past the window, like figures in a home movie, grainy and slightly

70

out of focus. She wished she could go back to the beginning and do it properly, do it perfectly, do it again.

Ethan sat in his room, among the bin bags and boxes. He should put everything away, but he knew he wasn't going to. Probably they'd be piled up in the middle of his room for weeks. Why not? He could take clothes out of his cases, then put them into a bin bag when they were dirty; when the case was empty, he'd go to the laundrette, which he could see from the window. It seemed like an efficient arrangement. And he could pick out books and CDs as he wanted. He leant back against the bed, pulled his iPod out of his backpack, plugged in the earpieces and turned it on. 'This is the first day of my life,' a light-timbred voice sang inside his head. 'Remember the time you drove all night just to meet me . . .' He winced and skipped to the next track, drank his tepid tea, then finished Gaby's. He put the two empty mugs on top of the tennis racket, beside the bag of shoes, and lit a cigarette.

If his father was here, he thought, tapping ash with a hiss into one of the mugs, he would be putting everything away at once, finding a place for all of Ethan's possessions, trying to turn the room into another home. He could imagine his frowning, concentrated face; the precision with which he organized things. He could be very purposeful, his father, like many of the adults Ethan knew. He strode through his days as if they were a road that led to a known destination and he mustn't turn aside or let himself be delayed. But Ethan liked the sense he had now of floating in the currents of this day, sitting in a heap in the warm room and having no idea of where

71

he should be heading and no particular desire to head anywhere. He could find a bar and stay there until it closed, nursing a beer and listening to other people's conversation; he could take a bath; he could knock on one of the doors in this corridor of identical rooms and make a gesture towards friendship; he could cook a meal at midnight, smoke a joint, cycle round the city with the map Gaby had pushed into the side pocket of his back-pack, go to sleep in this small, warm space, sitting on the carpet with his knees up in a bridge, and only rise as it got dark. Anything was possible.

He lit another cigarette, drew the smoke into his lungs, let it out in a dissipating bluish cloud. He thought of his mother's face as she left, screwed up in an effort to be cheerful. Then he reached over and took the pack of playing cards out of his backpack. He dealt columns and started to play patience, as his father had taught him many years ago. He must have played it hundreds, thousands, of times. He'd played it incessantly through GCSEs and A levels – for luck, as an omen, a ritual of superstitious distraction. Before each exam, he'd have to get all his cards out. And then there were those grey Sunday after-noons; those rainy camping holidays in Scotland and Wales. Fish with flabby, salted chips, damp clothes, and inside the humid tent, the cards tipping on the rucked sleeping-bag. He laid out seven more cards, liking the plasticky snap they made. Once he'd got out in a game, he told himself, he would do something. He'd go and knock on doors, meet neighbours, phone friends in other halls of residence. When the cards told him.

*

At last Gaby stood up, paid for the coffee and pastry, pulled on her jacket and left the café. Outside, the sky had darkened and it was trying to rain. A few large drops landed on her cheek and hair. Turning back on to the main street, she quickened her pace and headed for the station. She'd have time before the 16.22 arrived to buy a magazine or book, and she'd settle down in a window seat, drink brown tea, go home. It made her feel dreary, the thought of returning to her old life, as if nothing had happened. She pictured Ethan's dark, stripped room, fluff balls in the corner and dead flies on the windowsill, bare spaces along the shelves, and silence thick in the room, like an odour. She had insisted that Connor should go on his long-planned sailing trip, yet now she knew that he should have been there to mark this event. After so many years they were a couple living on their own again. They should have said goodbye to their son together, then taken a wild walk or gone swimming in the sea, got drunk, been undignified, booked into a hotel for sex, got on to a plane that would take them away to an unknown destination. Anything, rather than a dutiful return, back in time for a glass of wine and an early night.

She bought a single ticket to London, Paddington. She gazed round her, but nothing made sense and the crowds and bright lights wavered in her vision. Putting her fingers to her cheeks, she found she was weeping. The tears slid down her face in sheets, her throat ached, her heart was heavy. And then, over the loudspeaker, she heard an announcement: the 16.18 was due to arrive on platform two, calling at Plymouth, Liskeard, Par, St Austell, Truro, Redruth, St Erth and Penzance.

For a moment she stood, at a loss, while passengers flowed past her in both directions. Then, clutching her one-way second-class ticket to London, she went towards the train that would take her in the opposite direction, and sat down in the empty first-class carriage. She held her breath and pressed her nose to the window. Small rivulets ran down the glass; outside, figures wavered in the strengthening rain. She felt the engine vibrate and the people on the platform fell away as the train began to move towards Cornwall, slowly at first but soon picking up speed.

Sitting back in her capacious, illegal seat, she looked past her own fugitive reflection in the streaming window, out on to the sodden patchwork green of the countryside that flooded by under the leaking grey sky. In the incessant rain, it resembled an Impressionist painting, all smudged colour and light, like a landscape inside her head. A tremble ran through her, whether of happiness or sorrow she could not tell, and she closed her eyes. When she opened them again, it was her younger self she was looking at in the vague mirror of the window – the one she thought she had left behind, but who had been waiting for her to return. The train shuddered on, carrying her back into her past.

Four

It was Connor's watch. Stefan slept down below, wrapped in an old tartan blanket with his feet sticking out and one large hand curled round the side of his face, as if he was comforting himself. Every so often he flinched, shifted, half woke. The sea was quite calm tonight, the moderate waves lifting and dropping the boat, up-up and down again in a lethargic waltz. Even in sleep, Stefan could feel how the boat tugged forward with the wind, then went slack before picking up momentum once more. It was a rhythm he loved and tried to store in his body: the asymmetrical rise and fall while the water slapped against the bows and vibrated almost imperceptibly under the keel. The old wooden boat creaked.

It was the eighth year running that the two men had made the trip together. In the summer, after the university term had ended and Stefan was free, they sailed his small yacht to France. Connor would then return home, and Stefan would spend his holiday there, sailing into small ports and harbours, or simply pottering about. Sometimes a friend would join him, more often he preferred to be alone with his books, his thoughts, the salty wind in his face and the spray stinging off the waves. Then, in the autumn when the academic term was about to begin, Connor would fly out and they would sail back across the Channel, to the berth near Southampton.

As he felt himself falling back into sleep, he heard, far off, the muffled boom of a foghorn – too distant to worry about. Anyway, Connor was on deck. Stefan could imagine him sitting at the stern in his oilskin, one hand resting on the tiller, his eyes narrowed as he watched the compass, the horizon and the taut belly of the sail. They'd be all right tonight. He turned on his back, laid a forearm against his eyes, was pulled down into his dreams.

The boat bucked up against a steep wave, then shuddered into its valley. Connor felt it tug against the tiller. The wind was strengthening. Without looking at what he was doing, he poured coffee from the flask into the pewter mug, then shook a cigarette out of its packet. He put it into his mouth and, with one practised hand, struck a match. Gaby thought he'd given up, but for the few days each year when he was at sea with Stefan, he liked to smoke. Especially when he was alone on deck at night and all around him, in every direction, its edges bleeding into the sky, was the sea. There were times on the watch when he felt as if he was hallucinating, the world topsy-turvy and terrifying. The waves crested and tipped in a kaleidoscope of snow-capped mountains and craters, while the sky was a dark and watery ocean rushing above him. The liquid, shifting landscape seemed to flood into his brain, and his sense of who he was dissipated and dissolved. If he let himself go, it would be like dying. Then he had to blink, gulp the harsh coffee, light another cigarette and drag himself back to the precision and solidity of the present.

'Connor Myers,' he said aloud. 'Forty-four years old.

Doctor. Husband. Father.' Was that all? His life was an infinitesimal speck, tossed on the ocean.

But usually what he felt in these lonely stretches was the kind of clarity and contentment that he rarely achieved in his daily life. He lived so pressed up against the obligations of each day (seeing patients, hearing stories that made him feel helpless, all the increasing bureaucracy of the job, domestic chores, family crises). Only here, suspended between earth and sky with the cry of the terns and shearwaters rinsing through his mind, could he see himself whole and clear. He knew he was a taciturn man, often filled with a sudden, powerful anger, which he concealed under a tense impatience. He hated to lose control. He hated untidiness, disorder, things not going according to plan. He wasn't very good at taking pleasure in the small moments of life. He wasn't good, he admitted to himself, at being happy, although he could do grief exceptionally well. Ethan had once accused him of despising happiness, and although he'd denied it at the time, he knew it was partly true. Happiness often seemed to him to be a kind of laziness, a moral apathy or blindness. But maybe, he thought now, as he sat on the deck and watched the nose of the boat pushing into the water, then snouting up again, maybe what he really felt was that he had not earned the right to happiness and that he had not deserved his luck: not his beautiful, joyful wife, or his raw, romantic son who, even now, was leaving home.

If he had said such a thing to Gaby, she would have laughed and put her arms round him and told him he was a self-punishing, guilt-ridden, ridiculous Puritan and that it didn't work like that. He could imagine her so clearly that, for a second or two, it was as if she were with him on the boat; he saw the way she'd stand to absorb the motion of the waves, her hands on her hips, legs apart, hair tangled in the wind. She was good at being happy. She treated small moments as gifts and was grateful.

Yet it was wrong to reduce Gaby to 'happy', as if she was an unstained child who had not yet acquired all of the messy, furtive and ambivalent self-consciousness of an adult. She'd had her share of misery. After Ethan had been born – to Connor's shock and her own shame – she had plunged into a full-scale, weeping, catatonic post-natal depression that seemed bewilderingly out of character and had taken many months to lift. They rarely talked about it now. But for a moment her weeping, swollen face presented itself to him and he stared at it in the dark, full of tenderness.

Then, unbidden, another memory rose in him. It was so vivid that it was almost as if he were watching it on a screen. Ethan, who was eight or nine months old, was lying in his carry-cot in the living room, finally asleep after hours of struggle. They were sitting on either side of him, exhausted. There was a half-drunk bottle of wine on the table, and a fire in the grate, so it must have been winter-time. It was dark outside. Connor could see the reflection of the flames dancing in the window-panes. He watched himself get up and close the curtains. 'He's out for the count,' he said. 'Little bugger.'

'Thank God for that,' she said, sighing and sinking back in the sofa. 'I was about to suggest brandy in the milk. Sometimes I think I'm not cut out for motherhood.'

'Don't you dare say that! Don't. After everything you've gone through – well, you're a hero.'

'A hero?' A splutter of laughter came from her.

'Heroine.'

'Hero's better.'

He looked down at her, smiling. 'Hero.'

They stared at each other, the smile fading from his face, replaced by confusion. 'You look all in,' she said softly.

'I am. Done in.'

As if the strength had run out of him, he sank to his knees in front of her and put his head in her lap. She ran her slender fingers through his hair. Neither spoke, and it was in silence that he lifted his head and kissed her blindly, pushing her back against the sofa and clambering after her; in silence that she undid the buckle of his belt and that he pulled up her skirt. They clung together like drowning people, each trying to save the other, pull the other under.

'Oh, God,' he said, into the soft hollow of her neck.

'Sssh. Quiet now. Don't you go and wake Ethan.'

But Ethan had been fast asleep, his hands curled into small fists and his breath deep and even. There had been a quivering behind his eyelids to show that he was dreaming.

Connor blinked and shook his head. The images receded; he was looking out at the moon, broken up in the choppy landscape of the sea once more, a tiller in his hand and the main sheet coiled neatly at his feet. The wind freshened and the boat leapt forward. Connor felt the wind cool against his face. It was still many hours before dawn – that barely perceptible lightening on the horizon. Then he heard Stefan's old alarm clock give its tinny rattle, and Stefan's groan. Soon enough the sun would be up, and they would see other boats dotted around them. Soon he would be home.

Five

The notebook was no longer in the sequined pink bag. She bent inside the wardrobe and rooted around among the discarded clothes and shoes. It wasn't there, or in the chest of drawers, among the underwear or the T-shirts. She lifted up the mattress – that was where boys were supposed to hide pornography, wasn't it? – and looked under the bed, but all she found there was a sock. Then she looked in the schoolbag – a scruffy grey backpack, with writing in felt tip scrawled all over its fabric, torn along one seam – and that was where she found it, sandwiched between the physics textbook and the one for higher maths.

21 September 2005

Anyway, I suppose I should tell you something about myself. There's all the obvious boring stuff, and you know some of that already. I'm eighteen. I do well at school, mainly because I work hard (they've always called me boffin at school, and it used to make me a bit miserable, but then I decided to take it as a compliment and now it kind of has become one. I guess Mrs Sadler would see a moral in that: be true to yourself blah-blah). I am doing A levels in maths, chemistry and physics, and Mum and Dad think I ought to study medicine but, really, I want to be a scientist. Genetics, maybe. Who knows? I love books – I wanted to do English as well as science, but in the end I had to give something up. I swim for the school and for the last two years I've competed in the national trials. My best stroke is crawl, and I'm quite good at butterfly as well. I love swimming. It's the closest you get to flying. Sometimes I think I'm most like myself when I'm in the water. There we are – back to the idea of a 'self' again. I take lots of photographs and perhaps there's a particular reason for this, but that's another story. (Mum and Dad gave me a really good digital camera for my birthday.)

OK. What else? My closest friend is called Goldie – that's not really her name, of course. Her name is Emma Locks, but because she's got this rippling golden-blonde hair everyone called her Goldilocks, then just Goldie and it stuck. Most people don't even know her real name any more. We met each other when we were five; she's almost like my sister now, except we don't quarrel. I've got a boyfriend called Alex. He's clever and ironic and dry, and half the time nobody understands a word he's saying. Maybe it sounds strange to say this but I've always thought he'll be the one to finish it between us. One day he'll wander off and forget to tell me he's gone. Maybe I like him precisely because he's a bit strange and you can't explain him even to yourself or pin him down. He eats raw chillies at lunchtime.

None of this says that much about me, though, does it? I could be anyone at all. We did an exercise in creative writing at school once. We had to write a hate-list and a love-list. I can't remember what I put, but I'm going to do another for you, and try to be honest.

I hate: sand between my toes, tomato ketchup, rats, pebble-dashing, animal liberationists, thongs, cooked apples, itchy jumpers, supermarkets, hair sprouting out of noses and ears, designer labels on the outside of clothes, those wristbands with slogans on them that make you feel like you're doing something to help the world simply by wearing them, people who think they're radicals because they're wearing a Che Guevara T-shirt, fat African dictators in white suits who live in grand palaces and eat caviar while their country burns and starves, people using foreign words in their sentences to impress you, spittle at the corner of mouths, Christmas-tree lights that are all tangled up, drizzly Sunday afternoons, waiting for someone, those envelopes with grey fluff inside, golf, windscreen wipers on dry windows, the word 'minging' (and 'manky' and 'pikey' and 'scum'), hair in food, dog shit on the pavement outside my front door, November and February, theme parks, recorded advertisements on the telephone, bank statements, tepid baths, politicians looking sad during two-minute silences, arguments about whether Darwin was right, feeling jealous of friends, patchouli oil, chewing-gum (being chewed, or stuck under tables and seats), the soft-mushy sound people make when they eat a banana, party political broadcasts, trifle, the lottery, being told it takes more muscles to frown than to smile, being told to 'cheer up, it may never happen', being told that I'll change my mind when I get older, the smell of beer, sweet popcorn, strawberry creams, plasters in swimming-pools, asterisks replacing swear words, instruction manuals, new-year resolutions, my socks slipping down inside wellington boots, waking up and not knowing where I am, when I don't get the joke but laugh anyway, ulcers, Monopoly, the sound I used to make on the violin before I gave it up, white chocolate that sticks to the roof of your mouth, people claiming that climate change is still unproven, music in lifts, peanut butter, someone whispering and thinking they might be whispering about me, worrying about my weight, eggshell in my mouth, toothache . . .

I can't think of anything more right now, although I'm sure I will as soon as I'm not writing this.

I love: the smell of basil, the smell of coffee being ground, the smell of petrol and nail-varnish remover, clean sheets, hot baths in the winter after I've had a really long day, the times when I'm swimming well and I feel strong and supple and just right, getting a simultaneous equation to come out, Keats's poetry (and John Donne's and W. H. Auden's), fish pie, black-currant ice-cream, sour apples, the words 'clunk' and 'odd' and 'thwart' and 'fizzgig', the skin of baked potatoes, crying in weepy films, notebooks with thick white pages that haven't been written in yet, getting the giggles with friends, waking up in the dark and looking at the clock and seeing I've still got hours to go before I have to get up, May and early June, rock pools, warm evenings, receiving a letter in the post, the smell of grass after it's rained, thunderstorms, warm rain, weeping willows, firelight, the colour green, Italy, snorkelling, pistachio nuts, bread just out of the oven with lots of butter, cycling downhill (after I've gone up it), the sound when you cut through a hank of hair, good teachers, staying up all night and seeing the sun rise, dancing when you get the rhythm right and the music feels like it's running through your whole body, cherries, the smell of babies, doing cartwheels, mist in the early morning, sharpening pencils, swimming naked, cooking lemon drizzle cake, picking scabs, windy weather, elections, the Olympic Games, bread-and-butter pudding, little white clouds, my room when I've tidied it and every single thing is in its proper place, teat pipettes, strangers who smile at you for no reason, big soft towels, the bobbly scar on my index finger

84

where I grabbed on to a barbed-wire fence, white wine, New York (I've never been there), owls . . .

Do you know what I think? I've just read through both lists, and the hate-list seems much more revealing than the love one. Why do you think this is?

The real question, though, is what am I going to do next? And the answer is – I don't know. I haven't decided. It all feels too big and significant. It almost doesn't feel real. It's as if this is happening to someone else. Not me, Sonia.

She closed the book and put it back in its place, but for a long time she went on sitting on the bed, staring at her hands, her whitened knuckles, until she collected herself and left the room.

Six

'Ticket, please.'

Gaby handed hers over.

'This isn't for first class, madam.'

'No, I know.'

'And, here, it isn't for this journey, either. It's for London. I'm afraid you're on your way to Penzance.'

'Yes. It's very beautiful here, isn't it?'

'Madam?'

'I got on the wrong train, that's all,' she said. 'Sorry. I'll get off at Liskeard, shall I?'

'But you've already passed Plymouth. Why didn't you –?'

'I was in a bit of a dream. It's been a funny kind of day. My son – my only child – has gone off to university for the first time and my mind was on other things. Memories. But I don't want to lie to you – I knew it was the wrong train all the time.'

'I don't follow you.'

'I just suddenly got on it. It seemed the right thing to do, although I'm beginning to feel a bit foolish. Have you ever done anything like that?'

'I can't say I have.'

'Do you want me to pay for this journey?'

'If you get out at the next stop, I'll turn a blind eye. Considering everything.'

'You're a very nice man,' she said warmly, and he blushed and rubbed the side of his face in embarrassment.

'But you'll still need to go to the second-class carriage, unless you want to pay the extra, which will be –'

'No, it's all right. I'll move.'

But the train was already slowing and a voice announced over the Tannoy that they were coming into Liskeard. As she got out on to the platform, she noticed that it was already dusk. The nights were drawing in.

She didn't have an address or a phone number, just the name of a village a few miles from Liskeard. In any case, she certainly didn't want to phone ahead. That was out of the question. Never mind, she'd have to get a taxi to Rashmoor, then wander about until she tracked her down.

A few months previously, Gaby had been lounging on the sofa after supper, nursing a large glass of red wine and half watching the news. There was an item about the floods that had severely damaged several villages in Cornwall; some residents had even had to be rescued from their houses in boats. A female reporter, sloshing along in the muddy brown water and looking inappropriately jolly in bright red wellingtons that had obviously been bought for the occasion, said, 'I'm here in the picturesque village of Rashmoor, where dozens of houses have had to be evacuated. It really is an extraordinary scene.' The camera panned over images of a street that had become a stream, with the tops of cars, fences and lamp-posts poking out of its fast-flowing surface, and then of the inside of a house, water half-way up the stairs and a furious-looking woman standing a few steps up holding a bucket, before returning to the face of the smiling reporter.

At that point Gaby had sat bolt upright on her sofa, slopping her wine. For as she watched, a woman wearing boots and an oilskin walked past. She glanced fleetingly at the camera and, for a surreal moment, Gaby had the clear sense that she was looking straight at *her* – and then she looked away and quickened her pace. Even as Gaby a gasped and leant closer, the woman was gone, and the reporter was saying something about climate change and insurance companies. She hadn't seen her for nineteen years, yet the recognition was sharp and total: the square jaw and intense eyes, the colour of a gas flame; the way she had of carrying herself, back straight, head up, like a soldier on parade. She'd always done that, even as a girl. People had always thought she was taller than she was.

For a few minutes Gaby had sat on the sofa, startled with the shock of it. Then she drained her glass of wine, stood up decisively and pulled the large road atlas down from the bookshelf. She turned to the index and found Rashmoor. And there it was, a tiny dot near Bodmin Moor, a few miles from Liskeard and not far from the sea. Without giving herself time to think, she rang Directory Enquiries and asked for the number of Nancy Belmont, Rashmoor, Cornwall. 'Sorry, caller,' said the voice at the other end of the line, 'but that number is ex-directory.' So she had seen her: she did live there. After so many years of not knowing where she was, not knowing if she was in the country, not even knowing if she was still alive, Gaby had found her. Or, rather, she had appeared to Gaby, like an apparition. She had stared into her eyes.

But that had been many weeks ago now, and Gaby had done nothing about it. She hadn't even mentioned it to Connor, although she didn't understand why not. She'd practised the words – 'Guess who I saw on television?' – but never spoken them. Connor had told her often enough that she should let Nancy go. He had argued, reasonably, that whatever her motives Nancy had made it clear by her behaviour that their friendship was over. It was no good trying to persuade her to change her mind; you couldn't beg someone to be your friend or plead with them to like you. And neither had she told Stefan, for what was the point? She'd let the image go and it drifted slowly to the muddy depths of her mind where it lay out of sight.

But now here she was in Liskeard, on some madcap errand to find a friend who wasn't a friend and ask her – ask her what? Why did you leave Stefan like that? Why did you leave me? Why did you never write? What happened? She wasn't even sure any more that she wanted to know the answers. To make it worse, there wasn't a single taxi. It was getting dark, and Gaby stood indecisively, pondering. Perhaps she should get back on the next London train. She could be home before too late, have a long bath and watch a film or curl up in bed with a book.

But even as she was thinking this, she had turned her back on the station and walked towards the centre of the town. She had no idea of which direction to take – the atlas had shown that Rashmoor was north-west of Liskeard, but which was north-west, for goodness' sake? Connor knew things like that. He would frown for a few seconds, considering, then point decisively. And he was always bloody right. It was extremely annoying – like the way when he was driving and she was failing to find where they were on the map, let alone where they were going and what road to take, he would jab the page and say, 'We're about there.' Perhaps she could smell the sea and follow that, or perhaps she could orient herself by the North Star, if she knew which star it was. Wasn't it the bright one, low on the horizon, or was that the Pole Star – or maybe the Pole Star and the North Star were the same? She squinted up at the darkening sky hopelessly. She should learn about constellations, she thought, knowing that of course she wouldn't.

She went into the first pub she came to, making her way through the fug of cigarette smoke to the bar.

'Can you tell me the way to Rashmoor?'

'Rashmoor – let me see, it rings a bell.'

'It's near here.'

'Yeah – Vicky, do you know where Rashmoor is?'

'Isn't it the little village up past the old tin mines? The one that got badly flooded in the summer?'

'That's the one. I knew that, I knew it.' He leant across the bar to Gaby. 'Take the first left out of the town, drive up that road for a mile or two, then take the next right along a small road that follows the river. It's a bit isolated, mind.'

'Thanks. How many miles do you think?'

'Not many. It'll only take ten or so minutes I reckon.'

Gaby didn't tell him she was walking. She asked for a glass of white wine and a packet of dry-roasted nuts, and sat at a small table near the window, sipping the wine slowly and popping nuts into her mouth, crunching them. Then she stood up, waved at the man behind the bar and left.

Before long, she had left Liskeard. All around her stretched the moorland, scattered with the pale shapes of sheep, and above the great sky heaved with clouds. A bird flew low over the ground in front of her uttering a plaintive cry and once she thought she glimpsed a fox. As she walked, her feet becoming sore and blistered so she had to shuffle, she tried to plan what she would say to Nancy. But it was no good. Her mind refused to co-operate. She understood, but she still didn't truly believe that in a short while she might be standing face to face with the woman who for years had been her closest friend and who had nearly been her sister-in-law. She'd used to imagine the circumstances of their meeting (the party, the wedding or funeral, the moment in the street when they would find themselves face to face), and she'd practised what she'd say – whole, eloquent speeches that would make Nancy realize what she had done, the pain she had caused not just to Stefan but to her as well. She had long, impassioned sections about the meaning of friendship, its unconditional loyalty. Sometimes the words she wrote in her head were delivered more in sorrow than anger – but often they bubbled with rage. Now, walking over the moors towards her, she couldn't remember a word of them, and even if she could, she knew that they would be useless.

She tried instead to think about Nancy in the past, but even that was difficult. She found that, all of a sudden, she could not properly remember her face, either as a child or as a young woman. She summoned particular events to mind to see if that would bring back the image of her friend (their first day at secondary school, when Nancy had turned up with cropped hair and her leg in plaster; that bike ride they'd been on together when they'd cycled through a shallow-looking puddle and found themselves pedalling deeper and deeper into it, until at last they'd both toppled off, screaming with laughter; the time Nancy and Stefan had announced to her, with awkward formality, that they were – er – kind of, you know, seeing each other; a rare time when she'd seen her friend cry, though she'd never discovered the reason, and she'd been extraordinarily moved by the way her fingers had clutched a sodden, shredded tissue, which she used to mop her swollen eyes; Nancy's twenty-first birthday party when she'd worn a tux and danced salsa with Stefan to everyone's applause). But Nancy was like the person in the photograph whose features have been pixellated out. She was a smudge. The years they had known each other seemed to run together, all the separate episodes leaking into each other like colours mixing on a palette. Nothing of Nancy was distinct in her memory any more; everything was murky and undifferentiated. The only image that remained clear was the brief glimpse that Gaby had had of her on the television screen, when for almost two decades she had been a stranger.

Instead, Gaby found herself remembering Stefan's face on the day that Nancy had left him. That still lay clear in her mind. It had been a weekday night. Ethan was asleep in his room, the night-light glowing softly beside him, and Connor – who had been on duty for thirty-six hours

– had been in bed for an hour or more. Gaby was lying on the sofa reading a book (she even remembered which: *Innocence* by Penelope Fitzgerald, a lovely novel that she would associate for ever with betrayal). The rain had hammered down outside, but inside it was warm and messy, and she was sipping a mug of hot chocolate that she had made – with a sense of luxurious self-indulgence – with cream and chocolate melted over a double-boiler. She had been feeling as contented as a lazy cat. And then there had been an urgent rapping on the front door. She had pulled the belt on her dressing-gown tighter, taken a last thick gulp of her drink, and gone to see who it was. Stefan had stood on the threshold in the pouring rain, his hair flattened on to his skull. He had stared at Gaby, but she had had the impression that he wasn't really seeing her. A small frown puzzled his brow, but under it his eyes were empty. The skin round his mouth was slack, and he looked old, drab and hopeless. Gaby had tried to hug him, but he stood passively in her arms in his thick wet overcoat, his arms hanging by his sides.

Walking along the empty road now, Gaby felt the old anger flare up inside her, making her quicken her pace. There was one image of Nancy that she could vividly remember from the past, after all, and she held on to it. She had gone round to Stefan's flat, which until then had been Stefan and Nancy's flat, the following day, knowing from Stefan that she would find her friend there. Nancy had arranged a time when Stefan was at work to collect her possessions and drop off the keys. Gaby was struck by how efficient she was being – telling her brother in the evening, moving out lock, stock and barrel the next afternoon, not even keeping a key in case she should want to return. They had been together for five years, they had planned their future together, but now in a single day she was clearing away all signs that she had ever been there. Gaby was nearly too late. Nancy had arrived earlier and spent less time in the flat than she had anticipated, so Gaby came upon her pulling her last case into the back of the van, the engine already running and ready to go. She was wearing dark jeans, sneakers and a black leather jacket, and her hair was covered with a bandana. She looked agile, streamlined, vaguely piratical. When she saw Gaby she seemed neither startled nor guilty. She slammed the back doors shut, rubbed her hands on her jeans and stood back. 'Gaby,' she said, 'I thought it was better this way. A quick, clean break.'

'Better?' said Gaby, raising her voice and making Ethan, asleep in his buggy, jerk awake for an instant. 'Better?'

'Yes.'

'Easier, you mean. Creeping away like a thief in the night so you don't have to see the pain you're causing.'

'I know the pain I'm causing.'

'No, you don't. You don't know. You've got no idea.'

'But it doesn't matter anyway, does it? Pity doesn't make you stay with someone.'

'Why?' Gaby had said. 'Why, for God's sake? I thought you loved him. He certainly loves you. I thought you were going to stay together. It was all so good.'

'No, it wasn't.'

'Stefan thought it was.'

'Stefan would think things were good even if he was

94

drowning, as if hoping can make it so. I know you adore him. I know he's adorable – but that's what he does, isn't it? It's what you both do, and always have.'

Gaby gazed at her for a moment, her mouth open. Ethan stirred and she rocked the buggy violently until he whimpered in protest. 'Do you think I'm going to stand here on the pavement and discuss what's wrong with Stefan and with me?'

'That's not –'

'What about me?'

'You?'

'Weren't you going to tell me? We're friends, aren't we? We've always been friends.'

'You're right. I should have said. The truth is, I didn't know what to say, and I had to tell Stefan first. I was going to write to you later.'

'Write – what? A postcard or something, saying, "By the way, I've gone away. It's been nice."'

'Not a postcard, of course not. Gaby –'

'And you're Ethan's godmother – non-godmother, whatever.'

'I don't think he'll miss me.'

'Have you met someone else? Out with the old and in with the new.'

Nancy made a small gesture, palms up, but didn't reply.

'So – that's it?'

'That's it.'

'It's very cruel.'

'Life's very –'

'Oh, please, don't start spouting clichés at me!' She heard her own voice, ugly in its humiliation, then watched

95

as Nancy fished her keys out of the jacket pocket, walked up to the door of the flat, and pushed them through the letterbox.

'Will I see you?' Gaby asked. 'You don't have to chuck me, too. Things can't just *go* like this, as if they've been washed away by the tide. After all these years. Can they?'

There was a pause.

'I should go, Gaby,' said Nancy. Her voice was unwavering.

'You haven't even said sorry!'

'If it makes it better, I'm sorry. More than you'll ever know.'

'It doesn't make it better.'

The two women stared at each other. Gaby watched as Nancy stepped into the van, and revved the engine, then pulled out. That was the image she remembered now, Nancy's face behind the glass, implacable and composed. Seeing her face separated from her by the windscreen, Gaby had thought that perhaps something had always set Nancy apart – the same something that had drawn people to her, like a magnet with metal filings. She had a strange and alluring quality of being able to seem both intimate and distant; there was a kind of doubleness about her. She had never met her since.

Perhaps Connor was right, thought Gaby, stopping to take off her sandals and liberate her stinging feet. Nancy had become a myth, fixed by her absence into a series of rigid meanings. She shouldn't be going to see her because you can't go back to the past. On that wretched day outside Stefan's flat, the two of them had set out on different roads and every turning they had taken, decision they had made, person they had met, loss they had suffered, love they had gained and joy they had experienced without the other had made the difference between them greater. They would be awkward strangers, with nothing to say.

Yet she needed to see Nancy again, to turn her from the ghost she had become back into an ordinary woman. And, anyway, she had come this far and knew she wasn't going to turn back now.

It was dark by the time she arrived at the edge of Rashmoor and stopped to consider what she should do next. The village was larger than she had expected, and it lay along the river that had flooded it so disastrously a few months ago. It was hard to believe that the quiet, darkly glinting strip of water had caused so much damage, or that until recently the stone houses had been half submerged and the small, hump-backed bridge isolated like a serpent's coil in the rushing flood. Gaby was cold and tired and drained by the emotions of the day. She shivered involuntarily and pulled her jacket closer. The moors stretched round the houses in all directions, and the lights from the windows and smoke from the chimneys made the scene cosy, but at the same time alarming in its remoteness.

Gaby walked down what was clearly the high street, although it was deserted now, past several houses, most of whose curtains were drawn so that she couldn't see inside. There was a pub called the Green Man from which laughter and voices could be heard, a café with its blinds down and the 'closed' notice hanging on its door, a hardware shop, a grocery, a newsagent's and a small post office. When she reached the spot where she thought the cheery reporter had been standing in her wellington boots, she halted and gazed round her, trying to remember exactly where Nancy had been coming from, then she meandered uncertainly along the road, occasionally seeing through windows women who weren't Nancy. After about twenty minutes she knocked on the door of a house called the Rookery and asked the diminutive man who answered if he knew where a Nancy Belmont lived. He didn't. Neither did the family a few doors down, although they said the name rang a bell. At the third house, the young woman said that she thought a Nancy Belmont was living in the white cottage on the outskirts of the village. She pointed a finger. 'That way,' she said. 'I think.'

So Gaby walked away from the village and down a tiny rutted lane that led into the moors until she came across it. Dread settled on her, making her skin prickle and her heart beat faster. The house stood alone, set back from the track and in the middle of its own well-tended garden. It was small, more of a cottage really, pleasingly symmetrical, with white stone walls. Its upper windows were dark, but downstairs they were lit up, the curtains open. There was a Virginia creeper on one side of the grey door, and a small tree – Gaby had no idea what kind: she'd never been any good at identifying trees – in a pot at the other. A fire crackled and smouldered in the garden, and although Gaby couldn't make out its flames behind the hedge she could see the orange glow. There were rose-bushes, pruned back for the winter. Nancy had always loved yellow roses – yellow roses, peonies and sweet peas. She had grown herbs on the balcony of Stefan's flat. Gaby crept forward, taking care not to make any noise, then stopped a few feet from the gate that led into the narrow strip of front garden, obscured by the bushes. She leant her cheek against the trunk of a stout tree, appalled by an idea that had struck her. What had made her assume that Nancy lived alone? At the idea of stumbling in on her with her family the blood rose in her cheeks. She pictured falling in through the door to several pairs of eyes turned on her inquiringly, and Nancy's appraising, contemptuous stare.

But as she was thinking this, a figure moved into one of the illuminated downstairs windows. Gaby gasped, her hand going automatically to her mouth, and shrank back. She felt dizzy with shock. Nancy was standing at the window, just a few feet from her. For a suspended moment Gaby thought she must be staring out at her. But, no, she was looking down at something, and Gaby realized she was in her kitchen, standing at a work surface, mixing something in a large bowl. Her movements were unhurried, and Gaby remembered how everything that Nancy did had always seemed considered. It used to be relaxing just watching her wash up – the way she cleared surfaces in advance, filled the sink with hot water, started with the cutlery and glasses, then moved on to dishes and pans, and how she would rinse the sink after-wards, rubbing the taps with a cloth to make them gleam. She was working with the same calm purpose now, and Gaby saw that she was kneading the dough she had made, pushing her fists into its elastic surface. The light was shining on her so that it was like watching her on a large screen, her face perfectly in focus, her expression clear.

Gaby couldn't move. She crouched in the shadows, noticing every flicker that crossed Nancy's features. Every so often, she moved away from the window and back into the darkness, but then returned. Her face seemed thinner than Gaby remembered, but she still held herself upright.

She moved away from the window once more, but this time she didn't return. Instead, a side door opened and she walked into the garden, wiping her hands on the apron she was wearing. She stood by the fire, bending to pick up sticks that had fallen from the pile and throw them back on to the blaze. Then she walked out to the shadows cast by the tree that stood by the low drystone wall marking the garden's boundaries, where she reached into its branches. Gaby realized she was picking apples, twisting them by their stalks to test their ripeness and gathering them in the folds of her apron. When she had enough she walked back into the house, pulling the door shut. Then she was at the window again, this time peeling the apples.

Gaby stood up straight and drew a deep breath. Without giving herself time to think or change her mind, she walked briskly to the gate, rubbing her hands to keep them warm; and opened it, at the same time lifting her eyes to the kitchen window. Nancy was no longer standing there, and now smoke was coming from the chimney. Gaby marched to the front door, pushed the bell and rapped the iron knocker violently several times.

'Right,' she muttered fiercely, under her breath. 'Now we'll see.'

She was filled with the anger that had been lying like dry tinder for years and now had been lit.

Footsteps echoed inside the house. The door opened.

Seven

The two women stood face to face, just a few inches between them. Nancy was motionless, her eyes narrowed as if she was nerving herself for a sharp burst of pain. Gaby felt rather than saw a shiver pass through her. Then she nodded, as if she'd been expecting Gaby to arrive.

'Surprise!' yelled Gaby, in a bellicose manner.

'It is,' said Nancy, drily, still not moving. 'But I might have known you'd find me in the end.' Such a smile lit her face, warming her eyes, that for a moment Gaby forgot they were strangers. Then it faded and her face became wary once more.

'Your house doesn't look as if the flood damaged it,' Gaby said, fiercely polite. 'I suppose it's far enough away from the river, is it?'

'I'm sorry?' Nancy's eyes seemed to bulge in her face. 'You've come to ask me about the flood?'

'Well, no, obviously not. That would be truly mad. I've come to tell you that –' Her voice was harsh and cracked. No, that was wrong. She tried again, standing stiffly to attention and swallowing hard before she spoke. 'For a long time I have very much needed you to know that you –' Then she stopped, feeling the words clog in her throat and her shoulders begin to shake. 'Oh, bugger.' She gulped, rubbing her sleeve over her face to mop up the tears. 'I can't stop crying today. This isn't going the way I'd planned it.'

Nancy gave a little snort of laughter. 'You haven't changed a bit. I would have known you anywhere.' She stood back. 'You'd better come in, now that you're here.'

Gaby, still weeping, shuffled into a small hall with wooden floorboards and a large mirror on one wall, and Nancy closed the door behind her. Her sobs gradually subsided, until she was being shaken by the occasional spasm. Nancy stood beside her, saying nothing, not trying to comfort or hurry her.

'Sorry,' Gaby said at last, dragging the back of her hand across her snotty face, then pushing her bedraggled hair behind her ears.

'Do you want to wash your face, clean up?'

'What? Why? But I guess that's a good idea. It's been a long day.'

'It's in there. I'll be in the kitchen when you're done.'

'Yes. OK.'

Gaby locked the door and leant against it, trying to get her breathing to return to normal. Then she took off her jacket, letting it drop to the floor, and tightened the belt on her skirt. She took a resigned breath, and examined herself in the small looking-glass over the sink. Her hair was damp and hopelessly tangled, like a sodden nest of vipers; her freckles stood out in blotches in her peaky, smeared face. Mascara was smudged under both eyes; there was mud on her chin and a large streak of green running down her cheek, presumably from where she'd leant against a tree outside the house. And she smelt a bit like a dog that had been out in the rain.

'Oh dear me,' she said. 'What a terrible sight.' A giggle rose in her, hurting her throat and threatening to turn into another sob. She ran hot water into the basin, cupped her hands in it, and scooped it over her dirty face. Then she rummaged in her bag for a brush, but could find only a small plastic comb, which she tugged through the knots, her eyes stinging, until it snapped in her hair and she had to prise it loose. She put on some lipstick, but the effect wasn't what she had hoped for – it made her look more rather than less unkempt – then sprayed perfume liberally all over herself. Her blisters were throbbing now, and she loosened her sandals and looked down at her raw, mucky feet, with chipped orange varnish on the toenails. She was a mess, no doubt about it, top to tail.

Oh, well, she thought, and squared her shoulders, giving a last defiant glance into the mirror before opening the door.

The kitchen lay off the hallway and was clearly the biggest room in the house. On one side were the cooker and hob, the fridge and the scrubbed wooden work surfaces, and it was here that Gaby had seen Nancy standing. Apple peel was curled in the top of a plastic bowl, ready for the compost, and on a large wooden board a clean white cloth lay over the top of what must have been the dough. Everything was austere and absurdly neat, like an illustration from some fifties magazine. Racks of spices – alphabetically ordered, Gaby noted with horror – and bottles of oils, vinegar and seasoning stood next to the hob. There was a small shelf lined with cookery books.

Knives (in order of size, thought Gaby, once more seized by the urge to laugh) were stuck on a magnetic strip. The surfaces gleamed and the lighting was very bright, as if the kitchen was Nancy's laboratory. She thought of their kitchen at home, which, despite Connor's best efforts, was shambolic – drawers stuffed with bizarre cooking implements, leaflets and birthday-cake candles; shelves tottering with jars, chipped bowls, lids off lost Tupperware and discarded bills; work surfaces that were generally strewn with unkitchenly items (books, earrings and necklaces in bright heaps, towels, sunglasses, Ethan's piano music, a camera, a clothes brush, a T-shirt or two, a bit of makeup perhaps, holiday brochures . . .); a fridge that Connor cleaned once a month, his mouth pursed in disapproval, but which at all other times heaved with food past its eat-by date, bowls of leftovers covered with clingfilm, pushed to the back and forgotten, several half-consumed tins of sweetcorn or tuna and bottles of milk. Gaby remembered one time – Connor had been away at a conference or something – when she and Ethan had eaten their supper standing in front of the open fridge, simply pulling out items of food at random (a bowl of stewed apples, fresh anchovies, a hunk of chorizo) and eating them there and then. Ethan had stuffed several olives into his mouth and washed them down with a liquid yoghurt; she had taken a large bite out of a red pepper and posted a piece of goat's cheese after it, then pulled the tab on a can of beer.

At the other end of the room, down a couple of steps, the light was more muted and a fire burnt in a small grate, a sagging sofa to one side of it and, under the second

105

window, an old, rickety table, painted white, with two chairs pulled up at it and a bowl of dog-roses in the middle. On one wall there was a framed black-and-white photograph of the sea, with sun splashing light on to its surface. Gaby took all of this in, and at the same time she was aware of Nancy. She was dressed in a pair of old jeans and wore an oat-coloured pullover with white paint on one sleeve; her short hair was brushed behind her ears. No earrings, no bangles, no makeup. She was stirring apples in a pan, a glass of red wine at hand, and there was the smell of cloves in the air, with woodsmoke.

'You definitely do live on your own,' Gaby said. 'Don't you sometimes feel like running amok?'

'I've lived on my own for years,' said Nancy, not bothering to reply to the second question. 'Do you want some wine?'

'Yes.'

'You look as if you could do with some food as well.'

'Do I? In what way? Oh, never mind – I'm starving, actually.'

Nancy tipped some wine into a glass, then pulled open the fridge. 'There are some left-over potatoes, and a bit of gravy. How about that?'

'Like being back at school,' said Gaby, rudely. She was aware of getting the tone all wrong, hitting the wrong note, being puerile, but she had no idea how to behave or what to say. She had always thought that when at last she saw Nancy everything she had stored up would be released and the words would pour out; she would shout and cry and feel purged. But something about Nancy's gravity and self-possession thwarted her. She felt clumsy,

106

yet volatile – like a reactive chemical that was about to change its state dramatically. Would she shift from solid to liquid, or liquid to gas – or even gas to a spitting explosion?

'Here. Do you want me to heat it?'

'No. It's fine like this.'

Gaby chopped the potatoes into small chunks and mashed the gravy into them. Without bothering to sit down, she forked the mixture into her mouth ravenously, interspersed with gulps of wine. She didn't try to speak until she had finished.

'I took Ethan to university today,' she said at last. 'Big day. I hadn't realized how painful it was going to be.' She glared belligerently at Nancy to stop herself weeping; she felt as though there was a sea of tears inside her. 'I dropped him off and said goodbye and for a few minutes I thought I couldn't bear it; I literally thought I'd break into little bits because it hurt so badly. All that part of my life over, and why didn't I know how precious it was? Then I got on to a train to Liskeard. I hadn't known I was going to do it. It hadn't occurred to me. I thought I was going to go home, and all of a sudden there I was on a train going west.'

'How is Ethan?' asked Nancy.

'He's your non-godson.'

'I didn't say *who*, I said how.'

'I know, I know. I was just reacting like that because you were trying to steer it all back to safe ground and I don't want to be on safe ground – and, anyway, there isn't any safe ground between us. Nothing's solid.'

Gaby took another large mouthful of wine. This was

better. She was losing the horrible tight feeling and getting into her stride. 'Ethan's fine, if you really want to know, which presumably you don't, or only in a mildly curious way, or you would have found out before. He's a sweetheart, actually.' She heard her voice growing maudlin. 'My lovely only child.'

'Only?'

'Yes. You thought there'd be others?'

'I – well, I probably just assumed you and Connor would have lots.'

'Happy families. No. I had miscarriages instead of children.'

'I'm sorry.'

'I used to think it was my fault because of how I was after Ethan – as if my mind and body were in a conspiracy against me and knew I wasn't fit to be a mother. Well, that was then. And before you ask, Connor's fine too. OK? And so's Stefan. Stains on his tie when he wears one and he carries everything around in split plastic bags and forgets where he's parked his car, forgets his own birthday, even – but his students adore him. Well, as you once said to me and have probably forgotten but I haven't, he's adorable. Anyway, he's fine. So we've got that out of the way.'

'Is he –?'

'Married? Nope.'

'Do you want some fruit?'

'What? Fruit? No. I'd like some more wine, though. I seem to have finished the glass without noticing – you haven't. Yours is still half full, or should that be half empty? Anyway, the point is that you're sipping and I'm gulping, and you're saying a few cautious words at a time – most of them questions, by the way – and I'm talking nineteen to the dozen. You should really drink more quickly on an evening like this. It'd be better if we were both half sloshed.'

'Do you think so?'

'There you are! Do I think so? Yes, I think so. I haven't come here to have a polite conversation with you, filling you in on the headlines of what's been happening since we last met.'

'So why have you come, Gaby?'

It was the first time Nancy had used her name; hearing it, Gaby felt the atmosphere change. Even the light in the room seemed to soften round the two women, and for a moment they both stood in silence, simply looking at each other's older faces; lines that hadn't been there before marking the years that they'd both missed.

'Let's sit down,' Gaby said, taking her wine and moving over to the sofa, where she curled up with her bare, grimy feet tucked under her. Nancy followed with the bottle.

'Why did I come?' she mused. 'I don't know, really. I always thought I'd see you again. It seemed inconceivable to me that we would never meet, that we'd die without meeting. I met you when I was eleven. That's thirty-odd years ago. We always said we'd know each other when we were old. Do you remember? Do you remember in the tree-house we made a promise to each other? Do you?'

Nancy nodded.

'You were always there. You were there when I started school and don't forget, *you* chose *me* – you came up to me in the second week and said you thought we could be friends and would I like to share a locker. You were there when I had my first period. You were there when I had my first boyfriend, and you were there when I got dumped – I hate that word – we never used it, did we? "Chucked", that's what we said. Anyway. Exams, parties, shopping, cooking, dieting, everything. You were always at my house, sleeping over, doing homework with me, revising with me, sharing secrets, giggling, crying – you were my sister, the one I didn't have but always, always wanted.'

'Gaby –'

'No, shut up. Listen. And I think – I thought, anyway – that I was your sister, too. Especially after your mother started acting so oddly, going out with all those strange men and stuff, and we were your family, really. You practically lived with us. When I remember my childhood, you're in it. People often talk about how when their marriage splits up, one of the things that's so painful is that they've got no one to share memories with any more. All the things you did together don't exist any longer. But I think it's like that with friendships too. With our friendship, anyway. It was as if, when you upped and left, you'd rubbed away half of my life. It almost felt that it hadn't happened. Who could I say, "Do you remember?" to. Who'd get all the subtexts, all the stupid hidden meanings? You know that lovely feeling when you hear a phrase, or see a particular sight, and you can catch someone's eye and you know that they're thinking what you're thinking. But you don't have that with many people, and I thought I had it with you. I thought you had it with me.

I thought it was unconditional. The one area of my life I felt entirely certain about.'

She tipped back the glass and swallowed hugely, in uninhibited full swing now, the stiffness and fear dissolved by wine and tears. She felt liquid inside, all the feelings, memories and inchoate desires sloshing together in a dark, rolling wave of emotion. She could talk all night. She could talk for ever. She could change the past and set the future on a different course, just with the lava flow of her words.

'Please, Gaby –'

'Listen, will you? When you started going out with Stefan, it felt really, really weird at first. I worried that we wouldn't be so close. You had other loyalties; you wouldn't be able to confide in me – certainly not about your love life, anyway. I thought I wouldn't be so close to Stefan either, and you know how we are. It was always him and me against the world – though, of course, darling Stefan's not against anyone, is he? He doesn't have it in him. Maybe that was why you left him. Maybe he's just too nice for his own good. He wasn't even bitter or angry about you leaving like that – just bewildered and terribly sad. It was like seeing the lights turned out. He continued with everything exactly the same, but there was no life in it. Anyway, I'm getting away from the point. More wine, please. The point was, I can't remember what the point was. Yes. The difference it made to our relationship. It was all right. Wasn't it all right? We all dealt with it brilliantly, I thought. At first, I dreaded one of you finishing with the other, but after a bit I forgot to dread it. It seemed so solid, so good.

'I'm listening to myself speaking and I know I probably seem ridiculous to you. You're all silent and dignified and orderly, and I'm like some kind of bubbling Icelandic geyser. But I made a decision when I was walking here that I didn't care about being cool or pretending it's not a big deal. You know when people fall over in public and they're bleeding copiously or their ankle has swollen so much they can hardly walk? They jump up shakily and insist they're fine, it's nothing, because for some reason it's embarrassing to say it's really painful. I don't want to be like that. It's really painful. Do you hear me? Do you?'

She stood up suddenly and went to the window, pressed her hot forehead against the cool pane and looked out into the night. She could make out, through the reflection of her own face, the lane and the tree where she'd hidden, and beyond that nothing but darkness. Behind her, the fire crackled.

'Why have I come?' She turned back to face Nancy. 'Why? To be honest, I've no fucking idea. Not really, not the way you mean. I just suddenly found I had to. I didn't want you to fade to a distant memory and not to matter any more. I *wanted* you to matter, don't you see? I wanted to hurt about it, even though I should have grown up by now and accepted that it was all so long ago when I was a foolish young woman. I'm a foolish middle-aged woman now and I don't want time to heal everything. I hate that. It's crap. And I wanted to see if it mattered to you, too. I couldn't bear it if you'd forgotten about me and us, when all this time I've remembered. I wanted you to hurt, too. I've been waiting for this day. For this moment.'

'If you'll let me speak.'

'And I had to find out why you went away like that, and why you never came back.'

'I think –'

'I always expected you to come back. More wine, please.'

'I always expected to come back as well.'

'Did you?'

'And yet it seemed impossible – more and more impossible as the years passed.' Nancy was speaking quietly and slowly, not looking at Gaby but gazing into the distance. 'I've always been a bit of a bridge-burner. I'm good at beginning again. I've always been like that, you know it as well as I do. Even when I was young, if someone offended or insulted me, or if they did me wrong, that would be it.'

'But it was *you* doing the wrong.'

'Well, exactly. That made it even more imperative to start again.'

'So you just walked away.'

'You could say that.'

Gaby rubbed her face. The elated anger was dying down and she felt weary. One side of her was hot from the fire and the other still a bit chilly. 'But, Nancy, it was precisely the walking away that was the wrong thing. Leaving Stefan – of course that was awful for him, one of those everyday tragedies, but it wasn't wrong, a crime.'

'It felt like a crime.' Nancy levelled her turquoise gaze at Gaby; her voice was matter-of-fact.

'So you fled the scene?'

'Something like that.'

'And never came back?'

'And never came back.' Nancy poured more wine into

her own glass and held it up, squinting at it, then taking a sip. 'I didn't know the way.'

'Was there someone else?'

'No. It was just me.'

'Are you a lesbian? Is that what it was?'

'No. I'm not a lesbian. Anything else?'

'Do you have any kids?'

'No.'

'Didn't you want them?'

'That's enough, I think.'

'Do you? Have you been happy?'

'Happy?'

'In your life.'

'I don't know what that means.'

'Have you been in love?'

'Gaby –'

'What? Why is that a wrong question? I've come all the way from London. Why can't I ask you that, for God's sake?'

'Yes, I've been in love. Yes, I've lived with men. Yes, I live alone now.'

'And?'

'What? Yes, I've thought about you. Is that it? Does that make you feel better? I've thought about you, Gaby. So, then.'

She leant forward and stirred the fire with a poker. The flames leapt higher, casting writhing shadows over the room. 'Do you know what your problem is, Gaby?'

'I have lots of problems, but they're probably not the ones you're thinking of. I imagine you're going to tell me, though.'

'Your problem is that you always think you can make things better.'

'Oh.' Gaby looked down at her hands, noticing that there was still dirt under the nails. Connor had often said the same about her, and even Ethan had criticized her insistence that, when things were going wrong in his life, she could help him.

'And sometimes,' continued Nancy, 'trying to help doesn't. You can make things worse by meddling.'

'Am I meddling now? Is that all it is?'

'There are things you can't change.'

'What are you saying? That our friendship's over? I know it's over. I just want to understand why.'

'What more can I say? Perhaps there's nothing else to understand.'

A stab of pain hit Gaby between the eyes. 'Do you mean we're not even going to have the conversation?'

'You mean, the all-night-weeping-and-shouting-and-baring-our-souls conversation?'

'*Yes*, fuck it, that's what I mean. Don't sneer.'

'I didn't mean to –'

'You did. So that's it, is it? That's your summing-up of what happened. "Perhaps there's nothing else to understand." I'll leave and nothing will be any different, nothing will have changed. *I want to understand!*'

'Gaby –'

'Don't "Gaby" me in that patient voice.'

'Sorry.'

'No.' Gaby sighed. 'It's me. I'm overwrought. I hear myself sometimes and am appalled.'

'Do you want some more wine?'

'Maybe I shouldn't.'

'I'll make us some tea, then, shall I?'

'I said shouldn't, not wouldn't – but go on, then, tea would be good.'

'What does Connor think about your being here?' asked Nancy, as she filled the kettle with water and set it on the hob.

'He doesn't know. He's on a boat in the middle of the Channel with Stefan. It's Stefan's boat and they're sailing it back from France. They do it every year. They'll arrive in Southampton tomorrow, but he won't be back till Monday because they need to put the boat to bed for the winter. That's more information than you need, isn't it?'

'It's OK. So they sail together?'

'Yes. He'll probably think I'm daft when I tell him.'

Gaby watched from the sofa as Nancy poured the water over the tea-bags. The anger had drained away again. She felt quite peaceful and mildly detached, and the heat of the fire was making her sleepy.

'What do you do?' she asked.

'Me? I'm head teacher at a primary school near here.'

'But you were training to be a lawyer!'

'I began again, didn't I? It seemed more worthwhile. What about you?'

'Oh, me. This and that. I've never really settled on one thing. And then after Ethan was born, I took lots of time off, what with one thing and another. Well, that was when you were still around, wasn't it, so you remember all that? It was a miserable period. It took me a long time to realize how shocking it was. And then the miscarriages. Everything got a bit scrambled. I've ended up by doing lots of things not very well. At the moment I work for this little company – more like a one-man show than a company – that puts together cultural holidays for people from abroad. Mostly they're American, but not always. You know, Stratford and a couple of Shakespeare plays, London and several more plays, plus art galleries and maybe a literary walk or two. I like it, but I'm not very organized. I've made terrible mistakes. I'm OK at the creative and social side – maybe that's why Gil's kept me on. I decide what a group should see and I try to arrange for them to meet directors or actors. So you could say that I'm kind of working with the theatre, like I used to say I wanted to when I was eleven, though it never occurred to me then that saying and doing were entirely different things. I certainly get to see lots of plays.'

'You always did.'

'Yes.'

Nancy handed her a mug of tea. Gaby sat up straighter and wrapped both her hands round it.

'And Connor?'

She took a sip. 'Connor's still a doctor, of course. Obsessively so. He's a pain specialist. It's a big new area and he's one of the experts. Actually, he's the director of a pain clinic that's just been set up in central London.'

'The science of suffering,' said Nancy.

'Yes, I suppose so – except it's not as simple as a science, that's what's so fascinating about it. Pain's in the brain. It's very subjective. He's been involved in this survey which shows that if you tell one group of volunteers their pain is moderate, and the other group that it's severe, the moderate group will actually *feel* significantly less pain – you can tell it by the pattern in their brain. Isn't that weird? That's one side of it, and the other is very literal, trying to help patients who suffer terrible pain, sometimes for years, decades. He works with torture victims. He sees terrible things. The stories he tells me – you know, you could go mad thinking about all the cruelty in the world. The work he does makes what I do feel frivolous, stupid.'

'We can't all work with torture victims.'

'I know that, of course.'

'There's a little boy in my school. His name's Ari, and he comes from Chechnya. His parents claimed asylum here but his two brothers are still in Chechnya, if they're alive. When he first arrived, he didn't speak. Not a single word, no matter how hard we tried to draw him out. He has the most touching face, with enormous eyes that stare at you. It was weeks before he even said, "Hello," or uttered his name. At break he would simply stand in one corner of the playground with his arms folded across his body and not move – it didn't matter if it was freezing or raining. He was always perfectly polite. I often wonder what he's seen, what he's carrying inside him. A few months ago, he was on a school trip and it was night. He was staring up at the stars and the moon, and he suddenly said, "It's the same moon and the same stars as in my country." That seemed to make him happy.'

'How heartrending,' said Gaby. She thought: It's been nineteen years since I had a conversation with Nancy Belmont.

'It's late,' said Nancy, 'and I don't know about you but I'm exhausted. I assume you're staying the night?'

'I don't know. I hadn't thought.' She looked at her watch and saw it was one o'clock. She'd had almost no sleep since the night before last. 'I hope Ethan's all right,' she said, and imagining her son alone in his little room, surrounded by his scattered possessions, made her eyes fill with tears again. 'There was this woman, she was married to a famous musician but I can't remember his name now. When her children had finally left home she drove to a bridge somewhere, gave her car keys to a couple of teenagers, poor things, and jumped off. Just like that. I guess she didn't know who she was now that she wasn't needed as a mother.'

'Probably better to track me down in the middle of the night and shout at me, then.'

'Probably.'

They smiled at each other properly for the first time.

'I'll show you where your room is. Do you want a toothbrush? I always keep those travel ones they give you on long flights for times like this – not that I've had many times quite like this before.'

'That'd be great.' Gaby gestured at her bag. 'As you can see, I'm travelling light. I don't even have any keys.'

'This way. The stairs are rather steep so mind you don't slip.'

Nancy led Gaby to a small room with a sloping roof. The bed was under the window, with a small table next to the pillow, a bedside lamp that cast a pool of light when Nancy switched it on. On the opposite wall a single shelf was stacked with books on education, and lined up on the floor underneath were shoes – two pairs of walking-boots, one relatively new, the other split and scuffed, espadrilles, trainers and a pair of grey suede clogs. Next to them were two large cardboard boxes and a filing cabinet.

'I'll get you a towel. The bathroom's next door – you have to wrench the hot tap a bit to get it working.'

'Thanks.'

'Sleep well, then.'

'You too.'

Nancy pulled the door shut and Gaby was left alone. She sat down on the bed and closed her eyes. Her head spun in a kaleidoscope of images and thoughts, and she couldn't distinguish between misery and excitement, frustration and a certain sense of triumph that at least she had got here. She didn't know if she was glad to be sitting on this bed, in this strange room, in the middle of the night, or if she longed to be at home.

She took her mobile out of her bag and rang Connor. She knew he wouldn't answer – he was out of range, sitting on a boat somewhere. But at least she would hear his voice telling her that he couldn't take her call.

'Connor,' she said, to the voicemail. 'It's me. Everything went fine today.' She thought of the car wrecked in the garage, herself with Nancy in a remote village in Cornwall. 'More or less,' she added feebly. 'I'll talk to you when you get back. I just wanted to say that I'm thinking of you. Oh, and if you call me when you get in to Southampton, I probably won't be at home, but don't worry, I'll speak to you soon. Take care.' She turned off her mobile, which was running out of battery, and stood up.

After cleaning her teeth and washing her face, she came back into the room and took all her clothes off, leaving them in a heap on the floor. The curtains were open and the patch of sky was quite dark. Gaby could see her naked reflection, and for an instant she had the impression that she was staring at someone else. She pulled the curtains shut and climbed into bed. The sheet was cold against her skin, and she huddled under the light duvet, drawing her knees up and wrapping her arms round herself. She stared out into the bare room. Then she reached out and turned off the bedside lamp.

In London, it was never completely dark and never completely quiet. Here, the thickness of the darkness felt like a heavy blanket that had been thrown over her. Gaby strained her eyes, trying to pull a shape out of the inky void, a lighter shade of black. Nothing. She closed her eyes tight for a few seconds, then opened them again. There was no change. This is what it is to be blind, she thought. And deaf. No owl cry, no cat call, no car in the distance reassuring her that she hadn't fallen off the edge of the world. She couldn't even hear the wind in the trees. She could only hear herself breathing. She closed her eyes once more and waited for sleep to come for her.

Eight

'What we should do,' said the student who had said his name was Mal, and whose room they were sitting in, 'is go and get drunk.'

'No,' said the student who had said her name was Riva, or had Ethan misheard that? 'What we should do is cook ourselves a meal here.'

'And then go out and get drunk.'

'Why do you want to get drunk?' asked Lucy, who had the room next door to Ethan's.

'It seems like a good way of breaking the ice.'

'There isn't any ice,' said Ethan, thinking even as he said it that this was embarrassingly inane and meaningless. He grinned, shrugged and lit another cigarette, then glanced round the small room at all the unfamiliar faces. Would they be friends one day? He liked the look of Harry, who hadn't uttered a word so far and was slouching in the corner still in a long coat even though the room was overheated. And Renée from Paris, who had dark hair, dark eyes, crooked teeth and nicotine-stained fingers. He passed her a cigarette and the stale fug of the room thickened.

'Who can cook?' asked the shy Indian, whose name Ethan hadn't caught.

'I have a wok!' said Lucy. 'We can put lots of things in it and see what happens.'

'I think . . .' began Riva, briskly. She obviously had a plan.

'My aunt gave me a cookbook for my birthday,' said Mal. '*One Is Fun*.'

A hoot of laughter went round the room. The door pushed open and two young men came in carrying a plastic bag bulky with cans of beer, which they handed round. Ethan pulled the tab off his and watched the little spume of froth snake out. He didn't really know if he wanted to be here, after all. Was everyone else thinking the same thing? Were they laughing and chatting and pretending to have fun, and all the time wondering if they should be somewhere else? He caught Harry's eye and they smiled at each other. He took a long, warm pull at his beer and felt himself relaxing. Best to sit back and see where the evening would take him.

Four hours later, in a sharp wind that carried in its tail the hint of rain, Ethan found himself wandering the streets of Exeter with a group of about twelve other students. Harry had dropped away at some point, and so had Riva, but others had joined them on what had turned into an extended pub crawl. Mal was drunk and rowdy; Lucy was drunk and weepy – her arms were round the shoulders of Ethan and the shy Indian, and she stumbled along, her feet catching on the paving-stones, words jolting from her. Something about a boyfriend who'd let her down and why did she always fall in love with the wrong kind of person, and maybe she wasn't up to the university course she'd chosen. Ethan wasn't really listening any more, not to her and not to anyone. He felt mildly drunk and everything around him had become slow and dreamlike. His thoughts were muzzy, and he didn't feel like talking to anyone. He wanted to go to bed, but he didn't have the energy to unhook Lucy and set off on his own.

In any case, he had no idea of where they were. They were out of the centre where they'd started and now they were passing a car park that was empty except for a row of recycling bins. Mal and another man leapt on top of the bottle bank (for green glass only) and started clowning a fight. They pushed against each other, staggered, regained their footing.

'Come on!' they cried, and a few more of the group climbed on top with them. Mal took an ungainly leap on to the next one (clear glass only) and then the next (newspapers). Soon about eight students were following him. Their feet drummed on the metal surfaces and their voices rose in raucous jollity.

Ethan thought they sounded like seagulls circling a returning fishing boat. He took Lucy's arm gently from his shoulder, so that now she hung helplessly from the Indian's neck. 'I've got to go,' he said, and turned away. He headed for the cathedral in the distance, and was glad of the wind on his face as he walked. His footsteps echoed. In the distance, he could still hear the shouts of Mal and his group, but soon that died away. Before too long, he thought, he'd go to the coast for a day; it was so near, after all. Briefly, he allowed himself to think of his father, sitting on a boat surrounded by heaped waves. Would his father be thinking about him, too, wondering how he was getting on, or would he be pondering the pains and problems of humanity?

Ethan was meandering along a narrow street with old houses on either side and above him a strip of dark sky. Most of the houses' lights were off and the area felt almost deserted. He came to a small square where he stopped to sit on the low wall to one side and pull out his cigarettes. He smoked slowly, with a relieved sense of his solitude, and as he did so the moon rose above the roofs of the houses and hung above him, almost full, with a ribbon of cloud trailing across its face. The square was filled with its mysterious light. He stared up at it, tears pricking his eyes although he didn't think he felt sad.

Then, in the silence of the night, he heard footsteps coming towards him. He huddled on the wall, in the shadows, and watched as a young woman approached. She walked quickly, lightly, with her shoulders back. Her pale coat opened out from the waist, swinging, and her skirt rippled with each smooth step she took. One end of her narrow scarf blew behind her, like a pennant. Ethan watched, scarcely breathing. Now he could see her face, a young and creamy oval in the moonlight, her hair piled richly on top of her head, with little tendrils snaking round her cheeks, the column of her neck above a scrap of scarf. She moved lithely, like a cat or a ballet dancer, chin held high, feet seeming to glide over the ground. Her eyes – were they blue or green, grey or brown? he couldn't make them out – were looking into the distance. Her lips were held in a smile so small that perhaps he was mistaken and she was solemn. From where he sat, silent and absolutely motionless, she seemed like the source of the light that fell around her.

She flowed softly past on the other side of the street,

not glancing in his direction. Ethan waited until she was out of sight, the ash of his cigarette crumbling and breaking. A melancholy elation filled him and he stared at the space where she had been. He knew he was a hopelessly romantic fool, a sentimental idiot doomed to insomnia, disappointment and too many cigarettes. He didn't care.

Nine

It was chilly when Gaby woke, the unmistakable pinch of autumn in the air. She sat up in bed, pulling the duvet under her chin. Her mouth felt dry and her head thick, and she was still half tangled in the dream she had been having, so that it took her a few moments to remember where she was. Her watch showed her that it was nearly nine o'clock. She pulled the curtains apart a few inches and squinted outside, almost gasping at the colours that rolled away from the house. The green moors ran into the blue, bucking sea in the distance; the sky was a metallic grey, with patches of turquoise breaking through, the sun a vague yellow, still low in the sky and its shafts breaking through the trees. Low-lying pools of mist almost obscured the lane that led to the house, but soon these would burn away and the day would be sharp and vivid.

As she looked, a figure came along the lane. It was Nancy, cycling through the mist so that only her upper body was clear. The bike was an old-fashioned kind; indeed, Gaby could almost have sworn it was the same one that Nancy had ridden twenty years ago. It had a solid grey body and, attached to the front handlebars, a disintegrating wicker basket in which there was a towel and, on top of that, several large white mushrooms. Nancy sat upright, as she always had on a bike. Her back was straight and she was serene and quaintly dignified.

Her hair, Gaby could now see, was wet, and her cheeks flushed with effort. She watched as Nancy dismounted and bent down, apparently to retrieve the house key from beneath a small boulder that lay just inside the gate.

Gaby pulled shut the curtains and lay back on her pillow. Then she swung her legs out of bed and looked about for her clothes. They were all gone, but a blue flannel dressing-gown lay at the foot of her bed, and there was a pair of moccasin slippers on the floor. Nancy must have come in while she was still asleep and put them there for her. She put on the dressing-gown and shuffled to the bathroom, hearing the door downstairs open and close. There was no mirror, only a medicine cabinet above the wash-basin, which she opened out of curiosity and peered inside. Vitamin tablets, paracetamol, plasters, a razor and extra blades, two bandages, a thermometer, a linked chain of safety-pins, a small jar of Vaseline, a pot of moisturizer (not, she noted, one that was anti-ageing, as hers was even though she dismissed such things), three unopened bars of soap (evening primrose), two roll-on deodorants (natural), shampoo and conditioner for normal hair, a spare tube of toothpaste and dental floss, a small pot of lip salve, a tube of mascara and a couple of lipsticks, a box of Tampax. Once again, she was struck by the stern order of Nancy's life, which was such a contrast to the disarray of her own (in her medicine cabinet, which Connor hadn't got round to cleaning for several months, there was a jumble of odds and ends, from ancient prescriptions that needed chucking to dozens of little bottles of shampoo and body lotion that she'd taken from hotel rooms). Here, everything was kept in its proper place; everything had a function.

There was a small shower cubicle in the corner, and she let the dressing-gown slip to the tiled floor and stepped inside, turning on the tap and releasing a jet of cold water that gradually turned warm. She washed her hair twice with the shampoo she found on the small metal shelf, rinsed it thoroughly, soaped her body. She wanted to delay going downstairs for as long as possible because she felt awkward this morning, and anxious. Would Nancy be friendly, or cool and efficient the way she could easily be? Would they continue to talk to each other, or had the fever of the evening died away, leaving only its ashy remains? And if Nancy asked Gaby what her plans were, what would she reply? For what were her plans, after all? Was she leaving this morning on the first available train or did she want to stay longer, now that she was here? Surely she couldn't simply say goodbye and leave, but how could she remain, uninvited and probably unwelcome as she was? The truth was, she didn't know what she wanted, didn't understand her mood, which was agitated and yet at the same time lazy and lethargic. She shivered and pulled the dressing-gown closely round her. Her throat hurt. Perhaps she was coming down with something, she thought hopefully: a vague, painless illness that meant she had to lie in bed for a few days being looked after, making no decisions for herself. But she knew she was simply weighed down with emotion.

There were smells wafting up from the kitchen now – coffee, freshly baked bread, woodsmoke. And sure enough, when she went into the kitchen, Nancy had laid a small fire, which was not yet giving out much heat, and was standing at the cooker, stirring mushrooms in a frying-pan. A small white loaf stood plumply on a metal rack, and the kettle was starting to boil.

'I picked some parasol mushrooms on my way back,' said Nancy, not even looking round. 'I thought we could have mushrooms on toast for breakfast.'

'Lovely,' said Gaby. 'Way back from where?'

'I swim in the sea every morning. It's only a mile or so away.'

'Even in winter?'

'Especially in winter.'

'My God, how virtuous.'

'I like it.'

'I always think I ought to start doing some kind of exercise. All of a sudden everyone I know seems to have taken up running.' She heard the bright, meaningless words stream out of her. Shut up, she told herself. Just be quiet for once in your life. Let someone else do the talking. 'Connor runs practically every day,' she continued helplessly, as Nancy poured boiling water over the ground coffee. 'Even in blizzards. He looks happy when he runs – his face is settled and there's a kind of spring in his step.'

Be quiet! Oh, hold your wretched tongue. But still she went on talking, to cover up the silence of what seemed impossible to say this morning. 'Every time I try it, though, I remember all over again why I don't do it. I set off and I think, Oh yes, *now* I remember what it feels like. My legs get heavy and my lungs hurt. I'm like a rusty old lorry. People walk past me.'

At last she stopped, exhausted by herself.

'Coffee?'

'Mm, please.' She stood by the window, staring out.

'Why don't you come and sit down? The mushrooms are done. There's always one place that I find them at about this time of year.'

Gaby sat at the little wooden table. 'My clothes,' she said.

'I washed them after you went to bed, and now they're hanging over the boiler. They should be dry before long, maybe they are already.'

'Thanks, but there was no need . . .'

'Here. Eat this while it's still warm. Coffee with milk and no sugar, right?'

'Right. This is delicious.'

'Good.'

'I have to tell you, though, I feel a bit odd. Very odd.'

Nancy didn't reply. With immense concentration, she was cutting her mushrooms on toast into squares. Then she forked one square and put it into her mouth.

'I had this dream,' said Gaby, suddenly remembering it. 'I dreamt I was packing for Ethan but I kept on putting in things that he wore when he was much younger. Well, I guess it doesn't take a genius to interpret that one. I wish I had cheerful dreams. Do you?'

'I don't dream,' said Nancy, and put the next square into her mouth.

'Everyone dreams, they just don't remember.'

'Actually, some people don't dream at all. There's a woman who had a stroke and stopped dreaming. It didn't harm her.'

'You haven't had a stroke, have you? You must dream!'

'So maybe I don't remember.'

'You mean, you've never remembered dreams? Not ever?'

'No.'

'Not a single time?'

'No.'

'You've never even woken up and felt the images slipping away from you – so that you at least knew there'd been something going on inside your brain?'

'No.'

'Do you mind?'

'You've said yourself that most dreams are unhappy.'

'Even so, you're missing something extraordinary, aren't you? This vivid, jumbled mess of pictures. It feels better to have some kind of glimpse into what's been going on inside you – otherwise it's a terrifying blank. When you don't dream, it's as if you cease to exist. I think that's why children can be so scared of going to sleep.'

'More coffee?'

'I wonder what it means,' said Gaby.

'Why should it mean anything?'

'It must. Everything has a meaning.'

'Does it?'

'Maybe you don't want to remember.'

Nancy glanced up from her breakfast and raised her eyebrows.

'Or maybe you never wake up during dreaming sleep, only when that bit of the night is over – they say that's what makes you remember them. But surely it's impossible that in your whole life you've never been interrupted during dreams.'

There was a silence between them. Gaby felt that she had said something crass and inappropriate, but she didn't know what it was. Like the previous night, she had the impression of swinging helplessly between intimacy and alienation, of coming in too close or else standing back too far, but she didn't know how to correct herself. Wretchedness swept over her, and to conceal it she stood up abruptly and went to look out of the window again.

'Gaby.' Nancy's voice was suddenly gentle.

'Yes.'

'It's not your fault.'

Gaby didn't know what she meant by that. She pressed her forehead against the window. The mist had all but gone, just a few barely visible wisps lying like scraps of chiffon over the grass, where spiders' webs smoked and glistened in the sun. 'It was never meant to be like this,' she said at last.

'Listen, in about an hour's time, I've got to go.'

'Go?' Gaby turned round, bewildered. Nancy's face was kind, and that made everything harder. 'Go where?'

'I'm accompanying a group of year-sixes to camp in France for a couple of days. I do it every year.'

'Oh.'

She tried to keep her face expressionless, but knew that Nancy would be able to see the misery and humiliation that were sluicing through her. She was transparent – Connor often told her so, with rueful tenderness. But she didn't want to be transparent: she wanted to be like Connor could be, or like Nancy was now – discreetly packed into neat compartments, hidden away from prying eyes, locked in safely with her own secrets, unknowable, tantalizing, valuable.

'So you see . . .' Nancy didn't finish the sentence, just held out her hands, palms upwards, in a gesture that Gaby recognized from three decades ago.

'I should leave.'

'Yes, I think so.'

'OK.'

'Are you all right?'

'Why shouldn't I be?'

'I'm sorry.'

'But will we meet after – ?'

'I'm sorry,' Nancy said again. It sounded so final.

By the time Gaby was downstairs again, in her clothes, which were creased but dry and smelling of fabric-conditioner, Nancy's travel bag and leather briefcase were standing by the door and Nancy had changed out of her jeans and sweater into a dark skirt and a silky black mac; she wore flat suede boots and her hair was brushed away from her face. She looked, thought Gaby, pleasantly businesslike and attractively intimidating. Not someone to mess with, not someone whose shoulder you could cry on, or whose personal life you could interrogate.

'I've ordered you a taxi,' she said. 'I would have given you a lift to the station but I'm going in the other direction and there isn't time. There's a train that goes in forty-five minutes.'

'Fine. Thanks.'

'Do you want sandwiches for the journey?'

'It's OK. I can get something on the train.'

'I'll pick a couple of apples for you, then, shall I?'

Without waiting for an answer, Nancy went out into the garden. Gaby sat down on the sofa, next to the fire. She folded her hands in her lap and stared at the embers. This was it, then. Nothing had changed. She had found Nancy; she had cried in front of her and squeezed a few grudging truths from her – but that was it. She had imagined their reunion many times, and thought she had played through every variation – hatred, grief, rage, contrition, confession, some kind of blinding revelation. But always, in these scenarios, something would happen: their meeting would be like a hinge. A door would open; a world would change. Now she realized that in a few minutes she would leave and return to London, pick up her old life, and this strange interregnum would gradually come to seem like a dream, with no context and no apparent meaning.

'Here,' said Nancy, handing over two russet apples.

Gaby pushed them into her bag. She saw Nancy glance surreptitiously at her watch. 'I hope your camp goes well.'

'And I hope your journey back is all right. Did you say that Connor was home tonight?'

'Tomorrow, middayish. I'll have a chance to clear up a bit before he arrives. He hates coming home to chaos and I've a feeling I left things in a bit of disarray.' She thought of the unwashed breakfast things still on the kitchen table and the litter of objects that Ethan had discarded at the last minute and now lay in a trail round the house.

There was the sound of a car drawing up in the lane.

'That'll be your cab.'

'Right.' Gaby stood up and ran her hands uselessly down her crumpled skirt. 'I'll say goodbye, then.'

'Goodbye,' said Nancy. She held open the front door for Gaby.

'But will we see each other again?' Her voice was small and plaintive.

'Take care of yourself.' Nancy behaved as if she hadn't heard Gaby's words.

'I've got a friend who hates it when I say that. He always says, "Take risks," instead.'

'Gaby, the driver's –'

'And I agree with him. Take risks. That's going to be my motto. Or maybe, now I come to think of it, wake up those sleeping dogs. Yes. Don't let them lie.'

Nancy gave a small laugh, with no trace of irony or bitterness in it. 'How I've missed you, after all,' she said, as if she couldn't stop herself. Then her face closed once more; her expression became polite and distant.

'Listen, Nancy, we could –'

'You don't want to miss your train.'

'I don't care about my train.'

'Give my regards to Connor and Stefan.'

'Regards? Your *regards*?'

'Thank you for coming.'

'But we haven't even –'

Nancy kissed Gaby quickly on both cheeks, pushed her firmly over the threshold and shut the door on her. Gaby heard the lock click behind her, and she stumbled forward towards the cab waiting on the lane. She climbed inside, trapping her skirt in the door, and pressed her face to the window, gazing back at the house. But there was no face looking at her and no hand waving. Nancy had gone.

'The station, is it?'
  'Hmm?'
  Was that it, then? Was that all?
'Is it the station you're wanting?'
'The station? Oh, yes. That's it.'
She hadn't even given Nancy her address or ex-directory phone number. They had parted on a polite, nasty full stop.
  'Going somewhere nice?'
  'I'm sorry?'
  'I said, are you going somewhere nice?'
  'I don't know.'
She stared at the driver's fat white neck, flubbery beneath his thinning grey hair.
  'You don't know where you're going?'
  'Yes, I know that. I'm going to London.'
  'Is that where you live, then, or are you spending a few days there?'
  'What's that?'
  'I was asking, do you live in London?' The driver shouted the words slowly and crossly, as if to a deaf foreigner.
  'Yes. I'm sorry, but I think I've changed my mind.'
  'I couldn't live in London myself. It's all right for visiting, but not for living in.'
  'I've changed my mind.'
  'Changed your mind?'

'Please stop. I'm not going after all. I can't do it. I can't. Let me out here.'

He screeched to a halt and twisted round in the seat. 'Now, look –'

'I'll pay you what it would have cost. Here, take this.' Gaby pushed several notes at him, not knowing or caring how much she was handing over.

'Are you all right, if you don't mind me asking?'

'I'm fine. I just need to get out.'

'Here?'

'Yes.'

Gaby half ran, half stumbled back to the house. She estimated that Nancy would probably be there for maybe fifteen minutes longer, and although she had no idea of what she would say, she couldn't bear to part on that cool, well-mannered note: *Give my regards . . . !* Better to shout and spit at each other. *Thank you for coming!* No. It just wasn't possible to leave it like that.

She hurtled round the corner and down the lane. Small birds flew up from the hedgerow, in a fluttering crowd, and disappeared. Her breath was coming in uneven gasps and a nasty stitch made her press her hand into her side. At the gate, she took a few deep breaths, pushed her tangle of hair behind her ears and marched up to the house. She rapped on the door and stood back, waiting. She rapped once more, then a third time. She bent down and peered through the letterbox, but could only make out a strip of empty wooden floor. She walked through the flower-bed, her sandals becoming claggy with thick, wet soil, and pressed her face to each window in turn but could see nobody.

'Nancy!' she shouted to the upstairs rooms. Then louder: 'Nancy.'

She walked round the house, wondering where Nancy kept her car. There was no garage, but beyond the house, where the lane petered out into a footpath, there was a lay-by with the marks of car tyres in it.

'She must have left already,' Gaby said, out loud. 'Bugger. And now I've gone and missed my train.' She kicked at a stone with her sandalled foot and winced at the jab of pain. 'Again,' she added. 'You idiot. You stupid, stupid fool.'

She made her way back to the house and stood looking at its empty windows, and at the chimney from which a few curls of smoke still seeped. It had all been for nothing, she thought, and didn't know what to do with herself – with her tired body and her heavy heart, and with all the memories that she would now have to press back inside her. She rubbed her face, feeling ungainly with sadness. Then – without knowing what she was doing – she opened the gate and bent down to lift the small boulder lying just inside. The key she had seen Nancy retrieve earlier in the morning was there, and she picked it up, wiped it on her skirt, then walked up the path and opened the front door. It swung in with a small creak and Gaby held her breath, in case Nancy was still there after all. But the house was unmistakably empty, all the lights off and the fire dwindling in the grate. Their breakfast things were washed and placed on the draining-board, the two chairs pushed neatly against the table; the dog-roses had been thrown into the bowl for compost, along with the earthy ends of the stalks from the parasol mushrooms.

For a few minutes, Gaby stood in the middle of the room, at a loss. Then she sat down on the sofa and took off her jacket and sandals, wriggling her toes and letting a small thrill of illicit pleasure run through her: she was in Nancy's house, alone and uninvited, like a burglar. She noticed that she'd left muddy footprints on the floor, which she must make sure to clean up before she left.

'Now what?' She leant back and rested her head on the cushion. 'Coffee, I think.'

After the coffee, with milk heated in a small pan and the pan scrubbed, dried and put back in its exact place, Gaby allowed herself to scrutinize the objects in the room as she had not been able to do when Nancy had been there. First she stood in front of the bookshelf, her eyes going from title to title. Poems by W. H. Auden, W. B. Yeats, Louis MacNeice, Sylvia Plath, Thomas Hardy, John Donne – all writers Nancy had loved as a teenager. Several books on trees, birds, butterflies and wildflowers. Three shelves of alphabetically arranged novels, from Chinua Achebe to Edith Wharton. A large dictionary, a thesaurus, an atlas of the world and a road atlas of Great Britain; a miscellany of reference books; half a shelf of cookery books, all well thumbed. Further down there were biographies and history books, and as she looked, Gaby felt a shiver of surprise pass through her: *The Anabaptists*, by Stefan Graham, and *The Life of John Dee*, Stefan's first book. She pulled them off the shelf and leafed through their pages. So Nancy had been out and bought books by Stefan. She thought about him still, all these years later, though whether with idle curiosity or nostalgia or even regret she didn't know. She pushed the books back, lining them up with the others, and leant down to the bottom shelf, which was tightly stacked with Ordnance Survey maps. She tugged at a couple randomly – one of south Suffolk, one of the west of Sicily. They were torn at the folds and Gaby remembered the worn walking-boots in the spare bedroom.

After she had looked properly at the photograph of the seascape, she paused by another, much smaller one half hidden in the alcove near the fire. Gaby recognized it at once, because Nancy had always had it, ever since she could remember. It was black-and-white, and showed a young man on a beach, wearing a shirt with its sleeves rolled up and a pair of baggy trousers, holding the hand of a tiny little girl in a frilly swimsuit, whose legs were twisted round each other, feet digging into the sand. Gaby knew that the man was Nancy's father, who had died shortly after the photograph had been taken, and the child was Nancy. There had never been a matching photograph of Nancy and her mother, who had lived on for decades and was probably still alive. Nancy had once told her that she chose to think of herself as her father's daughter, although of course she had never really known her father, only invented him for herself to copy.

Her mother, on the other hand, she had chosen adamantly not to become: thin and glossy and sweetly pretty, with a perky, frantic kind of charm, she had had affairs or flings with almost all of the men she knew. Each man was going to be the one who would save her, love her, protect her from harm. She had a terrifying resilience: experience did not teach her to expect disappointment. Gaby had always thought that Nancy's moral sternness, her unyielding sense of who she was, stemmed from her mother's humiliating pliancy. She leant in to examine the faces more closely. The man was smiling at the camera but his daughter was looking up at him, her face shiny with pride. It was an expression that Gaby had never seen on Nancy's face in all the years she had known her.

Next, she examined the fridge. She always loved looking in people's fridges and she wasn't disappointed by Nancy's, which, although orderly, was also slightly unexpected. There were the obvious things, like strong Cheddar, rashers of dry-cured bacon, tubs of crème fraîche and Greek yoghurt, semi-skimmed milk, lettuce, cherry tomatoes, a cucumber, spring onions, grapes, eggs (free range, of course), a few red chillies, a bottle of vegetable stock, a Cellophane-covered pack of field mushrooms, unsalted butter, a bottle of white wine. There were also several film canisters stacked on one of the shelves, making Gaby think that the seascape had probably been taken by Nancy. There was a squishy yellow packet, which, on closer inspection, turned out to be a kind of bath jelly that was required to be kept refrigerated. And inside the egg carton there were three eggs and a little lump of shrink-wrapped cannabis.

So: Gaby knew that Nancy took photographs, went walking, read, or at least bought, books by Stefan and smoked dope.

She went over to the noticeboard by the door, on which Nancy had pinned invitations, reminders, newspaper articles, a couple of postcards. She knew that her prying was becoming more and more unacceptable. To look inside a fridge is one thing, to unpin a postcard and read it something else, especially, of course, when she had broken back into the house. But that was exactly what she did now, first the one with a painting by Caravaggio on the front and on the back a few scrawled words: 'Thinking of you; I hope you're thinking of me.' The postmark was Rome. Then the one from Edinburgh, in the same handwriting: 'Thank you for telling me. See you on Friday.' There was a signature this time but it was illegible.

A school photo pinned near the top of the board – several hundred children, arranged in descending size, and in their middle, among the other teachers and gazing straight ahead, Nancy. By the side of it, there was a passport photograph of a girl of about sixteen: she had dark hair and a firm mouth, and the defiant, fugitive look so often seen in passports. School timetables, a flyer for a classical concert in Newquay and a craft fair, an invitation to a party, a shopping list in Nancy's handwriting with items neatly crossed off, an obituary of a woman called Fenella Stock, furniture-maker, who had died aged eighty, and below it a newspaper clipping running over two columns and half folded in on itself. The headline read 'The Gateways of Pain'.

Gaby pulled out the drawing-pin and took the article to the window. Even in her confusion, she remembered that the following week she was due for an eye test. Soon she would be wearing reading-glasses, losing them everywhere she went. She squinted at the dense lettering, her gaze jumping through paragraphs. It was a piece about a newly diagnosed medical condition called reflex sympathetic dystrophy, a type of intense, chronic, incurable pain. Half-way down, Dr Connor Myers of the

London Pain Clinic was quoted as saying that 'Pain has been neglected by doctors and researchers. It's frustrating, a kind of medical failure that we don't like. What's more, pain is subjective: everyone has their own pain threshold, and usually it is not measurable. Until a few years ago, it didn't even have its own speciality. Now, however, we're beginning to find out more about the biology of pain. RSD, which is a kind of maladaptive pain, may give us a window into understanding some of the fundamental aspects of the nervous system.'

Her hands were trembling, shaking the paper so that it was hard to make out the words. Very carefully, she replaced the cutting in its original position, pushing the drawing-pin back into place. So, now she knew that Nancy walked and took photographs and smoked dope; that she read Stefan's books and cut out articles about Connor, which she put on the noticeboard. Gaby felt a quiver, like an electric buzz, down her spine, but she couldn't identify the feeling behind the sensation. Excitement? Happiness? Apprehension? Pity? Nancy hadn't forgotten about them, after all. She'd ruthlessly burnt her bridges, yet she'd looked back across the impassable river to the land she'd left behind, and was still doing so two decades later.

Gaby hadn't meant to go upstairs, just as she hadn't meant to get out of the taxi and return to the house, pick up the key, let herself in. She was watching herself behave in a way that disquieted her – no, that appalled her. Later, she could tell herself that it had all happened as if in a dream she was powerless to halt, and it was true that she moved slowly, in a hallucinatory drift, into Nancy's bedroom. It was large and light and the air was tangy with cleanliness, woodsmoke, lemon and pine. There was a spacious chest of drawers, a wooden wardrobe with a mirror on its door, a desk under one of the windows. The floor was uncarpeted, but a thick cream rug lay across most of it, and Gaby curled her toes into it as she stood, looking around. The large bed lay under the window; its white duvet was folded back and Gaby thought she could still see the shape where Nancy had lain. She pulled open the wardrobe door, so that her own image swung past her, and then she riffled her hand through the clothes hanging inside – dresses, skirts sensible and chic, shirts, the flash of colour interleaved between more sober greys and browns. She brought out a blue summer dress, held it up against herself, then pulled the door to examine her reflection in the mirror. If she put it on, would she look more like its owner? But where Nancy was slim and neat and structured, she was always messy and without real edges. Even in her thin phases, she looked plump. Even when she was trying to look elegant, she couldn't quite manage the sculpted chic she saw on other women. She tended to cover herself with overlapping layers – like now; she was wearing a camisole under a strappy top under a shirt. The first time Connor had undressed her, unbuttoning one blouse to find another, he'd compared it to peeling an onion and never quite getting to its centre. She hung the dress back in the wardrobe and closed the door, then faced the room again.

The four pillows were stacked at the head of the bed invitingly. She moved over and sat on the edge, looking out of the window at the grass still steaming in the bright morning. She shifted her weight, then found she was lying down, her head sinking into the softness of the pillow. The sheet was cool against her raw feet, and she felt her heavy limbs relax. From this position, she could see another large black-and-white photograph on the opposite wall, this time of a V-shaped flock of birds against the sky. It was as if she was staring up into space. She closed her eyes against the dizziness, and for a few seconds still saw the skein of birds imprinted on the lids, amid circles of light. She told herself she would lie there for a few seconds, then leave discreetly, and no harm would have been done to anyone. She turned on to her side, drew up her legs, pressed her face into the pillow and fell asleep.

Ten

They always had a cooked breakfast on their last morning aboard. It had started out as bacon and eggs but over the years Stefan had added to his repertoire and now, sweaty, red in the face and triumphant, he produced grilled tomatoes, sausages, mushrooms, black pudding and baked beans as well, leaving in his wake a mess that was second only to that which Gaby made when she cooked. Connor used to tell Gaby that if you clean up any existing mess before you begin, then clear up as you go along, it was easier in the long run, but he had long since given up and resigned himself to the havoc she could create in an astonishingly short period of time. Stefan obviously had the same cooking gene as Gaby, using a large amount of energy, making a drama out of a boiled egg or a salad.

Usually Connor was the chef on board, as well as the person who cleared away and tidied. He loved to cook and did so with the dedication of the self-taught. He bought cookery books, cut recipes out of magazines and followed them meticulously, collected tips from friends, was proud of the collection of oils and the sharpness of his knives. He rarely had time during the week, but at weekends he might spend an entire day going to the market for food and coming home to cook it. Gaby would tell him to give himself a break, scramble an egg or order a takeaway, but it was the act of preparing an elaborate meal that relaxed him. In his head, he had already planned the supper he would make the following night for himself and Gaby: Moroccan chicken, he thought, cooked with saffron, cinnamon, ginger and preserved lemons. He imagined himself, bathed and rested, in clean clothes, sitting across the table from her. He could suddenly see her face quite clearly: the tiny scar across her lip that whitened when she smiled, the tendrils of her hair snaking down her freckled, blemished, generous face.

There were only two tiny gas-rings on the boat, so some of the ingredients were cool and congealed by the time they made it on to the plate. The yolk of Connor's egg had split and oozed stickily into the sludge of beans. The toast was burnt and the sausage pink on one side, charred and split on the other. The instant coffee was bitter and tepid. It didn't matter, for the two men were hungry and weary after their nights of snatched sleep, and from days spent in the wind. They sat on deck, plates balanced on their knees, with creased, ruddy faces and sour morning breath, and ate wordlessly, wiping their mouths on their sleeves. They had tied up in the port a few hours ago, and other boats bobbed on either side of them; the clink of their halyards and the voices of the crews floated towards them over the calm water. The boat rocked gently under them.

Connor liked the way that Stefan could go for hours without talking. During the days that they spent together each year, it was almost an unspoken rule that they should not discuss work, politics or ideas. Their normal life receded, and in its place was the confined and complicated world of the boat, surrounded by the indifference of the sea. They discussed the weather, the forecast for tomorrow, the night watches, the state of the engine, the bilge pumps, the rigging of the main sail, spinnaker and jib. They tied knots, coiled ropes, mended damaged lockers and replaced cleats, scrubbed the deck and sometimes peered at the chart they spread on the table. Sailing up the coast, eye on the depth-sounder, they looked out at the tiny fishing villages and the deserted beaches; in open sea, they pointed out sea birds, or ships on the horizon, commented on the shape of the clouds or the way the sun splashed dabs of silver light over the water. They watched for squalls ruffling the waves into a corrugated darkness. They made each other endless cups of coffee and tumblers of whisky. In the evenings when they were moored in a small port, they would often play chess or backgammon before climbing into their narrow bunks and listening to the creaking of the boat's timbers and the slap of water against her bows. Now, however, no longer at sea, both men could sense their lives pressing in on them again. As they ate, they were thinking of appointments and tasks, people to see and phone calls to make. Connor had already tried to ring Gaby, but there was only an answering-machine at home and her mobile was switched off.

He watched Stefan sitting across from him, plate balanced on his lap. The lick of dark blond hair fell over his face, but his expression was contented as he chewed his half-raw, half-burnt sausage. Connor wondered what he was thinking of. Even after twenty years, he found his brother-in-law mysterious. At first glance, he seemed straightforward: a candid, dreamy, clumsy man without an unkind bone in his body. He'd steered his way through the rancours of university life by not noticing them, the way a boat will sail serenely among a buried landscape of icebergs, its hull passing within a millimetre of being pierced. He was generous to colleagues and helped students with an unstinting avuncular benevolence. He was courted by eager women who wanted to mother him, but appeared rarely to notice them either. He could lose himself in his own mind, or in the book he was reading or the period he was studying, so the outside world almost ceased to exist. Gaby worried that he sometimes went for entire days without a meal, because he had forgotten about food; at other times Connor had seen him consume two lunches in quick succession, because he had not remembered he had eaten. Occasionally he wore inappropriate outfits – grey suit trousers and a brown suit jacket to a meeting, a thick jersey on a summer day, a thin T-shirt in the middle of winter. Clothes had frequently lost their buttons or come unravelled at the hem, but he never bought new ones. Almost everything he wore had been got for him by Gaby and their mother. Often, he wouldn't shave, so a thick almost ginger stubble grew; once or twice he had cut his own hair with kitchen scissors, giving himself a radically skewed fringe. He could look as unkempt as a tramp. His study was almost impossible to enter: books teetered in towers or lay in collapsed heaps across the floor; pamphlets and letters, ripped folders and yellowing newspapers barricaded the entrance. At his university, he was famous for the mess of his room and for his habit of forgetting he was supposed to be giving a lecture (just as he was famous among family and friends for failing to meet appointments). Yet the work he produced from such disorder was vivid and lucid; his largely unscripted lectures were widely admired; the books he had written were praised for their scholarly clarity.

But Connor had thought for a long time that something else was going on underneath the ramshackle kindness of his brother-in-law, and on the weeks that they spent together in Stefan's boat, he watched him. Although Stefan would discuss ideas at excited length, he never talked about his own feelings, or even about events in his life, like friendships or relationships – and, indeed, he rarely used the word 'I', as if he was trying to erase himself from himself. Connor had seen him cry at films and books, and once at a painting they were standing in front of in Pisa, but never at something that had happened in his own life. And he could only remember seeing him lose his temper on one occasion, long ago: he'd looked out of his window on a rainy summer evening and seen Stefan hitting a shrub outside his and Gaby's front door, violently and repeatedly, with his umbrella. He could still see the expression on his face, of rage and humiliated despair. But Stefan hadn't known anyone was looking, and a few minutes later, sitting in the kitchen with Gaby and Connor, he had been as sweet and sunny as usual.

That scene had haunted Connor through the years, and when he could not prevent himself remembering it, a chill would spread through him and leave him wretched.

For there was a forlorn quality about Stefan, though he couldn't put his finger on it because it wasn't displayed in his cheerful behaviour or even his expression. It was as if the sun had gone down on him and he was now standing in twilight. Although he would never agree with Gaby when she said the same thing, Connor knew that Stefan had not been like that when they had first met all those years ago, outside Gaby's shared house, and Connor had assumed he was Gaby's lover, not her adored brother. But then, of course, Nancy had been with him and Stefan had shone with grateful happiness. Something had changed in him the day she left. Optimism had become instead a kind of eagerness; joy had turned into cheerfulness; patience had mutated into stoicism. It was like the lights being turned down in a room, so that while nothing else alters, the atmosphere becomes subdued.

'What will you be doing this time on Tuesday?' he asked.

'Tuesday? That's – um –'

'Tomorrow, when we go home, is Monday,' said Connor, helpfully.

'Yes. Let's see. I think I have a faculty board meeting to go to on Tuesday. It rings a bell, anyway. Beginning of the academic year, all of that. There are so many meetings. I could spend my entire teaching life not teaching and researching but going to meetings about teaching and researching. Sometimes I go and I don't say a single word, except "thank you" when they give me tea and biscuits. Always those chocolate Bourbons and custard creams.'

'We have chocolate Bourbons and custard creams, too, at our meetings.'

'Horrible things.'

'Are they? I've never really had strong opinions about them.'

'I always seem to lose mine when I dunk them, and then I have to fish around with a spoon and make a mess in the process. So, Connor, the last night on board until next year. Pub meal or are you going to cook?'

'Your choice.'

'I think I'd like you to cook, you know. Nothing complicated. How about a steak? Steak and bread and red wine.'

'I can go to that butcher's in town that's always open on a Sunday.'

'Sometimes, in the middle of winter, I find myself thinking about the boat all alone and empty in the boatyard, waiting for me. Anyway, what about you?'

'Me?'

'On Tuesday. What's waiting for you? Apart from Gaby, I mean.'

'Oh – a few patients. And then meetings, I expect. Letters, forms to fill in, emails to go through. Bureaucracy.'

'Hmm. Don't you want that bacon? Because if you don't, do you mind if I have it? Thanks. Does it get you down?'

'My work?' Connor thought about a recent patient who had lost both legs in an accident. He was a middle-aged man, a successful middle-class professional who was articulate and apparently in control of his life. But when Connor had first met him, he had lost the power to communicate except in whimpers and cries, like a baby before it learns how to speak. It was as if he had become the pain, inhabited it entirely, and there was no bit of him that could stand outside it and observe it.

'Doctors often don't listen to their patients,' he said now to Stefan, not really answering his question but following his own train of thought. 'Especially when severe pain has smashed their ability to describe what they're going through. They think that patients are unreliable narrators of their own experiences and that objective science holds the answers they seek. I used to think that too. But pain can't be tracked like that. It moves around. It lives in people's bodies very differently. It's not just about bravery, stoicism, whatever. Your pain isn't mine: it's unique to you. You have to trust the human voice. That's what I've learnt over the years.'

When the man he was thinking of, the amputee, was able to talk again and describe how he was feeling, it was a sign of his recovery. The pain was still there, but it no longer possessed him. Connor thought about all the cries and whimpers he had heard as a doctor, all the terrible sounds that people make when they're in agony. Everything else disappears; they have no story left to tell. All they can do is moan like an animal in distress.

'Pain obliterates,' he said. 'It's very lonely. You can't share it. I once had a conversation with a philosopher and she said something that I'd never even thought of, not in all the years I'd been working in the field. She said that pain has no outside object – I mean, you feel fear *of* something, you feel love *for* somebody, yet you simply feel pain. You can't refer it to anything outside you. Just imagine how many people are in pain, and it's invisible, contained within the body. Stand in the Underground and probably someone just a few feet away is hurting, and you've no idea. It's a strange thought, isn't it, that great gap between their reality and yours? You can't bridge it but, as a doctor, you can make it a little less lonely by recognizing it, at least, though doctors aren't very good at that sometimes – sometimes they almost seem to do the opposite. And you can help ease it, even erase it. Although, as Chekhov once said, where there are hundreds of remedies, you can be sure there is no cure. There are things we can do now that people wouldn't have believed even a decade ago . . . And imagine if you'd been alive two hundred years ago – or in your period, five hundred years ago. Imagine even commonplace events, a breech birth, say, or toothache.' There was a silence. Stefan was frowning into space, his face wrinkled in thought. Connor picked up the last slice of sausage and popped it into his mouth. He chewed slowly, then tipped the last of the cool coffee down his throat.

He himself had never experienced severe, or even moderate, physical pain. He'd torn a ligament when skiing, sliced open a finger cutting up vegetables, had wisdom teeth removed, suffered hangovers and sore throats, ached for a while with flu. But the kind of hurt that he witnessed as a doctor every day was utterly unfamiliar and unimaginable to him, a foreign land that he knew, one day, he would probably have to visit. When he'd watched Gaby in labour, he'd been horrified by her howls and screams and ferocious obscenities (Gaby hadn't even tried to hold back: she'd been stupendously uninhibited in her public demonstration of pain), by the way she'd writhed and thrashed on the bed like a landed fish, and most of all by the way her face, which he'd thought he had seen in every shifting mood, had become unfamiliar to him, her mouth drawn back over her teeth in a snarl.

'I'll go and get the steak in a minute,' he said.

'What about pain that isn't physical?' asked Stefan, suddenly, turning towards him.

'Ah, now.'

'What you're saying – well, can you say the same about that?'

'I don't know,' said Connor. He stood up and brushed crumbs from his clothes. 'I'm a doctor not a priest.'

Eleven

Where on earth was she? She struggled up to a sitting position and blinked in the shafts of light that slanted through the window. For a moment, everything was a bleached-out dazzle, which gradually took shape. A bed, photographs, a wardrobe and a chest of drawers; through the window, a stone wall, grass, small thorny trees and a distant sea. She'd been sleeping with one hand under her head and now pins-and-needles were tingling through it. She rubbed her fingers together, then swung her feet to the floor and stood up, face creased, dazed, a stale taste in her mouth, staggering like a jet-lagged passenger emerging into a new temporal zone.

In the bathroom, she discovered that Nancy had already thrown her disposable toothbrush into the bin, cleaning her away as soon as she had left. Gaby retrieved it, brushed her teeth vigorously, dropped it back into the bin and splashed cold water over her face. Only then did she look at her watch, squinting to make sure she wasn't mistaken. It was nearly half past two: she'd been fast asleep on Nancy's bed for hours. Indeed, she saw now that, outside, the sun had moved across the sky and was already quite low and yellow as a yolk, sending its long fingers across the moors, filtering softly through the trees. Gaby fumbled for her mobile and scrolled down her address book to the number for National Rail Enquiries.

She asked for trains from Liskeard to London, this after-noon, and was told that there were no further trains that day because of works on the line. What about a replacement bus service? she asked. There was one to Plymouth but it had left twenty minutes ago. The next train from Liskeard to London was the following morning.

Gaby stood becalmed at the top of the stairs, wonder-ing what to do – although she already knew, even as she knew that she shouldn't, she mustn't. She would stay here, in Nancy's house. She would sleep in the spare room and make sure the duvet was pulled back exactly as it had been. She would buy supplies from the shop in the village, assuming it was still open at this time on a Sunday, then clear away the meal, replacing everything neatly, rubbing away any tiny stains. She would leave no trace and tomorrow she'd sneak out of the front door, lock it and leave the key under the boulder. No one would ever know. It would be her secret night, shut away inside herself.

The first thing to do was to buy food, for she was already ravenous and she didn't want to raid Nancy's cupboards. She found her jacket hanging in the hall down-stairs and then, feeling chilly, she pulled one of Nancy's coats over the top, and pocketed the key and her wallet. She slipped out of the house like a thief, casting nervous glances around her, and walked briskly back to the centre of Rashmoor, past the pub and the antiques shop, to the grocery and off-licence she'd noticed last night. It was surprisingly well stocked for a village shop, with fresh vegetables and locally baked bread, and was still open, although the woman behind the counter was packing things up and while Gaby was still inside turned the 'open' sign to 'closed'. Gaby bought a wholemeal baguette, four tomatoes, a packet of ham, some Cornish cheese, a small jar of instant coffee, a half-litre of milk and a bottle of red wine. As she was about to leave, she turned back for ten Silk Cut and a box of matches.

As she walked up the lane, a few leaves spun slowly through the air towards her. She held out a hand and caught one for luck. She wanted it to be evening, so that she could sit in the small house with her picnic and her wine, and look out at the darkening landscape and the stars becoming visible, one by one. But it was barely three o'clock and she felt fidgety and full of unsatisfied energy. She went out into the garden, where the bonfire from last night was still smoking and giving off heat, and smoked the first of her cigarettes. The rush of dizziness pleased her, and she leant against the apple tree pulling smoke into her lungs and gazing out at the sea in the distance. She wanted to be in those waves, salt water in her eyes, gasping with the cold and facing out to nothingness.

Before she had time to change her mind, she went back into the house and found Nancy's swimsuit and her towel, still damp, hanging above the boiler. The bike was in the lean-to at the back of the house, and she rolled the costume into the towel, pushed it into the basket. Through the gate, and having put the key to the front door under the stone, she hoicked her skirt up and was off, wobbling over tree roots and boulders. She didn't really know where she was going, simply headed for the sea, which disappeared from view as she went down a steep hill, then re-emerged, glinting in the sun. Eventually, she dismounted and pushed the bike over a recently ploughed field, the mud sticking heavily to her sandals, and left it leaning by the fence, which she climbed over, tearing her skirt and stinging her calf on a nettle as she did so. But there at last was the sea, down a steep, rocky bank, through vicious thornbushes, which grabbed at her hair and snagged her shirt, then on to a crop of land between two rocky stretches, too gritty and small to be called a beach. Waves slapped the shoreline, leaving a crooked necklace of seaweed in their wake.

There was no one to see her. Gaby tugged off her clothes, hearing a button pop and her skirt rip even more. Her skin was pale and covered with goosebumps and the churning sea looked inhospitable, the rocks on either side menacing. But she reminded herself that this was what Nancy did every morning and strode towards the water's edge, wincing as sharp stones pressed into her soles and giving a small shriek as the first wave curled over her foot, then sucked back. A few paces more and she was up to her thighs, giving ineffectual hops every time a wave threatened to break over her, crossing her arms over her chest to shield her breasts.

'After the count of three,' she instructed herself. 'One, two, three . . .' But still she didn't submerge herself and start to swim until she lost her footing and sank, eyes stinging and choking on a mouthful of water. She thrashed back to the surface and saw that the undertow was already pulling her strongly towards the rocks. She flailed her arms in an approximation of the crawl, but she was a weak swimmer, a sunny-day floater in summer shallows, and now the sea was pulling at her and she could feel the colder current under her feet.

She tried to stand and found that she was out of her depth already. She turned to face the shore, although the sun in her eyes made it hard to see. There was the small disc of the beach, and there were her clothes in a tumbled heap. There was the slope she had struggled and slipped her way down, before a nasty little wave tossed itself into her face, into her stinging eyes. She spluttered and swallowed more water, struck out blindly.

Swimming lessons at school: other girls with their streamlined bodies and slick black swimming caps, arms raised, hands together, entering the water with never a splash, just a neat hole that opened at the touch of their steepled fingers and closed in on itself as their pressed-together feet dissolved from sight. And then they were the flickering, subterranean figures shifting along the floor of the pool; shape-changers, underwater birds. While she – hair cascading loose from the pinching cap and fingers wide open, as she had been told they should never be, her flesh soft and full, mouth open in a silent laugh of embarrassment at her own clumsiness – would go in, limbs flying apart and silver leaps of water all around her, then the sudden turquoise silence of the underwater world. If she had tried harder then, she wouldn't be in this pickle now.

Now she closed her fingers, pulled at the swirling water and kicked her legs. Connor would be on the deck, holding heavy coils of rope, gathering heaps of sail into the bags. Ethan – where would Ethan be? Was anybody thinking of her right now? The sun was a yellow orb dangling inside her skull and the sky a metal sheet shimmering above her; the waves tipped and chucked her. For a moment, she thought that she would die out there and no one would ever find her, or even know where to look. Not waving but drowning. Then her feet scrabbled on the bottom and she was standing up, up to her waist. Below her waist, even — she could have stood before. She'd been splashing around in a frantic panic when the ground was beneath her feet. She gave a sobbing cough and waded against the tug of the tide up the shore, half falling, then stumbling on. She reached the pile of her clothes and turned to look back at the sea. The waves were small, the rocks mild, and it seemed so tame and easy.

She wrapped Nancy's towel round her and stood, her limbs trembling with cold and shock, her teeth chattering. Then she rubbed herself dry, wincing as sand scoured her skin. She wrung out her hair and wrapped it, turban-like, in the towel. The sea had come in far enough to douse her clothes with spray, so that they were now wet and sandy. It was difficult to pull them on over her chilly, damp flesh, and the sandal straps rubbed against her gritty, blistered feet. This hadn't been such a good idea, after all. Yet it had looked so beautiful from a distance, green-blue, welcoming and still.

Gaby's skirt tore further on the bike ride home, when the hem caught in the bike chain. Her hair lashed her cheeks. Water dribbled down her neck. She was thankful when she arrived at the house and, with numb fingers, unlocked the door. She put the key under the boulder, for she wouldn't need it again before she left in the morning, then squelched into the hall, leaving a watery trail behind her. She kicked off her sandals, then made her way upstairs to the spare bedroom, got undressed and wrapped herself in the dressing-gown she had used before. Next, she rinsed all her clothes and hung them over the boiler with the swimsuit and towel. She turned the hot water on at the immersion heater, boiled the kettle and poured water over a herbal tea-bag, then ran herself a deep bath, adding plenty of lavender bath foam.

Oh, but it was lovely. She held her nose and slid under the surface, staying there for as long as she could manage. This was her kind of water, hot and fragrant, making the tips of her fingers shrivel. She could stay there until it got dark, turning the tap with her big toe when the water cooled, watching day turn to evening out of the window, letting her flesh melt . . .

Later, she wouldn't be able to remember what came next: it was simply a kaleidoscope of memories and feelings that glittered in her mind, forever rearranging itself into a different pattern. Did she have a glass of the shiraz, or was that after she had opened the first cardboard box in the spare bedroom and pulled out envelopes, folders of bank statements and bills, bundles of letters – all carefully ordered, some labelled and dated? Did she sit in the garden with a cigarette, watching the smoke coil into the air and dissipate while the stars hung low in the sky, or did she leaf through the photographs, one by one? There were so many, an album of a life thus far, and there's something powerfully emotional about seeing a familiar face grow older under your fingers. Older, and perhaps less happy, or was that just what happened to a face as it left youth behind and gathered up the years in the creases round the eyes and the brackets round the mouth? Photographs of Nancy with her father, with her mother, with other tiny children – cousins, perhaps, though Nancy had never mentioned cousins – and with other, unfamiliar, adults.

It was with a jolt that left her breathless that Gaby was suddenly looking at her own life as well, her own face getting older: for there she was with Nancy, and Cindy Sheringham, sitting on the swings in the playground behind her old house. And there she was again, arm in arm with Nancy, in shorts and a T-shirt, and for a moment she was in Brighton again, on that day long ago. And again, a few photos later, she was with Nancy and with Gaby's entire family – her mother partly obscured by an enormous brimmed hat that made her look like a gangster, her father blurred, and her three brothers tall and grinning in front of them. Stefan, Antony and Max. How young they all were then, how hopeful and boyish. Now Max was a banker, Antony sold cars and Stefan taught history at a university and never wore matching socks. As for Nancy, she stood very straight, her chin up in the pose Gaby knew so well, and stared intently at whoever had been taking the photograph. Then they were teenagers, their lips were red and they had earrings in their lobes and a more knowing way of posing for the camera. Gaby could hardly bear to look at some of the pictures, for they brought memories flooding back so strongly that she felt they might choke her. Ah, here was Stefan again – and no longer just one of Gaby's brothers but Nancy's boyfriend. Gaby knew that many of the photographs had been taken by Nancy; she even remembered her doing so – even thought she could hear the click of the button as she depressed it. And gradually she saw how she slid out of the pictures, or was on the sidelines. It was Stefan – at that twenty-first birthday party, in a suit, in swimming-trunks, at graduation, holding a bottle of champagne, sitting at a table outside a café in some foreign town, even out of focus on a bike. Every so often it was Stefan and Nancy in a group or posing together: an official couple, holding hands or smiling towards each other. And studying them, one after another, Gaby saw how in several of the photographs Nancy was looking at the camera, head lifted and gaze steady, while Stefan was turned towards her. It was two decades ago, but Gaby could see the contentment in his face. He felt safe. Even now it hurt to see it, knowing how it had ended.

There were several pictures of Gaby and Connor. How intense he was as a young man, thought Gaby, studying her thin, dark-haired husband; how full of angles and fierce desires. He rarely smiled in photos, but there was one in which he gazed at the younger, grinning Gaby with a look of agonized delight as if he thought that she would melt away; in others, he scowled at the camera as if it was threatening him. She recognized that expression still, although as he had got older Connor had learnt how to mask some of his feelings, present an acceptable face to the world. She came to a photograph that made her flinch: Ethan as a tiny baby, lying swaddled in her lap and fast asleep. But was that really her? She was like an effigy who'd been propped up in an imitation of life. Her face was pasty and dull between the curtains of greasy hair, her expression fixed, her shoulders slumped. She had let herself forget the depths of her post-natal misery, but this picture brought it sharply back.

Then, abruptly, Gaby was no longer in the photographs, nor Connor, nor Stefan. They were out of Nancy's life as if they'd never been there and in their place were strangers. Gaby felt her eyes burning with unshed tears. How could it have happened? How could all those rapt, smiling faces, all that seriousness of passion, have disappeared? The photographs that followed were more spaced out and better composed, as if Nancy was creating an acceptable version of her life with the messy bits left out, until at last Gaby was looking at what were clearly carefully selected printouts from a digital camera, often in black-and-white, and often of landscapes empty of human life. But here – then here, and here and here again – was a young man. Nancy liked to photograph him unawares, even in one photograph from behind, simply the fall of his dark hair over his neck and his broad shoulders as he faced the rippling sea. She examined each image carefully, noting the thick brows, the open face, the smile that put a dimple in one cheek. Nancy's lover, then.

Certainly there had been a glass of wine after the photographs, probably drunk too quickly in cool, thirsty gulps, and another cigarette, with the window opened wide to let the smoke drift out into the autumn night. Gaby was ravenous to the point of faintness, so she made herself a thick and messy sandwich, stuffing as much ham, cheese and tomato into the baguette as she could, then liberally smearing it with mustard that she found in the cupboard. She looked around the kitchen and living room and saw that she was creating her characteristic mess, but she couldn't deal with that at this moment. She'd clean up later. She ate standing up, pushing the bread into her mouth and chewing hungrily, washing it down with more wine.

When she had finished, she returned to the filing cabinet and the boxes, taking the wine with her. She was increasingly conscious of how badly she was behaving, but she was compelled by the urgent sense that she could find Nancy among the documents of her life, and make sense of the fugitive past. Then, at last, she would be released from it. For she had lost something when Nancy had abandoned her – not just that friendship, but with it a sense of certainty, a knowledge of being loved as she was, with nothing to prove. People can be felled by the death of a spouse, or by divorce, they talk about it endlessly, as if by putting it into words they can make the loss more bearable. But Gaby thought that being left by a best friend could be equally painful, yet there was no proper way to mourn or express it. Connor had never fully understood how she had felt about it – how could he? He didn't have best friends like that. He had dozens of colleagues and acquaintances, and with each one he expressed a different side of himself. But Gaby had always felt that Nancy saw her whole. She had been the only person in the world that Gaby didn't try to charm. The pledge they had made that they'd still know each other at ninety, and the loss of that relationship, which should have stretched from childhood to old age and death, still haunted Gaby, but it was only now, riffling through Nancy's life like this, that she realized how much.

She didn't open the envelope that had the word 'Will' printed on it, and she put to one side all the folders that contained the deeds of the house, the details of the mortgage, life insurance, car insurance. She barely glanced at the bank statements, only noting that they were – as she had expected – arranged in chronological order. One drawer of the cabinet was given over to Nancy's work and she didn't bother with that, but she did open a hard-backed notebook whose pages were unlined and thick. On the first page, there was a pen-and-ink drawing of Nancy's house, and on the second a half-completed watercolour of a church. Then there were several pages of sea birds, meticulously drawn. Gaby turned the pages slowly, stopping when she came to words, arranged like a poem but not really reading like one, although she spoke them out loud: '"It can be hard to get from day to day or, at least, it is never simple. I must have lost the knack somewhere along the way. I look at people and I wonder how they do it with such apparent ease. I wonder what is happening behind their cheerful faces. Are we all just pretending? Are we all made up of secrets and of lies? Or is it only me?"' Gaby read it again, to herself, then turned the page and saw a doodled portrait of a face she didn't recognize. Opposite it was another, more intricate, drawing, of a door with carved panels, and words scrawled underneath: 'I close this door.' Then sea birds again, curved beaks and delicate long legs, and a final pencil sketch of a male body, sitting down but bowed over so that only the back of the head, the serrated spine and the muscled, outstretched arms could be seen.

Gaby pushed away the book and poured more wine. She sat with her back against the bed and sipped it slowly, closing her eyes and feeling tiredness gather in her skull. Nancy had told her that she never dreamt, but surely that couldn't be true. Everyone had dreams. She turned her attention to Nancy's school reports. What a good student she had been – teachers who had called Gaby 'indolent' and 'irrational' and 'messy' used words like 'exemplary' for Nancy. But school reports rarely yield up a person's secrets. Gaby soon tired of flicking through the years, following her friend's sure progress up the school, her prizes and medals and positions of responsibility.

Then there were the letters, a great many, held in separate bundles by thick rubber bands. Gaby pulled one such bundle out and peered into the first envelope. The writing was spidery, and in faded blue ink, and she saw that it wasn't addressed to Nancy but to an Emily; the 'E' was curled and the 'y' trailed its tail back under the name. There was a date at the top: 19 April 1958. The signature at the bottom was hard to make out, but Gaby assumed that these must be letters from Nancy's father to her mother, well before Nancy was born. She slid the pack back into its place and randomly pulled out another, much slimmer one. The first letter was from a woman called Janet, writing from New York and describing a visit to the Frick Museum in too much detail. The next was from Mexico and this time was a mini-lecture on the murals of Diego Rivera. Gaby had never heard of Janet and she couldn't think why Nancy should keep such pompous

169

epistles. There were a few from Marcus – presumably an old flame, for between paragraphs of news there were endearments. He missed Nancy, he said; he thought of her face on the pillow. Gaby read only one of his letters. She found it strange that there had been men like Marcus in Nancy's life, and she hadn't known.

It was with a prickly sense of disquiet that she recognized her own handwriting when she was eleven, and pulled letters from herself out of the drawer. She couldn't remember writing so many, yet here they all were and she could follow herself from a child, letters round and unformed and smeared with ink, to a teenager and into her twenties. There were postcards from summer holidays in Wales and Brittany and, once, Spain, describing blue seas and yummy crêpes and gales that had blown down the whole camping site. There were airmail letters on flimsy paper, the sides gummed together, and there were letters from university. She told Nancy about things she could no longer remember – parties, grades, boys, holiday plans. About Connor. She made arrangements. And finally – on one side of cream-coloured notepaper, in a large and almost illegible hand – she had written: 'Nancy, please please please please get in touch. Please.' No name at the end. She had sent that letter to Nancy's mother to forward and never even known it had arrived. But here it was, and Nancy had never answered.

She didn't read Stefan's letters; couldn't bring herself to commit what seemed like a double betrayal. She only glanced at the dates to see if he had written since Nancy had left, and it was when she was replacing the bundle that she found a single letter that she almost didn't bother to read, because it was typed and looked formal and, anyway, she was becoming queasy about her spying, and could feel the ominous first throbs of a migraine above her left eye. She could so easily have overlooked them – the words that, however much she stared at them, however much she shut her eyes, then opened them again, still read:

Dear Nancy Belmont,

As you must know, I turned eighteen a few days ago, and you have probably been wondering if you would hear from me. At least, you posted your details on the Adoption Contact Register and so did I. So, several days ago I was given your name and address, and it was up to me whether to use them. I think I would like to meet you. There are questions I want to know the answer to. Could you write to me at the above address to let me know if you will see me? I don't know when – we live a long way from each other and, anyway, I don't think I am quite ready yet. Please do not telephone or anything like that. It wouldn't feel right. And my parents do not know that I am contacting you.

I look forward to hearing from you.

Yours sincerely,

Sonia Hamilton

Twelve

<u>25 September</u>

I used to have these two particular emotions when I was a child. The first was that I would feel guilty, really horribly guilty, but I didn't know what the guilt was for. It happened most often at night and it sometimes made me anxious about going to sleep. I would wake up and it would be dark outside and my heart would be pounding away as if it was going to burst through my chest, and I'd feel that I'd done something badly wrong. I thought if I could work out what it was – like being mean to someone or lying or stealing or cheating or bitching about a friend behind her back, anything, really – the feeling would go away, or at least it would get less, until it was a manageable little ball of worry and not a thick blanket of fog. And if I knew what it was, I could do something about it, like confess or apologize. Atone, that's the word. I could atone, like Catholics have to when they go to Confession. My friend Lorrie's a Catholic and even though she doesn't really believe in anything any more, she still likes going to Confession because she says she feels clean afterwards. When I was still quite small, I'd sometimes wake Mum and she'd come and sit on my bed, and put her hand on my forehead to see if I had a fever. I'd try to tell her what I was going through, but there wasn't really anything to say, except 'I feel guilty.' Maybe lots of people feel like this. I don't know. I've never really talked about it to anyone. I still get it sometimes, although not quite as often. It's like a sense of foreboding – but not foreboding about something that's about to happen, or that even has happened. Maybe it's a foreboding about myself. Perhaps it's because of who I am, or am not. Perhaps there's something monstrous about me that I don't know, something lurking inside me, and one day it will come hurtling out like a prisoner who's burst their chains.

The other feeling I've always had is that I'm waiting. Waiting for something to happen, as if life hasn't properly started yet or something. Recently I've wondered if what I've been waiting for is you. I tried talking about it to Alex and he said it was just existential <u>Angst</u> and a condition of being alive. Very helpful.

<u>26 September</u>
You're not my mother, you know. Don't you ever go thinking that. You can only have one of those and I've got mine. She might not be particularly beautiful or clever or well-off or anything, but she's my mother and I don't want anyone else, no matter who they are. But I'm your daughter. I'll always be your daughter.

PS I got your reply. It was very businesslike. What else did I ever expect?

Thirteen

The house was a mess, thought Connor, irritably, dropping his bag in the hall, stopping to pick up the mail, then stepping over a pile of laundry on the way into the kitchen. The sink was full of dishes, the ashtray was full of cigarette stubs, and the remains of a cooked breakfast were still on the table, along with Gaby's house keys. The air was thick and stale and he unlocked the door into the garden and pushed it open, noticing as he did so that Gaby had left washing hanging on the line. He had spoken to her earlier, as Stefan was driving him home. She'd been on her mobile, her voice crackling, and had said she was on a train. In fact, she said, she was in the dining car, eating porridge and looking out at green fields, where cows were lying down in the drizzle. Connor, bewildered, had started to ask where she was and where she'd been and when she'd be back – and why on earth, for that matter, was she on a train when she had his car? But she'd interrupted him to say that the line was breaking up and a few seconds later the call was disconnected. When Connor tried her again, the phone was turned off.

Clearly, in spite of her keys on the table, she had not been at home since she left on Saturday morning to take Ethan to university. There were signs of a hasty departure everywhere. Cupboard doors were open, surfaces littered with objects Ethan must have discarded at the last minute.

Upstairs, their bed was unmade and the wardrobe stood ajar, with a colourful pile of Gaby's clothes on the floor beside it. Connor frowned. He had imagined opening the door to a warm, tidy house and Gaby's smile, her hand on his shoulder as she asked him about his week and told him about hers. He ran the water in the kitchen and discovered it was cold, so he turned on the immersion heater and set about clearing up before Gaby returned; he needed everything to be in its proper place before tomorrow morning when he went back to work. Although he gave a heavy sigh as he set about the task, Connor enjoyed cleaning. He liked taking mess and turning it into order. He was very methodical. He put on a wash, stacked the dishes in the dishwasher and left the dirty pans beside the sink while the water heated, then took his bag upstairs and unpacked his own clothes before hanging Gaby's in the cupboard.

There was an empty chocolate box on Gaby's side of the bed and a hot-water bottle on the floor, and Connor saw her lying back, popping truffles into her mouth. Where was she, though? He shook out the duvet on their bed and plumped up the pillows. Wiping surfaces, vacuuming the floors, filling the sink with hot, soapy water to wash the pots and pans, returning Ethan's belongings to his room, putting CDs in their covers and books on the shelves: mess made him feel that he had lost control, but neatness restored it. The washing-machine hummed; the row of glasses gleamed beside the sink. Clean, empty surfaces, chairs pushed back under the table, old newspapers put into the recycling bag, the satsumas he'd bought yesterday arranged in a bowl. Soon he'd reward himself with a cup of tea and then he would go down the road to buy a chicken for the supper he had planned. He would have a long bath and shave. But he did wish that Gaby would come home. He opened the fridge. A tub of goat's cheese shot out and hit him in the stomach.

He saw her first half-way up the magnolia tree by the side of the house. For a moment he said nothing, just stood and stared at her, feeling strangely happy. She lay across a branch like a cat, her ripped skirt twisted round her bare legs and her hair piled on top of her head. 'I left the door open in the kitchen for you when I went to the shops, just in case.'

'Connor, you're back!'

'So it seems.'

'I meant to be here when you arrived.'

'You can come down now.'

'I'm not sure I can. It's always easier to climb up than get back again. They say that in walking and climbing guides, don't they? Make sure that every step you take is reversible.'

'Shall I give you a hand?'

'Please.'

He put down his shopping bag, held out his arms and she slithered from her perch, scraping her calf. 'This isn't quite what I expected,' he said, his arms still round her, his face in the fragrance of her hair. She smelt of woodsmoke and salt, and her face was pale and tired.

'I know. I'm sorry. I didn't either. And the house must have been in a terrible mess when you got back; I meant to clean everything up but it's all been so – well, let's go in and then we can talk. You look all tanned. Was it lovely? Did you miss me? I missed you.' She stopped suddenly and kissed him full on the mouth. 'It's been odd,' she said. 'Ethan, and then – well, anyway . . .'

'Here, let's not stand outside. Yes, the house was dreadful. You and Ethan are as bad as each other. Is he all right, by the way? I've been thinking about him. I'm sorry I wasn't there.'

'I'm sorry too.'

'I should have been. And of course I missed you. What have you been up to?'

'Up to?'

'Where have you been?'

'Oh, well, you see –'

'And where's my car?'

'Ah.'

'Gaby?'

'It's in the garage.'

'But –'

'In Exeter.'

'In the garage in Exeter. What happened? Did you have an accident? Is that why you look so done in?'

'Not an accident as such. Shall I make us tea?'

'Gaby –'

'It kind of blew up on our way.'

'What d'you mean, blew up?'

'I drove it in the wrong gear. The one for towing things.'

'Oh, fuck.'

'Sorry.'

'How can you *do* things like this all the time?'

'Sorry,' she repeated, her voice wobbly.

'Time and time again.'

'I know. I said to Ethan you'd be furious.'

'Do you blame me?'

Gaby rubbed her face. 'No,' she said wearily. 'Of course I don't blame you. I drive myself mad as well. Listen, Connor, I'm really, really sorry. That's all I can say. We can hire another car on our insurance until it's mended, and I'll go and fetch it when it's ready, of course.'

'If you'd only thought for a –'

'It needs a new engine.'

'Jesus.' He sat down at the table, squeezing his ear-lobe between thumb and forefinger and frowning at her. 'Is that why you're home late?'

'Well, not exactly. It's kind of a long story. I can't say it in a sentence. It's going round and round in my head and I need to – Look, why don't you have a bath and I'll make us tea. We can talk about it later. And you can tell me about your week. Yes?'

'All right.'

'Let's not ruin the first evening back. There are more important things than broken cars.'

'Hm.'

'Connor –'

'What?'

'Oh, nothing. You're filthy. Get into your bath and I'll bring you your tea.'

'Thanks.'

'I can't tell you how lovely it is to have you back.'

*

Sitting on the train, Gaby had worked out the dates. There was no way round it: Nancy had been pregnant when she had left. It must be that Stefan was a father – a father who didn't know he was a father; a father who wasn't a father. Or had he known? No, surely that was out of the question; it would make no sense. He had loved Nancy, adored her like a besotted fool. She had left him because she had discovered she did not love him enough to stay. Presumably the pregnancy had pushed her to go when she did. But why on earth had she not had an abortion? What had possessed her to have a baby in order to give it away? Nancy wasn't religious; more than that, she had always been a fierce advocate of women's right to choose. It didn't make sense at all. As Gaby sat at the kitchen table, waiting for the kettle to boil, she put her head in her hands and felt the thoughts churning in her brain, a seething froth of half-formed ideas and half-remembered words. What had Nancy said to her about Stefan, in that level voice and looking at her with her turquoise gaze: leaving Stefan had felt 'like a crime'. I bet it did, she thought bitterly. You were carrying his child and you knew how much he longed to be a father.

The kettle boiled. She made tea and took a cup up to Connor, where he lay perfectly still in the bath, eyes closed, the water lapping at his sides. While she'd grown softer and rounder, he'd become more gaunt with the years, muscles in his legs and sharp ribs. Gaby looked down at his brown forearms, brown neck and ruddy face, his shocking white body with the fuse of hair running down his belly. His genitals bobbed gently in the water.

She put the cup down on the edge and his eyes opened. He looked at her and smiled and she leant forward through the steamy air and kissed his moist cheek. 'What long eyelashes you have,' she said.

'All the better for closing my eyes.'

And he did just that, and slid further into the water.

She should never have gone to Rashmoor in the first place. She should never have tracked down Nancy and thought that somehow it was her right to push and prod her for secrets. She most certainly should never have broken back into her house in secret, like the vain and foolish girl in Bluebeard's castle, and gone through her belongings like that, trying to winkle out some simple answer to the question that had dogged her through the years. Never, never, never. For now she knew and couldn't unknow, couldn't turn back the clock and not get on the train, not sneak into the house, not lift out that letter and read the few typed words. She knew, and the knowledge poisoned her. She could feel its toxic juices inside her, seeping through her body, oozing into every cavity of her brain, staining the past and corrupting the future. She knew what she had no right to know, and what should she do now? She had got so much more than she had bargained for that she was choked with it. She didn't know how to tell Connor, how to begin – because then she would have passed the secret on to him, like a virus that would infect him too. And what about Stefan? Didn't he have a right to know? The thought of it made her breathless with panic. For now, through her ignorance and folly, she had an unwanted power and there was no way of not using it. To withhold the secret had it own consequences: she would be denying her brother insight into his own life, and if he was ever to find out, then discover she had known all along, how would he feel? Yet the idea of saying to him, 'I think you have a daughter,' felt impossibly cruel. Anyway, he didn't have a daughter: Nancy had given her away.

So Gaby did not tell Connor, not that evening at least. She glossed over her delayed return – the car, she mumbled, and then complications with the trains on Sunday, you know how it can be, finding a little place not so far from Exeter; she didn't exactly lie, but her heart pounded with the deception and she was surprised that Connor didn't pick up on her anxiety. They ate Moroccan chicken and talked instead about Ethan, and about Connor's time away with Stefan, and what the week ahead held for both of them. They were tired out, and after supper and the news, they went to bed. Connor set the alarm clock for seven o'clock, then turned on to his side, laid a hand on Gaby's hip and went to sleep. But Gaby lay awake for some time, staring into the darkness.

Fourteen

After the first structureless weekend, Ethan got into a routine of a kind – or, at least, a routine was imposed upon him by his timetable of lectures, seminars and tutorials, and the essays he was immediately set. He had always been a nocturnal creature, and he met most of his deadlines in the early hours of the morning, in a blue haze of cigarette smoke, while around him lay the contents of his room. He still had not bothered to unpack and it was becoming increasingly difficult to find a space to work. Every so often he would pile books higher and throw a few clothes back into his case; he put the notes he made at lectures and in the library into a cardboard box and promised himself that one day, soon, he would create a filing system. Colour-coded folders, he thought. Highlighter pens. When he had more time, more inclination; when he had properly settled in.

There wasn't really a centre to his life yet, but he didn't mind, telling himself that that would come later. He was meeting people on his history course, going to parties, drifting amiably in and out of social groups, making tentative friendships, coming back to his room to eat cold baked beans straight from the tin, drink beer from the can or wine from the bottle. He didn't see much of the other residents on his floor, although they bumped into each other in the corridor, the bathroom and kitchen.

The only one from the first evening he ever saw socially was Harry, who was caustic, clever and spectacularly cynical. They had played squash together a couple of times and now Harry had invited him to have a meal with him and some friends at a Mexican restaurant. He let drop that it was his birthday and Ethan had bought him a book about mathematical paradoxes and ethical dilemmas that he and Connor loved. He didn't have any wrapping-paper, so he pushed it into a paper bag he found in the corner of his room and wrote 'Happy Birthday' on the outside in large letters.

He seemed to have got through a surprising number of clothes since he'd been there. His laundry lay in a large heap by the door and it was hard to find anything clean to wear. He rummaged in his bag for a shirt his mother had given him a few months ago, shook it vigorously, and pulled it on. He found socks under the bed. In the absence of a brush, he ran his fingers through his hair. His stubble was turning into something more like an unsatisfactory beard, but he didn't have time to shave. Harry had said he should be there by eight, and he was already running late.

By the time he arrived fifteen or twenty people were crowded round the table at the back of the restaurant, young men and women who'd already got through several bottles of wine and whose spirits were high and cheeks flushed. Harry waved him over, hugged him in an uncharacteristic outbreak of sentimental friendliness, and tried to introduce him to his friends – several of whom, Ethan gathered, had been at the same school as him.

But he stopped hearing the names and he stopped seeing their faces. They became a blur; their voices a vague and distracting background hum. For she was there – the nameless she, who had walked with such soft steps past Ethan on that first evening and whose luminous face had been in his mind ever since. Half-way to his chair at the corner of his table he halted. She had a smooth, pale, oval face, made even paler by the black shirt she was wearing, and autumnal auburn hair; her grey-green eyes were large. She made Ethan think of moonlight and cool, secret shadows. It seemed to him that there was a mysterious radiance about her, setting her apart from the jostling noise and hot, grinning faces around her.

'I saw you,' he tried to say, but was drowned out.

'Sit down, then,' someone was yelling, and his chair was scraped back for him, a large glass of rough wine poured out.

He let himself sink down, and now he could barely see her any more. What was her name? Who was she? He half thought that, out of his sight, she might dissolve and disappear, like a ghost. There was a toast to Harry and everyone raised their glasses. Plates of tortillas and tacos were being slammed on to the table. Ethan turned to the person sitting on his left and tried to smile. 'I'm Ethan,' he said.

'Hi. Amelia,' she said.

'I don't know anyone here, only Harry. Tell me who everyone is.'

She laughed and said he'd never remember, but did so anyway, like a litany. The names flowed over him. Harry, of course, then Daisy and Faith, and Boris from LA; Cleo and Chloë and Dan times two; Coralie from France, Mick, Lorna, Penny, Morris, Irish Maeve.

'Lorna like Lorna Doone,' said Ethan, stupidly.

'Sorry?'

'Nothing. Nothing at all.'

Ethan started off tongue-tied, then segued swiftly, with no intermediary stages, into a garrulous tipsiness. He spoke loudly, so that Lorna would notice him. He got to his feet to propose another toast, so that she would look at him. He told jokes to make her laugh, mentioned politics so she would know he was thoughtful, and gave Harry his present half-way through the evening, because he wanted her to see what he had chosen. He ordered more wine, so that he could lean across the table, over the remains of the meal, to pour it into her glass and see her look up and hear her say 'Thank you', in a voice that was soft and clear, and fell like fresh water into the brackish confusion of his mind. Later, he wouldn't be able to remember what anyone had said to him. He had no appetite for the food, but he drank wine and smoked too many cigarettes, once finding himself holding two at the same time.

When someone – Tom or Dan or Boris – said they should all go back to his room and continue the evening there, Ethan agreed eagerly. Of course the evening mustn't end. He imagined sitting on the floor a few inches from her; he imagined touching her hand as if by accident. The very thought sent an electric thrill through him.

But what was this? Harry wasn't coming, and neither was Lorna. 'We're a bit tired,' said Harry. *We?* The casual intimacy of that 'we' was like a bucket of ice thrown over

Ethan's hot head, dousing every fantasy, and he was suddenly stone-cold sober and wretched. He watched as Harry helped Lorna into the light-grey coat she'd worn when Ethan had first seen her, then wrapped her scarf round her neck for her. She lifted her chin to let him do it, smiling very slightly. Ethan wanted to howl like an animal as Harry led her from the restaurant. A few moments later, they passed the window holding hands, lacing their fingers together and matching their strides.

Back in Tom's room, Ethan continued drinking, but the alcohol only gave him a heavy, metallic headache and thickened the sour taste in his mouth. He smoked a joint, two, to make the pain more distant. He lay back against a cushion. People spoke to him and he replied. They laughed and he laughed too. More people arrived. The room was crowded now. There was music and he let himself be pulled to his feet to dance. Someone kissed him and, obediently, he kissed her back.

It was dawn, drizzly and grey, when he let himself into his room, drank three glasses of tap water, then lay down on his unmade bed in his damp, smoky clothes. He put his pillow over his face, closed his bloodshot eyes and, in the tipping room, he dreamt of Lorna.

Fifteen

For three weeks, Gaby said nothing and did nothing about what she had discovered. Her life continued as normal. She went to work each day; two or three nights a week she saw a play, usually taking a friend with her. She met up with people, and talked and laughed with them as if nothing had changed. Read books, went for walks on Hampstead Heath, gossiped on the phone, called Ethan to check he was all right, started going to an art class with two friends every Tuesday evening, tried and failed to take up running, organized a small party and baked a large chocolate cake to celebrate Connor's birthday. She and Connor saw each other early in the mornings and late at night; they told each other about their day and fell asleep together, their bodies touching. Nobody, looking at her, would have known that inside she was turmoil and dismay. She had discovered that she could lead a double life: smile, talk, listen and yet feel continually shadowed by dread. Sometimes she wondered, if she simply let the secret lie inside her like a package dropped down a well, whether it would gradually decay and dissipate. In a year or two, say, would it no longer exist in its original state but have been mixed in with the rest of what was inside her mind? Like salt, or like a soluble bitterness. And if that happened, did it mean that she had been forever corrupted, her whole make-up changed by reading the letter?

She saw Stefan several times during those three weeks. Once he came over for supper when Connor was working late. He arrived with a bottle of white wine and a bunch of dahlias: he always brought flowers when he came for dinner. He would present them to his sister with an embarrassed half-bow and be surprised and delighted when she hugged him exuberantly in thanks. He told her of the next book he was planning tentatively to write; she outlined a new project that she and a director-friend had recently embarked on, trying to involve constantly truanting pupils in theatrical events. 'It could be extremely exciting. But, of course, it depends on finding sponsors,' she said, all the time thinking about Nancy, about Nancy's daughter.

Suddenly the secret that had been lying quiescent inside her felt like steam under pressure. 'Do you ever think about Nancy?' she asked abruptly, tipping her chair back and not meeting his eyes.

The question hung in the air. Stefan prodded at a tiny shred of lettuce on his plate. 'Nancy,' he repeated musingly, as if he was trying to remember who she was.

'I know it was a long time ago, but all the same –'

'It was a long time, yes.'

'Eighteen years. And two-thirds.'

'Is that right?'

'Yes. So, do you?'

'Now and then,' he said vaguely. 'She's in my attic, as it were.'

'Attic?'

'Junk room. Memory bank. Whatever. Things don't just disappear, do they, although they might get mislaid for a bit among the extraordinary, multitudinous space of one's brain? Imagine all the things I don't remember that I remember, if you see what I mean. You say a name, mention an event far back in the past, and I rummage around, pull open a few drawers, lift a few lids and find it.'

Gaby sighed. He wasn't going to tell her anything.

'What sometimes bothers me,' continued Stefan, 'is our ability to find memories that aren't really there. So if I say to you, "Remember my blue jacket?" You might search through your memory and eventually find a blue jacket hidden away there, although I never actually had one. It was brown. Hypothetically, of course, because I do have a blue jacket. At least, I think I do.'

'You were wearing it this evening. Do you ever think it was Nancy who stopped you meeting someone else?' Gaby said doggedly.

'I meet people all the time.'

'You know what I –'

'How do you know I'm not seeing someone at the moment?'

'Are you?'

'Not as such. But you shouldn't worry about me so much. I'm quite all right. I like being on my own, you know. I don't think I'd be a very easy person to live with. Shall we watch a film? I brought a selection of DVDs with me.'

'OK, I won't ask you anything else.'

'I don't mind you asking.'

'You just don't want to answer.'

'There's nothing to answer. It's a question of patience. I know you're not a great fan of patience. But in the end the pain goes away.'

The trouble was that Gaby remembered the address on Sonia's letter. The more she tried to forget it, the more she remembered, until it was branded on her mind. She could see it now, printed at the top of the page: 52 Willow Street, Stratford-upon-Avon. And what was more, she had to visit Stratford quite regularly for her work. She would be there the next day, for example, to meet the actor who was going to talk to her current group of Americans about Shakespeare's problem plays before they saw *Measure for Measure* in the evening, and to check out a couple of restaurants where they might eat. She would be alone, with time on her hands.

So it was that at half past eleven the following morning, Gaby found herself standing in a neat suburban street on the outskirts of Stratford, where plane trees lined the road. The door to number fifty-two was dark blue, with a brass knocker in the shape of a fox. A car was parked outside, but she could see no sign of life within. In fact, the whole road felt deserted.

She should turn round and go about her business. She had no right to be here. Yet even as she thought this, she felt the familiar gulp of excitement inside her, like a bubble forming at the bottom of a beaker and slowly glinting to the surface. She stepped forward, raising her hand as if to press the bell, then stopped dead. No, this was wrong, quite wrong. As she stood there, appalled by her own folly, the door opened and she found herself face to face with a middle-aged woman, a few years older than herself, but plumper and with short grey hair and glasses hanging round her neck. She wore the kind of coat — thick and shapeless — that makes middle-aged women start to seem invisible, but her face was strong and her grey eyes shrewd. She looked faintly surprised to see Gaby standing on the path.

'Can I help you?'

'No. Sorry, wrong house.'

'I see. What number are you wanting?'

'Forty-three,' said Gaby at random.

'This is fifty-two.'

'Yes. Stupid of me.'

The woman's eyebrows rose.

'I'll be on my way, then,' Gaby said, backing away. 'Sorry.'

She walked off in a daze, trembling at her own reckless-ness. Looking back, she saw Sonia's mother get into a red car and drive in the opposite direction. It was a cold day, with a sharp wind and rain in the air. Dead leaves blew round her feet. She shivered, put her hands into the pockets of her jacket for warmth, and found the last of the cigarettes she'd bought in Rashmoor. Without think-ing about it, she stuck one into her mouth and, turning her back to the wind and shielding the flame with her hand, lit it. A familiar vertigo hit her as she took a deep drag. She'd smoke it and then go, she thought. But as she walked slowly back down the short street, she saw that in the house where Sonia lived a curtain was being pulled open in an upstairs window. She halted. Now, as she stared, she saw a young woman with dark hair at the window, looking out on the bare street. Gaby drew a sharp breath and turned away, though her limbs felt heavy and she moved as if underwater. She had seen Sonia. She knew it. And now that she had, Sonia was no longer just the indistinct face in a miniature photograph tacked to Nancy's noticeboard but had become real and solid – flesh and blood in Willow Street.

A youth passed her, coming from the other direction; she glimpsed a hawkish nose and very pale eyes that met hers briefly. Then he was gone and she found herself at the end of the street, where it joined a busier road, full of shops and cafés. There was a bus shelter at the junction, with fold-up seats inside; Gaby collapsed on to one, pulling her jacket closer round her and trembling. Her legs weren't working properly. Her mouth was dry. She sat there, waiting for her breathing to return to normal, and then she smoked another cigarette, relishing the slight ache in her lungs as she sucked at it deeply. A few drops of rain spat at the bus shelter's window and the sky darkened further. She should have brought her umbrella with her; she was definitely going to get wet.

As she stood up to leave, she could not resist looking back down Willow Street. A young couple were walking towards her, not touching, but close to each other and talking animatedly, and as they drew nearer she realized with a jolt of alarm that it was the pale-eyed youth and the girl she had seen in the upstairs window. Sonia – daughter of Nancy and Stefan, unexpected time bomb ticking away in Gaby's life – was about to walk past her. Gaby pressed a hand against her heart. A skinny, loose-limbed, knock-kneed girl she was, wearing a colourful ra-ra skirt over leggings and Converses, and a bomber jacket on top. Her hair was dark and spiky and her jaw firm, just like Nancy's. There was a stud in her nose, a large ring on her thumb. She looked like an urban elf. Her eyes were turquoise-blue. She smiled at something the youth was saying and her angular face was transformed.

They sauntered past, ignoring the rain that was splattering down on their bare heads. Gaby held her breath. If she put out a hand, she could touch her. She could call out her name and the girl would turn. She watched them go by, feeling a tear roll down her cheek, into her mouth. They linked hands loosely and she saw them stop before a café a little further up the road. He was saying something and she was nodding. Then he gave her a kiss on the mouth and she went into the café alone.

Gaby sat and watched the rain streaming down the windows. There was a hollowness in her stomach; maybe it was hunger. She thought about getting some fish and chips before her early-afternoon meeting, something soggy, salty, greasy, comforting. She and Ethan often used to get fish and chips when Connor was out; they would sit companionably in front of the TV with the warm damp bags on their laps, and a can of beer each. She wondered what he was doing now. It was odd how you don't realize that they are leaving. The day creeps up on you in a version of Grandmother's Footsteps, softly, softly, until it pounces. Once she had known everything about his life; he had been part of her. When he cried, she fed or changed him; when he held out his arms, she hugged him; if he fell over, she lifted him up and comforted him. She walked him to school in the morning and collected him in the evening, and knew every lesson he would have that day. He would tell her his secrets, climbing into her bed and pressing his mouth against her ear, whispering what was inside him until she felt that it was inside her as well. Bit by bit, it changed. He stopped holding her hand. He stopped calling her 'Mummy'. He stopped telling her things. He locked his door. But now he was in another world entirely. He had friends she would never meet, interests she could never share. Soon there would be another place that he would call home, while for her home would never have quite the same meaning again.

She was glad. Of course she was glad. But sad, too. Something was over and it would never come again. She understood now that she should have been better prepared; should have rehearsed for this moment of her life, had other interests and plans to fill the emptiness she felt. One of her friends, when her daughter had left last year, had hurled herself into new projects with almost alarming vigour, filling her evenings and weekends with piano lessons and Italian classes and some extra-energetic type of yoga. She said she was refusing to pine. Gaby had always assumed that she would be like that too – she had no intention of being a moper, an abandoned mother in the grip of maudlin nostalgia: when Ethan left, she would decide what she was going to be next, who she was going to be; doors that had been closed would swing open and she would step into whole new landscapes of possibility. The chance of self-renewal had always excited and cheered her. One stage of her life would be over, but the next just beginning. So what was she doing now, sitting in a bus shelter in the outskirts of Stratford, spying on the daughter of her ex-friend, groping around in the treacherous and incomprehensible past? It was no way to behave.

She stood up and stepped out purposefully into the steady downpour. Almost immediately, she was drenched. People were walking fast, umbrellas up and heads down. Gaby hurried past the florist and the Oxfam shop, past the pub. Past the café. But, no, not past the café. She stopped dead at its entrance and tried to see inside, the water plopping on to her from its awning. Of course, she had known all along that she was going to push open its door and take shelter from the rain; take off her soaking jacket and hang it on the coat-stand, shake her head so that her dripping hair scattered droplets of water over the floor; sniff the aroma of coffee and pastries; look for Sonia.

Sonia wasn't sitting at any of the tables. She was standing behind the counter in a white apron, working the espresso machine, which hissed and frothed from its various nozzles. Gaby hesitated, then sat on a tall stool at the counter. The girl glanced at her. 'I'll not be a moment,' she said, and her voice had a slight burr.

Gaby watched her. She was wearing a buttoned blue T-shirt under her apron; her shoulders were thin, her collarbones sharp, but her breasts were soft and round and her neck smooth. For a moment, Gaby was reminded of Ethan, with his lanky, effortless grace. Her hair was damp from the rain, and drops still sparkled in its blackness, so dark it was almost blue. She had a straight nose, and her brows were thick and dark over Nancy's eyes. She handed the cappuccino across to the customer, and

Gaby saw her bony wrists and long fingers, with their bitten nails.

'What can I get for you? Here – take some of these paper towels, you're soaked through.'

'That's kind. A hot chocolate, I think.'

'Coming up.'

'With cream.'

'And marshmallows?'

'No – oh, why not?'

'Good for you.' Suddenly Sonia smiled at her across the counter, a broad smile showing even white teeth. Her triangular face lit up and she was nearly beautiful.

'And some of that carrot cake, please.'

'OK.'

'Can I buy you some hot chocolate too? You look as though you got caught in the rain as well.'

'That's very kind, but I'll have something later.'

She turned away to make Gaby's drink and Gaby put her elbows on the counter and propped her chin in her hands, watching her from behind.

'Here.'

'Blimey, that looks bad for me,' Gaby said, as she slid over the money.

She sipped the foaming creation, feeling its creamy richness slide down her throat, then picked at the carrot cake. The girl wasn't paying her any attention, but drying espresso cups and putting them back on the shelf. Maybe it wasn't even her, after all, and she was reading significance into something that had none. She waited until she had handed another customer his spinach-stuffed croissant, then leant forward. 'My name's Gaby,' she said.

It came out louder than she had intended, nearer a shout than a murmur.

'Oh. Well – hi.'

Gaby felt like a middle-aged man trying to pick up the nubile waitress. She slurped her drink once more to hide her embarrassment and wiped away the chocolate moustache, then said, 'You're supposed to tell me your name now.'

'My name?'

'Unless you don't want to.'

The girl stared at her, frowning, biting her lower lip anxiously.

'Sonia,' she said.

'Sonia? Ah.'

'Yes. What is it? Why do you ask?'

'Nothing. Just – nothing. It's a nice name, that's all.'

This time the look Sonia gave her was one of panic, as if Gaby might be mad and dangerous. Gaby saw herself through the young girl's eyes – a middle-aged woman in damp clothes, desperate for company – and felt a flush spread over her face, her whole body, but she persisted. She was waiting to see Stefan in the girl. Anything would do, just a glimpse, a gesture, a certain way of smiling. Then she would know.

'And have you worked here long, Sonia?'

'I'm sorry?'

'I was asking, have you worked –'

'I heard what you said. I just didn't know why you said it. Sorry, that sounds rude. I'm tired today, distracted. No, not long. I'm still at school – this is my half-term. I'm saving up for my gap year.'

'Where do you want to go?'

'Where?' Sonia pulled her ear-lobe and her face brightened with the anticipation of the year ahead, making her look younger, a child still. 'Well, all over really, but first of all . . .'

She started to say something about Africa, Botswana, a project with HIV women that she'd already signed up for, but Gaby wasn't listening. The words slid in and out of her consciousness. The café blurred and quivered; she blinked hard but it remained queasily without edges, and she thought for a moment that she would faint. Her whole body was tingling, as if she had pins and needles over every inch of her skin; her forehead was clammy; inside, she felt bubbling hot and liquid, as if everything that was solid about her had dissolved into a rushing deluge. Only her heart remained, swollen and huge, thumping away like a hydraulic pump. The hands on the counter: they were her hands, but they looked and felt like the hands of a stranger. She put two fingers against her lips; it was her mouth, but it felt numb and rubbery and she was sure that if she tried to speak, only gibberish would come out, in a voice that no longer belonged to her. She stared at the floor beneath her feet and it seemed impossibly far away. If she fell, she would crash to it and break into a dozen pieces.

'Are you all right?'

'Hnnn,' she managed, and felt herself trying to smile; her face buckled with the effort. Sonia stared at her, her face a Cubist painting, everything familiar rearranged into strangeness.

'Are you ill? You've gone all pale.'

'I don't –'

'Do you want to lie down? Or can I give you some water?'

Water. Gaby thought of a well, a stream, cool clear depths. She gripped the edge of the counter and pressed hard. Her breath came in ragged gasps. Then, suddenly, the world steadied and she was herself once more, surrounded by sights and sounds that she could touch and name. This was a knife, this a plate, this a cup. The girl opposite her was Sonia. Everything was distilled into that one gesture: the glimpse she had been looking for and now would always see, the little flash of knowing that, for a pulse-beat, had thrown a wild light over her entire world, making the tame landscape seem suddenly sinister and full of dark, guttering shadows. She stared at the concerned young face, into the pale, long-lashed eyes.

'Sonia,' she said.

'Can I call someone?'

'No. Just a funny turn.'

Sonia laid a slim, cool hand over hers; her bangle pressed against Gaby's skin. 'But you –'

'No, I said!'

Gaby jerked away her hand and stood up, stumbling, waiting beside her stool, one hand holding the counter, until she was sure she could walk steadily to where her jacket hung on the coat-stand. It was still damp, but she had only been in there for a few minutes. She thought how strange it was that a few minutes could be like a crack running through your life; the point at which you break. She thought of one of her friends, Helena, whose second child had been run over by a bus: for months

199

after it had happened, she had talked obsessively about how a single second had changed everything, as if by talking about it she could alter it, wind back the clock to that place and that time and place a hand on her boy's shoulder, keeping him by her side. The bus would rumble past. One second earlier or later, she had said, and nothing would have happened. After a little shudder of dread at what might have been, life would have continued as before.

But it wasn't chance that had made the crack in Gaby's life; it was Gaby herself who, with the persistence of the zealous cop, had refused to let old secrets hide in the deep corners of the past. She had found Nancy's child and now she wondered if she had known all along, not with her head but in her blood and in her bones and where the nerves meet and where the gates of pain opened.

All these thoughts shimmered in her, like points of light glancing off the surface of the sea, before she reached the door of the café. Through the glass she saw that the people walking past, umbrellas up, huddled into themselves, were blurred by threads of rain so that they looked unreal. She stepped out on to the pavement and tipped her head back to feel the cool drops on her cheeks, on her eyelids, running down her neck and soaking into her layers of clothes. The weariness that she sometimes felt at having to be herself overcame her, and for several minutes she simply stood in the downpour with her eyes shut, thinking of nothing but being wet.

Sixteen

<u>24 October</u>

I wonder if I will stop writing this once I've met you. I'm only writing to you because you're still no one, everyone, a blank page, my inner thoughts, my ideal, the woman I love, the woman I hate, the woman who's me, the woman who made me and lost me and whom I've thought about ever since I knew about her. If I'm honest, there are times when I want you to hurt when you see me. I want you to realize what you lost when you gave me away.

I'm pretty nervous about our meeting – are you? – and I keep trying to work out what it is that I fear so much, that makes me wake up night after night in a sweat. What if I hate you, or just find you boring and irritating, someone I don't want to know? What if you're fat and greasy-haired and slack-jawed and stupid, some kind of lowlife? Or one of those dried-up, prudish, priggish, beady-eyed women who some-times come into the café and look at me as if I'm Jezebel because I'm wearing a short skirt or a stud in my nose or some-thing? All that sounds cruel or shallow, I know, but I'm only writing this to you – that is, to me – so I'm trying to say what I really think, not what I ought to think. Or what if you're all glamorous and glossy and hard, and you've pushed everything you've ever suffered and felt and believed behind that painted crust and I can't get beyond it? What if you're right-wing? Or racist? Or really religious, so all the things I love, you think are sinful, and all the things I want to talk about are out of bounds? If you were my real mother – I mean, like Mum is, even though she isn't, if you see what I mean – then I'd have grown up with what you were like and then I'd probably just accept those things. Or at least, not accept them but not see and judge them in the same way. But if I see you and think you're dull and ugly or just not very nice, then what does that say about me? I've come from you, after all. You made me. You've been coded into me.

But there's something that disturbs me even more than disliking you. What if you're tormented about losing me and in some way or other want me back in your life, want me to be family? What will I feel then? And what if I like you – really, really like you? What if you're similar to me and I sense an immediate connection with you – what will that mean? I don't want to feel you're my real mother because I've already got a real mother and she's loved me for all of my life. Every second that she's known me she's loved me and cared for me and never abandoned me. She's been unconditional.

That's what mothers are supposed to be, isn't it? Unconditional. I've thrown everything at her – maybe more than I would have if she'd been my biological mother – because I continually wanted her to prove to me that she loved me just as much. I had tantrums; I had adolescent storms; I can be rude and sulky and secretive. And she's never wavered. I love that word, 'unwavering'. It makes me feel a bit weepy, and I think it's because I've so badly needed someone to be unwavering for me. You didn't love me, you didn't want me, you gave me away when I was a few hours old, you weren't even conditional. You weren't anything except an absence, a powerful, powerful absence, like God. But she was there. She was always

202

patient, always present, never asking for anything in return, never even asking for my gratitude or my love. I think it is only now that I'm about to meet you that I understand what she's done. So now, if I meet you and I feel you're my 'true' mother, if I recognize myself in you, what does that make me feel about my 'real' mother? Will I lose her in some way?

A woman came into the café the other day and I thought she might be you, because she acted so strange and she kept asking me questions. Of course, as soon as I thought about it, I knew she couldn't be because I didn't think you'd be so stupid as to sit in front of me and say you were somebody else just before meeting me properly. That wouldn't make sense. But for a few moments I did wonder, and I was looking at her and thinking, Is this my mother? She was rather lovely in an odd kind of way, quite a bit younger than Mum is, but not as young as I'd imagined you would be (I always thought you were probably just a teenager when you had me, maybe even fourteen or something like that), and a bit wild and romantic and haphazard. She had this smile that made her whole face crinkle up. I found myself thinking that I'd quite like her to be my mother, partly because I liked the way she looked and partly because she wasn't anything like me, but almost my opposite.

I keep trying to work out the questions I want to ask you when we do eventually meet. Ever since I can remember I've been asking them in my head, and I don't want to let them slip away just because I'm nervous. I don't want to not ask you things that I really want and need to know. And I want to know even if the answers are painful.

Why did you give me away?

How old were you?

Was it difficult to decide?

Did you mind? (Did you cry? Did you want to keep me? When I was born, no longer an idea but your child, did you love me? Or maybe you hated me because of what I'd done to your life.)

Are there things I should know about you? (Like: have you got any inheritable diseases or disorders? Are there any mental-health problems in the family? Are there any suicides or things like that? Are you particularly clever or talented in any area, or particularly bad? Are there odd behavioural traits you have that I may have too? Stuff like that.)

Have you thought about me? How much? Do you feel guilty? Do you have regrets? (I don't know if I want to ask that question.)

Am I like you?

And then there is this whole other category of questions that kind of go together. What are my grandparents like? Do I have brothers or sisters? Do they know about me, and if they do, do they mind and do they want to meet me – or do they dread meeting me? Who else knows about me? Am I real in other people's lives, known about and talked about and cared for, or am I forgotten and hidden away like a dirty secret? The Unmentionable Me.

And OK, then, there's the big question, and perhaps you don't know the answer or it's like a multiple choice and you aren't sure. Who is my father? (Then, of course, all the above questions begin again, asked of him this time.) I've always thought about you, not him, but suddenly, now that I know I'll meet you, he's in my life at last. It's as if you've been standing directly in front of him all this time, blocking him from my view, and now you've moved forward and he's half visible at last.

There are other things I want to ask, things I never will, though, because if I did you couldn't answer, and if you did answer I'd hate you because you don't have the right. Like: am I pretty? Am I clever? Have I done well? Will I be all right? Do I make you proud?

I'm going to end this now because it's late and I'm tired and I have to get up early tomorrow to work in the café.

26 October

A few hours ago I told Mum and Dad. I should have told them ages ago. The trouble was that the longer I waited the harder it became to say anything. I'd never even said to them that I wanted to meet you one day. They probably knew. I think, looking back, that they've kept on making openings for me to say it but I felt I couldn't, as if it was a kind of betrayal. It's so odd. I've always known I was adopted. I never found out; there was no point at which I discovered. They probably told me on the first day, when I was a prune-faced baby, and never left off telling me. And yet we haven't ever talked about it properly, and nor have I talked to my friends. They know, of course. I've never hidden it; the opposite, really. I mention it when I first meet someone, as if it's something I have to get out of the way. I kind of blurt it out. When Alex asked me out, I said, 'I'm adopted, you know,' before I said yes – as if he might think of me differently once he knew. But, then, we don't really discuss it. I don't know why. Probably my parents are waiting for me to bring it up, if I want to, and I'm waiting for them.

So I told them. We were having supper. Cauliflower cheese – I made it. I'm practising my cooking skills for when I leave home; I'm good at things with white sauce, and pasta, and different kinds of eggs, and I've started doing lots of marinades to go with chicken breasts, like lime and chilli and garlic and ginger. Anyway, I told them. I did what I always do when I'm nervous about saying things. I just dropped it like a bomb into the conversation and waited for it to go off. We were talking about what I was doing at the weekend and I said, 'By the way, I've been in touch with my birth mother.' Birth mother: it sounded so official. There was a silence. Dad put this huge forkful of cauliflower cheese into his mouth, then stared at me without chewing, cheeks like a hamster's.

But Mum stood up and came round the table to me. It seemed to take ages, and she had to push the chair back with a loud scrape and her feet clipped on the lino. Her face was calm and smiling, and I realized that she'd been waiting for this moment for ages and had practised in her head how she was going to deal with it. She'd washed her hair but not dried it, so it was plastered to her skull and she wasn't wearing any makeup or earrings or anything, just this old red pullover she's had for as long as I can remember and a pair of grey cords that have gone saggy. She looked plain and worn and familiar, and when she reached me she put her arms round me and her pullover itched against my skin and her wet hair made my cheek damp. And I burst into tears and then she did too, and we hugged each other, crying and then giggling like we haven't done for ages, while Dad went on looking at us with his bulging cheeks and bulging eyes.

You know, they suddenly seemed so old and defeated, and I felt so young and strong and powerful. It was horrible.

We didn't talk about it after that. We blew our noses and dried our eyes and grimaced at each other sheepishly. Dad made us all a pot of tea and we drank it and dunked Diges-tives and scooped out the bits that dropped in with a teaspoon. And we played cards for ages: rummy and racing demon and three-person whist, all our old favourites, things we've played since I was little. It made me remember camping holidays and caravan holidays and eighteen years of Christmases and rainy Sundays. No one wanted to go to bed. It was dark and gusty outside; we could hear the wind in the trees and rain pattering against the window-panes. But inside it was cosy, sitting round our kitchen table with mugs of tea and the dishwasher chugging away and Dad pretending to be worse at cards than he is (which is bad enough anyway), and Mum's watery smile and pink eyes. I looked at everything as if I was looking at it for the last time: the stained old mugs, the peeling lino, the biscuit tin with roses on it, the wooden table with scratches from all our meals together, the photograph of me on my first day at school. George was under the table, his head on my foot, whimpering and shifting in his sleep. The clock ticked on the wall, seven minutes ahead of time as usual. I wished I was a little child again, when everything was simple and everything was safe; when if anything went wrong, I had known my parents could make it better. I wished you didn't exist.

Seventeen

For several days and weeks, Ethan had mooned around the university, his shirt half undone, his hair unbrushed, his laces trailing, his bag flapping open, his cheeks flushed, his lips in a vague, bemused smile and his eyes darting about for Lorna. He thought about her all the time. He woke up groggily and her face would form in his mind, becoming more beautiful with every day he didn't see her. He sat in lectures and, like a thirteen-year-old lovesick boy, wrote her name in hatched letters in his otherwise blank notebook. Lorna Vosper. He circled the words and wondered where the last name came from. He wrote essays about the rise of the dictator in modern history and thought about the way she smiled. He paced the streets at night, plugged into his iPod and smoking roll-ups, hoping to catch a glimpse of her. He persuaded Harry to play squash daily, in case Lorna turned up as well, and when she didn't, he lumbered round the court missing shots and crashing into walls. He meandered into cafés and pubs, bookshops, libraries and women's clothes shops, and when she wasn't there he meandered out again. All he thought about was seeing her again – but she was going out with his friend and he knew that to be with her would only stoke his desire and increase his wretchedness. He could scarcely bear to think that all this fierce anguish and hopeless hope would be wasted and that nothing would happen. But it didn't matter because he wanted to be in agony and to long for untouchable Lorna. He didn't eat and couldn't sleep; he lay on his bed and songs rolled over him and every word was about him or her. He sat at the grand piano in the music department and played Debussy and Chopin; his fingers knew the notes although his brain didn't; he remembered what he didn't know.

One late Sunday morning, when he was still lying drowsily in bed, there was a knock at his door. He groaned and squeezed open his eyes. Last night, he'd gone to a party and several people had ended up back in his room, smoking and drinking and playing poker until the early hours. He had a vague memory of losing a fair amount of money and of drinking someone's truly disgusting Chinese brandy out of a teacup. Saucers full of ash were scattered round the room; empty and half-full glasses of various liquids stood on his desk. His clothes lay in a heap by the bed, the laundry piled in the middle of the room. CDs lay everywhere; his piles of books had been toppled. There was a pair of women's patterned ballet pumps on his chair, and a saucepan containing the crusted remains of a can of baked beans next to them. Even Ethan could see that the mess had got out of control.

He closed his eyes, but the knock sounded again, longer and louder, and someone called, 'Oi, Ethan, I know you're in there!'

Harry's voice. Ethan sat up and slid out of bed, narrowly avoiding a bowl of cereal that had been there for a few days and stepping instead on his half-finished assignment on Mussolini. 'Coming,' he said.

He was only in boxers, so he pulled on a grey T-shirt before negotiating his way across the room.

'We need coffee,' Harry was shouting. 'Hurry up.'

Ethan registered the plural a second or so before he pulled open the door. Harry and Lorna stood before him, smiling and fresh. She smelt of flowers, he thought groggily.

'Oh,' he mumbled, stepping back to let them into the stinking chaos. His legs were trembling; he felt crumbs and grit under his bare feet.

'Jesus, Ethan, I knew you were untidy but this is wild,' said Harry, sounding almost impressed.

'Is it a bad time?' asked Lorna.

Were those the first words she'd spoken to him? She had a husky voice and he let the few syllables sink into him, smiling beatifically at her. 'No,' he said. 'No, come in, please come in.' He caught his reflection in the mirror – the grubby T-shirt and boxers, his hair half over his eyes and stubble on his cheeks. He looked at the disaster of his room, then back at Lorna, her rippling hair and creamy skin. 'I was just going to clean up,' he said, stumbling across and opening the curtains; the shafts of light only made the mess look worse. He wrenched open the window, then kicked the overflowing bags of dirty clothes towards the edge of the room; he picked the women's shoes and the saucepan off the chair. 'Sit down,' he said. 'Or on the bed. Here.' He scooped away more clothes and pulled up the duvet, smoothing it. 'I'll make coffee. You both want coffee? Do you want coffee, Lorna?'

There. He'd called her by her name. He was looking

into her eyes and she was smiling at him and saying something back.

'And then we thought we could all go to the sea,' said Harry. 'Marco's got his old car. I said we'd meet him in half an hour. Are you free?'

Ethan thought of his essay, due in tomorrow on a grudgingly extended deadline. He thought of the arrangement he'd made with friends to go to the cinema later, then out for a meal, and of the phone call he'd promised his parents. 'Yes, I'm free.'

'Good,' said Lorna. She eased herself down on to his bed, pulling off her jacket. She was wearing a green shirt; her arms were smooth and strong and there was a bright bangle on her left wrist and a man's watch on the right. Her jeans were old and worn at the knees and she wore scuffed baseball boots. Ethan stared at her, transfixed. Everything about her seemed mysterious: the tiny mole under her ear, the way her hair was soft and darkly chestnut, creating a shadow round her face. 'You were at that meal, weren't you? I've been wanting to meet you properly. Harry's squash partner,' she said.

'I saw you,' began Ethan, in a strangled voice. 'I saw you before we ever met. I –'

He found he was blushing – not just an ordinary flush to the cheeks but burning up from head to foot. He could feel the sweat on his brow; his face was on fire, his body was overheating like a boiler whose thermostat had broken. Harry and Lorna were both staring at him, Harry smiling ironically, and he felt that he was standing naked before them, pitifully obvious and exposed. He might as well have declared his love outright.

'Coffee,' he managed at last, turning away and letting the autumn air from outside cool his cheeks. 'Milk and sugar? I guess I'd better put some clothes on.'

'Maybe.' Lorna was smiling at him and his cheeks flamed again.

He picked up a pair of jeans, a shirt and his toilet bag, and left them in the room together. In the bathroom he scrubbed his teeth and gargled furiously with mouthwash, then examined himself in the mirror. His stubble was nearly a beard, but if he shaved he'd make himself look even more eager and ridiculous than he already did. Anyway, his razor was blunt – he was sure to nick himself and have to stick tiny shreds of tissue on to the cuts. He made do with running a nailbrush through his unkempt hair and splashing his face with cold water, staring into his eyes as he did so, trying to see himself as a stranger might – as Lorna might. His jeans were loose on him; he must have lost weight. He pulled on his shirt and a button flew off.

It was cold by the time they arrived at the coast, and beginning to drizzle. They walked along the ragged hem of the tideline drinking beer from bottles. Harry and Marco had a stone-skimming competition. Lorna sat down cross-legged on the damp sand and shivered. Ethan ripped off his jacket and offered it to her.

'Don't be daft. You'll freeze.'

'I'm warm.'

'Really? You don't look it.'

'Take it. Do you want a cigarette?'

'OK, then.'

'They're in the pocket of the jacket.'

She pulled out a squashed packet, handed it to him, and he tapped out a couple.

'What else have you got in here?'

'Nothing very glamorous. Probably just tissues.'

'Coins. Matches. What's this? A watch without a strap. How odd. It's one hour behind.'

'The clocks go back soon anyway.'

'And a pen – it's leaked everywhere.'

'Never mind.'

They leant together so their heads were almost touching while he lit a match into his cupped hand. She leant in to it and Ethan was a few inches from the crown of her head. He could smell her shampoo. He closed his eyes, didn't breathe and didn't speak. Harry and Marco seemed far away, bent double over the waves with their flat stones.

'I love the sound of waves,' she said dreamily. 'I love the sea. I love its endlessness. Don't you?'

'Yes.' There must be something else he could say. For he did love the sea – its great waves, its glittering calm, its briny smell and knifing winds, the sound it made from a distance and the mystery of all the things that swam in its depths or sailed on its surface or flew above it in wheeling, crying circles. In his recent travels he had slept several nights on beaches, wrapped in his sleeping-bag; he would never forget how the moon hung above the ocean, throwing silver fingers across the dark waters and how close and thick the stars had seemed. Should he tell her that? No.

'"Milly and Molly and Maggie and May,"' he began,

running sand through his fingers. '"Went down to the sea one day to play, and Milly befriended . . ." No, even that's wrong. My mother used to recite it to me. I can't remember how it goes now. That's the thing with poems. I forget them. I learn one and it pushes the others out of my head. I know how it ends, though.'

'How does it end?' Her hair fell over her face.

'"For whatever we lose, like a you or a me, it is always ourselves we find by the sea."'

'Who wrote it?'

'I can't remember that either.'

'It's nice. But strange as well. It sends a little shiver down my spine.'

'Happy-sad,' said Ethan.

'Something like that.'

'Everything that's properly happy has to be sad as well.' I'm happy now, he didn't say, and sad enough to weep. 'Did you know,' he said instead, 'that there are more people alive now than there are people who have ever been alive?'

'You mean we outnumber all our ancestors? Can that be true?'

'I read it somewhere. Did you know that it's a myth that you can see the Great Wall of China from the moon?'

'No, but did you know that dust is mostly made up of dead skin?'

'Or that the universe is infinite but bounded? Or that when we look at stars we're seeing them as they were millions of years ago? Maybe they've all gone now.'

'I saw the eclipse a few years ago,' said Lorna. 'It wasn't a clear day. For professional eclipse-watchers, it was a bit of a disappointment. But I thought it was – it was so weird and scary. It made me think about dying and being dead. The birds really did fly off. Everything went cold and still and grey, and then it went dark. Dark and silent. I was with my family and my cousins. Nobody spoke. Nobody made a sound. I think we all stopped breathing. Then the sun slid out again and the birds flew back and the cock crowed and the air became warm again and it was over. But for a moment it was like life had stopped. Oh, it was spooky.' She gave a little laugh.

Ethan moved his fingers through the sand towards hers, but he didn't touch her. He didn't believe in love at first sight, and he didn't believe in soulmates. He knew this feeling would die away one day and that he'd look back on it with rueful amusement. He told himself, and knew it was true, that the torment would fade; it was just the rush of chemicals through his body. But his heart hurt and it felt like love. All he wanted was to put his arms round her and feel hers round him and press his rough cheek against her pale, smooth one.

'Once,' he said, in a voice that trembled slightly, 'when I was little – just eight or nine – I went with my parents to the far north. My father was giving a lecture in Stockholm and then we went up above the Arctic Circle for a couple of days. My mother had this thing about being there on the shortest day of the year. She wanted to see the northern lights. We didn't see them although she made us all sit up through the night waiting, but it was amazing anyway. It was so very cold, steamingly, blastingly cold, almost like walking into a furnace of ice. I'll never forget stepping outside. Everything that wasn't wrapped up in thick layers of clothing froze. My eyelashes froze and my hair turned to frost and there were icicles in my nose and when I breathed, my breath froze in the air. And it should have been dark. There was no sun at all, just the moon all through the day that never became day. But because of the snow, everything glowed with this blue light. Lunar beauty,' he said, raising his eyes to her and hearing the phrase as he said it, absurdly poetic and freighted with too much meaning. Then he heard himself say, 'How did you and Harry meet? Are you in love with him?'

Lowering her eyes and letting her hair fall over her face, Lorna pretended not to hear. '"In the cold cold night,"' she half spoke, half sang, in her husky voice, 'would you rather die of heat or die of cold?'

'Cold is better,' said Ethan, authoritatively. 'You become slow and dreamy and peaceful. It's like dying into sleep.'

'Slow and dreamy and peaceful sounds all right.' They smiled at each other, then both looked away.

That was what Ethan would remember, when he tried to reconstruct that afternoon later in detail. He couldn't recall what he had said, and in truth he'd been largely silent, or what Harry and Marco and Lorna had talked about. He pushed from his mind the journey back in the dark, when he had sat in the front with Marco and Lorna and Harry had been in the back, not speaking. When he'd glanced behind he'd seen Lorna's head on Harry's shoulder and Harry's hand on Lorna's thigh. He knew where they'd go after they had dropped him off at his room and what they'd do. He mustn't let himself picture that – the fall of her brown hair over bare skin, the swell of her breast in the curtained dark. No. Instead he held in his mind those few soft and unironic moments when he and Lorna had huddled on the beach with their cigarettes, sheltering each other from the wind. He still didn't know much about her, but he had seen her close-up smile, he'd breathed in her perfume, he'd felt the brush of her hair against his cheek.

'Mum?' he said. 'Mum? Did I wake you?'

Gaby knew at once that something was up. His voice sounded so young. 'No,' she lied, struggling into a sitting position and pulling the duvet up round her. Connor groaned and turned on his back. 'Are you all right?'

'Fine, really fine. I know you tried to call me a few times and I just wanted to say hello. Um, hello.'

Gaby squinted at the radio clock. It was twenty to one. 'Are you really all right?'

'Yeah, honestly. Great.'

'Your work's OK?'

'Kind of. I need to catch up a bit. I'm writing an essay at the moment. I guess I'll be up all night, but that's OK. I'm not tired. I quite like going a night without sleep sometimes. It makes my brain fizz.'

'Is that good?'

'Interesting.'

'What about your social life?'

'Great.'

'Have you met people you think you can be friends with yet?'

'Sure. A few, anyway.'

'I'll be coming down soon to collect the car, I expect. I'll take you out to lunch or something.'

'Lovely.'

'The house feels very quiet and empty without you. I can't get used to it.'

'I'll be back in a few weeks. Then I can play loud music and keep you awake and give you lots of dirty laundry. I ought to go to the laundrette, actually.'

'I'm trying not to imagine the state of your room. Did you ever unpack?'

'Not as such.'

'Not as such. Hmm. Are you cooking much?'

'To use the word "cooking" is to glorify the heating of beans and microwaving of packets.'

'But you're OK?'

'You keep asking that. I'm OK. I'm not lonely. I'm not starving. I'm not injecting myself with heroin. I'm doing my work, kind of, and I like it. And I'm having fun. I'm beginning to find my way around, to know what I'm doing.'

'Good. That's good.'

'I went to the sea today.'

Gaby heard the change in his voice. 'Did you?' she said carefully. 'How lovely. Who with?'

'Oh, just some friends. Harry – I've told you about Harry. And this guy Marco. I hadn't met him before. And Lorna.'

'Lorna,' Gaby repeated.

'Harry's girlfriend.'

Gaby grimaced tenderly down the phone. So that was

why Ethan was ringing. He was a young man of heart-break and extremes.

'What about you and Dad? All OK there?'

'Dad's a bit overworked.'

'What's new?'

'And I've been working quite hard too. Not just with the cultural groups – I'm trying to get this idea of working with truanting kids off the ground. It's quite exciting, and it would be good for me to have a challenge like that. An adventure.'

'But you're OK? You're not sad or anything?'

'I'm not sad, my darling.'

'You promise?'

'I promise.'

'I've just seen the time. You *were* asleep, weren't you?'

'It doesn't matter at all. You can ring me up whenever you like.'

'Sorry. I was just feeling a bit – you know – Sunday nightish.'

'I wish I could click my fingers and be there.'

'Hmm. Even you wouldn't like to be in my room right now. Once I've finished my essay I'm going to have a binge clear-up.'

He took three bags of clothes and bed linen to the laundrette and for an hour sat on the bench and watched as they churned sudsily round. Then he went back to his room, made his bed, unpacked his remaining clothes, put his shoes in pairs at the bottom of the wardrobe. He emptied all the ashtrays, collected plates, bowls and mugs from under the bed and washed them in the kitchen. He sorted scattered sheets of scrawled-on notepaper into piles; later he would get round to buying folders and files. He opened the windows wide, then hoovered the crumbs and grot off the carpet. He even wiped down the washbasin with some lavatory paper. The room still didn't look immaculate, but it was no longer squalid.

Then he showered, shaved, dressed in clothes still warm from the dryer. He made himself a cup of coffee and sat by the window with a cigarette, watching the smoke curl out into the cold air and dissolve. Now Lorna could visit. He was ready for her.

Eighteen

'Nancy?'

'Speaking.' Nancy knew at once who was on the other end of the line, but she waited to hear her say it.

'It's Gaby. We have to meet.'

'I don't think that —'

'It's not a request. *We have to meet.*'

There was a silence.

Gaby imagined Nancy's frowning face as she assessed the situation; Nancy pictured Gaby's flushed and emotional one.

'All right. When?'

'As soon as you can make it. I can be flexible. Name a day, and we can join up somewhere in the middle. Where's the middle between Cornwall and London? Or I can come to you. Whatever.'

'No. Listen, I'm going to a conference about boys' literacy in Birmingham next Tuesday. If it suits you, we could meet there at lunchtime, middayish. I think it's only about an hour away from London and —'

'Tuesday in Birmingham's fine. Where?'

'Perhaps you could come to the hotel.'

'No. In the station is best. There must be a café. I'll meet you at the end of platform one at half past twelve, all right? Shall I give you my mobile number?'

'No need. I've said I'll be there.' Nancy paused. 'By

the way, I know you were in my house. You never were very good at tidying up after yourself. That was wrong, you know. Very.'

'Twelve thirty on Tuesday.'

The line went dead.

On Saturday Gaby went skating with two friends. She was even more exuberant and reckless than usual, and fell over thirteen times, eventually twisting her ankle so that she had to hobble off the rink and sit at the side. She and Connor had people round for a meal in the evening. Gaby lit candles so the room glowed mysteriously. Dressed in a long silk skirt and a shirt with widely flared sleeves that she'd forgotten she owned, she sat in the softly guttering candlelight, ate with gusto and drank several glasses of white wine; at the end of the evening she recited 'The Highwayman' from beginning to end without a falter, to great applause. Everyone agreed that she was on fine form.

On Sunday she drowsed in bed late, half asleep in the rumple of her duvet and listening to Connor in the kitchen, clearing up from the night before, then making his way up the stairs to his study, the ping of his computer being turned on. She didn't need to see him to know how he'd looked as he'd patiently emptied the dishwasher, washed the pans, wiped every surface clean, then gone to his desk with his thin, clever face alert.

When she got up she made scrambled eggs for them both on buttery brown toast, read the Sunday papers, and went to a garden centre where she spent far too much money on tulip bulbs to plant ready for the spring. In the evening, she read *Jane Eyre*, a novel she'd read seven or eight times before and whose familiarity and suppressed rage gave her comfort. She went to sleep quite early but was woken after midnight by a phone call from Ethan. From the first syllable she knew he was in distress. After he finished the call, she lay awake for a long time thinking about him. Only the sheer impossibility of it stopped her from leaping into her clothes and getting herself to Exeter there and then.

On Monday she went to work early and came home late. Connor was still out and she had a long bath, washed her hair, painted her toenails, drank a spicy tomato juice and sat for a while in the emptiness of Ethan's room, which still smelt of him even though the window had been left open for days. She went to bed with no supper, curling herself into a ball. Connor always said that nobody liked to lie in bed with their arms outside the covers. He said that everyone needed to protect themselves with their hands as they slept; it was a human instinct.

On Tuesday she took the train to Birmingham and at half past twelve exactly she was standing at the end of platform one.

They sat on hard chairs in the station café, which was half open to the crowded concourse, full of the blue haze of tobacco smoke and the smell of burnt coffee. In the cavernous, echoey space, they had to speak up to make themselves heard, and every so often announcements for trains forced them into awkward silence. Nancy hadn't taken off her thick coat; above its turned-up collar, her face was pale and wary. Gaby noticed that she had a few

223

grey hairs and that there were little creases above her upper lip, faint brackets round her mouth. How has that happened? she thought. How have two decades gone by so fast? Where are the young women we were just a blink away, the flat-chested girls? Lying in a hammock together in Gaby's garden, drowsy in the heat, sticky with lemonade, and giggling as they swayed under the green leaves, splashed by the sun. Swapping secrets and making plans; blithe for the future.

'So,' she said. She was surprised by how calm she felt, in control at last. 'Sonia.'

Nancy's expression didn't waver. She picked up her orange-coloured tea, then put it down again without drinking any. She thought that Gaby, with her hair pulled tightly back and her face naked of makeup, creased with anxiety and puffy with tiredness, had never looked so striking. 'I gather you read her letter, then.'

'Yes.'

'I thought you might have done. You shouldn't go doing things like that, you know.'

'I know. But I did. I can't undo it now or unknow what I know. That's the thing about time – it's a one-way road.'

Nancy regarded her steadily. 'So, then, what do you know, my old friend? That I had a baby when I was young. A very long time ago.'

'Yes, it was a very long time,' said Gaby, softly. She was holding off the words for as long as she could, letting herself drift in this curiously restful moment before she took the next step along the one-way road. Out in the station, people hurried past with newspapers, briefcases,

224

backpacks, all on their way somewhere else. 'Eighteen years.'

Nancy said nothing. Outside, a distorted voice boomed news of a delay. Apologies for any inconvenience this might cause.

'You could have had an abortion.'

'I could have, yes.' Her mouth closed firmly.

'But instead you chose to escape and have your daughter secretly and give her away.'

Nancy said nothing.

'I can't imagine how that must feel. Going through a pregnancy and a birth and then letting her go.'

'Probably not.'

'Or, at least, I can begin to – because of having Ethan and even when I was so ill I felt sick and moony with love for him. And then the miscarriages, of course.' She waited a few seconds. 'I was pregnant when you left. That day when we met, I was feeling so sick and I thought I might be. I went straight home and did the test and I was. So, for a couple of months we were both pregnant at the same time, though you were further on than me, of course. I've been thinking about that.'

'Gaby, if you –'

'Sssh. Listen. Of course, when I read the letter from Sonia, I thought about Stefan. I didn't tell him, though, if that's what you've been wondering. Well, of course you've been wondering. Or Connor. Isn't that strange? The two people I tell everything to. You'd have thought I couldn't hold it back for a moment. You know that feeling when there's a secret inside you and you can feel it growing and growing in the darkness until you're sure it has to burst out of you? That makes it sound rather like pregnancy, now I think of it. Anyway, I've had this secret inside me. Your secret. What a secret. Did you tell people? Were there friends after me you could turn to and pour out your heart to? Or were you like King Midas, whispering it to the rushes, and thinking that it would shrink away and one day almost feel as if it didn't exist? If it had been me, I would have spilled it out sooner or later, but it wasn't me, and you're so very different from me. That's why I loved you so much, I guess. You're all that I'm not. And you've always been good at secrets.

'Anyway, I didn't tell them. I still haven't. Every time I saw Stefan I would feel so scared of what he would feel if he knew, even after so many years. He always wanted children, a family, and there he is, lonely and defeated, and sometimes I think he's such a sad man underneath the good cheer. It sounds ridiculous, but because I didn't tell Stefan, I didn't tell Connor either. Somehow I couldn't. I felt filled up with this poisonous secret and I didn't want to pass it on. I didn't know what to do with the knowledge that I suddenly possessed.' She gave a giggle and took a gulp of her cool coffee. 'I tell you, Nancy, it's been a very odd few weeks. I've been like some ridiculous spy, creeping round in disguise, pretending to be me. I can't believe no one noticed. Maybe nobody knows me as well as I always thought. Maybe I've got to stop being so naïvely romantic about human relationships. What is it you always used to say? In the end everyone is alone.'

'So you decided to talk to me,' said Nancy, hurrying her along in a clipped tone. She was sitting up straight in her chair, her hands on the table in front of her. To look at her, they might have been in a business meeting.

'Oh, no. No, that's not what I did.'

'No?'

'No. I went and found Sonia.'

There was a small gasp and the table rocked; tiny ripples spread across the surface of the orange tea. Nancy's hands clenched. Gaby saw the knuckles whiten. Nancy didn't speak. Her face had gone chalky and pinched; the lines round her mouth stood out and she looked suddenly older and smaller. Gaby almost felt sorry for her. Almost.

'I thought if I saw her I would know,' said Gaby.

'Know?' Nancy managed, in a whisper.

'Yes. Know if she was Stefan's. I had this belief that I'd be able to tell. Have you met her yet?'

'No,' Nancy gasped. She leant forward, her face screwed up in pain. 'She wasn't ready. I can't believe you went and –'

'Don't worry, I didn't tell her who I was or anything. I just wanted to see her. And of course she's not Stefan's, is she?'

'I don't know.' The words came out in a croak. 'I don't know who the father is, Gaby. I don't know.'

'I do. Not Stefan's, that's for sure. I should have known all along she couldn't have been Stefan's, of course – or, at least, that you weren't sure she was. Maybe but maybe not. Is that it? I just wasn't thinking straight. Why on earth would you have done a runner and cut all ties if she'd been his? What did you say when we met? You felt as if you'd committed a crime.' She sighed and sat back in the chair. 'It's funny, but when I dropped Ethan off at university, we had this lovely talk. Really lovely – the kind you can't ask for but sometimes just happens and you know even at the time that it's precious. He said when he was growing up he'd sometimes wished he wasn't an only child but had a brother or sister to keep him company.'

'Gaby, please.'

'Hang on. Sonia. She's lovely. She has your eyes, you know. You probably couldn't tell that from the little passport photo she sent you. And that jaw of yours. I'd have recognized her anywhere from it. I bet she's stubborn, just like you. I keep on reading pieces in the newspaper about new theories on genetics. I used to believe – because I wanted to, probably – that we can choose who we become, but a lot of scientists say that it's almost all genetic, as though we're a computer that's been programmed, and we're not really free at all, we only think we are – and even thinking we are is part of the program, if you see what I mean. Before I went into labour with Ethan, my left leg began to tremble violently; when I told my mother, she said exactly the same thing had happened to her with the four of us. Even that tremble was genetic. And Ethan – he used to be so close to me it was as though he was invisible. I was looking into him not at him. But now that he's older and so much his own person, I can see myself in him quite clearly – or I look at myself and it's his face, too, that stares back at me. He's not much like his father, neither in looks nor in character. I used to mind that for Connor sometimes. There were occasions when he seemed the odd one out in the threesome – so dark and precise and intense and troubled and self-contained and needy. You remember.'

She stopped and held her breath. The objects round her seemed clear and yet far off; Nancy herself seemed etched and unreal. She need not speak. She could do as Nancy had done and seal the secret inside her, plug the holes through which it might escape. Until now, a small part of her had resisted the revelation she had had that day in Stratford, turning it into a story, a dream that would fade away on waking. She knew that saying the words out loud to Nancy would move it into the outside world and make it solid, public and inescapable. So she paused. She looked across at Nancy with shining eyes. She felt the words from inside her and she opened her mouth: 'But Sonia's just like Connor.'

Into the silence a voice boomed, announcing the late arrival of the train from Worcester. Nancy was absolutely still, as if the words had cast a spell over her. Even her hands on the table didn't move. Perhaps she wasn't breathing.

At last she gave a small sigh. 'Is she?' she said. 'Is she really?'

So I'm right, thought Gaby. I thought I knew, but now I know that I know. Not even a hairline crack for hope. I'm right, and my husband and my best friend were lovers. Under my nose, in my house, while I was suffering and they were looking after me and saving me from harm, and of course I never suspected because I loved them, and I knew they both loved me; even now, I can remember them loving me and I know it's not a lie. They were my safety. They were my home.

'Oh, yes,' she said to Nancy, smiling. 'She's thin and dark and spare like him. She might have your jaw, but the shape of her face is his, and although she's got your eyes, she's got his brows and his long dark lashes. She even –' Gaby gave a tiny laugh that turned into the start of a sob, which she bit down, '– she even pulls at her ear-lobe the way he does. When I saw that . . . Anyway, it's more than that – it's like she's shot through with Connorness. Once I knew for sure, I could almost feel him in her. The thing that made me fall for Connor, as if I was falling down a sheer cliff, his prickly vulnerability that made me want to hold him in my arms and make him better – she's like that, I'm sure she is. Wait one moment. Hold on.'

She rummaged in her capacious bag and pulled out a new packet of cigarettes, put one into her mouth and lit it, dragging the smoke deep into her lungs, then letting it out slowly. 'I've recently taken up smoking again. Maybe it makes me feel that I might be someone else, a stranger I've only just met. I don't know why on earth that should be so comforting but it is. Anyway, I've really only got two more things to say. Or ask, really. Then I've done. All talked out. Was Connor going to leave me?'

'Gaby, if you had any idea how –'

'*Was Connor going to leave me?*'

'These are the things you have to ask Connor, not me.'

'Don't worry, I will. I just thought I'd ask my ex-best friend first. Was he?'

'No. *No.* You're the one he always loved. He never stopped loving you.'

'Don't tell me about love right now. The other thing I want to ask is: does he know about Sonia?'

'No. I promise you.'

'He doesn't know he's got another child?'

'No. When I left, I hadn't even told him I was pregnant. I never told him.'

Gaby started to giggle, though it hurt her throat and her eyes stung. 'Then he's in for a big surprise. Oh dear.'

'Gaby.'

'Shut up.'

'Please, darling Gaby. It was a long time ago.'

'I know it was – does that make it better or worse? What's the point in saying that? Don't say anything. Don't talk to me.'

'I don't have the words –'

'Then don't speak. What use are words anyway?'

There were other questions, of course. Even as Gaby sat and stared across the table at Nancy, they crowded into her mind. What would she say to Connor, and what would she do? What would she say to Stefan? Would Sonia want to meet Connor too, and would he want to meet her? And what about Ethan? Should he know? Her heart contracted at the thought of her son. Did he have to know? He had a half-sister now: of course he had to know. What would he say? What would he think? Her old life, which had once troubled her because it was so straightforward and predictable, now seemed sweet. Sweet and false; simple and untrue; happy only because it was complacent and bathed in ignorance.

What else was there to discover? she wondered queasily. For, after all, this was what all life must be, in the end: an elaborate charade in which everyone hides their true feelings and their secret actions beneath the acceptable surface of their public selves. It's all a necessary fake: we survive by pretending to feel what we don't feel, like whom we don't like, desire what we don't want, be who we aren't. It's not just about showing different sides of oneself, depending on whom you're with. It goes further than that. Gaby thought of the friends she had whom she didn't particularly like or even wish well; she thought of the times she'd lied to Connor, out of kindness – or, at least, the wish not to be unkind; she thought of the way in which she tried to court the world with her act of spontaneity. All deceit, she thought – and we don't only pretend to others, but to ourselves, so that we come to believe in the lies and the self-justifications we're peddling. As she sat at the table, watching a fat pigeon lurch across the concourse outside, the world seemed to drip with hypocrisy and cruelty that most of the time we have to choose not to see, because to see it would be unbearable.

Her best friend had slept with her husband. It was a cliché, a monstrous stereotype of betrayal. Her best friend had borne her husband's daughter. This happened to other people; you read this story in women's magazines and it's a grotty little tragedy, a grim little farce.

'Gaby –' Nancy was saying.

Gaby forced Nancy's stunned face back into focus, wincing. 'How could you? You were always the moral one. We looked up to you. You were so sure what was right and what was wrong – a bit like Connor, I guess. I was a bit flaky. You could never be sure that I wouldn't go and do something stupid, but not you. You were the rock, the one we trusted to behave properly. When you left, I thought it must be something I'd done. It had to be my fault. I adored you. Then this, this –' She choked and stopped, then lifted her eyes to Nancy's. 'How could you do it?'

Nancy cleared her throat. Her face was working and a small blue vein throbbed in her neck. When she spoke, her voice was dry and husky. 'I'm not going to ask you to forgive me. What I did was unforgivable. I know that. I'm not going to try to make excuses for what happened or in any way reduce the pain you must be feeling now –'

'Oh, please get on with it, Nancy. You're not in a court of law, you know. You don't have to give a speech on abstract things like forgiveness and guilt, and I'm not a tribunal or a judge or anything. I'm me. Gaby. Remember? We shared toothbrushes.'

'OK. OK. You're right. Maybe I sound like that because I've been making speeches to you in my head ever since it happened, although I hoped I'd never have to do it in real life. I wanted you never to know. I thought at least I could do that.'

Gaby broke in abruptly: 'I don't think I want to talk about all this now. I can't. I've kind of had enough. I need to get away to think.'

'Of course.'

'I don't know, Nancy.'

'You don't know what?'

'I just don't know. I don't know, I don't know, I don't know. Anything at all. I don't know what this means. I don't know what'll happen. I don't know who I am any more, or what my life is. I'm tired. I want to go home.'

But the word 'home' brought tears to her eyes. It didn't have the same meaning now, but fell with a soft, drab thump in her heart. Home had always been where Connor and Ethan were. But Ethan had gone – and Connor had changed for her. In her mind's eye, she saw her husband's pale, attentive face; the way he looked as he sat at his desk, frowning into the distance; the way he was with a person in pain – expert, but solicitous too. He might be prickly and difficult, but he was kind, he was honourable, he cared about other people, he was *true*. She'd always felt proud that it was her he had chosen to love.

'I'll be in touch,' she said, struggling to her feet, feeling ungainly and skew-footed. The ground seemed to shift under her weight. The walls of the room leant towards her; the ugly yellow lights throbbed in her skull.

Nancy stood too. 'I'm going to see Sonia soon.'

'I said I'll be in touch.'

'Shall I give you my email? That might be easiest.'

'OK, then.'

They swapped email addresses, Gaby stuffing the scrap of paper into her coat pocket, next to her train ticket.

'So,' said Nancy. She buttoned up her coat and picked up her briefcase.

'So,' said Gaby.

'Will you be all right?'

'Will I be all right?' she repeated.

'Getting home, I mean.'

'Yes – I'll be fine getting home.'

She turned on her heel and walked out of the café, into the station's dark and vaulted cave where sound bounced off the walls and voices were a babble around her. She could hear her heels clipping sharply beneath her and in the window she caught her reflection: her swinging coat and her tidy hair. She was surprised by how strong and in control she looked as she smiled and raised an arm to herself in salutation and farewell.

Nineteen

Connor ran. He started at the door of the hospital and ran up the road towards King's Cross, jogging on the spot at the lights, then weaving his way through the pedestrians. Past the shop selling chess sets, over the arterial road thick with cars and loud with blaring horns. An icy drizzle fell on his bare forearms.

He ran four times a week, without fail. In blizzards and heatwaves, on holiday and during sickness, he ran, up hills, along canals, round training grounds, through fields and parks, by the sea and along the edge of a mountain. He had run since he was sixteen and sometimes he would think about the distances he had gone and the gradients he had pressed into his bones. He had the impossible sensation that all of his journeys were still inside him somewhere. If he ever missed a session, he would feel itchy and full of a restless, peevish rage that he knew was ridiculous but which gripped him neverthe-less. On Tuesdays he had an hour free at lunchtime and always did a six-mile circuit of Regent's Park, coming back in time to shower quickly and be at his desk, clean and virtuous, by two.

The first mile was always the worst. There was a stiff-ness in his muscles and a tightness in his thoughts. But gradually he relaxed. His stride lengthened and loosened; his mind, which had been full of neurotic lists and snagging anxieties, expanded and breathed; images sailed through him and the ideas with which he had been struggling flowed more easily, as if they had been silted up but were now unblocked. He dodged a cyclist and made his way through the gates and into the park. He found his rhythm. Some days, he would feel sluggish and heavy-footed, but today was good for running: he was light, quick; energy ran in a clear channel through him. He thought of the patients he would see that afternoon, and the lecture he had to give tomorrow; he would have to write it tonight, at home. He thought about Ethan and wondered why he had hardly talked to his son since he left home. Gaby had, of course, and she was always topping up communications with emails, texts and postcards with two illegible words scrawled on them. She hadn't let go properly, and she missed him through details – the shut bedroom door, the emptier supermarket trolley, the napkin ring on the side, the evenings she now spent alone when once she'd often spent them with Ethan. Her energy had turned to a kind of restlessness, and Connor had noticed that she was more than usually distracted. Sometimes he would say something to her and she would stare at him with a wild vagueness, as if she didn't know who he was or what he was doing sitting opposite her.

He felt a pang of guilt and tenderness when he thought of his wife, as if his heart was bruised. It had been more than twenty years since they had met. Her generosity and sweetness then had been a gift that redeemed him and he had not thought he could repay her, or realized that she, too, needed nurturing. Perhaps the mystery of those early days had gone, rubbed away by years of use, and in its place was intimacy. He had slept next to her night after night and seen her body split open by childbirth. He knew each fold in her flesh, each blemish on her skin. He'd seen her with greasy hair and puffy eyes, witnessed her moods of elation and weepiness, suffered her untidiness, her repetitions and exaggerations, forgetfulness, indolence, and the bursts of excitement that seemed to him, in his painstaking precision, to be random. When she spoke, he heard the subtext; he could see her wince or flinch when it was invisible to anyone else. Years of history were piled up in each word.

But she'd lightened his life. She'd mocked him when he took himself too seriously. She'd charmed his friends and colleagues. She'd made him laugh. She'd been fun. They both had: his son and his wife. There had been times when they had been like a double-act put on the earth to torment and delight him. He remembered a supper when the pair had sat solemnly with dishcloths on their head, or another when Gaby had put on the radio and Ethan had stood on the table and danced with a theatrical intensity that had embarrassed and moved Connor. He should have taken Gaby away when Ethan left, he thought, or at the very least done something dramatic and emotional. She had always cherished rituals and he had come to understand that she needed them in her life.

The drizzle thinned to nothing; the sky was clearing ahead of him and now there was a light sheen of sweat on his forehead. He ran past a pair of men jogging slowly along the path, then a greyhound sniffing at an upturned poodle who was waving its short legs in submission. He could feel his heart beating fast but steadily.

Connor believed that most people judged everyone else too harshly and forgave themselves too easily. There was a great deal written by armies of therapists and pseudo-therapists, philosophers and journalists about guilt, but not enough about its absence. He and Ethan had often discussed the capacity of humans to justify themselves to themselves – to push the blame on to others and to feel misunderstood, however terrible their actions. We all have strong defence mechanisms to prevent us seeing our own wrongs too clearly. Studying twentieth-century history, Ethan had become impassioned with the zeal of a teenager who wanted to change the world about atrocities committed with unflagging self-righteousness. Closer to home, Connor recalled the case that had occupied him and Gaby recently. One of their near-neighbours had been an old woman, Mary, who lived alone and had no family. Over the years, she had become increasingly forgetful, wandering the streets swaddled in dirty clothes that were voluminous on her shrinking frame, wearing a vague, baffled smile. It was clear that she was no longer able to look after herself, but she had a horror of going into a home and would get agitated whenever it was suggested. The street had rallied round, and arranged a rota, cooking and cleaning for her, taking her for slow walks, from lamp-post to lamp-post, and making sure her bills were paid. Every Thursday, Gaby had spent the early evening there, toasting crumpets and listening to Mary play the piano with her arthritic fingers. Then she had died, leaving no will, and it had taken weeks to track down her nearest relatives, a well-off couple from Reading who, as far as Connor knew, had never met Mary or even known she existed. The house, although it hadn't been renovated since the fifties, had fetched a fair amount of money when it was put on the market, but when residents had written to ask the couple to donate money towards Mary's headstone (she had left detailed instructions as to her funeral and burial) they had replied that it was not 'appropriate' for them to give anything. Gaby had been so outraged at their pompous selfishness ('appropriate' was the word that chafed her into action) that she had gone to their house the following weekend to confront them. She had come home spluttering indignantly, saying that they had been unwavering in their pursed-lipped belief that they were doing nothing wrong; they believed themselves to be moral and decent citizens who would always do their duty. Indeed, by the end of the encounter, they had seemed to think they were the victims of this flush-faced madwoman who'd broken into the peace of their Sunday with her accusations, and threatened to call out the police.

But there were things that Connor himself had done that he did not allow himself to think about. He consciously did not think, for instance, about Nancy. The memory was like a shadow on an X-ray that, although he was aware of it, he chose not to examine. He saw but would not look. He did not remember but he had not forgotten. Every so often, a kind of breathlessness would come upon him, and he understood that he was remembering what had happened between them all those years ago, but the memory and the guilt were surfacing without his consent, like a subterranean event that works its damage invisibly.

Now he was by the boating pond. Ducks flew above him on heavily beating wings. A beautiful young man with a wispy beard hanging from his chin stood by the path crouching low and stretching out his hands in some Oriental exercise. Connor lengthened his stride and pushed out, wanting to exhaust himself. He thought about the afternoon and evening ahead. He reminded himself to take home the papers he needed for his lecture. Maybe he *should* take Gaby away somewhere. Morocco. Iceland. Somewhere far off and strange. Somewhere just for the two of them, and they could sit over a table and he could relax in her smile and tell her everything that was in his mind, however strange and however small. Except that.

Twenty

Gaby was always impressed by people who seemed to understand what their lives meant. She listened to television interviews with artists and writers in which they would fluently describe the trajectory of their development, in which the road they travelled and the choices they made led to the present moment. They pointed to watershed events, divided their experience into periods, paid tribute to their greatest influences, explained what impact suffering and triumph had had upon their ideas and their world-view, traced how they had changed and why. They had strong opinions and kept to them. They were able to stand back from the self in order to understand it, and to tell themselves as if they were a shaped story. Sometimes she thought that there was a fraudulent or complacent quality to their eloquent self-analysis, but most of the time she was just envious of it.

She didn't know what her life meant and she had no idea of how she had changed or whom she had become. She didn't have strong opinions so much as strong emotions, and when she tried to examine herself, what she saw was a not-unhappy mess. In her past, she didn't see a pattern so much as a shifting kaleidoscope of memories; swirling darkly between these bright fragments were all the things that she had let herself forget and perhaps, she thought, the seas of forgetfulness had formed her just as much as the fenced and tended patches of memory. Certainly she often felt that she lived much of her life in a state of unarticulated emotion.

Maybe her helpless sense of not-knowing came from an excess of stability in her background. Her childhood had been undramatically contented. They say that you remember the sudden changes in your early life, the crises and bereavements, but for Gaby there hadn't been any such change. She was middle-class, comfortably off, white, privileged. Her parents hadn't divorced, and they were both still alive, living in the house in which she had been born. Her three brothers had been protective of her, the baby of the family and the only girl. She had never been bullied, never been abused, never been ostracized. She had never failed at anything, although neither had she triumphed. Her parents had cared for her, helped her, encouraged her and believed in her. Above all, they had loved her.

She had read stories about refugees of fourteen walking alone across continents to find a new home; of eleven-year-olds looking after an alcoholic mother and four siblings; of child soldiers in Angola. One of her best friends at primary school had grandparents who had survived Auschwitz. Another was very poor. Nancy's father had died when she was very young and her mother had turned to sex and anger for comfort. Gaby's immediate neighbours came from Macedonia and Brazil; they had chosen to begin again in another place. Ethan's great friend Ari had come from the Congo aged thirteen, with nothing more than the clothes he had fled in and a Bible. One of Connor's colleagues, who advised him on his work with victims of torture, was a young Iraqi doctor who had been tortured himself when he wasn't even out of his teens, and who was blind in one eye because of it. These people, with their scars and their journeys, had a sense of themselves and of the life they had lived. Gaby, who had been brought up with a consciousness of her entitlement, felt that she did not. She had been too lucky and too untested for that. The one rupture in her life had been her post-natal depression, but even that seemed indistinct now, a dark blur rather than an event that had changed her: if she looked back at that time now, she could not recall episodes or images; she just remembered the dull weight of time, when the sky pressed down on her and it seemed impossible that she could get through an hour, a day. She had always thought that eventually she would arrive at a place where everything became clear but, if anything, the reverse had proved true. The older she became, the less she knew.

Connor was not like that, she thought, as she sat on the train that was taking her back to London, sipping coffee that was bitter, boiling and burnt her lips. He thought of his childhood as something he had escaped, wriggling free of poverty and misery into a world of his own making. You could see it even in the way he dressed – his soft, sober suits and plain, expensive shirts, the hand-tooled leather shoes that he buffed lovingly in the mornings – and in the way he cooked elaborate meals, warily following recipes as if one slip with the ginger or soy would result in catastrophe. He had hauled himself up, hand over hand, into his life of hard work and planned leisure. He made sure he was armed with information; his opinions were the product of thought and lacked the reckless, sometimes foolish, spontaneity of Gaby's – she was illogical, impassioned and contradictory.

Well, she thought, pushing the paper cup under her seat, that was how it had seemed. Everything had changed now; the ground beneath her feet had shifted and she felt dizzily precarious. It reminded her of the times when she had had a fever as a child and her bed had seemed to tip underneath her, as if it would fling her on to the floor, which also appeared to writhe like the sea. The one thing she had known, in her world of unknowing, was Connor's fidelity. As a young man, struggling towards his new self, he had chosen her. She had held out her hand and pulled him up the last few rungs of the ladder into her arms. She still remembered the way, during those first few months together, he had buried himself in her with a passion that was desperate and grateful.

Although the train carriage was warm and stuffy, Gaby felt chilly. She leant her forehead against the smeared window and felt its vibrations run though her like an electric current. In a short while she would arrive back home and she had no idea what she would do then. Every time she tried to think about it, her mind became sluggish and she would stare out at the green fields or houses flowing past outside and let her body be rocked by the train's motion. She sat up straighter in her seat and tried to concentrate. Beside her, a very fat man lifted the last of his fried chicken out of its cardboard box and bit into it.

She imagined the scene ahead of her. She and Connor would sit at the table in the kitchen with their glasses of wine, and into the pool of domestic tranquillity she would drop her boulder and wait for the waves to spread out to every shore: 'I think there's something we need to talk about.' No, impossible. Or: he would open the door and she would loom towards him out of the darkness and slap his face hard. No. She would lie in bed crying until he came to find her and, wrapped in his arms, she would sob out what she knew and ask him how he could have lived with what he'd done for so long and never breathed a word. She would hurl all the plates and glasses at his feet. She would attack him with a knife. She would make a phone call ('By the way, I know you had an affair with Nancy . . .'), or write a letter ('Dear Connor, you have a daughter . . .') and leave it for him to open while she stalked the empty, lamplit streets. She would say nothing and wait – but for what? She would get blind drunk on warm neat gin and wreck the house. She would run away. She would forgive him. She would never forgive him. She would leave him. She would stay. She'd be pious (impossible), understanding (ha!), insane (that was more like it). She would scratch his face, hurt him, make him weep, hold him, comfort him. She had absolutely no idea what she would do, and didn't know what she wanted. She only knew what she didn't want – to be here, to be now, rattling towards London with night falling over the past and the future dropping away precipitously in front of her.

When Gaby and Connor had first moved into their tall, narrow house in a street of tall, narrow houses in north London, they had knocked through all of the partition walls the previous owner had put up on the ground floor to create a long, airy space with facing windows, wooden floorboards, sagging sofas, low tables, piano and bright woven rugs. Gaby – who had grown up in a warren of dimly lit rooms cluttered with mysterious junk – had always loved the way the light fell peacefully across the floorboards and the white walls. However much mess she imported, it remained calm and uncluttered. She had often curled up in the sofa with a book, or half dozed contentedly, like a cat in a puddle of sunlight, while Ethan played the piano hour after hour. But now she was struck by the thought that it was a bit too much like a beautiful double-page spread from an interior decorator's brochure, not like a home at all. For a moment, when she got home from the station, she stood in the bright space, looking around her. Things she had lived with for so many years were now unfamiliar, and she felt like a shabby stranger stranded among all the middle-class comfort and careful elegance. This wasn't her, she thought: the paintings on the wall, the dahlias in a glass vase on the table, the framed photos on the mantelpiece of the three of them – and what a small family unit they were, as they stood side by side and smiled their public smiles. It was a fraudulent attempt at being someone she wasn't, someone grown-up and classy, even intimidating. She picked up a translucent jade bowl that Connor had brought back from Japan some years ago and examined it closely. It was very beautiful, she thought; very delicate. She dropped it on the floor. It cracked and exploded into several shining fragments. She knelt down and picked them up one by one; they pricked in her palm as she carried them into the kitchen and put them into the bin. Nobody would notice.

She looked round the kitchen. She could remember where and when they'd bought almost every object, from the large teapot (Devon, when Ethan was a toddler in a buggy and Connor a young doctor) to the green glasses (Prague, two years ago). A door led to the long strip of garden outside; she unbolted it and stepped out on to a carpet of soggy, mottled leaves and damp grass. She registered the signs of her neglect: the grass was long and the last of the roses were turning brown on their stems. Most of the apples had fallen from their branches and lay in a russet circle on the ground. Very different from Nancy's impeccable plot, she thought sourly, sitting down on the wet bench and pulling out the packet of cigarettes she had bought on her way home. Briefly, she worried about Connor discovering her smoking, which made her give a bark of grumpy laughter. That was the least of her concerns. She struck a match and pulled the smoke deep into her lungs, then let it out and watched it drift towards the empty sky. Her mind was curiously blank. She was waiting to find out what she would do.

Events decided for her. Going back into the kitchen, she noticed that the answering-machine was flashing, and when she pressed 'play' the first voice she heard was Connor's. It made her jump. For a moment, she thought he was going to confess.

'Hi, it's me. I've just come back from my run and I wanted to remind you that your brothers are all coming round tonight so there'll be seven of us. I'll try to get back before they arrive. Do you want me to pick anything up to eat, or have you got it sorted? I'll get some good cheese, anyway, so you don't have to worry about pudding. Hope you've had a good day. See you later. Oh, and by the way, the car's ready to collect from the garage in Exeter. But we can discuss that later.'

No, she hadn't got it sorted because she had forgotten. After an initial spasm of panic – Connor and Stefan at her table together, today of all days – she found that she was bizarrely relieved, even elated. Now she didn't need to make a decision; she could put it off until tomorrow and spend what was left of the day buying food, having a bath, pottering round the house in her dressing-gown before they arrived. She could avoid Connor without appearing to do so, and comfort Stefan without him knowing he was being comforted. One more evening of pretending that everything was normal. She would drink, laugh, swap ancient family anecdotes, lure them into staying too late. Her spirits rose; she could feel a bubble of excitement in her chest.

She realized she was starving and couldn't remember when she had last eaten a proper meal. Not today and not yesterday. Maybe she'd become gaunt and tragically glamorous, every cloud has a silver . . . She pulled open the fridge door and took out a half-full carton of semi-skimmed milk, which she gulped without bothering about a glass. Milk splashed over her coat, and she wiped her lips on her sleeve when she'd finished. She peeled clingfilm off a small bowl on the shelf, picked a meatball that had seen better days out of its tomato sauce and popped it into her mouth. She crunched her way through a carrot that had gone bendy with age. That was better. She peered deeper into the fridge to see what else was in there. Parmesan, the remainder of the rabbit casserole Connor had cooked on Saturday, an egg box with no eggs inside, several yoghurts long past their sell-by date. She peeled the lid off one, dipped in her finger and sucked it thoughtfully. Strawberry-flavoured – horrible. What could she cook? A simple meal for a Tuesday night. A chicken; she was good at chicken. But she'd done chicken last time her brothers and their wives had come, and probably the time before. Fish, then. Did they have fish? She yanked open the door of the small freezer: two salmon fillets, some smoked eel that Connor had put there when he came back from Amsterdam, a bag of peas, ice and various bottles of spirits. That wouldn't stretch very far. She'd have to go to the shops.

It had turned into one of those flawless late-autumn afternoons, crisp and bright. Gaby walked slowly down the road, relishing the warmth of the sun and the jostle of children who'd come out of school and were now making their way home in noisy groups. She went into the local butcher's and asked him what she should buy. 'You know me,' she said, 'something simple and foolproof – but not chicken.'

'Lamb fillets,' he instructed her. 'Already marinated. They need half an hour or so in the oven. And here's some mint sauce to go with them.'

'Perfect.'

Next door, she bought salad and a bag of limes; at the baker's, three baguettes. She made her way to the florist and stood in the moist green interior, breathing in the fragrance. There were buckets of roses, chrysanthemums, freesias, dahlias, lilies, irises; green fronds and purple-stemmed foliage. She picked out two bunches of freesias, and another of yellow roses.

'Is that everything?' asked the florist.

'Yes. No. No, it isn't. I'll take some bronze chrysanthemums as well. That's it.'

'Shall I put them all together.'

'Oh – and those floppy pink flowers, I never remember their name.'

'Lisianthus.'

'That's it. I love them. Two bunches.'

'Are you celebrating something?'

'Not exactly.'

She meandered home, the shopping-bags in one hand and the vast bunch of flowers held in triumph. Every so often, she stopped to change hands and to bury her face in their smell. A curious smile curled round her mouth. She was thinking of the evening ahead; her heart skipped a beat.

First, she lit the fire that Connor had already laid in the grate. Even so, it took several goes to get it alight, and by then the room was full of smoke and she had to open windows to get rid of it.

In the kitchen, Gaby swept the papers and letters on the table into a pile, which she deposited in a cardboard box, then set seven places – three couples and Stefan, the onesome of every group. She put the flowers in vases and jugs and placed them around the kitchen and living room, then rummaged in various drawers for candles.

A long, hot bath, till her fingertips shrivelled and her head swam. She washed her hair, towelled it dry, scrunching it to make it curl more, then stood at the window in her dressing-gown, gazing out at the fading light; there was a violet streak along the horizon. A full moon, so pale it was scarcely visible, floated in the sky. What to wear? Pulling clothes from her wardrobe, she held them against her in front of the mirror and dropped them to the floor one after another until she was standing ankle-deep in a puddle of garments. She ended up choosing a brightly striped long skirt and a wraparound top with flared sleeves and velvet hem, then festooned herself with bangles and beads that resembled boiled sweets. She looked, she thought, with satisfaction, like a fortune-teller in a circus tent. Nancy would never wear anything like this: she was stern and lean and tasteful. Leaning into the mirror, she drew lines round her eyes, smeared blusher along her cheekbones, squirted perfume behind her ears, on her wrists, down her cleavage, into her damp hair. Lip gloss; she pressed her mouth on to a tissue and saw its red shape blotted into a bold kiss.

She poured herself half a glass of red wine while she prepared the meal. But half a glass wasn't enough. It only lasted long enough for her to slice the cucumber and shred the lettuce into the salad bowl. She needed more while she crushed the garlic and made the salad dressing. Either she was moving very slowly, or time had speeded up, because now it was half past seven and there was a knock at the door. She knew it was Stefan, because he always rapped out the same rhythm: slow-quick-quick-slow. Was that a fox-trot? He stood on the doorstep with a bemused smile on his face, as if he wasn't quite sure that he'd come to the right place.

'Stefan!' she cried, drawing him out of the cool night

into the warmth of her hug. 'Come and sit by the fire and I'll get you a drink. Here, give me that coat. What lovely flowers.'

'You seem to have got rather a lot already,' he said. 'And you're – um – rather festive. I haven't forgotten someone's birthday, have I?'

'Yours is next week.'

'That doesn't count.'

'I thought I could make us a *caipirinha*.'

'What's that?'

'It's this drink they have in Brazil, with lime and rum and crushed ice. I had it the other week and it was so wonderful I went and bought a bottle of the special rum, but I forgot about it until now.'

'It is Tuesday today, isn't it?'

'Yes. Why?'

'It's just . . . That sounds a bit Fridayish to me.'

'Live a little.'

'All right,' he said doubtfully. 'Just a little one. I'm in my car.'

'Leave it here and take a cab. Or get a lift from Max. You squeeze the limes. They're over there and the lemon-squeezer's on the side. I'll do the ice.'

Gaby snapped the cubes out of their containers and wrapped them in a dishcloth, then took the hammer from the tool drawer and started smashing them vigorously. Tiny dents appeared in the wooden work surface and shards of ice scattered over the floor.

'Maybe it would be better with a rolling-pin.'

'This is fine. There's the door again. Will you get it for me?'

Max and Antony with their wives, Paula and Yvette, gathered round her in the kitchen, taking off their jackets and exclaiming at the flowers and candles. They stood in their sober, weekday clothes and watched as Gaby applied herself to the ice like a blacksmith at his anvil. Her long sleeves dangled on to the wet surface and her hair fell over her flushed face. 'There,' she said at last. 'That'll do. Bring me those glasses. I think it's just a handful of ice, like so. Then you share out that lime juice, Stefan. Stir in some sugar – you can add more if you want. And finally,' she took a slim bottle from the freezer, 'the rum.' It was viscous with cold and she glooped it into each glass. 'Cheers,' she said. She clinked her glass against the others and held it up.

'What are we celebrating?'

It was Connor, smiling in the doorway. He was still wearing his overcoat and his cheeks were bright with cold. Gaby thought he looked more handsome the older he got, his hair silvering at his temples, his face thin and mobile. There had been something callow about him when he was a young man but now he was easier in himself and carried himself with a certain authority. She watched as he shook hands with his brothers-in-law and kissed Yvette and Paula.

'You're just in time,' she said, as he bent to kiss her. His lips missed hers and grazed her cheek. She smelt his aftershave, felt the fine stubble on his jaw. 'Here, take your drink. What are we celebrating? Anything. Everything. Do we need a reason? Why don't you choose something?'

'Give me a moment,' he said, putting the bag of cheese on the side and unbuttoning his coat. 'There.' He remembered how he had been thinking of Ethan on his run, and raised his glass. 'To absent loved ones,' he said, with a half-ironic solemnity, trying to meet Gaby's eye.

'Perfect!' Gaby chinked her glass against his, eyes on his chin, the knot of the tie she'd given him several years ago. 'To absent loved ones. Wherever they may be. Whoever they may be.' She felt on fire already, and shouldn't drink any more. Not tonight. She put the tumbler down carefully out of her reach.

'Absent loved ones,' everyone else echoed dutifully.

For the rest of the evening, Gaby tuned in and out like a mobile phone going through dead zones. Later, there were patches of it she could scarcely recall. They'd talked about their mother, of course – they always did nowadays, for Samantha Graham was sliding into forgetfulness. What had seemed for several years like a benevolent vagueness, inevitable in old age, had become an act of disappearance. She was losing parts of herself – whole sections of memory were gone, chunks of vocabulary, all sense of future purpose. Their father insisted that he could look after her, but although he didn't complain it was evidently becoming more difficult. Gaby didn't attend to the discussion, but she knew what would have been said, what she herself would have said, because it was the same every time they met. Max thought their mother should, sooner or later, go into a home because before long their father would no longer be able to cope; they should plan ahead rather than react instinctively and chaotically to events. Antony responded heatedly that they couldn't decide for their parents what was best for them. Stefan listened perplexedly to what each person said and often rephrased it to clarify each position. Gaby insisted they should live with her and Connor whenever it became necessary. She would not hear of her beloved mother going into a home, even if one day she no longer knew where or even who she was. She became angrily emotional and even rude when Max turned over care options, or when Antony pointed out that perhaps their parents wouldn't want to live with Gaby and, after all, it was up to them. Their partners were on the sidelines, throwing the ball back into play every so often when it was booted out. Everyone knew in advance what would be said, and also that nothing would be settled, but the discussion had to run its course. Connor was always the referee, so Gaby supposed that he was that evening as well. She couldn't remember. She only knew that he kept trying to catch her eye, but she refused to respond. She served the lamb and watched as Connor poured red wine into everyone's glass. It was impossible for her to eat: the meat tasted of leather, the baguettes of cardboard, the salad of nothing at all.

It was strange to be there and yet not there, in her body and floating outside it. She knew something that nobody else knew and which, once it was discovered, would change their lives. She could almost feel the secret lodged inside her, ticking away. Every so often she imagined opening her mouth and saying, in a conversational tone, 'By the way, Connor, I met your daughter the other day.' What would people say if she did? What would happen to the expressions on their faces? She thought of Stefan's habitual beam fading and her heart constricted. As the evening progressed she became increasingly terrified that she would actually speak the words; she could taste them in her mouth, and sometimes she almost fancied she was saying them out loud. At last, she was reduced to a paranoid silence, even putting her hand across her mouth to prevent herself blurting out the truth. She sat hunched and still, as feelings strobed through her: fear, rage, misery, guilt, panic, love.

'Are you all right?' murmured Connor at one point, as he leant across her to take her plate.

'Fine,' she replied loudly and brightly. 'Just fine. Why do you ask?'

Maybe she should take herself off to bed, she thought, looking at the untouched slabs of cheese on her plate. Maybe she should crumple up and cry and let someone else take care of the sorry mess of it all. She prodded the goat's cheese with the tip of her knife and felt the words rise once more until they were at the back of her throat, like an unconquerable nausea.

The many candles guttered and threw strange shadows across the faces, making them mysterious. Wax puddled and hardened on surfaces. Then – after the clink of coffee cups and something about when they would all meet again and something about a lovely meal but tomorrow was a working day, and something about the evenings getting even darker, colder, longer than they are now – they were going, gathering up jackets and coats, kissing Gaby, hugging her hard so that for a few moments she felt solid and real again, opening the door.

The night was cold and clear; the moon was high in the sky and nearly full. The world was silver and black. Gaby waved them out, her flared sleeve like a flag and her painted smile wide; Connor came and stood behind her, putting his arms round her waist and his chin on the top of her head as he had done so many times before. She could look back across the years of their marriage and see them standing at the threshold, saying goodbye to guests, then turning to go inside together. Her eyes stung. Fear slithered under her skin. Now. Any minute.

Twenty-one

The door shut. They were alone in a house that was too big for them. She took a deep breath and waited to hear what she would say next.

'You go upstairs.' Connor put his hand fondly on her shoulder. 'I'll clear up. You seem tired.'

'Do I?'

She still didn't know what the words would be. For a frantic second, she imagined never saying anything, just hiding this away inside her for ever. Would that be saintly in its self-negating forgiveness, or simply odious in its moral sanctimony and fraudulent virtue? She'd never do it, though. For better or worse, she knew she was about to take the pin out of the grenade.

'Nobody else would have noticed. But I did. Are you feeling OK?'

'I – I do feel a bit odd, it's true.'

They stood at the foot of the stairs and he felt her forehead with his warm hand. His concerned smile wrinkled the crow's feet round his eyes.

'You're a bit hot. Maybe you're coming down with something.'

'No.'

'Shall I bring you tea in bed?'

'No.'

'Gaby?'

'Yes.'

'I know you're missing Ethan. I know that we haven't talked about it enough and I've been too busy, but that's no excuse. I should have been with you. I should have been more attentive. I was thinking about it today when I was out running.'

He loves me, she thought. I've never doubted it and still I don't. He's always loved me and always looked after me. Whatever else has happened, that remains true.

'No. I mean – no, that's not it. Connor –'

'We should go away together. Just you and me. No Stefan, no Ethan, no broken-hearted friends and lonely acquaintances.'

'I – I've got to –'

'I know – up to bed with you. We can talk about it tomorrow. I won't be long. Don't wait up.'

'But –'

'Away with you!'

He put his hand at the base of her back and gave her a push. Gaby started to trail up the stairs, her hand clutching the banister. The hectic euphoria of the early evening had gone and in its place was a dazed sense of unreality. She brushed her teeth, washed her face, rubbed anti-ageing cream that she knew didn't work under her eyes, unhooked her earrings, unwound her beads, peeled off her flamboyant clothes. Usually she slept naked, but tonight she pulled on an old flannel nightshirt, tied her hair loosely back, then sat heavily on the bed. She was cold and her hands were shaking. She stared at herself in the wardrobe's long mirror. She looked like a woman on stage, she thought, waiting for the curtain to rise and the drama to begin. She locked her hands together and listened to Connor downstairs. Of course she couldn't scream, howl, break windows, scratch his face or cry. She must simply tell him what she knew.

Then she listened to Connor coming up the stairs, light on his feet. She knew when he opened the door that he would be smiling at her and tugging at the knot of his tie.

He thought, entering the room, that Gaby was beautiful. No makeup, no finery, sitting at the base of the bed in an old striped nightshirt, her tumbling hair tied back like a schoolgirl's. One bare leg was curled under her, her hands were pressed together as if in prayer, and he could see the swell of her breasts under the flannel. She looked at rest and he was filled with a sense of happiness and gratitude.

She turned her face to him. It was grave.

'You should be in bed,' he said. 'It's past midnight.'

'No. Not for this.'

'What is it? Are you ill?'

'No, Connor. I'm not ill.'

Now the moment had come, Gaby was perfectly tranquil.

'What is it?'

'We have to talk. You may want to sit down.'

He sat on the bed beside her and took her hand. 'You're alarming me,' he joked.

But she took away her hand.

'I have to tell you something. I don't know how to do it and I know I should have said something before, when I had only discovered a few things, fragments and moments and not the full story.'

'What full story? What are you talking about?'

'When I took Ethan to Exeter and wrecked the car, I didn't just come home late the way I said. I still don't understand what came over me, but on the spur of the moment I got on a train to Liskeard.'

'Liskeard?'

'Yes. In Cornwall. I went there because a few months ago I was watching the television news and there was an item about the floods in a village near Liskeard. Rashmoor it's called. And I saw Nancy. She was wading along the road, which had become a river. I recognized her at once.'

She looked at Connor and he looked steadily back. In the silence that was so thick she could almost touch it, she could hear her own heart beating.

'I've never got over Nancy,' she said. 'I never knew what I'd done wrong. It's haunted me. Well, you know all that. You told me I had to let her go, didn't you? Maybe you were right, although maybe for the wrong reasons. But I don't let go, do I? I never leave well alone. It's my curse. Our curse. The curse of everyone who has ever known me. So I went to see her and it was quite painful. I felt – what are the words? I felt bereft all over again. Lonely and abandoned and foolish all at once. Well, if that was all, I would have told you, of course, and you could have comforted me. That would have been one ending to this story. But I didn't leave it at that. I stayed the night, and then the next morning she kind of chucked me out because she was leaving to go somewhere or other and I – well, I went back. It was over so abruptly and I wanted to have some kind of last word, I think. You know. So I went back, but she wasn't there. I did something really terrible. Unforgivable. I let myself in. I missed the train. I stayed there for another day and night. I rode her bike. I borrowed her swimsuit. I poked around in her wardrobe. I lay down on her bed. I –' She sighed heavily. 'You think you know what I'm going to say, anyway, don't you? I don't know why I have to go through this just to get to the point of the tale. I snooped. Read letters and stuff. I read a letter from a girl called Sonia.'

Connor's face was blank. She said in a deadpan tone, 'Sonia is Nancy's daughter.'

The two of them gazed at each other. Not a muscle of Connor's face moved.

'She is eighteen now, so she could track Nancy down. I thought about Stefan, of course. It seemed to me then that he was at the centre of the story, and perhaps he almost is, but not in the way I had imagined. I can't explain why I didn't tell you about it when you came back from sailing. It was too big, somehow – like a shape that's so vast and so close up you can't make out what it is. But the fact is, I thought I would tell you and then I simply couldn't. Maybe my blood and bones and buried memories knew what my brain didn't. Instead I went and saw Sonia. She's got Nancy's amazing eyes, turquoise. But in other ways she's the spitting image of you.'

A hoarse sound came from Connor. He held out both hands, palms up, as if he was offering something to her.

'Today I met Nancy again. We talked.'

'Gaby,' he managed, in a gasp.

'I understand things now. I look back and I see things

more clearly. Everything means something different. I know you had an affair with Nancy when I was sick. And you need to know that she had a child. A daughter.'

She stopped. They sat a while and she felt a strange urge to put her head on his lap and sleep. Connor said nothing; his face was still inscrutable and his body stiff. Gaby thought that if he were to be given a prod, he would topple like an unrooted tree. Pity surged through her; she wanted to wrap her arms round his shrunken body, cradle him to her and comfort him for the suffering that lay ahead.

'That's all,' she said at last. 'But I'm not sure what we do now. What do we do, Connor? Where do we go from here?' She waited, then said, 'But if you say that it was all a long time ago, I promise you I will walk out of the door and never come back.'

'Don't.'

'Don't what?'

But he couldn't say any more. She stood up and looked at him, frozen and wretched on the bed. 'I'm going to sleep in Ethan's room,' she said softly. 'You should try to sleep too. We can't talk now. Did you hear me, Connor? Connor? Oh, this is stupid.'

She knelt down and undid the laces of his lovely polished brogues, then tugged them off his feet. When she touched his skin he jolted in shock. She pulled off his cotton socks and threw them into the corner of the room. Slipped off the loosened tie and let it glide through her fingers on to the floor where it curled like a snake. Very delicately, she undid the buttons on his shirt and eased it off, turning the sleeves inside out as she did so. He looked thinner and whiter than he had the night before. She undid the fastening and zip of his trousers.

'Stand up,' she said, and he did so.

She took off his trousers, lifting each foot in turn. He stood before her, his whole body trembling, as if electricity was shimmering through him. Their eyes met and held and she knew they were both remembering other occasions when she had undressed him like this, then pulled down his boxers, taken him in her mouth and he'd groaned like a man in pain.

'Lie down,' she said, and steered him towards the bed, turning down the duvet, then covering him. His hair was black on the pillow and his face stared up at her.

'Don't,' he said again.

'Sleep, Connor,' she ordered. 'We'll try to talk tomorrow, when it's sunk in a bit.'

She turned off the bedside light, left him there and padded into Ethan's room. The bed wasn't made up, so she rolled herself in a blanket and lay on the mattress. Her feet were cold, though the rest of her was warm. She pulled up her knees and wrapped her arms round them, holding herself tight. The curtains were open so she could see the clear, glittering sky, the stars that pulsed over the chimneys and even the faint gauze of the Milky Way. This was the first night in the whole of their marriage when they'd slept together under one roof, but apart. Other couples she knew went to separate beds when their children crawled between them, or when one of them was ill, or snored too loudly, or had to get up early. They'd never done that. They'd lain side by side in fever, insomnia and discomfort. Now Connor was just a few feet away and he wouldn't be sleeping either. She could picture his wide-open eyes staring glassily into the dark room. What was he thinking? What was he feeling?

Twenty-two

Connor gazed at the strip of paler darkness between the curtains. Words from Emily Dickinson, which he had written out and stuck up on his noticeboard in his study to aid him as he worked, ran through his mind: 'After great pain, a formal feeling comes.'

'A formal feeling,' he whispered to himself. Did that describe the dark, shapeless dread that had seized him?

When Connor taught students about the treatment of pain, he would talk to them first about pain's immeasurability, inexpressibility, invisibility. As a subjective sensation that cannot be shared, it isolates its sufferers, and it often robs them of language. People in great pain are returned to their animal self – they cry and howl and whimper but they don't speak. Now Connor heard himself whimper, like a wounded dog. He heard a moan escape from him and he was reminded of all the men, women and children who had come to him making exactly that sound.

Like most doctors, he used a questionnaire with his patients that had been developed a few decades previously, to give an internal event an external reality and to put inarticulate agony into words, usually by finding comparisons and metaphors. He told his students that this was the first step towards rescuing their patients from that agony. The McGill Pain Questionnaire was quite simple; by now he knew it practically off by heart. It divided pain into categories, then divided each category into ascending levels of pain. For 'temporal pain' a patient can choose between 'flickering', 'quivering', 'pulsing', 'throbbing', 'beating' and finally 'pounding'. Or for 'constrictive pain', the options run from the mild 'pinching' to the extreme 'crushing'. The familiar words went through his mind: 'searing', 'lacerating', 'sickening' . . .

What terms might best describe the sensation that now gripped him like physical torment? Throbbing. Pressing. Gnawing. Penetrating. Aching. Heavy. Suffocating. It was like a hungry, sharp-toothed, stinking animal inside him, taking all the oxygen, chewing at his innards and scraping at his sorry heart. He tried to breathe steadily, as he often told his patients to do, but still his breath came raggedly. He tried to step outside the gobbling pain and look at it calmly, but it clawed him back and he was filled with a fresh sense of horror and shame.

You tell those in pain to place it on a scale of one to ten. Most people, even those who are howling, would say seven. Seven for a flashing migraine, seven for a lancinating toothache and seven for cancer that had got deep into the bone, where the drugs couldn't follow. That wasn't because they were being brave, but because they could always imagine worse. They were never at the end.

Seven, he thought. This feeling rates a seven, which means there could be an eight, a nine, a ten. What would ten be? Would ten be Gaby leaving him, Ethan hating him, Stefan suffering all over again? Or was that just an eight? Could anything be worse than losing everything he loved, or was there always something more?

The riptide of emotion that surged through him made Connor feel physically sick. It was as if he was being turned inside out, and he pulled the pillow to him and curled round it for comfort. He wanted to cry but the tears were frozen inside him. He closed his eyes and lay quite still, listening to the sounds of the night outside the window; he opened them again and looked at the green digits on his alarm clock clicking round. At 2.29 he sat up, knowing he would not sleep and unable to lie in bed any longer. He turned on the bedside lamp and blinked in the sudden dazzle, then swung his legs out of bed. It was chilly, and he felt an eerie sense of emptiness around him. He looked out of the window; below the flawless moon, the houses stood in darkness. A cat stalked along the road beneath him, its tail held high, and Connor could see its yellow eyes.

He put on the dressing-gown Gaby had given him last spring, not for a birthday or Christmas but because she'd fallen in love with it and bought it on impulse. It was long and sumptuously scarlet, and she said it made him look like a medieval knight. He pulled it tight round him and thrust his feet into the slippers at the foot of the bed, then made his way softly out of the room. For a few seconds, he stood outside Ethan's door and held his breath, listening, but hearing no sound. Maybe she was asleep, or maybe she was simply lying in bed with her eyes open waiting for morning. He went downstairs, leaning on the banister to lighten his weight and listening for the creak of floorboards underfoot.

The embers still glowed in the grate and he paused to warm his hands, then went into the kitchen and put on the kettle. He turned on the boiler for hot water, in case Gaby got up early and wanted a bath, then ground some coffee beans (putting two tea-towels over the grinder to muffle the noise). While he was waiting for the water to boil, he emptied the dishwasher he'd put on a few hours previously, and cleared away the pots and pans from the draining-board. He didn't want Gaby to do it in the morning. He kept out one of the tumblers and poured himself a generous slug of whisky. The coffee was strong enough to make him wince, and the whisky burnt his throat. He took both drinks upstairs into his study and closed the door. There was a large black-and-white photograph of Gaby on the wall facing him, taken several years ago by a photographer friend of theirs. It was summer, and she was sitting cross-legged on the lawn outside wearing old jeans and a white T-shirt; her feet were bare; there was a chain round one of her ankles. One tendril of hair snaked down her cheek. He'd caught her unawares; she wasn't looking at the camera but at someone out of shot, and smiling delightedly. Her left hand was held out in an exuberant gesture of welcome that Connor recognized. He sat at his desk, cupped his chin in his hands and gazed up at his wife. He had forgotten how gorgeous she could be, how warm and generous, with her mess of tawny hair and her wide, wholehearted smile.

He didn't know how long he sat like that, but when he glanced at the clock on the wall it was past three o'clock. He finished his coffee, now cold, tipped the last of the whisky down his throat, turned on his computer, put on his reading-glasses. He cleared his throat as if he were about to give a lecture, then started to type.

'Darling Gaby,' he wrote, and deleted it.

'Dear heart,' he wrote. No. Delete.

Or: 'I can't sleep, so I thought I should put down some of the –' Delete.

'I have lived for eighteen years with this terrible thing and now that you know –' Delete.

'Are you asleep now, or are you awake like me, my most precious Gaby . . .'

He turned off his computer and pulled out a sheet of paper. He took his fountain pen – which Ethan had given him when he turned forty and which he rarely used – out of the desk drawer. In his small neat handwriting, he began.

It's three in the morning and I'm writing this letter because I have to talk to you. Perhaps you're lying awake at this moment, and I should go and sit beside you and speak the words instead. But I'm not very good at expressing myself. Besides, I'm scared. I'm scared of hurting you more, and of losing you if I haven't done so already – and just plain scared. I know that I have behaved terribly and that I have hurt you (the person in the world I least want to hurt). I don't want this letter to make that worse, but I am going to try to be clear and honest.

There are two things, and I'm trying to hold them separately in my mind, for the moment at least. First, there's the fact of my affair with Nancy, nearly nineteen years ago. Then, there's the fact that I suddenly discover I have a daughter. Or, rather, that I am the biological father of a young woman who you say is called Sonia. I did not know this before tonight. I have not spoken to Nancy or been in any kind of contact with her since she left. And before anything else, I should tell you that I have not had an

affair of any kind before or since this one. I have not even been
tempted. You are my first and only great love. The great ambition
of my life is to make you happy and to deserve you.

Connor rubbed his eyes. He went back down to the kitchen with his tumbler and refilled it with whisky. He rummaged in Gaby's voluminous leather bag and found the cigarette packet he knew she'd been hiding in there, and shook out a couple of cigarettes. Back in his study, he lit one and took a sip of whisky. Then he resumed writing.

The affair with Nancy – if you can call something that lasted
a few days and I have regretted for the rest of my life an affair –
took place when you were ill after Ethan was born. This is not
an excuse, rather the opposite. At the time you most needed me,
I betrayed you. I simply want to describe what happened. When
I first met Nancy, I liked her because you loved her. Soon, I
liked her even more because I could see that she loved you. Then,
I simply liked her. It was only when you were ill and she was at
the house so much, looking after you and helping me look after
Ethan, that I thought of her sexually.

Connor scribbled out the world 'sexually' until it was illegible, and put in its place 'in any other way'. He dragged the smoke deep into his aching lungs and gulped some whisky.

I was exhausted, emotional, confused and scared by what was
happening to you. I think Nancy was as well, although of course
she must speak for herself. We had sex three times, over a period

of two weeks. I knew immediately what a terrible thing I was
doing, and so did she. It wasn't about pleasure or desire or love.
I don't know if you will understand when I say that our guilt,
which should have prevented us, actually and paradoxically drew
us together. We were partners in crime. I was filled with
self-hatred and self-disgust and the only person with whom I could
share this was her, because she was feeling the same. I don't
know if that makes sense to you. I don't even know if it makes
sense to me any more or if it is just a foolish self-justification. It
was quickly over and I was relieved when a few weeks later she
left the way she did, although I knew that you would be upset —
as of course you were. I know that by sleeping with Nancy I not
only deceived you and endangered our marriage, I doubly betrayed
you because I also took away your dearest friend and damaged
your brother's chance of happiness. I never told you because I
could not tolerate the anguish I would cause on both these counts.
I still do not know if that was the right or wrong thing to do.
There have been many times over the years when I have nearly
spoken about it; moments when I felt particularly close to you
and suddenly realized there was a large part of myself that I was
withholding. I felt at such moments that I'd poisoned the source
of myself. In part, I wanted to tell you because I wanted you to
forgive me (I cannot forgive myself). But that seemed a selfish
reason. I have tried since then to be a good husband — it is an
absurdly old-fashioned phrase but I can't think of a better one.
I never for one moment stopped loving you.

Connor lit another cigarette. Blue smoke drifted above
his head. He thought he heard a sound from Ethan's
room, but when he listened, there was nothing.

Then there's the fact that apparently Nancy gave birth to
Sonia and I am the biological father. Frankly, Gaby, I do not
know what to do with this information. My mind quite literally
goes blank with incomprehension when I think about it. When I
was lying in bed, trying to understand its significance, I could only
ask myself questions. Does it change what I did, nineteen years
ago? Does it make my actions worse? And then, of course, there
are other questions now, like does she want me to meet her?
Should I meet her? Should I meet Nancy? I realize that in some
sense these are not questions for you to answer, yet without
talking to you about it I feel I don't know what I think. I am
adrift. The idea of not having you there to turn to for advice and
comfort terrifies me more than I can say.

Connor's hand was aching. He laid down his pen and
read through what he had written. It seemed woefully
inadequate, expressing only the perimeters of his thoughts
not the dark vortex at the centre; barely beginning to
describe his guilt. He saw that outside the sky was becoming lighter; there was a thin strip of grey on the horizon
and the stars were going out. He picked up the pen once
more.

It's nearly dawn now and I am going to go out for a while.
I'm not sure where, but I don't want to be around when you
wake up, in case you don't want me to be. I will come home
before midday and I hope you will still be here and we can talk
properly.

He wanted to write, 'I can't live without your love,' but
that would seem like an appeal for sympathy or pity. He

274

wanted to write 'Don't leave me.' He hesitated, looking down at the densely covered pages in front of him.

You are the loveliest woman I have ever known.

He couldn't think what else to say, so he stopped on his name, put the letter in an envelope, wrote 'GABY' on the outside and slid it under the door of Ethan's room. Then he dressed hastily in his jogging trousers and long-sleeved running top, slid his wallet and keys into his deep side pocket and let himself out of the house.

Twenty-three

Gaby woke to the sound of the front door shutting. Her body remembered before her brain; there was a weight in her chest and a hollowness in her stomach. She couldn't believe she had managed to sleep. She had heard Connor going downstairs, and then a few minutes later entering his study. She had almost decided to go to him there, because it was unbearable to lie in bed and wait for the morning. And now she looked at her watch, which she'd forgotten to remove, and it was nearly six o'clock and the window was a pale grey patch in the room. The moon had gone and so had the stars, but the sun was not yet near the horizon. In the countryside, cockerels would be crowing in farmyards. She could hear birds singing outside. Her throat was sore, as if it was full of drawing-pins. Her legs itched from the rough blanket she had lain in.

She rolled out of bed and stood in the middle of the room. There was a white rectangle on the floor by the door that turned out, when she took a few steps towards it, to be an envelope. She picked it up and turned it in her hands without opening it. Then she put it carefully on the desk where Ethan used to work and wandered muzzily into the bathroom. She gazed helplessly at her puffy eyes and dry lips, and splashed cold water over her face. She sensed that there was no one in the house but her, and was filled with a desolation that made her feel old, frail, lonely.

In their bedroom, the bed was empty, the duvet pulled up over the pillows. She sat down on it, suddenly breathless. On the table at Connor's side, there were two books, both with markers in, and a medical journal; stuffed on to hers and overflowing on to the floor, there were the piles of books she was going to read soon, the magazines she hadn't quite got round to putting away, the notepads scrawled with lists she had made and not looked at again. She sighed and made herself get up, pulled on her old dressing-gown and went back to retrieve the envelope. Running her finger under the gummed flap, she pulled out the sheets of paper and looked at Connor's familiar, slanted writing. But the words blurred. 'It's three in the morning,' she made out. She took the letter downstairs to the kitchen, where it was neat and orderly and fragrant with the many flowers she had bought yesterday; the dishwasher had been unloaded, the surfaces cleared and the boiler was humming. She made herself a large pot of tea and sat at the table with the mug cupped between her hands and the letter spread in front of her. The steam made her face damp as she read it through slowly, word by word; then she read it again.

After she had finished, she didn't know what to do with herself. It was only half past six. In the houses around her, people lay fast asleep. The lamps were still lit on the street. She ran herself a bath, but as soon as she lay down in it she wanted to get out. She put her dressing-gown back on and made herself a piece of toast and marmalade, but after one mouthful she threw it into the bin. She picked up the phone to ring in sick for work, but as it was ringing realized that of course no one would be there yet, so she left a vague, apologetic message on the answering-machine and promised she'd call again later. She found the packet of cigarettes in her bag and smoked one down to the filter. Then she stood up decisively, found the scrap of paper with Nancy's email address written on it in the pocket of the coat she had worn yesterday, and went to Connor's computer, which she used when she needed it. She pressed 'new' on the message box and typed in Nancy's address. 'I told Connor last night,' she wrote, then sent it before she could change her mind. She thought about Stefan. He would have to know. There was a momentum about things now that none of them could stop. Connor would meet Nancy again, maybe he would meet Sonia, Stefan would discover the truth, then Ethan would find out. The secret had been spilt and now it was spreading over everything.

She got dressed in brown cords and a thick, shapeless pullover – the oldest, plainest clothes she could lay her hands on. The sight of all her bright, complicated things hanging in the wardrobe made her feel weary and jaded. So much effort, so much theatrical dressing up and showing off, and for what? She tied her hair back and coiled it into a stern bun. It was still not yet seven o'clock. Standing at the window, she stared out blankly at the street, which was filling with figures: men and women leaving early for work, moving briskly in the cool air; a teenager on a bike, with a bag of newspapers slung over his shoulder. The postman walked up the path to their front door and a few seconds later Gaby heard the clatter of mail falling on to the hall floor. She lay down on the bed and put her hands behind her head.

Connor ran. Through Camden, up Kentish Town Road and towards the Heath. He made himself go as fast as he could, so that his chest ached with the effort. He went up Parliament Hill, then towards the opposite side, where you can believe that you're in the countryside. Almost no one was around yet: a few dog-walkers, a tramp trailing his sleeping-bag, a young man sitting on a bench given in remembrance of 'our darling Gail, who loved this place'. Connor ran past the ponds, scattering ducks and fat pigeons, and along to the tennis courts. It wasn't enough. He retraced his circuit, his calves aching with the effort and his knees sore. The tramp had gone but the youth was still there, just sitting, and Connor wondered why he was so pensive. As he slowed down to a walk, at the exit to the Heath, he looked at his watch. It was not long past seven. He certainly couldn't go back yet; Gaby might still be asleep and he wanted to give her time to read his letter and prepare for his return. He had to behave with great caution now. He remembered how delicately he and Gaby had treated each other at the start of their relationship, how attuned they had been to the other's mood, knowing that they were holding each other's heart in their hands. Later, of course, that had necessarily worn away. They had had arguments in which they traded crude insults; they had behaved carelessly or unsympathetically and stopped treating each other as precious and vulnerable. But throughout they had had a sense of the comradely robustness of their marriage: they had teased each other, laughed at each other, had sometimes taken each other for granted but rarely taken offence. Now Connor felt returned to the exquisite frailty of their beginnings, when the heart is a bruise and love an open wound.

There was a café up the road where he and Gaby sometimes went at the weekend because it served thick soups, vegetarian stews and large salads, and in the summer they could sit outside on the pavement and watch the world pass by. He went there now and although a 'closed' sign hung on the door, he could see a woman moving around inside, preparing to open up. The sweat cooled on his forehead as he waited; the heat from his run was ebbing away. But the clichés were true: it did make a difference that the darkness had turned to day; it did help to exercise until your body ached.

The woman turned the 'closed' sign to 'open' and Connor stepped into the snug interior of dark wood, white walls, sofas and chairs. He asked for a glass of water, which he downed standing at the counter, and a cappuccino; then, seeing her frown, he added a toasted cinnamon-and-raisin bagel. He sat at the table by the window and made his coffee last as long as possible, sipping its warmth through the frothy surface. He tore off a shred of bagel and tried to chew it but couldn't swallow it. The café was beginning to fill and Connor wished he had a book or a paper so that he could pretend to read. Instead, he gazed out of the window at the people striding busily past and thought how long it had been, years indeed, since he had sat like this, doing nothing. Everything he did, from working to cooking his meals, was planned and had a purpose. Even when he went for a walk, he did so quickly and efficiently, rarely loitering. All of that seemed a different world. Time, which used to go so fast, had slowed to a dawdle; his purpose had narrowed to a single domestic point. Gaby.

At eight o'clock he put a generous tip on his table and left the café. He trailed along the road, stopping to get a newspaper that he tucked under his arm after glancing at the headlines and thinking about buying a bunch of roses from the kiosk outside the Underground station, but Gaby had turned the house into a florist's yesterday and, anyway, to do so would be to reduce the magnitude of what he had done – the contrite husband handing over the bouquet. Sorry, darling, but here's a present to make up.

At the front door, he fumbled in his pocket for keys, then changed his mind and, like a stranger, lifted his hand and knocked.

Twenty-four

<u>9 November</u>

I am about to ring you up. Mum and Dad have both gone out to the cinema and I'm alone in the house. They asked me to go with them but I said I was tired. I think maybe they guessed but they didn't push me. I don't think I can put it off any longer. I nearly did it a few minutes ago, I even started to dial the number, but then I slammed the phone down. I need to think of the first few words I will say to you. I have to practise saying them out loud and in the right tone – self-confident but not too loud – so that I don't stutter and go tongue-tied the way I do sometimes when I'm nervous. I know it doesn't really matter – I mean, I don't have to impress you or anything. Why on earth should I care what you think of me? Hello, can I speak to Nancy Belmont? My name is Sonia. It's perfectly simple. But maybe you won't even be there.

<u>Later</u>

So I've done it. I feel all trembly, as if I haven't eaten for ages. You answered almost at once and you just said, 'Yes?' in a curt voice, and for a moment I couldn't speak. When I did, my voice was pathetic and a bit squeaky. I must have sounded about nine years old. But I managed to stammer out my sentence. I think I wanted you to sound flustered or anxious, but you didn't. You were more like someone arranging a business meeting, very quick and efficient. Well, that was probably right, I guess – I certainly didn't want to start having an emotional conversation about how weird all of this was, blah-blah. But to be honest, I didn't particularly warm to you. You must have thought it all out beforehand, though. You had your suggestions of places to meet, and it was probably a good thing to agree in advance on how long we should be together, so it didn't dribble on with neither of us knowing when to leave. It felt a bit like a dentist's appointment or a maths tutorial or something. One hour, late morning, on the steps of the British Museum. And now I keep thinking of what I should wear. Isn't that stupid? Alex would be very disapproving of me. He hates vanity. But I think that probably it's just a way of thinking about who I should be when we meet, if that makes sense. I have to prepare myself: shall I be cool and punky me, or neat and organized me, or emotional and vulnerable me? I wonder if you're thinking the same, but you didn't sound like that on the phone. You sounded like you probably know exactly who you are and I bet you'll be wearing something sensible but quite expensive and whatever I've chosen will suddenly feel all tacky and wrong. I already feel clumsy. I'll spill my coffee and mumble my words and cry.

12 November

Yesterday me and Alex took George for a long walk. George can't move very fast any more: he's too old and fat and the vet says he's arthritic as well. But it was good. It was windy, and the leaves were flying up in front of us as if they were great flocks of birds and the light was thick and dramatic. I told him everything that's been happening with you. I didn't tell him before because I hadn't spoken to Mum and Dad and somehow it felt all wrong that he should know when they didn't.

His reaction was interesting. When my parents heard that I'd made contact with you, I could tell they were a bit hurt that I'd kept it secret for as long as I had, though they never said so. But with Alex it was the opposite. He loves people being mysterious and unexpected. He says that everyone should have secrets and hide bits of themselves away. Anyway, he seemed really chuffed and impressed by my news. Sometimes I think he would never have been interested in me in the first place if I hadn't been adopted. I'm not just this ordinary girl from the outskirts of Stratford, whose mother is a librarian and father an accountant and who lives in a semi with an old dog: I'm also someone with a mysterious background, who might have come from anywhere and be anyone.

I've tried to tell him that I don't want to be a mystery to myself but I don't think he takes it in properly. And he certainly doesn't understand the dread I feel at meeting you and perhaps having to redefine myself; for him being forced to redefine himself would be a wonderful adventure. The fact of not knowing is what I hate about myself and what he loves. Well, love isn't the right word. It's not a word he ever uses, and even when he's at his most tender he somehow manages it with raised eyebrows and a knowing smile – as if everything has to be framed by the knowledge that he's always being a bit ironic, a bit theatrical. He's very suspicious of love – he says it's a sentimental word and a dirty word and usually a lie and almost always a trap, and people do terrible things to each other in its name. I think if I told him I loved him he'd be out of the door faster than I could say, 'Just joking!' I don't tell him, but not because I think he'll disappear. I don't tell him because I don't know what I feel. Sometimes, when I see him walking towards me down the road with his beaky nose, looking eager and vulnerable (God, he'd hate to think he looked like that, which makes him even more touching), my heart contracts and I want to wrap him up in me and keep him safe from harm. Is that love? Or is that just the way so many women feel about men? Women want men to need them, and men dread women needing them. I was talking about that to Goldie yesterday – how one of the biggest insults a man uses about a woman is that she's 'needy', which means he's gone off her. It seems cruel that the more you love and need someone the less likely it is that they'll love and need you back. Auden wrote once about having to be either the one who loves or the one who's loved. He chose to be the one who loved. I don't know what I would choose. Neither. I want it to be equal. Why shouldn't it be? I think Mum and Dad love each other equally; they're not sentimental towards each other. You wouldn't look at them and think, There's a great love story. But they seem to belong to each other and to know each other inside out. They finish each other's sentences sometimes, and have these shared stories that go back through all the years they've been together. I can't imagine what will happen when one dies and leaves the other alone. It doesn't seem possible that either could be single and independent again. It's like all their little habits and rituals have grown up around them like a shelter – which is probably my shelter, too, now I think about it. I read this quotation in the papers today, in an article written by a woman who'd lost her husband after something like forty years of marriage: 'I am rich in all that I have lost.' It made me feel quite weepy.

I'll tell Goldie today as well. It feels better if the people I'm close to know what's going on. And, anyway, she can tell me what to wear!

Twenty-five

'How's Lorna?'

Ethan tried to make the question casual, blurting it out as he raised his cup of coffee to his lips, and taking a gulp before her name was properly out of his mouth, then busily lighting a cigarette. He and Harry had had an arduous game of squash (won, as usual, by Harry), and the flush that rose to his forehead when he mentioned Lorna could, he hoped, be put down to exercise.

'Fine.' Harry picked up the chocolate-chip cookie he'd bought, broke it in two and put one half into his mouth. His next words were muffled and indistinct. 'She was away the last couple of days, visiting her father.'

'Yeah?' Ethan stared intently into his cup.

'She goes quite a lot. It's a bit of a drag. But her mother died and she's the oldest of four girls. I think she feels a bit guilty that she's not there to help out any more. She's a responsible kind of person.'

This last was said with a faint suggestion of a sneer, but Ethan's heart was hammering at the thought of Lorna having a dead mother, a forlorn father, three younger sisters in need of her protection. He sighed blissfully, imagining himself accompanying her to a tiny, run-down house where the fridge was empty and the heating broken down. He would cook, clean, bring comfort and cheer to the motherless girls, be a stout companion to the father. He would rescue them and she would love him for it.

'How long ago?' he asked.

'How long ago what?'

'Did the mother die?'

'Oh. I dunno. A year or so. Cancer, I think – it usually is, isn't it? She doesn't talk about it much. I only found out when she was on the phone to her little sister, trying to calm her down about something or other.'

'Poor thing,' said Ethan, filled with melting tenderness.

'Oh, boy,' said Harry, smirking in a way that made Ethan feel uncomfortable.

'What?'

'Nothing, nothing. Just – oh, boy.'

'I don't know what you're on about.'

'Ha!'

Ethan finished his coffee, stubbed out his cigarette and fiddled in his pockets for coins. 'I guess I ought to go. Richelieu beckons.'

'We need to find you a girlfriend.'

'I don't want a girlfriend.'

'Yeah, you do. You're pining.'

'Crap.'

'Wasting away. Smoking too many cigarettes.'

'Look who's talking.'

'"I hear singing and there's no one there,"' Harry warbled, in a comic falsetto, ignoring the stares.

'Stop.'

'"I smell blossoms and the trees are bare."'

'I'm really going now.'

'"All day long I seem to walk on air."'

'Right. That's it.' Ethan stood up.

'She's not a goddess, you know, Ethan.'

'Who? What are you going on about?'

'She's not even all that beautiful.'

'I'll see you around. But why are you with her if you don't think she's beautiful?'

'So you do know what I'm going on about. Lorna's nice-looking, but she's not like – like that Elizabeth on your course, for example. She's a stunner. She likes you, by the way. Why don't you ask her for a drink or something?'

Ethan stared at Harry. Elizabeth was tall, dark-haired and striking, but not a patch on Lorna. A tiny window of hope opened in his mind: if Harry didn't think Lorna was beautiful, he shouldn't be with her. And if he could talk about her so casually, as if she was dispensable rather than unique and precious, he certainly didn't deserve her.

''Bye,' he managed.

'But hands off, Ethan. OK?'

'I'd never – I'd never try to . . .' He trailed to a halt and stared at Harry. The atmosphere between them was suddenly cold.

'I watched the way you were with her on the beach that day. Huddled up together and whispering sweet-nothings in her ear.'

'No!' Ethan was aghast at how Harry's version dirtied the few minutes he'd spent with Lorna, which he had relived many times since. 'We were talking, that's all.'

'Yeah, right. That's why she kept asking about you afterwards.'

'You're my friend, Harry! I'm not like that,' Ethan said, while he stored away the words for later: she had asked about him. Did that mean she liked him?

'Just thought I'd warn you, in case.'

'You didn't need to.'

'Fine. So it's clear.'

'Clear.'

They met by chance in the bookshop. Ethan often spent hours in there, picking books that caught his interest off the shelves and reading them while he leant against a pillar in his coat and scarf. He had read the whole of *Homage to Catalonia* earlier in the week, and a sizeable portion of an idiosyncratic history of salt. Today he'd come in from the wind and rain to take refuge in the warm comfort of the shop. He was cold and tired – probably cold because he was so tired – and at a loose end. He had no plans for the rest of the day and didn't want to go back to his room yet, where he knew he would not work but instead would brood, eat cold baked beans or Pot Noodles and smoke too many cigarettes.

He picked a collection of Raymond Carver's short stories from the shelves, and a psychology book about the trustworthiness of intuition, then wandered further into the interior of the shop, where the wind didn't sweep over him every time the door opened. At the children's section, in an alcove at the back, he saw half a shelf of thin, brightly coloured Dr Seuss books and pulled several out, smiling to himself. Strange, bright-eyed, outraged, baffled creatures; fish with smiles; turtles and long-haired, long-legged, spindly hump-backed waifs and mongrels.

Such skippety rhymes. *The Cat in the Hat*. He opened the book and found the picture he remembered of two children looking in a woebegone fashion out of the window at the rain. Then along comes the cat, walking on its hind legs with a glint in its eye, to wreak havoc and bring fun. 'Fun is good,' it says. That was what his mother used to say, laughing over her shoulder at his frowning, captivated father.

He flicked through the pages, and his early years seemed to return to him. Tucked up in bed with his mother sitting beside him, sleeves rolled up and slippers on her feet. *Green Eggs and Ham*: he'd loved that book. And here was *Horton Hatches the Egg*, the story of a patient elephant sitting on an egg in the place of the feckless mother-bird, and finally, after pages of adversity and woe, hatching out an elephant-bird. His father would always say that the book was about being a stepfather, really: it's love, not biology, that counts. His mother had read all these to him when he was little, over and over again. They'd known whole chunks off by heart, and he could still remember fragments, as if they were hard-wired into his brain. Probably when he was on his deathbed he would still be able to recite, 'Bump, Bump, Bump, have you ever seen a Wump? We have a Wump with just one Hump . . .' He opened up *One Fish*, *Two Fish* and found the poem, murmuring it to himself out loud: '"But we know a man called Mr Gump, and Mr Gump has a seven-humped Wump . . ."'

'"So if you want to go Bump, Bump, just jump on the Hump of the Wump of Gump,"' a voice joined in. 'Do you always go about reciting things, Ethan?'

He turned, open-mouthed and flame-faced. 'Lorna.'

'Because this time I can compete. "Sighed Maisy the lazy bird, hatching her egg, I'm bored and I'm something and I've something or other and rum-te-tum . . ."'

'"I'm tired and I'm bored and I've kinks in my legs, from sitting just sitting here . . ."'

'OK – "Day after day. It's work, how I hate it, I'd much rather play . . ."' I don't know any more. Except "An elephant's faithful . . ."'

'". . . one hundred per cent."'

They stopped, grinning at each other, then abashed and awkward.

'Hi,' he said.

'So you like Dr Seuss too.'

'My mother used to read them to me. Things you love when you're little – you never forget them, do you? They stay with you.'

'My mother used to read them to me, too,' said Lorna. 'And one day I'll probably read them to my kids – if I have any, that is. Handing things down.' She took one from his hand and looked at its jacket. *Thidwick the Kind-hearted Moose*. 'Except I always used to insist that Thidwick was a goat, not a moose.'

'That must have played havoc with all the rhymes.'

'I guess so.'

'I'm sorry about your mother,' Ethan said awkwardly.

'Thanks.' She pushed the book back into its space on the shelf.

'Was it recent?'

'A year ago, more or less. Is that recent or is it a long while? I don't know.'

'Time's odd like that, I guess. It goes slowly and quickly all together. It seems pretty recent to me, though.'

'She was ill for a long time before she died. We knew it was coming, like a juggernaut rumbling over a hill – but you're never ready, however much you think you are. She certainly wasn't ready. She thought she would hold on till we all left school, and she said she was going to insist on having at least one grandchild before she went.'

'I'm sorry,' Ethan repeated. 'Were you close?'

'Yes. But in a different way by the end – I couldn't be a raging adolescent or anything when I knew she was dying, so there was a way in which we didn't share the things we would have. I thought I had to protect her; now I think she would have preferred it if I'd let her protect me. I almost stopped her being a real mother to me, so in a way she was gone before she was gone or something. I don't know. Why am I telling you all this? I hardly know you. Most people don't ask – they just mumble something and change the subject.'

'You must miss her.'

'Are you going to buy any of these?'

'Sorry, I didn't mean to –'

'I don't want to cry in a bookshop, that's all.'

'OK. Well, I wasn't going to buy them. I just read them in here.'

'Don't they mind?'

'I don't think they notice. I like it here, among all the books. I like the smell and all the nooks and crannies. And the thought that there are hundreds of thousands of ideas and images and facts packed away and you just have to open the pages to find them.'

'I'll leave you to it, then.'

'No. No, look, Lorna –'

'What?'

'How about if I buy you some of these Dr Seuss books? For the memories.'

'Don't be daft.'

'Really. Unless you've still got them.'

'I haven't but –'

'Please let me, then. For you to read to your children one day.'

'Ethan!'

'I'd like to. Really. Let me.' In his eagerness, he took several and held them out to her. 'Which ones are your favourites?'

'OK. You can buy me one if I buy you one.'

'But –'

'Take it or leave it.'

'All right, then. I accept.' He gave a small bow and she smiled at him with her generous mouth, and her beautiful almond-shaped eyes shone and he saw how smooth and pale her skin was and how delicate her collarbone and . . . He gulped. 'Which one will you have?'

'Oh, that's so hard.'

'Take two, three. As many as you like!'

'It's got to be *One Fish, Two Fish*.'

'Right.'

'What about you?'

'The same.'

'The same?'

'Yes.'

'Then we can't lend each other our copies.'

'Were we going to do that? Then I'll choose something else. Of course. Um, *Horton Hatches the Egg.*'

'Good. I was hoping you'd choose that one.'

'You were?' He almost took her in his arms right then.

They queued to pay and then, rather formally, they handed the books to each other.

'Thank you,' said Ethan, gravely.

'And thank you.' Lorna hesitated. 'Do you want a cup of coffee?'

'Oh.' He remembered Harry, heard his words: 'Hands off.' Saw his cold eyes. 'I don't think I can . . .'

'Don't worry.' She half turned from him. 'It was just a thought.'

'No! Actually, I'd love to.'

'If you're busy . . .'

'No. I'm not busy. Not at all. Nothing happening. Coffee's perfect. There's a lovely place down the road. I go there a lot. They do the best chocolate cake. I sometimes have it for breakfast.'

Out in the street, he walked beside her and thought, his heart bursting with terrified pride, that people who saw them might assume they were together. Her shoulder brushed his; her right hand nearly touched his left; little wisps of her hair blew against his cheek. He matched his stride to hers so they were walking in rhythm. In the coffee shop, he ordered a double espresso for himself, a cappuccino for her and a slice of chocolate cake to share. Then they sat opposite each other in a dark booth in the smoking area at the back of the café. He looked at the tiny band of froth on her upper lip, a crumb of cake on her cheek, then down at her hands, which lay on the table a few inches from his own. If he moved his a bit he could touch her. If he shifted forward in his seat, their knees might meet.

He sat up straight and offered her a cigarette.

'No, thanks. Maybe later.'

Later – was there going to be a later? He lit his own cigarette and dragged smoke deep into his lungs, tapped non-existent ash into the ashtray, looked intently at his coffee as if something of great interest was in there, waited for his heart to stop thudding.

They talked about other books they had loved as children (him, *The Phantom Tollbooth*, *Winnie-the-Pooh* and later the *Northern Lights* trilogy; her, the Moomintroll books and *The Little White Horse* – all of which her mother had read to her – and books by Michael Morpurgo, David Almond and, later, Agatha Christie thrillers in the bath). They talked about their gap year (him, travelling through Eastern Europe, sometimes with other people – he didn't mention that 'other people' actually meant one person, Rosie – and sometimes on his own, ending up in Moscow; her, the final days of her mother's life and then a period in which she mourned, worked in the local supermarket and took care of her father and her sisters). They swapped bands they liked, drew up a list of the five worst films of the last year, agreed that the planet was being poisoned, discussed the meaning of dreams, found out they both loved Thai food and sushi. And suddenly Ethan realized that it was dark outside. Evening had fallen; the world had become more dangerous. He mustn't forget Harry's words, or he would lean towards her right now and touch the curve of her cheek. He clenched his fists.

'How long have we been here?' he asked.

'I don't know. Are you meant to be somewhere?'

'Not as such, but –'

'Can I have that cigarette, then?'

He shook one out of the packet, handed it to her and struck a match. His fingers trembled and she put her hand round his to keep the light steady and, for an instant, they gazed at each other through the orange flame. The rest of her face was close up and blurred, but her eyes were clear and he could see his face reflected in them. He moved towards her; he felt her breath on his skin and his heart pounding in his chest; he felt a groan force its way up his throat.

Abruptly, he removed his hand from hers, lit his own cigarette, blew out the flame with a sharp, emphatic puff, sat back from her. 'I've got to go in a minute,' he said briskly.

'Oh – all right, then.'

'Work. I'm behind.'

'Work,' she said. 'I see.'

'What are you up to this evening?'

'Well – I said I might meet Harry later.'

It was the first time Harry's name had been mentioned and Ethan felt himself flinch. 'That's nice,' he said.

'But I had this thought that –' She stopped.

'What?'

'It doesn't matter.'

'Harry's great.'

'Yes.'

'Great,' Ethan repeated, more loudly. He heard himself boom on in an absurd, avuncular tone: 'One of the nicest people I've met here.'

'He's fond of you too,' said Lorna, dutifully.

'Good,' said Ethan. He stabbed his cigarette into the ashtray and ground it down. 'That's good. To have friends.'

'Ethan?'

'What?'

'What's wrong?'

'Wrong? Nothing. Nothing at all. Why should anything be wrong? Everything's fine. Really fine.'

'You've just gone a bit –'

'A bit what?'

'I don't know.'

'Go on, tell me.'

'A bit odd, that's all. Have I said something to offend you?'

'No! Honestly. What makes you think such a thing? I have to go, that's all. I have to work. I'm behind with everything. I keep thinking that if I work all night without stopping, then in the morning I'll be almost back on track, but then I'll be so bloody knackered that I'll let it get out of control again.'

'You're going to work all night?'

'That's what I say now. I'll probably wake up with a jerk at dawn and realize I've been asleep for hours and got nothing done. I'd better get going now.' He rose to his feet and put on his coat.

Lorna stood up, too, and edged out of the booth. 'It's been nice,' she said, suddenly shy. 'Thanks.'

'Yes,' he said. 'It has been nice. Really nice. Lorna –'

'Yes?'

'I didn't mean to be odd. I just –'

'Just?'

'Nothing.' He pulled open the door. 'I think we go in opposite directions from here.'

'Do we?'

'Yes.' He shuffled awkwardly. 'So – goodbye, then.'

'Goodbye. Unless you want to go and see a film with me or have something to eat maybe? Before working all night, that is.'

'No!'

'All right. It was just a thought.'

'I mean – I can't.'

'Don't worry – I've got the message.'

'Lorna, you don't understand – I'd like to – I'd love to.'

She shrugged, suddenly cool. 'Yeah, well. Another time.' And turned to go.

'Christ, Lorna!' The fury in his voice spun her round to face him again. 'I can't because I want to so much.' Ethan felt all his resolution leaving him, like water finally breaching the dam. Words gushed out of him. 'Don't you understand? All I want is to be with you, it's driving me mad, I dream about you for God's sake, don't smile like that, I know it's stupid but it's how I feel, and anyway you're going out with Harry and Harry's my friend, and even if you felt one iota of what I feel about you – no, don't say anything, *don't say anything*, and don't look at me like that, I know you don't, of course I know you don't – but if you did, I still couldn't go out with you because he trusts me. Well, maybe he doesn't really trust me, but he should, he should trust me not to – not to – I know you wouldn't want it anyway, I'm not assuming anything,

I hope you don't think that – oh, God, Lorna, just tell me to shut up. I'm his friend.'

'Faithful one hundred per cent,' said Lorna.

She smiled, stood on tiptoe and kissed his cheek, just to one side of his mouth. Then almost before he realized what she was doing, she left him standing there and walked away. He watched her go: the straight-backed, light-footed glide he'd seen on that first evening, her soft hair shimmering under the lamplight, until she melded with the other figures in the street and at last disappeared. Still he stood and stared, imagining that she would change her mind and return to him and put her arms inside his coat and hold him tight.

At last, he sighed and stirred, glanced at his watch. It was time to go and work, as he had said he would. He would stay up all night because he couldn't imagine sleeping now. He would smoke too much and drink too much instant coffee and his eyes would sting with tiredness and emotion. He felt sick with her absence and his foolishness. He felt sick with hope and loss.

'Hello? Hello, Ethan my darling. It's me. I hope you get this soon. Your mobile always seems to be turned off. I'm planning to come up tomorrow to collect the car and I want to take you out for lunch. Or tea. Or both. Whatever you want. Let me know as soon as you can because I've got to leave first thing tomorrow and I don't want to come if I'm not going to see you and I know you're probably busy with work and stuff so I don't want to get in your way but it will be *lovely* to see you. I hope you're OK. Are you OK? Ring me. 'Bye. Oh, and, Ethan, tell me what you want me to bring you – I mean, do you want any special food, or anything like that? Or if there's anything you forgot to take and you've discovered you need – this is going on too long, isn't it? Sorry. I'll go now. Lots of love. Take care.'

Ethan, listening to the message, imagined his mother as she left it – her hair would be coming undone at the end of the day, she would be gesturing as she talked, or walking around the room with the phone. He felt a sharp stab of homesickness. He didn't want to be here, in his messy room, crumbs on the carpet and a bin full of beer and beans cans; he didn't want to sit up all night with his history essay, or to fall asleep fully clothed and wake up to a corridor of other students whose lives occasionally brushed against his. He didn't want to be in love with his friend's girlfriend. He didn't want to be in love at all. It was too tiring and bewildering. He wanted to be a child again, living peacefully at home, in the room he'd had almost all his life, surrounded by familiar objects. He wanted to hear his father at the computer in his study, or listening to his beloved Bach, and his mother singing in the shower or laughing with friends downstairs, or calling up to him to come down for supper.

He looked at his mobile to see the time. Eight o'clock. What would they be doing now? Probably his father would be cooking something, slicing red peppers into thin strips, carefully mixing cardamom and cumin in his mortar, peeling and crushing garlic, never hurrying; the fragrant steam would be rising into his concentrated face and every so often he would take a sip of wine from the glass at his elbow. And his mother, she'd be curled up on the sofa with a book most likely, or maybe lying in a luxuriously hot bath with candles and foam. If he was there now, he might be playing cards with her, or sitting at the piano and letting his fingers range over the keys. He'd go to sleep on clean sheets and wake to the smell of coffee being ground.

He sat on the bed, still in his coat, and keyed in the home number.

'Hello, Ethan.' She sounded breathless.

'Mum, sorry, I've only just got your message.'

'So, then, are you around tomorrow?'

'Yeah. When do you reckon you'll be here?'

'I can fit myself round you. I'll get an early train and be with you whenever. But if tomorrow's no good I can always come another day. Whatever's best for you.'

'No – tomorrow's good.'

'Tomorrow it is, then. When do you want to meet?'

'You said lunch – is that still OK for you?'

'Of course. Shall I come to your room?'

'Why don't you ring me when you get here and then we can decide?'

'Fine. And are you all right?'

'Yeah.'

'Really all right? You sound a bit subdued.'

'Mum, I'm good. A bit tired, maybe.'

'What can I bring?'

'I can't think of anything I need.'

'How about marmalade? Or coffee? Have you run out yet? Some ready meals? Biscuits?'

'Tell you what, surprise me.'

'Fine. What are you doing tonight?'

'Working.'

'But everything's −'

'Mum, everything's good. Honestly. We can talk tomorrow.'

'You're right. I'll ring when I arrive, then. Hope your work goes well.'

'Thanks. See you.'

He disconnected and lay back on his bed, with his hands behind his head. In a few minutes he'd raise himself, make strong coffee, sit at his desk with his laptop. No, not at his desk: it was piled high with books, files, clothes, cups, scraps of paper, CDs. He closed his eyes and let himself, for just a few seconds, remember the feel of Lorna's lips on his skin. Her face glimmered behind his eyelids.

He worked through the night, drinking coffee until his head buzzed, smoking cigarettes until his throat was sore and his chest ached. He plugged himself into his iPod and didn't answer his phone. He ate two stale custard creams to keep him going. At just before half past six, he had finished. He transferred his work to his memory stick, turned off his computer and closed its lid. He felt empty rather than tired; his body ached as if he'd been for a long run. Later, when he drew back the curtains, he saw that it was getting light outside. The sky was a clear turquoise, with tiny scribbles of clouds like white runes along its horizon. He rubbed his eyes and opened the window, leant out to feel the wind fresh against his prickling skin.

He pulled on his shoes, and the coat he'd left in a heap

on the floor, and went out on to the deserted campus. His footsteps echoed in the silence. With each gust of wind, leaves floated silently down. In the branches of one tree, stripped almost bare for winter, dozens of small brown birds bunched and swayed like unpicked fruit. Ethan walked for a long time. He didn't know where he was going, or what he was thinking. He just wanted the clean air to pass through his tarry lungs and his fevered brain. At last he stopped at a diner to buy a bacon sandwich and a cup of tea, which he had standing at the counter. The bacon was salty, the bread plasticky and the tea stewed enough to make him wince, but he felt himself revive, and the sense of being disassociated from the world receded. The vague drift of melancholy emotions sharpened into thoughts. He looked at his watch, and saw that he must hurry if he was to shower and dress in clean clothes before his tutorial.

Twenty-six

'You still haven't unpacked!'

'Not as such. I tidied up for you, though.'

'Thank you,' said Gaby, doubtfully. 'You've lost weight.'

'I was going to say the same to you.' Ethan scrutinized his mother. Her face was thinner, so that her eyes looked large and her cheekbones more prominent. And her clothes were loose on her, as far as he could tell. 'Are you OK? Have you been ill or something?'

'Ill? No, I've been fine. Maybe it's because I've been dashing around – or maybe I haven't been eating so many puddings since you left. Anyway, it's always all right for a woman to lose weight,' said Gaby, cheerfully. 'You know what they say in Hollywood: you can never be too rich or too thin.'

'Well, they don't say that anywhere I care to be. What's in the box, then?'

'Lucky dip.'

He put his hand inside. 'Hazelnut and chocolate-chip cookies,' he said. 'Sardines. Tuna with mayonnaise. Jelly – why have you brought me jelly?'

'Not so you'll make it or anything but it's good for energy. A few squares can keep you going. Actually, I left before the shops opened this morning, so it's a random selection from the cupboards at home.'

304

'This is like Christmas. Dried chillies. What am I going to use dried chillies for? Do you think I cook real food? Marmalade, made by Dad – great. Marmite. I've still got a whole giant pot of Marmite; with this, it'll last me till I graduate. Dark chocolate. Sweetcorn. Pasta. Pasta sauce. What's this?'

'I don't know. What is it?'

'Harissa. What's harissa?'

'Something Dad bought.'

'Maybe you should take it back to him.'

'Nonsense. You have it.'

'What'll I do with it? It smells odd.'

'I don't know. It's Middle Eastern – you add it to things.'

'Add it to what – baked beans? Coffee? Take it back, Mum. How is Dad anyway?'

'Fine.'

'Just fine?'

'He's good. You know – busy, happy, fine.'

'Send him my love.'

'Of course. Where are we going to eat?'

'I thought we could walk down to the quayside. It's really pretty there. You'll like it. And there are some nice cafés – you don't want anything grand, do you?'

'Do I look like I want something grand?'

'Not really.'

'Mum?'

'Mmm?'

After lasagne and garlic bread, which neither of them came near to finishing, Gaby had insisted on buying

Ethan a large slice of cheesecake. To see him eat made her feel better herself, less hollowed out by strangeness. But Ethan took only one bite, then laid down his fork.

'Can I ask you something?'

'Of course. Though I might not have the answer.'

'Say I liked someone, OK, and say she was already involved with someone else, what should I do?'

'Do?'

Ethan picked up his fork, then pressed it lightly into the top of the cheesecake, leaving four small punctures in it. 'Yeah – I mean, should I leave it? I should, shouldn't I?'

'Does she like you too?'

'I don't know – maybe. There was a moment when I thought she might, but she probably doesn't, not in the way I like her. She's just being nice to me and I'm reading all sorts of things into it.'

'This other relationship she's in, is it serious?'

'No – well, I don't think so, not on his side, anyway. He's not like that. He's too – too detached. Everything's like a game for him.'

'You know him, then?'

'Um, well, yes. That's how I met her. He's my friend. Harry.'

He saw Gaby wince. 'He's your friend?'

'Yes. OK, OK, don't look all pensive like that. I should leave it. I knew I should anyway. I didn't even need to ask you. Maybe asking your advice is my way of telling you about it. Not that there's anything to tell. Nothing's happened. Nothing will happen. It's just – I like her. I haven't felt like this for ages. I know it'll blow over, but I don't believe it.'

'Does she know you like her?'

'Yeah,' said Ethan, wretchedly. 'I kind of blurted it out. I didn't mean to. But, anyway, she probably knew. I'm just a fool.'

'No, you're not.' She paused, then said: 'Friendship's important.'

'I know.'

'You don't want to do something you'll feel rotten about later.'

'Right.'

He put his elbows on the table and cupped his face in his hands.

'On the other hand –'

'What?'

Gaby wanted to reach out and put her arms round his body in its crumpled jacket. She wanted to hold his sweet, familiar face between her hands and tell him that everything would be all right, she would make sure of it. As she looked at him, she was assailed by memories of all the other times he had sat like this before her, troubled and woebegone and asking for help. When he'd woken up out of nightmares, when he'd fallen over and grazed his knees, when boys at school had pushed him around the playground, laughing at his distress, when he'd felt bad and sad and worthless. At two, you can help a child, pick them up and make it better. At four you can speak to the teacher about bullies or comfort them after night fears. At seven, your power to intervene is already on the wane, however you might still hang on. Later, there's nothing you can do but watch and listen and be there. When Ethan was little, he had been shy and dreamy, and

Gaby had feared for him because he lacked the protective skin that other children had, their worldliness and resilience. Even now, a young man who to all appearances was confident and popular, he seemed raw and vulnerable. He could be lifted up by waves of joy or dragged under by misery, and had no defence against either. But perhaps all mothers think that about their sons, she thought — perhaps even the coolest, toughest, most streetwise teenage boy has a mother at home worrying that he will be hurt by the world's callousness.

After the past few weeks, Gaby felt that she, too, had been flayed of her skin, exposed to the bright horrors of the world. She told herself constantly that what had happened to her was negligible compared with the upheavals of most people's lives — an injury had been done to her many years ago and now, like a piece of shrapnel, it had worked its way to the surface. Yet as she tried to reduce the significance of what had happened, she was in a state where anything could hurt her, the lightest touch and the smallest word. She had to carry herself carefully, avoiding injury. The frown of a stranger could make her flinch. The sight of a mother hand in hand with her toddler, say, or a couple walking along together, smiling at each other, turned her helplessly tender and nostalgic, although at the same time she observed herself and knew she was being foolishly sentimental. Tears would fill her eyes when she read about wars in far-off places or saw photographs that showed the grieving faces of parents. She went out for dinner with a friend who had recently lost her mother and the two of them sat holding hands over their salmon, fat tears rolling down their cheeks. A piece of music would fill her with such painful longings that she preferred silence, although in silence her thoughts heaved and surged and images she was trying to hold at bay broke over her. Most of all she was charged with a hopeless protective love for Ethan that made her rock herself from side to side. He thought he was their only child and would now discover that he wasn't, not really; he thought that their home was his safe haven and would see now that there were jagged rocks under the surface of the smooth water.

She looked at him, his creased face and bitten nails – the defeated hunch of his shoulders – then leant across the table and pulled the collar of his jacket straight, taking an imaginary hair off its lapel. 'What I really think, Ethan, is that I don't know. I simply don't know. These things are so complicated.' She fumbled for the right words, which all of a sudden seemed barbed and dangerous. 'You can't take advice from anyone else. Everyone has their own memories and agendas muddled up in it. You have to decide what's right for you and good for you – what will make you happy. For all sorts of reasons, which I can't go into, I'm the last person to know what you should do.'

'I know. I don't think I can eat all this cheesecake. Sorry.'

'Not to worry.'

'I ought to get back in a minute.'

'Of course. And I've got to collect the car.'

'Was Dad furious about it?'

'A bit annoyed, understandably.'

'It would have been nice if he'd come down too.'

Gaby turned up her palms in a gesture of helplessness. 'His work,' she said.

That was a lie. For the first time in his life, Connor was neglecting his work. He had taken half-days off to spend with Gaby. He had turned off the alarm clock and rolled over on to his side in bed, gazing at the wall for hours. But today was different. Today he was meeting Nancy. He had shown Gaby the letter, which although it was addressed to him was clearly written to the two of them, carefully setting out the situation as Nancy understood it and explaining that, very shortly, she was going to meet Sonia and would like to talk through the implications of this in advance. She was sure that Sonia would want to know who her biological father was, and she needed to know what Connor's – and Gaby's – thoughts were on this. She also wrote that she would quite understand if Connor chose not to meet her, or if he wanted to bring Gaby with him. But Gaby read the letter carefully, then told Connor he should obviously go alone. She said that of course Sonia must know who he was; now the secret had been breached, anything else was unthinkable. She knew – they both knew – that this would very likely mean that Sonia would want to meet Connor as well, perhaps Ethan too – she had no siblings of her own, and he was her half-brother, after all.

'Work,' Ethan repeated, with an ironic shrug. 'As ever.'

'He wants to come and see you soon. He misses you.'

'Does he?'

All of a sudden, Ethan felt tears pricking his eyes. He blinked furiously and clenched his hands into fists.

'Of course. What do you think? You're his beloved son.'

'Sorry. I don't know what's the matter with me today. You came on the wrong day – if you'd come tomorrow or something, I would have been completely different. I'm tired. I didn't get any sleep. Everything's good, really. I'm good. I like it here. I'm being stupid. This'll pass.'

'I know.' She laid her hands over his fists. 'Tiredness can often feel like grief.'

'Right.'

'And, of course, so can love.'

'Very mystical. Let's get going, shall we? Now that I stayed up all night doing my essay I don't want to be late handing it in.'

At the door of the café they hugged each other. She breathed in the smell of his sweat, his cigarettes, his hair, his aftershave, his nearness.

'Take care,' she said, smiling hard and bright, and they walked away in opposite directions.

Twenty-seven

<u>15 November</u>
It's funny, but today I feel quite peaceful about it all – or if not peaceful exactly, something like steadfast (I love that word; my parents are steadfast). Steadfast about meeting you, I mean, and finding out about me. I know I'm loved; I don't need your love. So I'm kind of ready for you and somehow, after all the fretting and scrabbling around for meanings and torturing myself with imagined scenes and dramatic resolutions, I feel small and clean and simple, like a child who's been scrubbed in the bath, then wrapped in a big soft towel and put in front of the fire to get dry.

We'll see.

Twenty-eight

Connor stood in front of the long mirror and tried to fasten the blue and silver tie that Gaby had given him. His fingers trembled; he couldn't get the knot quite right and today it seemed important that it should be perfect, that his white shirt was ironed, his face smoothly shaven and dabbed with aftershave, his shoes polished, his hair brushed. For the past few days he'd been untypically shabby, but now he thought it was only the punctiliousness of his preparation that was holding him together – take away the sober suit and knotted tie and he'd fly apart into many fragments. He looked up briefly to meet his own eyes, then glanced rapidly away. He did not want to see his thin, tense face, the face that had acquired so many lines and wrinkles over the years and that she would be seeing in less than an hour. What did she look like now? He hadn't asked Gaby, and Gaby hadn't told him. He tried to imagine the young woman he had known – the blazing eyes in the sculpted face – and superimpose two decades on to its youth, the way they can do on a computer program to mark the passing of years: carve brackets round her mouth, furrows between her eyebrows, add a slackness to that stubborn jaw, put weight on the slim, hard body, turn her hair grey. Maybe she'd be matronly, with wide hips and a soft shelf where her shallow breasts had been, or perhaps skinny, all bones and loose flesh, with a knuckly grip. For a moment he thought of his long-dead mother and shuddered.

And what would she see? He lifted his eyes once more and this time made himself examine the self that gazed back from the mirror. He was thin, as if time had pared him back. The skull beneath the skin. There were frown marks corrugating his forehead and fine smile lines round his eyes, which were bloodshot after days of little sleep. He leant closer, pressing his fingers against the tiny wrinkles in his cheeks, trying to smooth them. His dark eyebrows were turning silver, his hair had grey in it and was starting to recede. His teeth had fillings in them. His sight was fading and he needed glasses to read or write. For a moment, he saw with perfect clarity the young man he had been when he first met Gaby and Nancy – a coiled spring of energy, anxiety and burning hope. And he saw them: two beautiful young women, arm in arm and laughing at him in the sunshine that poured from the imagined sky on to their soft hair and smooth skin. He felt their bright eyes on him, and even now, so many years and so many regrets later, he felt himself blush with delight under the teasing kindness of their regard.

Connor groaned and pressed his forehead to the mirror. Then he straightened and went slowly down the stairs. Gaby had already left to meet Ethan and collect the car, so the house was still. Usually he treasured the rare times when he was alone in the house but today it filled him with a premonitory dread. This was what it would be like if she were gone for good – silent, the air pressing round him, his footfall loud on the stairs, rooms empty and lifeless, and all the routines they'd built up together over their marriage meaningless, serving only to remind him of what he'd lost. He prepared the breakfast he had every morning: two oranges, freshly squeezed (with which he swilled down the omega 3 and vitamin E he took religiously, though he had little faith in their power to hold off age and decay), brown bread toasted, with marmalade (made by himself last year), a large cup of coffee with heated milk. He turned on the radio for company but, after hearing a few words from an unctuous politician spouting clichés, quickly switched it off again. Then he sat at the table with his breakfast in front of him. He looked at it for several minutes, then lifted the cup to his lips and took a cautious sip of coffee. He put it down and wiped his lips with a napkin, then sat perfectly still, his hands lying on either side of the plate, the amber capsules just above his left thumb. Finally he stood up, swept the toast and pills into the bin, put the glass of juice into the fridge and poured the coffee down the sink.

He and Nancy had arranged to meet outside Tate Modern; if it was fine, they could walk along the river, and if wet, take shelter in the café. It was important to Connor that they were meeting in a place that held no memories for either of them. He left the house early to walk there, for he could not bear to be pressed up against a crowd in the Underground on this particular morning. Anyway, he wanted to steady himself before the encounter. It had rained in the night, but now the day was fresh and bright. The sun shone on the wet road and turned it into a stream of light. Birds swayed in the branches of the bare plane trees, sending down tiny silver drops of water that burst on the pavement. Connor walked at a brisk pace – through Camden towards King's Cross, then down to Blackfriars and the river. Though the traffic was thick, the river was calm and golden. The people crossing the bridge were dark silhouettes against the sky, and small waves thwacked against the bank.

Now – glancing at his watch to make sure he was in good time – he slowed and forced himself to think about what lay ahead. Not just Nancy in a few minutes' time, but after that telling Ethan and then Stefan, as he and Gaby had agreed he should do. For years now Connor had been the one to receive the confessions and pleas of others. He had sat in his small room and heard his patients tell him the stories of their lives and bodies. He had given them news about what was going on inside themselves; looked into their eyes when he told them it wasn't good. He had watched them cry and, laying a hand on their shoulder or leaning towards them with a tissue or a glass of water, had offered them advice, consolation and help. He was the good doctor. Like a priest, he was there at the end. Now, though, instead of being the calm, dependable figure of authority, he had become a ragged, weeping supplicant, festering with the sins he'd hidden in the dark all his adult life. He had pretended to be blameless and wise, until he'd almost believed it himself, but the time had come at last for him to lay his misdeeds and his guilt at the feet of the people he loved and wait for their verdict. He tried to imagine looking into Ethan's face and telling him he had a half-sister somewhere. Or Stefan – what would Stefan say? He always insisted on thinking the best of everyone and had a guileless admiration for Connor. He would probably not be angry; his shy face would sag with sadness instead, or defeat and retrospective humiliation. Connor knew that look. He knew that in the small hours his brother-in-law probably saw his life as a failure. He was not-a-husband, not-a-father. He was a lonely, dreamy academic in a small, untidy house, whose sister bought his shirts and whose students thought he was a 'teddy bear' and 'darling'. And maybe he, Connor, was the agent of Stefan's private wretchedness.

He slowed to a halt and stared out over the broad Thames, watching as a boat passed. A few weeks ago, he and Gaby had walked together over this bridge late at night. They'd stopped at its highest point and looked down to see a leisure boat crammed with dancing people and in its centre, raised on a circular dais, a woman in a low-cut dress singing into a microphone. The music had filtered up to them. They'd leant on the railings and gazed down at the party as it chugged slowly past, until it was a miniature bauble of light in the distance. He'd put his hand on the small of Gaby's back and she'd turned her head towards him and smiled, then straightened up and taken his hand. Connor, a single child from an unhappy home, was perpetually moved by the way a good marriage becomes filled with shared experiences, the same memories lodged in two minds. But that comradely moment on the bridge lay in a past from which he was now separated by a deep crevasse. He had not known at the time how precious it was.

Connor walked over the Millennium Bridge with a stream of other people. He narrowed his eyes and squinted at the entrance of the large building, where she would be waiting, but could not make her out. He fiddled with the buttons on his coat to make sure they were done up properly, cleared his throat, made himself breathe steadily. Stepping off the bridge, he thought he saw her a few feet away, then realized that the woman he was looking at was in her early twenties, as Nancy had been the last time they'd met. She wasn't there yet; after all, he was a few minutes early. He put his hands into his pockets, bowed his head in the wind, and waited.

That was how she first saw him, standing absolutely still, face set in granite composure. She stood for a moment, watching, then walked up to him. He turned.

'Hello, Connor.'

'Nancy.' His voice choked. There was a pebble in his throat, a boulder in his chest, a mist in front of his eyes.

'You've hardly changed,' she said.

'Nor you,' he replied formally, wondering if they were meant to shake hands or kiss each other's cheek.

He had tried to imagine how she would look, but when he had pictured her, her face had taken on either a fierce beauty or a dramatic malevolence. He had made her firm jaw firmer, her eyes blaze like a blowtorch, her hair shine like a helmet. Now she stood before him and she was smaller than he had remembered, and less extraordinary. Her face was weathered, her hair short and neat, her eyes – which were looking at him – not as piercing as he'd drawn them in his mind. She was wearing a black coat, belted at the waist, and a scarf in muted greens and golds round her neck. He looked at her and Gaby's mobile, despairing, joyful face came into his mind. Relief surged through him, making him feel dizzy: he felt nothing for this woman. Neither love nor hatred, desire nor disgust. She was a stranger, and it was hard to believe that he had lain sobbing in her arms.

'Shall we walk?' she asked, and he nodded.

Neither knew how to begin, though both had rehearsed this moment. For several minutes, they walked in silence along the riverbank. Eventually Connor spoke: 'You should have told me.'

'Should I? Of course, now that it's discovered, it's easy to say that. But if it had never been discovered – if Gaby hadn't turned up on my doorstep the way she did, never mind rooting through my private papers – nobody would have known and perhaps it would have remained better that I didn't say.' She stopped and made an abrupt gesture. 'Oh, shit, this is starting off wrong, Connor. I've lain awake night after night thinking how to deal with this meeting and the first thing I want to say is that I'm sorry.'

'It's for me to –'

'Listen. Let me talk first, then you.'

'All right. Go on.'

'I'm sorry in many ways. I'm sorry for what we did. I've always been sorry and I always will be. It was wrong. I'm not really saying sorry to you, of course. It wasn't you I wronged, nor me that you wronged. We have nothing to forgive each other. We're not the victims. Gaby and Stefan were – and still are. I'm just expressing my profound regret. And I'm sorry I got pregnant and you didn't know. Once I decided to keep the baby – actually, "decided" is not the right word, but leave that. Anyway, once I knew I was keeping it – her – you had a right to know. I see that. I just thought that other things

319

were more important than your right to know. Like Gaby, for instance. I didn't want — I couldn't bear to think —' She bit her lip, looked fixedly out at the river, steadying herself.

'And I'm sorry, too, that it had to be found out. I thought the secret would stop with me and no one else would ever know. I made that decision and I was going to carry it through until the day I died. But one thing I've been thinking, Connor, is that the fact of Sonia doesn't make what we did any worse.'

'I don't know.'

'It just makes it more complicated.'

'It reverberates,' said Connor.

Nancy glanced at him, her brow furrowed. 'You really haven't changed,' she said, almost affectionately.

Connor winced at her tone. 'It means the past can't be left behind,' he said. He was finding it hard to keep his voice even. His breath was coming in unsteady gasps, and he was reminded of how he used to feel before he gave a talk in public. 'We can never be free of it. Perhaps that's always true of the past, however we try to hide from it. But in this case —'

'In this case, it's visited on other people.'

'Yes,' said Connor.

'And then there's Sonia.'

'Sonia,' repeated Connor. He couldn't look at Nancy. He had to stare straight ahead, at the winding river and the layers of bridges, the spires, towers and familiar landmarks of the city. He and Nancy had a daughter, theirs but not theirs. Mentally, he shook himself. 'It seems to me,' he said, in a businesslike voice, 'that what we need to talk about is Sonia. How this affects Gaby, Stefan and Ethan, of course, is not for us to discuss. I've talked everything through with Gaby and we're agreed that soon I will have to tell them, but that's for me, not you.' His voice became harsh. 'You're not in their lives, after all. They don't know you any more.'

'True.'

'But about Sonia we do need to talk.'

'Do you want to see her photograph?'

'What?' He stopped dead and glared at her. 'What's that?'

'I've got a small photograph here with me. Do you want to see it?'

'A photo of Sonia? No. No, I don't.'

'OK.'

'Does she look –?'

'Like you? Yes, I think so. And Gaby recognized she was yours at once, you know.'

'All right, then. Show me.'

'Sure?'

'I said, show me.' Nancy took her wallet out of her bag, unzipped the inner compartment and drew out a passport-sized photograph. She passed it to Connor.

He turned away from her. Dark, spiky hair, a triangular face, a defiant look. He was shocked by the thrill of pride that ran through him. 'Thanks,' he said, handing it back.

'I'm seeing her later today.'

'Today?'

'Yes.'

'I see.'

'Connor, she'll probably want to know about you. She

321

might ask your name, want to meet you. I would if I was her. Have you thought –?'

'Yes.' His voice grated. 'I mean, yes, I've thought about it and, yes, you can tell her about me, if she asks.'

'And if she wants to meet you?'

Connor swallowed. 'Yes,' he said. 'But –'

'But?'

'But not with you.'

Nancy gave a short snort of laughter, and he was catapulted back to the days when he and this woman had been simple friends, and they would sit around a table, the four of them, and Gaby would throw back her head and peal out laughter and Nancy would give her sardonic snort of comic delight, while Stefan beamed beside her. Those were happy days, he thought.

'You mean, you don't want us to be like a little alternative family together? Of course I agree with that.'

'Good.'

'So I can give her your address?'

'Yes.'

'Does –?'

'Does Gaby know of my decision? Of course she does. It was Gaby who insisted on it, in fact. She's being very honourable.'

'I'm sure.'

'Nancy?'

'Yes.'

'Why didn't you tell me?'

'I don't know.'

'You have to say more than that.'

'I don't. I can't. It was so long ago. What's the point

in knowing, anyway? What difference does it make now? It's all over and done with, long ago.'

'It doesn't feel that simple,' he almost shouted. 'You left years ago. You disappeared out of our lives. I thought I'd never see you again, never have to think about what happened. Then all of a sudden – this. Like a bomb in the middle of my placid life, everything blown apart. Everything. And I don't know what's the right thing to do. I've tried to do a thought experiment on myself. Why are you smiling like that? Is it so ridiculous? I've asked myself that if God were looking down on this situation, what would he say was the right thing to do? The ethical thing. But God doesn't seem to know. Should I see Sonia or not? Tell Ethan and Stefan or not? Talk to you and walk with you like this or not? If I behave well to one person, I hurt another. It's as if I'm in a thick fog, wandering around and not knowing where I'm going. Everything's so –' He passed a hand over his face. 'I don't know,' he said eventually. 'I don't know any more. I don't know what I think and I don't know what I feel and I don't know who I am.'

'I'm sorry,' she said gravely, and Connor shrugged.

'Why didn't you have an abortion?' he said, in a weary tone.

'You mean, if I'd had an abortion you wouldn't have to be going through all of this?'

'No, of course not. I just don't understand why. You always used to be vehemently pro-Choice.'

'I still am. Maybe without the vehemence.'

'So?'

'I don't know that, either. I thought I would, but I kept

323

delaying it. I didn't understand it myself. I left it till it was too late for it to be a simple procedure – and then I left it even longer. And then – well, then I went ahead with it because it was the only thing left to do. Perhaps I was punishing myself.'

'But you never wanted to keep it?'

'Her.'

'Her. Never wanted to keep her?'

She wheeled to face him, putting a hand across her stomach as if the memory of her pregnancy was a physical presence inside her. 'What do you think, Connor? Of course I fucking wanted to. Do you have any idea what it feels like to go through a pregnancy and give birth, then give your baby away? The violence of my loss was like – never mind. That's over. I didn't know what else to do, is the real answer. It was your baby. Gaby was the person I loved most in the world. Stefan was the person I thought I loved second best. We'd wrecked all of that – and I didn't know what to do. I was on my own.'

Connor looked at her. The austere face seemed to have fractured, and now he did not feel that she was a stranger any more. He saw the lines on her face and the grey flecking her hair and was filled with a heavy, melancholy affection. He put out a hand and touched her shoulder. 'I'm sorry too,' he said. 'I'm so very, very sorry for all you've been through. And I'm glad I know. In spite of everything, I find I'm glad.'

She took his hand then and they walked along the path together, not saying anything.

He felt her warm fingers between his. 'What time are you meeting her?' he asked at last.

'In about an hour and a half.'

'So soon! Where? Not here?'

He had a vision of the girl seeing them together like this, hand in hand. He let go of her fingers and put his hands back into his pockets.

'No, not here. Can I ask you something?'

'Go on.'

'How's Gaby?'

'She's – I don't know. She's calm.'

'Calm?'

'I know. Not like her, is it? She's calm and kind and practical. And almost, well, pitying. She pities me.'

'Oh!' said Nancy. She bit her lip.

'It makes me feel ashamed.'

'Will you and her – will it be all right?'

'I don't know. Sometimes I think that it was all so long ago, and we've been so good to each other since, how can it not? And sometimes I think that something's been broken and, whatever I do, I can't put it back together. It feels wrong, telling you this.'

'I understand. Sorry, I shouldn't have asked.'

'It's not your fault. I should go now. I have to get to work.'

'Connor?'

'Yes.'

'You're not a bad man, you know.'

'Goodbye,' he said. She could see that there were tears in his eyes. 'I don't know if we'll –'

'No, nor do I. Good luck with everything.'

'And to you. Take care.'

'I did love you,' she said in a rush, as he started to walk away from her, then put her fist into her mouth.

He turned. 'What's that?'

'Nothing,' she managed to say. 'You must go now. Goodbye.'

He set off along the riverbank and she watched as his thin figure, in its dark overcoat, melted into the crowd.

Connor walked until he was sure he was out of sight, then stopped. He had no idea what he was feeling, except that he was sick and empty and tired. He left the river and walked up towards St Paul's, where he stood for a few minutes, at a loss for what he should do next. Perhaps he should go inside and kneel down in the cold, lofty space, bend his head and pray. But he never prayed. He had no God, nor had he ever had. He had had only a belief in himself, ever since he was a small boy striving to escape the grim world his parents had given him. What would he say to God? Make it not have happened, make Gaby love me the way she used to, make Ethan never have to think of me as the man who hurt his mother, make Stefan live a happy life, make me someone else, turn back the clock, undo the past, make it all right in a way that it never can be.

There was a stall selling coffee, and he asked for a cappuccino. When it came he wrapped his hands round the cardboard cup and felt warmth return to his fingers. He lifted the plastic lid and leant over the steam to let it lick his face. Then he shuffled a few paces and sat on a wooden bench in the lee of the cathedral and closed his eyes. He saw Nancy's forty-year-old face and Gaby's. He saw their younger faces. His cheeks were wet and when he felt them with his fingers he discovered he was crying.

The salt tears stung his skin. He put the coffee, half finished, on the ground, and bent forward on the bench with his face in his hands. Tears dripped through his fingers, and his shoulders were shaking. Small whimpers were coming from deep within him, like the first warning sounds of a great quake. The whimpers grew louder and now his whole body was shuddering. He was dimly aware that people would be passing the bench and looking curiously at the well-dressed middle-aged man weeping like a baby. He didn't care. He pressed his head deeper into the cup of his hands and was in his own warm, wet, private darkness. His throat was sore and his chest ached. His eyes hurt and against his closed lids he could still see the faces of those he loved, his own private film of anguish.

'There, there,' someone was saying, more like a rustle of leaves than a voice.

A hand was on his bent head, stroking his hair. For a mad second, he thought it was his mother, comforting him as she never had when he was little. His sobs grew louder.

'There, there.'

At last he lifted his face from his hands and looked around through his watery, bloodshot eyes. A woman was sitting on the bench beside him. She was tiny and ancient, wrapped in a thick, oversized coat tied at the waist with a length of rope and her feet stuffed into moth-eaten slippers. An absurd hat, more like a grubby turban, was perched on her head, and her lined, weathered face reminded Connor of an onion. Her little blue eyes peered at him. 'Hello, dear,' she said. 'You needed to get that out of you.'

'Sorry.'

'When you want to cry, you have to cry or it poisons your insides,' she said. 'Me and Billy have a good weep together sometimes, don't we, Billy?'

Connor stared around, bewildered, then saw a small, scruffy dog sheltering between her legs, its face peering out from between the flaps of her coat.

'Sometimes I sit on this bench all day,' said the woman, 'and no one even looks at me. They walk by me and their eyes go right through me. I'm invisible. They even drop litter at my feet. Once someone threw an apple core and it landed in my lap and they didn't even turn and say sorry. People are very rude nowadays. My name is Mildred May Clegg. I have a name. My mother gave it to me eighty-eight years ago, but there are days when I have to go and stand outside a shop window so I can see my reflection in the glass, just to make sure I'm still there. I say, "Hello, Mildred May." Maybe I wave at myself. People think I'm not right in my head. They walk in a wide circle so they don't come anywhere near me. There's nothing wrong with my head, is there, Billy? There, Billy can tell you. He knows. Dogs see more than people. Billy recognizes when someone's a bad one. He snarls or backs away. He likes you, though. Look, he's wagging his tail, that's a sure sign he thinks you're all right. It doesn't matter what they look like, they can be dressed up all fancy and speak ever so proper, but he can tell what they're like inside. People can't do that, can they? Or not many, anyway. I reckon I can. I've had practice. Years of practice. I used to sing, you know, when I was young. You wouldn't think it, would you? I wasn't always like this. I was a pretty girl and I sang and everyone said I'd go far. Life doesn't turn out the way you think, does it? It was the drink that did for me, or the death. Death first, and then drink. That was the order, though the order's got muddled up since then and, anyway, nobody cares to ask any more. They used to care. They used to say, "Mildred May, you have to pull yourself together." They were probably right. I mean, if you don't pull yourself together quite quickly you stop remembering how to do it. Since then, I've sat on this bench and watched people. It's a bit like watching the river after a bit. Faces flow by, they do, and mostly you don't properly look at them. A tide of humanity,' she said, shaking her head from side to side and winking at him. 'Just a tide passing by.'

Connor stared at her with his throbbing eyes.

'But some you notice. They jump out at you, look into your face, and after that they're inside your head. When I die, a lot of people die with me.'

'Can I get you a cup of coffee?' he asked politely. 'Or something to eat?'

'Billy would like a doughnut from there.' She nodded at the stall where Connor had bought his cappuccino.

'A doughnut for both of you, then?'

'And one for you, young man. You need feeding up. Don't you have a mother?'

'No.'

'Everyone needs a mother. I was a mother once, you know.'

'Were you?'

'My little Danny boy.'

'What happened?' His voice was gentle.

'My father used to tell me that nobody owns anybody else. You're here for a while and then you're gone. Gone without a trace.'

'I'm sorry.'

'It's a vale of tears, my dear. Never you mind.'

'I have a son called Ethan,' Connor said. 'He's nineteen. He's left home now.'

Once again, fat tears began to roll down his cheek.

'An apple one for me, and a jam one for Billy.'

'Very well.'

Connor bought three doughnuts wrapped in paper napkins and returned to the bench. He sat down beside Mildred May, close enough that their thighs touched and he could smell the sweet stench of alcohol on her. 'Here.'

The old woman took the jam doughnut and held it out. Billy crept from the shelter of her coat and grabbed it before retreating again. Then she tore her own in half and posted the first portion into her pursed mouth, making a smacking sound as she ate. She pulled a glass bottle full of clear liquid out of one of her pockets and took a gulp, then put it away again. Connor took a bite of his own doughnut. It had been many years since he'd eaten one and its fried, doughy sweetness comforted him.

'There,' said Mildred May. 'Shall I sing for you now?'

'That would be a treat,' said Connor.

'*Quid pro quo.* That's what I say. You gave us doughnuts.'

She stood up, scattering Billy from the tails of her vast coat, and turned so that she was facing him, ignoring the glances of passers-by, their sneers and sniggers. Placing one hand on her heart, she took a deep breath, opened her mouth and began to sing. Her voice trembled and sometimes almost disappeared before returning louder than before; her eyes shone. Billy wailed at her side. She sang 'My Bonny Lies Over The Ocean' and then 'Foggy Foggy Dew'. She sang 'Early One Morning' in a quavery, broken-backed high pitch, before looping round again to 'My Bonny', her voice giving up by now. They were all in their own ways songs about absence and heartbreak. Connor gazed at her diminutive, rotund shape; her crinkled, battered face folded round the blue slits of her eyes, the puckered mouth in a choirboy's 'O' of rapture. She lifted her dirty hands into the air and gazed past him, at some distant point only she could see. Perhaps she was on a stage, a young woman again with the world before her, or perhaps she was singing to her lost Danny boy. Perhaps she had never been a singer and never had a son, never had the life she'd lost.

When she finished, Connor clapped loudly and she gave a little bow. Behind them a group of teenage girls were giggling helplessly. Connor and Mildred May ignored them.

'Thank you,' he said, standing up, taking both her hands in his and holding them there. 'That was a great pleasure.'

'We all have to spread what cheer we can,' she said. She was panting and there were red blotches on her cheek. 'In this cold and ragged world.'

'Indeed,' he said. 'Can I come and visit you again?'

'You'll find me and Billy here most days,' she said, 'on and off. Don't wait to be invited.'

'I won't, you can be sure of that.'

He bent down to kiss her on both pouchy cheeks. She lifted her hand and pushed his hair away from his forehead. 'You'll do very nicely,' she said.

'Will I?'

'Of course. Won't he, Billy?'

Twenty-nine

Stefan was sitting in his kitchen under the naked bulb with a giant sandwich in front of him into which he had stuffed any ingredient he had found in his fridge: chorizo sausage past its sell-by date, mozzarella (ditto) and Cheddar, a few lettuce leaves, tomatoes, mayonnaise, pickle, mustard and some aged gherkins. But he had taken one vast, oozing bite out of it, then pushed it away for later. He was practising his knots. He had about twenty smooth, thin lengths of cream-coloured rope, whipped at the end to prevent fraying, and was tying them, one by one, into different shapes. He had started with the simplest, and they lay in a line beneath his sandwich: the overhand knot, the sheet knot, the figure-of-eight, the reef knot and the halyard. These he could almost do with his eyes shut; the challenge was to make them as pleasingly supple and symmetrical as possible. Now he was practising his bowline: he formed a loop a short distance from the end of the rope, passed the end through the loop as though making a half-hitch, then pulled it round the standing end and back through the loop. There, it was easily done and he laid it alongside the other knots.

He opened his can of beer and licked away the plug of foam before taking a warm gulp. The clove hitch, the two half-hitches, the sheepshank – he often had trouble with that one. A blackwall hitch and a rolling hitch and a slippery hitch, a fisherman's knot and a fisherman's bend, a lariat loop, a lark's head. This was the way time ticked by. One by one, he laid them before him. A marlinspike and an intricate surgeon's knot. He finished with an improved blood knot, for which he used two very thin pieces of rope, almost string. He twisted the strands together ten or twelve times, separated the central twist, wriggled the two ends through the space, then tugged them sharply. He sighed in satisfaction at the neatness of the plait before him, then placed it carefully at the bottom of his grid of knots.

Picking up his sandwich with both hands to prevent its contents spilling everywhere, he opened his mouth as wide as possible, then took a determined bite. He swilled down a bit more beer and picked up the book he was reading, taking care not to spread grease over its pages. When Gaby read a book she would open it wide so that its spine cracked. You could always tell when she'd had a particular book – it would be scuffed and stained and its pages turned down to mark particular passages. She read books the way she ate meals, greedily and with avid attention. If he tried, he was sure that he could chart her life so far through images of her deep in a book: up a tree; sitting on the lawn with her legs apart and a novel propped on her knee; lying on sofas or snuggled into armchairs, every so often putting out a hand and feeling for a chocolate; at a table, her head cupped in her hands; in a bath, the steam softening the pages. She would lose herself while reading. You could call her name several times before she heard and looked up, as in a stupor, her eyes unfocused. He thought of his sister and frowned.

Something was bothering her. He wished she would tell him her troubles, not try to protect him.

The sandwich was too large, too messy and the bread was stale. Stefan left it and went into the sitting room, which also served as his study. Books were in heaps everywhere – he could never go into a shop without buying several; he pottered for hours in second-hand shops, rooting out forgotten volumes of essays or remaindered novels from before the war, and he never could bring himself to throw books away. There were piles of scrawled-upon leaves of lined paper on and around his desk. He reminded himself that he had essays to mark, emails to answer, journals to catch up on, a meeting to prepare for, a lecture to write and a paper he needed to research on radical religion in the Middle Ages. He lived much of his life in the past, in a world of words and ideas, and sometimes he wondered what it would be like to deal with people and objects, the mess of everyday life. He thought of Connor pressing his hands against a patient's stomach, or probing flesh for an area of pain. He thought of all his family looking after their children as babies, spooning gunk into a small mouth and wiping away drool with the corner of a bib, or changing a nappy, deftly gripping two ankles in one hand and lifting the squirming body, wiping the red, wrinkled bottom and smothering it with thick cold cream. He'd done it a few times, of course, especially with Ethan when Gaby was so ill, but he'd been horrified, incompetent and scared of his own size and clumsiness. Nancy had pushed him away. He could hear her voice now: 'You're hopeless,' she'd said, laughing at him. 'Let me do it.'

He knew that he was hopeless in many ways. He was vague and dreamy and the practical arrangements of his life floated out of his head, like so many dissolving clouds; he broke things and spilt things and forgot where he was supposed to be. He could tie knots and read charts and sail a boat round the point, avoiding jagged rocks, but he tripped over his shoelaces and lost his keys. He could read twelfth-century texts and understand the life of a miller in Somerset, but he couldn't understand the lives of his colleagues – their rivalries, affairs and subtle intrigues.

The phone rang, and it was Gaby. 'Stefan? I didn't wake you, did I?'

'Wake me? No. What time is it, anyway?'

'Half past eleven.'

'I thought it was about nine. Funny, these long dark evenings – you lose track of time. Well, I do. How are you? Are you all right?'

'Fine – well, OK. There's something I want to talk to you about. Connor and I want to talk to you about, actually.'

'All right, then.'

'Not now, not on the phone. Do you want to come round to ours or shall we come to you?'

'You mean tonight?'

'No, it's not urgent like that. It's just – well, something.'

Stefan glanced round the room. He thought of his kitchen, in which the only calm spot was the grid of knots on the table.

'I'll come to yours, shall I? When?'

'Are you busy tomorrow evening?'

'I have a feeling I am. There's a supper I was invited to. Hang on, let me look in my diary. Where's my diary? I can't find it. I was sure I put it – but hang on, let me have a look in my briefcase. Here we are. No, I can't do tomorrow, I'm afraid – though I could always make an excuse.'

'No, you mustn't do that. How about the next day?'

'Thursday? I think so. There's a word scrawled on that day but I can't for the life of me read it. What would it be? Persephone or something? No. Anyway, I'm sure I can come then.'

'Seven o'clock?'

'I might be a bit later. It says here I have to be in York that afternoon. Make it seven thirty.'

'Seven thirty, then. We can have a bite to eat.'

'Right.'

'Stefan?'

'Mm?'

'I just want you to know that I love you very much.'

'Oh – well, yes. Thank you. Um, you know that I –'

But she was gone.

Thirty

<u>18 November</u>

When I got back today it was already dark. It gets dark so early now, and light so late. I hate it. I spent the train journey just sitting there, with my face pressed to the window, watching the sun sink, then disappear. The horizon was a kind of mauve and there was a very pale moon, like a stencil in the sky. I looked at the fields going past, the houses and the cars and the trees and the sudden canals and the footpaths snaking their way into the distance – and gradually it became dark. Once, a train going in the same direction drew level with mine, and for a few minutes it was as if both trains had come to a stop. I stared in through the lighted window of the other compartment and a girl of about my age was sitting reading a book. She looked up and saw me staring at her and for a moment our eyes locked and then she smiled, as if we were friends and would see each other again one day, and looked away again. It was really strange.

I had imagined I would spend the journey thinking about the day I'd had, but I didn't. Instead, I remembered things from the past. Odd things that I hadn't even known I remembered, like sitting in the garden with a girl called Kelly from primary school, and pretending we were dentists and that bricks were faces; we spent hours poking at their surfaces with teaspoons, telling them they had to be brave. Or going swimming with Dad at the seaside; I don't know how old I was but I do remember that he walked into the water backwards, holding my hands and the waves broke against his legs. Or being ill once with flu and lying in bed feeling hot and dizzy and very strange; the room seemed to be tipping and I kept thinking there were these slimy boulders shuddering on the floor. I had ulcers all over the inside of my mouth. Mum made soup and I had to suck it through a straw, and she kept telling me to drink lime cordial. I remember her hand against my burning forehead: cool and soft, smelling of soap and hand lotion.

I don't know why I'm telling you any of this. None of it matters to you, does it? Maybe I'm trying to say all that I felt after I left you, because you're receding and I'm empty of you, and scared, and trying to get you back. But you should know that now I've met you you're no longer in my head like you used to be. You're outside me, a real person, your own self, flesh and blood. My flesh and blood.

When we arrived at Stratford, I nearly didn't get off the train. I thought I could stay where I was and be taken north to all the places I've never been that are just names on the loudspeaker, and go on staring out of the window until we arrived at a destination. But of course I did get off; I always knew I would. I walked home from the station, even though Mum had said I should call her and she would collect me, no matter what the time. I didn't feel ready to say anything to her. I didn't want to describe the day or somehow find a way of giving it a meaning. I didn't know what its meaning was. I just wanted to sit huddled up on the sofa with a blanket round me and a mug of warm soup, and watch mindless TV and not say anything and not have anyone looking at me in a concerned kind of way, or every so often laying a hand on my knee.

Though the day had been sunny, the night was cold and calm. There wasn't any wind. Usually I don't notice things like that, but tonight it was so still and quiet it was as if I had stepped out of my normal world and into a black-and-white photograph – or not quite black-and-white: the moon, which had been so pale, was low and huge and a lovely yellow colour, like the kind of round yellow moon you draw when you're a child.

So, anyway, I walked home very slowly. Although it was quite dark, it wasn't really late, yet there was hardly anyone around. My footfalls echoed as I went. Goldie gets scared when we're walking at night and no one's about, but I don't mind it. I like the dark. It feels secret and protective. You can hide in it. You can wrap yourself up in it like a velvet cloak and feel safe. I stopped at the bottom of our road and looked up it. Everything that was so familiar also seemed strange.

When I got to the house I looked in at the front window and Mum was sitting on the sofa staring at the TV, which wasn't turned on. Just sitting and staring. I wanted to cry at her face, which was so sad. But she must have felt me there, because she turned towards me and I saw her expression change. She made herself be all cheery and calm, as if it was just another day and I was coming home from school or some-thing – which is what I would have been doing, of course, if I hadn't been to see you. She stood up and tugged her skirt straight, then wiped her palms on it. I knew she had probably been sitting like that for hours, waiting for me to phone her. And I knew, too, that she would never tell me all the things she had been thinking while she was waiting like that. Goldie's mother tells her everything – about how her dad shouts at her when he's drunk, or how she was bullied at the office or how she's worried about money and doesn't know what she's going to do. Goldie knows about the boyfriends her mother had before she met Goldie's father. She says her mother tries to treat her like a friend, when what she really wants is to be treated like a daughter – scolded and comforted and given rules she can keep or break. Mum never tells me stuff like that, or shares her worries with me. Now that I think of it, I've hardly ever seen her cry. She protects me, so when I saw her face tonight, it was like being given a glimpse of a whole other person.

She came to the door wearing her cheerful face and gave me a hug – but not one that went on too long or that would make me feel smothered. I knew she was being careful to behave exactly right, and she'd probably been planning it while she sat in front of the blank TV. Then she said that there was a ginger cake just out of the oven and would I like a cup of tea and a slice of it. I didn't have the heart to tell her I wasn't at all hungry, so I sat in the kitchen and she made tea and chatted about this and that so I didn't have to speak. Then she put the cake, which was still damp and warm from the oven, in front of me and poured me a mug of tea, and sat opposite me and said, 'Do you want to tell me how it went, then?'

I didn't know what to say, where to begin. I prodded the cake and put a few crumbs in my mouth.

She said: 'You don't have to tell me anything if you don't want to. There's no way I want to pester you. As long as you know that I'm here if you feel like it. There's nothing you can't tell me, nothing that will offend me.' Then she got up, kissed my cheek, and started wiping all the surfaces in this busy way, although everything was perfectly clean. I fed the cake to George, who was under the table, and I'm sure Mum saw but she didn't say anything, except 'Why don't you have a long soak in the bath?'

I want to tell her everything, but how do you discuss your mother with your mother?

So I had a bath. I could smell something cooking from the bathroom. Tunafish bake – that's what I always asked for when I felt in need of comfort and that was what she was making now. Then I heard the front door open and shut again: Dad was home. I heard him and Mum talking together downstairs, and although I couldn't make out what they were saying, I knew they would be talking about me.

Later I went into the kitchen and said I couldn't talk about it yet, but that wasn't because I didn't want to – just because I felt so tired and empty that there wasn't anything inside me to say. I said it had been fine and that we would talk about it soon. And that I loved her very, very much and that she and Dad would always be my mother and father. Nothing would ever change that.

What is there to say?

That you have my face, my eyes, and when I look at you I can see me there? It sounds stupid and obvious but I've never had that feeling before, and it made me feel I'd missed something huge. I wanted to cry – not just for myself, but for Mum and Dad for even thinking that way, when they've tried to give me everything a parent can give a child. The one thing they couldn't give me was that primal sense of the self – the self that's handed down from generation to generation, continued, replicated. I grew up feeling unique and alone, a person who'd started from zero, and suddenly I saw that I was a link in a great chain, stretching back into the past and – if I have kids myself, which I hope I do – forward into the future. But

Mum and Dad weren't part of that. I was linked to you instead.

That you told me the whole story? I hadn't really expected you to, and I didn't even know if I wanted to hear exactly how I came about and why I was given away. But I asked, and you told me. You must have decided in advance what you were going to say, because you talked for what seemed like ages. You made what happened into a story, with a beginning, a middle and an end. A friendship, a brief, guilt-ridden affair with the friend's husband, a parting – and me. That's what I came from, that intense and tragic mess, which damaged everyone: the friend, her husband, her brother, you. You were calm and factual and didn't try to appeal for my sympathy and I liked that: it was honourable and it showed you were thinking about me and not yourself. At the same time, it made me uncomfortable, because you were behaving the way a mother should, and I don't want to think of you as my mother.

That I have a father? I mean, of course I have a father some-where, but on the birth certificate it said 'Father Unknown' and I assumed I'd never find out who he was. But, again, I asked you and you told me. It was as simple as that. I have a name, an age, an occupation. I have an address and a phone number. I know about his life and also that he looks like me. Or I look like him. His hair, his brows, his ex-pression. He knows about me now. He's waiting for me to get in touch.

That I have a half-brother? Oh, God, that makes me feel peculiar, half glad and half full of fear, I'm not sure why. You haven't seen him for eighteen and a half years. You don't even know if he remembers your name and he knows nothing of me, but you think that one day soon he will. Poor thing. Poor all of you. Have I done wrong?

That I don't know what I thought of you? You were so cool and self-possessed when we met, but I thought that was maybe because you were being honourable, if that makes sense. In fact, that's the strongest impression I took away with me – that you had a kind of integrity and were someone that people would trust, even if they didn't particularly like you. That you wouldn't let people down but kept your word. That you said what you believed and didn't mind what people thought of you. A strong woman. A bit hard, maybe. A bit sad. But perhaps I'm inventing that because I know what you went through. I could see how it felt so painful for someone like you to behave like that, to betray your friend and your boyfriend in the way you did. You must have felt terrible.

What did you think of me? Did you realize I was so nervous I could hardly speak? My tummy turned to liquid and my tongue was sticking to the roof of my mouth and my throat went dry as chalk. Did you know I wanted to hug you, hit you, run away? I wanted you to be proud of me, and I desperately wanted not to care. Did you see that I was trying not to cry? It wasn't anything you said in particular, it was everything. The sheer fact of us. I looked at my hands on the table and then at your hands and they were the same. I looked into your eyes and they were my eyes. I listened to your voice and it was telling me my story. I've been waiting for this moment for so long, for almost the whole of my life, and now it's come and I don't know what to do with it any more. I thought it would feel different from this.

It's half past three in the morning, the dead hours. I've been writing this for ages. My hand feels cramped and my fingers are stained with ink. I've come to the end but I don't want to stop, because when I do I'm alone with myself and it's hours till morning and I don't know what to do. I can't sleep, not tonight. I don't want to dream.

Thirty-one

Ethan left his tutorial and unlocked his bike. It was half past three and he hadn't had much sleep the night before – his habit of binge-working was continuing. Yet he didn't feel tired any more: rather, he was full of a restless, churning energy. At six o'clock he had arranged to meet friends in the pub, and he didn't know what to do with himself until then. In other circumstances, he would have tracked down Harry and persuaded him into a game of squash – but he didn't feel like seeing Harry and, besides, he was very likely with Lorna, and he most certainly didn't want to see Lorna, not when she was with Harry, anyway, and not after their last meeting. His cheeks burnt when he thought of it, and his heart pounded uncomfortably hard.

He had to get away. He got on to his bike, and started to pedal, although he had no idea where he was headed, and he didn't care. All he knew was that the wind blew into his face and his legs ached from the effort. Before long, he found that he had left Exeter behind him and was headed into open countryside. If he looked back, he could see the city in the distance, with its soaring cathedral and its widening river, and he found it strange to think of himself there, pacing its narrow streets, feverish with unrequited love. The light was thickening and he could feel that soon dusk would fall. Already, the vivid greens of the fields and the rich golds and browns of the trees had become muted in the fading day. He was wearing a light jacket and no gloves and was starting to feel cold, although his face glowed with effort.

He took lefts and rights at random, cycling at full speed down narrow lanes with hedges high on either side, bending over his handlebars, seeing only the road in front of him. Fields and farms flashed past. Woolly sheep and cattle with long horns. Cars passing in the other direction. Signposts signalling the way to villages with unfamiliar names. Crossroads where he stopped, then turned in whichever direction looked emptiest, wildest, most full of promise.

At last he came to a halt and dismounted. His eyes were watering in the wind and he could no longer ignore how dark it was, or how cold he felt. His fingers were white claws from where they had clenched the handlebars and he blew on them to warm them, stamping his feet. He had absolutely no idea of where he was, not even of the direction in which he was going or of how many miles he had come. His watch told him it was nearly six o'clock: at this moment, he should be walking along a well-lit, populated street towards the pub to meet his friends. There were already pale stars low in the sky and the sun had sunk below the horizon. Cursing, he fumbled in his pannier, brought out his mobile and tried to turn it on, but he had failed to recharge it and the battery had run out.

It seemed to him that he was in the middle of nowhere. The lane was sunken, the hedges high and obscuring, so he could get no sense of where it came from or led to, or remember how many lefts and rights he had taken to lead him to this remote spot. He pushed his bike along the road until he reached a gate, which revealed only a patchwork of fields that rolled away to the horizon.

He remounted his bike and cycled in the direction from which he had come, but the network of lanes was like a maze and after several minutes he felt almost sure that he had looped back on himself and was as far away from the main road to Exeter as he had ever been. What was more, it was becoming increasingly difficult to see. The landscape around him had lost all colour and was a dark grey; trees were massed shapes in the hedgerow; the road twisted away from him.

'I'm lost,' he said out loud, and felt unaccountably contented. He biked fast up a small hill and at the top propped his bike against a stump and climbed on to the gate beside it. He eased his cigarette packet out of his jeans pocket and, after several failed attempts, lit one. He took a deep drag, then let the smoke curl out into the twilight and dissolve. As he sat there, cold and tired, he was filled all of a sudden with a piercing happiness that was, at the same time, a deep melancholy. He felt that he was at the heart of life's meaning, where happiness and sadness met, and where the sense of one's self blurs – and yet he knew he was being ridiculous, infantile and was overwrought.

From where he was perched on the cold bar of the gate, he realized he could see lights twinkling in the shallow valley below. He threw his cigarette on to the damp grass, jumped off the gate, and set off once more to ask for help and directions. It was oddly hard to find the source of the lights, for they disappeared as he descended the hill, and it was only after a couple of wrong turns up muddy tracks that led nowhere that he found himself cycling up a driveway towards a building with lights glowing from the ground floor. There was a tractor with vast wheels and several pieces of farm machinery in the muddy stretch of land in front of the house and to one side a shelter with a corrugated-iron roof, so Ethan assumed it was a farm, but if so it was small and run-down. A dog barked ferociously as he approached, then came belting out, a large shape with white teeth and shining eyes.

'Good dog,' he said nervously, braking to a halt and dismounting.

The shape lunged towards him and stood a few inches off, growling and giving intermittent, sinister barks of warning. Ethan did not move.

'Who's there?' called a voice.

'Sorry to bother you,' Ethan said, though he could still see no one, 'but I got a bit –'

'What's that? Come on out of the shadows and let me see you.'

Ethan took a small step towards the house. The dog bared its teeth and let out a truly menacing snarl. 'Your dog. Do you think you could call him off?'

'Him? He wouldn't hurt a baby.'

Ethan took another step. The dog half squatted as if to spring. 'Good dog,' he said again, in a high, scared coo. 'Good dog.'

'Oh, for God's sake. Come here, Tyson.'

'Tyson? As in –'

'Don't worry, he's a softie at heart.' The man who came loping out of the yard was tall and thin with long

349

white hair that blew back from his face and sunken, pitted cheeks. 'Here, Tyson,' he said sharply, and yanked the dog by its collar.

'Thanks. Sorry. I'm not used to dogs.'

'What can I do for you?'

'I've lost my way,' said Ethan. 'I need to get back to Exeter, but there don't seem to be any signposts – or not to anywhere I've ever heard of, anyway.'

'You've come a fair way.'

'I know.'

'And it's dark.'

'Yes. I didn't realize how late it was.'

'Come in,' said the man, and swung round, letting go of the dog, which scuttled towards the yard.

'But I just wanted to know the way back.'

The man didn't respond, simply led Ethan through the yard, still wheeling his bike.

'Really,' said Ethan, 'it's very kind of you, but if you'd just tell me . . .'

'Now then,' said the farmer, as he opened the front door on to a small utility room full of old jackets, muddy boots and several torches ranged along a shelf. 'Lean your bike there and step inside.'

'I don't think . . .' began Ethan, wondering if he'd stumbled into some spooky fairy story '. . . I don't think I really have the time to . . .'

But he was inside and the door was shut behind him.

'Look at the state of you,' said the farmer. 'In you come.'

The kitchen looked as if it had been last decorated in the fifties and not touched since. It had a low ceiling. The walls were brownish-yellow and Ethan couldn't tell if that was the way they had been painted, or if it was the result of years of smoke and grease. A small, antiquated Aga was against one wall; a clatter of pans hung above it and several pairs of socks were arranged along its drying pole. A small fire burnt in the grate.

'I'll put the kettle on, shall I? You take the weight off your feet and sit by that fire now. Put some warmth back into you.'

'Really, I don't want anything to drink,' said Ethan, hovering by the kitchen door, with the dog eyeing him suspiciously from across the room. 'And I don't want to sit down. I just want directions back to the main Exeter road.'

'Reginald,' said the white-haired man. 'And you are?'

'Ethan.'

'You're not from round here, then, Ethan?'

'No, I –'

'You'll be from London, I reckon.'

'Yes, that's right.'

'My wife was from London. Enfield.'

'Oh,' said Ethan.

'She died five years ago. Cancer. She never took any notice of the pains and by the time she went to the doctor it was too late to do anything. Don't look so anxious. I'm going to make you something to warm you up, then give you a lift to Exeter in my truck. How's that?'

'No! You don't need to do that. Honestly, I just need directions. I certainly don't want to put you to any bother.'

'Bother?'

'Yes.'

'What do you think I'm going to do with my evening?'

'Well, I –'

'Wait for it to go by until it's bedtime, that's what. To have a young body like you in my kitchen adds a bit of life, even if you do look like something the cat brought in.'

'It's very kind of you,' said Ethan, weakly. He moved across to the fire and sat before it, holding his hands out to the warmth of the flame. The dog slunk over and settled by his feet. 'I really am grateful.'

'Do as you would be done by, that's what I say. If I was wandering round like a lost soul I hope someone would do the same for me.'

'The kindness of strangers,' said Ethan. As clearly as if she was in the room with him, he could hear his mother's voice as he uttered the words.

Reginald looked at him. 'That's it,' he said. 'That's the thing.'

'Thank you,' said Ethan. He stroked the dog's flank cautiously and Tyson lifted his head blearily, then laid it on his paws once more.

The heat was licking one cheek and his fireside leg felt hot under his jeans. Reginald put a mug of strong tea on the arm of his chair and he took it between both hands. Tiredness settled over him.

'Now then, bacon and eggs or scrambled eggs – or I've got a bit of ham in the fridge?'

'No, really . . .' He saw Reginald's worn face. 'Scrambled eggs, then. Just a bit, though.'

'I never cooked while my wife was alive. Now I like it. It gives a shape to the end of the day, cooking. Especially when you're on your own. I can do all sorts. I made steak pie the other day. I had to give most of it to Tyson, though. You don't need much for one.'

He pulled a pan on to the hob and put in a pat of butter, which sizzled briefly.

'Do you have children?' Ethan heard himself say, out of the muggy tiredness that was wrapped round him.

'A son in America.' Reginald cracked two eggs into the pan and stirred them briskly. 'The trick is to cook them slowly. I read that in a colour supplement. Imagine, me reading recipes in a colour supplement! He's in something to do with advertising. I don't understand it at all. He calls me once a week and sometimes he comes over and I've been there a few times, though I prefer him coming to me. He's got two children and a stepson. They're good kids, but they grow up so fast nowadays, don't they? And they have so many things. Computers and bicycles and TVs in their bedrooms and drum kits and – toast with your eggs?'

'Just eggs, thanks.'

'They don't taste right unless they're on hot buttered toast.'

'Toast, then.'

'I never knew I was happy until I wasn't any more.'

'I'm sorry,' said Ethan, awkwardly. If Gaby were here, she would know what to say and do in this room that was thick with loneliness.

'You just take it for granted. People think it doesn't matter when old people die. Not that she was that old, only sixty-eight. That's not old these days, is it?'

'No, I guess not.'

'We had a good-enough marriage. Ups and downs. Now I think of all the things I didn't tell her.'

'I'm sure that she –'

'I haven't cut my hair since the day she died.'

'Really? But why?'

'I don't know. I used to get it cut once a month, without fail. My son keeps telling me I ought to get it cut. He thinks I look – what does he say? Disreputable. Unkempt, like an old tramp. It makes him worry about me.'

'I like it,' said Ethan, on surer ground now.

'You do?'

'You look cool.'

Reginald gave a wheezing little laugh.

'Nobody's ever called me cool before.'

'Like a rock star,' said Ethan. 'Or the Ancient Mariner.'

'Well. I'll have to tell my son that. Here, your eggs are ready.'

'You could tie it back in a ponytail sometimes, if it gets in the way.'

'A ponytail?'

'Yes.'

'Hmm.'

'Or you could grow a little goatee.'

'What, like a beard?'

'Yeah, on your chin, here. These eggs are great.'

'Not done too much?'

'No.'

'Or not enough?'

'No, they're perfect. Just what I needed.'

'You weren't properly dressed for a bike ride.'

'I wasn't thinking properly.'

'Girlfriend trouble?'

'Yes.' He fed himself a forkful of egg. 'Or no. She's not even my girlfriend. Just a girl.'

'You're sweet on her.'

'So sweet my teeth ache.'

'Your teeth ache!' Once again, Reginald gave a chuckle and his weathered face creased into a map of all his smiles and frowns.

'I'm like my mother. I can't step back and take a long view. I'm no good at waiting for things to pass. I feel I have to do something *now* or I'll go mad.'

'What can you do?'

'That's it – nothing. Except cycle very fast until I'm completely lost.'

'So here you are.'

'Here I am. Can I use your bathroom?'

'Up the stairs on your left.'

Ethan put his plate on the floor by the chair and heaved himself up. The stairs were steep and narrow, the carpet threadbare. He was struck by the oddity of being in a stranger's house, far from anywhere familiar, with night falling outside and the wind blowing over the moors. And when he looked at his face in the cracked oval mirror above the sink, he was unfamiliar to himself: young and distressed, with anxious eyes.

On his way down, he glanced into the living room on the other side of the stairway. 'I see you've got a piano,' he called into the kitchen.

'My wife used to play a bit,' said Reginald, joining him by the stairs. 'Just simple tunes. It's not been touched for years. Do you play?'

'I try to.'

'Do you want to have a go now?'

'No, no!' said Ethan, but he wandered into the dingy living room, which had a chilly, unused air, and lifted the lid. It had dust all over it. He ran his fingers over the yellowing keys of the upright piano. Several didn't work, only gave a dull plonk as he depressed them. The rest were tinny and out of tune. He sat down on the stool and picked out the first few notes of the Intermezzo by Schumann, which he'd played for his grade-eight exam two years ago. If he'd been asked whether he still knew the piece, he would have said he didn't – but his fingers remembered it long after his brain had forgotten, in the same way that he had remembered the words of Dr Seuss only as he had said them.

Something touched him about the thought of this ropy little piano standing unopened for years, in a room that itself was clearly unused for months on end. Probably the last fingers to have touched the keys were those of Reginald's dead wife. What had she played? Simple tunes, Reg had said. Ethan's fingers drifted out of the Inter-mezzo, into 'My Old Man Said Follow The Van' and then, before the chirpy melody had properly taken hold, 'How Many Roads Must A Man Walk Down'. He stopped abruptly, closed the piano lid, using the tail of his shirt to wipe away the dust, and stood up. 'Do you want to go now?' he asked, as he went back into the kitchen.

'I could make us some more tea.'

'I ought to be getting back,' said Ethan, trying not to see the need in the old man's eyes.

'It's as you wish.'

Ethan bent down and stroked Tyson's muzzle. The dog looked up at him, then sank his head back on his paws. 'He is a softie, after all.'

'I told you. You shouldn't judge by appearances.'

'It's been very kind of you.'

'You can come again, if you want.'

'Thank you,' muttered Ethan, knowing that he wouldn't and already feeling guilty.

'I'm usually here in the evenings.'

'Right.'

'When you're feeling blue about the girl that makes your teeth hurt.'

'I hope I won't be,' laughed Ethan. 'They say time heals everything.'

'They do.'

'Don't you agree?'

'Time and whisky.'

'I'll remember that.'

'Time and whisky and keeping busy. You have to keep busy. Don't stop. It doesn't really matter what you're doing, just do it the best you can and the hardest you can.'

'Right.'

'Chocolate's good, too.'

'Chocolate.'

'It comforts you. And baths – long, hot baths.'

'Chocolate, whisky, baths and being busy.'

'Yup. You have to find ways of filling the time. When my wife died, I spent the first few months waiting for time to go by. Every morning I'd wake early, and I was looking out over the day and it was a desert. It stretched ahead with nothing in it except flatness and grief, and I didn't know how to get across it. I didn't even think to call it grieving – all I knew was that she'd died and now I had to get on with it on my own. One day and then the next and the next. What did they mean, all these days, going on and on and I couldn't see the end? When I was young, I used to long for time to relax and do nothing, like you now, and when I had it, I found it was horrible. All the things you do together and take for granted. Habits that used to irritate you. Who makes the tea in the morning. Who washes the dishes. Who takes the dog out at night. How thick you spread your marmalade. Which bit of the paper you read first. What you both remember about the past. Silly jokes. Getting on with little things together. Being in the room and not having to talk. Making arrangements. Even the little squabbles are part of it. When all of that goes, there's this great big space you have to fill up. And not just with memories and tears.'

They stood by the door, looking at each other.

'So you have to keep busy,' said Ethan, lamely. He wished he could think of the right words, the ones that were like a thick blanket on a cold day, sun in winter, cool running water in the endless desert that Reginald had described.

'And have a dog,' said Reginald, recovering, trying to smile. 'Dogs are good for lonely old men like me.'

'Dogs, being busy, whisky, chocolate, long baths,' said Ethan. He put his hand on the door knob. 'And growing your hair, maybe.'

'And that thing you said.'

'That thing?'

'The kindness of strangers.'

'Yes.'

'Come on, then, let's be getting you back. You need a good night's sleep.'

When he reached his room, he didn't see the note that had been pushed under his door – just a scrap of paper torn out of the back of a diary. It was half hidden under the pile of notes he'd been working on from the night before. So he didn't read, '7.30 p.m.: I came to see you but you were out – if you want to see me, please call a.s.a.p. Lorna xxx.' He stumbled into his bed, pulled the pillow across his sore eyes and plunged into sleep, like a patient going under before surgery, sinking into a deep shaft of unconsciousness.

Thirty-two

Stefan knew something was wrong as soon as he stepped in through the front door and saw how tidy everything was. That wasn't like Gaby. Even after Connor had thoroughly cleaned a room, she managed to put her mark on it at once – maybe a scarf trailing across the floor, shoes left at the bottom of the stairs, the contents of a bag emptied on to the kitchen table, mugs unwashed on the mantelpiece. It was as if blank surfaces bothered her and she had to mess them up, just a bit, to feel comfortable. But this evening, the living room was immaculate and in the kitchen everything was clean and ordered. The orange and bronze chrysanthemums that Stefan had brought stood on the bare table. Even the fridge, when Gaby pulled open its door to bring out a bottle of white wine, was half empty and pristine. It felt as if Connor and Gaby were going abroad for a long while and had left the house ready for strangers to occupy.

'Are you going away?' he asked.

Gaby looked startled. 'I don't think so.'

'It's so tidy.'

'Oh – that. I know. It's surprising, isn't it? Wine?'

'Please.'

At first, Gaby had planned to be out when Stefan arrived. She thought it might be easier for Connor to talk about what had happened without her present, and perhaps it would be easier for Stefan as well. Yet what had happened had involved her as well as him. She was part of the story. And she wanted to be there to comfort Stefan if that was what he needed. Connor had always wanted her to be there – not to make things easier for him, though, rather the opposite. He seemed intent on not sparing himself, like a medieval flagellant welcoming pain. So she had returned home from work to the unfamiliarly tidy house, hung her coat on its hook in the hallway, rather than slinging it across a chair as she normally did, and waited for the two men to arrive. Connor had said he would cook, though Gaby couldn't imagine how anyone would eat a proper meal this evening. She felt both hollow and nauseous, as she had for several weeks now. Her clothes hung off her and her face, which usually glowed with health and vigour, was thin. Sometimes she would stand in front of the mirror and be shocked by the middle-aged woman who looked back. She felt furious with her appearance – she was like someone who had suffered, like a hollow-cheeked victim of a disaster. That wasn't her at all, to lose her greed and her delight. She tried to continue as before, eating chocolate in the bath, making herself bowls of pasta that she couldn't finish, pouring large glasses of wine that she pushed away. She painted her toenails, daubed red on her lips, hung jangly earrings on her lobes, wore her most colourful clothes and ridiculous shoes. But it couldn't disguise the change in her.

Connor had arrived back with salmon fillets and purple-sprouting broccoli. He'd kissed her cheek and asked about her day. She had made him a cup of Earl

Grey and asked about his. They were very polite with each other, considerate and self-conscious. While he was slicing potatoes thinly and layering them in a dish with salt, black pepper and knobs of butter, she went into the garden, because she didn't want to sit and watch him in the way that she used to – quizzing him, mocking him, flirting with him, making him feel foolish and warm.

Outside, it was dark and cold. It had been a beautiful day, one in a long, shimmering string of beautiful days, and now it was a still night, full of stars. Ethan had once told her something about how the night sky proved that the universe was infinite but bounded, because if it wasn't, all that we would see would be dazzling light. She hadn't understood that then, and didn't now. She tried now to make out the Great Bear or the Seven Sisters, but couldn't, only the North Star, just above the chimneys and trees. Looking up at the sky always made her feel vertiginous and – in a tranquil kind of way – scared. She asked herself what point there was in the frantic emotions of the past few weeks if in the end she was just a pinprick on a dot in a galaxy that was itself negligible. All the scrabbling around, the desperate search for happiness, meaning and union – while around us the millions of stars shine on, implacably distant and remote. We desire and love and hate and quarrel and deceive and weep – and in a short while we're gone and our lives leave no trace, and all those tears and all that laughter might never have happened. Even those who know us forget us soon enough, and then they are snuffed out in their turn. How strange, to care so passionately and yet to mean so little and to die alone and go where no one can follow. She shivered and turned back to the house. She could see Connor's face through the window and it brought back the memory of watching Nancy as she stood in her kitchen, kneading bread with an expression of concentration.

She went inside. Connor had put the greens into a pan, and the salmon, covered with pulped ginger, crushed garlic and coarse salt, into an oven dish. She could smell the potatoes cooking. Three glasses were on the table and a small bowl of olives. Everything looked so civilized and welcoming. All they needed was Stefan – and at that moment the bell rang and she went slowly to open the door, knowing he would be standing there with a smile already on his face and a bunch of flowers in his hand. And, indeed, there he was, and as if it was any other day, they kissed and hugged each other and he handed over his bouquet with an awkward, ducking bow and wiped his feet on the mat.

'Connor!' Gaby called up the stairs, before leading her brother into the kitchen. 'Stefan's here.'

Connor had rehearsed his first sentence, but when he finally uttered it – after a swift glass of white wine and several bolted olives – it sounded high-flown and insincere.

'Ever since I met you, I have always loved you, as Gaby's brother and my friend, but I have also done you an injury.'

There. It lay between the three of them. Gaby looked from brother to husband, then down at her wine glass. She twisted it between her fingers until she heard it squeak. Stefan gazed at Connor with a glance of benevolent inquiry, but said nothing.

Connor swallowed hard. 'When Gaby was ill . . .' he said, then stopped, putting his hand over his heart and grimacing.

'Yes?'

'When she was depressed after Ethan was born,' he said, looking away from both the faces opposite him, 'I did something very wrong, which I have never ceased regretting. Wrong to Gaby and wrong to you.'

There was silence. Gaby could hear the drip, drip from the tap in the kitchen. Connor took another deep breath but before he could say the next sentence, Stefan interrupted him: 'I know.'

'No, Stefan, listen, will you? I – with Nancy –'

'I know,' Stefan said again. He sounded quite calm.

'You know?' whispered Gaby.

He turned his face towards her. 'Yes. I'm sorry.'

'I don't understand –' began Connor.

'You mean, you've always known?' interrupted Gaby.

'I suppose so,' said Stefan.

'How?' Connor managed to ask.

'I saw you together.'

'Oh, no!'

'I'd arranged to meet Nancy at yours and the meeting I was supposed to be at was cancelled so I came round earlier. I saw you through the window.'

'But you never said – I never knew –'.

'I went away and came back at the expected time.'

'You never told me,' said Gaby, gripping his forearm. 'Why, for God's sake? All these years!'

'Well.' Stefan blinked and took a sip of wine. 'That's a complicated question. There are lots of answers to it, and some are more important than others. Do you know? I can barely believe I'm having this conversation. I've had it in my head so many times. I wanted it and dreaded it – dreaded it more than wanted it, I guess, because every time I thought I had to speak to you, I found I couldn't. I quite simply couldn't. One answer to your "Why?" is that you were so wretched and frail that of course I couldn't say anything at the time, and then later – well, later it was too late and I couldn't see that it would serve anything except some abstract, rather cruel principle of openness. Another is that I thought – I hoped – that if I said nothing and never let on to anyone, it would die down and disappear and we could go on as we were: me and Nancy, you two together. Which half happened anyway. And then I persuaded myself that it was for Connor and Nancy to decide what to do and I tried to behave as if I hadn't stumbled across their secret. It was something I should never have seen, a bit like reading someone's diary. It was easier than I thought it would be, actually. It slipped away into the background until I pretty much forgot.'

He frowned. 'No. Maybe that's not quite true. I remembered, I always remembered, but the memories gradually became like a background to my life, rather than vivid, painful things that would stab at me, as they were to start with. I suppose you could say that I learnt how to live with them and in the end I almost forgot what it had felt like, before I knew, before I saw you together and before Nancy left me. It was a different life, and a different me who was living it. Does this make sense?'

He stared at Connor, biting his lip.

'I did once almost confront you, as a matter of fact. Nancy had left me, and you and Gaby seemed back on an even keel. She was Gaby again.' He turned to Gaby and smiled at her with great charm. 'Sorry – not *she, you*. You seemed happy again. I had been sitting alone in my room and I'd had a few glasses of wine. I guess I had been brooding over things and suddenly it seemed to me intolerable that you, Connor, who had behaved so badly and caused such suffering, should get away scot free, while I –' he faltered '– I, who had tried to be good, to do the right thing by everyone, should still be unhappy, should still be alone. It was as if everything I had pushed down inside me, pretending to myself and to everyone else that I was all right, was finally erupting. I felt as if I should explode with terrible anger and despair if I did nothing. I actually ran all the way to your house. I remember it was a wet night and the rain was pelting down on to me and I still felt as if a fire was blazing inside me. I got to your house and it was the strangest thing. I heard Gaby laughing. She – *you* – have a lovely laugh. And I couldn't do it. I still felt full of anger and misery, but I literally couldn't bring myself to do anything to jeopardize her.'

He gave a smile.

'I beat your shrub to the ground with my umbrella instead,' he said. 'I don't think it ever recovered. And then I knocked at your door and you let me in and we had a pleasant evening together.'

I saw you, thought Connor. *I saw you on that evening. I should have known. I should have guessed.*

'The fact is,' said Stefan, 'you two seemed happy. I thought I'd made the right decision and that time had proved it so. You were happy, weren't you?'

'Yes!' cried Connor, in a voice of agony. He looked across at Gaby.

'Yes,' she agreed, wistfully and quietly. 'We were.'

'I don't get it,' said Connor. 'I don't understand anything. I thought – I always thought – Christ, Stefan, didn't you hate me?'

'Of course not.' Stefan was genuinely shocked.

'Why not? I hated myself.'

'I knew that. I could see it. Maybe that's why I couldn't,' said Stefan. He looked across at Gaby and asked, 'Are you all right?'

'Yes,' she said. 'Kind of. Better now you're here.'

Connor saw the way they smiled at each other as if no one else was there. He poured himself a second glass of wine, took a deep draught of it, then got to his feet and left the room, pulling the door shut behind him.

Stefan half stood up to follow him, but Gaby held him back. 'Let him go,' she said. 'He'll be back in a minute. He's pretty near breaking-point.'

'Is he?'

'Yes.'

'And you? Have you been near breaking-point too?'

'No,' she said. 'I don't think so. I've been worrying about you. I feel a bit more peaceful now I know that you know, I'm not quite sure why. Are you all right? Your hands are shaking.'

He held them out in front of him. 'So they are. I'm fine. Gaby, you do understand, don't you, why I didn't –?'

'Yes. Yes, I do. Every time I think about it, it has a different meaning. To begin with it felt very close, too close to see properly, and very painful. Right now, it all feels far off.'

'How did you find out?'

'It's a long story – which, now I come to think of it, shows me behaving in exactly the way you decided not to behave all those years ago. I pried and snooped and went to see her and dug up old secrets – oh, I behaved very badly all round because I couldn't bear not to know. It's what I'm like. I can't leave well alone. That's what Nancy said to me when I went to see her and she was quite right. Once I knew a bit I had to know everything. Pandora's box. Everything flew out, all the things that would have stayed under the lid if it hadn't been for me. But listen, Stefan, there's more to this story.'

'More?'

'Yes. Wait. Connor has to be here for this.'

'How, more?'

'There's a reason why we're speaking to you about this, rather than keeping it secret between us – keeping it secret from you like you've been keeping it secret from us. You knew and I knew but I didn't know you knew and you didn't know I knew . . . Oh, God, it hurts my brain, Stefan.' She gave a giggle that turned into a sob.

'What's the reason, Gaby?'

'Hang on, here he is. Are you all right?'

Connor's face was chalky, but he gave a nod and sat down. 'Sorry,' he said. 'The reason, Stefan, is that Nancy had a baby.'

Gaby was watching Stefan's face as he heard the news

and she saw the expression that flickered across it – simultaneously horrified and full of hope. 'Connor's baby,' she said quickly, to douse the hope before it grew any stronger.

'I see. I see. Yes.'

'She had it adopted at birth.'

'Her,' put in Connor.

'Her. Sonia. She's eighteen now and –'

'Yes,' said Stefan again. He blinked hard, took his reading-glasses out of his jacket pocket and started to polish them on the hem of his shirt. 'Yes, indeed.'

'She's been in touch with Nancy and she knows about Connor. Probably she will want to meet him too. And Ethan – he and Sonia both have to know they have a sibling. So, of course, we had to tell you, too.'

Stefan put on his glasses and peered over the top at them owlishly. He rummaged in his pocket and took out a length of thin, flecked rope and started to twist it in his hands. 'Thank you for telling me,' he said formally, as a knot formed between his deft fingers.

'Tell me what you're feeling,' said Gaby urgently. 'Please, darling Stefan.'

'I don't know,' said Stefan. A little furrow knitted his brow. 'A bit dazed, perhaps. But it's all right, it really is. I think so, anyway. It'll take time for this to sink in. I've lived so long with a different version of the past. So Nancy had a girl. I never – And you're quite sure she's Connor's?'

'Yes.'

'Well, well. Sonia, you say?'

'That's right,' said Gaby. She reached over, took his

fretting hands between her own and held them tightly. 'Are you OK?'

'Mm? Me? Yes. What about you two? This must have been an enormous shock.'

'Don't be so bloody English and polite!' Connor shouted, banging on the table hard with his fist so the glasses rattled. 'For Christ's sake, don't be so nice and forgiving all the time, Stefan! I can't stand it.'

'I'm sorry,' said Stefan.

'There you go. Shout at me, hit me, anything but your terrifying kindness.'

'I don't know how,' said Stefan. He placed the knot on the table. 'This is called a fisherman's eye, by the way. It's quite hard – I've been practising. I'll teach you next summer, Connor, when we're on the boat together. I lack the shouting gene.'

Connor groaned.

'It's true,' said Gaby. 'And the hitting gene.'

'It's not necessarily a virtue,' said Stefan. 'Some people might consider it a fatal flaw.'

'So what do we do now?' asked Connor.

'Drink?' suggested Gaby. She topped up everyone's glass. An unaccountable hilarity rippled through her and she felt as though she might open her mouth and let out a howl, a hyena's shriek of mirth.

'Eat?' said Stefan.

'You want to eat now?' Connor stared at him with a glazed expression.

'I can smell something in the oven. It's making me hungry.'

'That's Connor's potato dish. Shall I take the foil off the top so they go crispy?'

'If you want,' said Connor, dully.

'And put the salmon in?'

'All right. Top of the oven.'

'There you go. What about the broccoli?'

'The broccoli?'

'Shall I cook it?'

'I was going to steam it,' said Connor. 'I'll do it. You sit down.'

'Maybe we should have whisky or rum or something stronger than wine. What do you reckon, Stefan?'

'Remember that I'm driving.'

'No, you can't. You're already over the limit as it is. You'll have to stay the night.'

'Will I?'

'Yes.'

'You two don't want to –?'

'What?'

'You might want to be alone for a bit.'

'I don't think so,' said Gaby. 'No. You stay. Here, finish that wine.'

'You're both quite mad, you know,' said Connor. He suddenly felt ill, or perhaps just so weary he could scarcely keep his eyes open. All he wanted was to crawl into a dark, quiet room, pull the duvet over his head and sleep for hundreds of hours.

'In a good way, you mean?'

'In the best way. I need to go and lie down for a bit. Can you keep an eye on the salmon?'

'Are you feeling all right?' asked Stefan.

'I don't know. I feel odd. A bit –' He passed a hand over his forehead and found it was clammy with sweat.

His legs were trembling and there was a burning sensation in his throat. 'I think I might be sick. Bad timing. I'm not running away. Sorry. Sorry for everything. So very, very sorry.'

'Sometimes I imagine being on my deathbed. Not in pain or anything. When I picture it, it's always very peaceful and solemn. I'm just slowly dying. I know that's unlikely – I'll probably thrash around in pain and terror and scream obscenities. Anyway, I've always imagined Connor and Ethan would be sitting on either side of the bed and holding my hand.' She took another gulp of whisky and let it trickle down her throat.

'The past is made up of many hidden things,' said Stefan, taking a large mouthful of whisky as well. His voice was slightly slurred. 'You think you know your life and yourself, but that's an illusion. As a historian, I often have the sense that I'm looking through a peephole at a small segment of the past. It's the same with life. Most of it is quite obscure. Probably better that way too.'

'But maybe I'll be alone,' Gaby continued, 'and recently I've been thinking that perhaps it doesn't matter so much. Ethan and Connor can't accompany me over the threshold anyway, can they? What do you think?'

'What do I think?'

'About dying.'

'I don't think about dying.'

'Never?'

'I never think about dying. I think about being dead.'

'Ugh, no, I can't do that. The mind balks, it refuses.

It's like a physical impossibility to think about not being alive to think. To think about nothing.'

'I think about being absorbed back into the earth and the air. In the end, I'll be a raindrop.'

'A raindrop!'

'Yes. What?'

'I don't know. We haven't had much of Connor's meal, have we?'

'Is he all right?'

'I think there's nothing left to be sick.'

'Maybe it's a virus.'

'Maybe he literally makes himself sick. I'm serious.'

'Are you two going to be all right?'

'I can't tell you the answer to that. I'm not furious. I don't feel betrayed the way I would have felt if I'd known at the time. I'm simply – well, I don't know, Stefan. Something's changed, that's all I can say.'

'Of course.'

'More whisky?'

'I've had quite a lot already.'

'Can I ask you something?'

'What?'

'Do you think you've never lived with anyone or married because of Nancy?'

'I haven't been unhappy, you know.'

'That wasn't what I was meaning.'

'It was, really. You think I've missed out on something.'

'Have you?'

'Only in the paths-not-taken kind of way.'

'Really?'

'And I always thought I would have children.'

'I know.'

'I've got nephews and nieces, though. That's good enough for me. Speaking of which –'

'We're going to wait until he's home for Christmas. It's only a few weeks now. We wouldn't tell him at all except – well, he's got a half-sister. And she probably wants to meet him one day, and he's going to find out sooner or later so we figured it had better be sooner.'

'It doesn't necessarily need to be made into a huge, tragic thing.'

'No. That's it. I mean, it'll be odd for him.'

'Of course.'

'It's odd for all of us, isn't it?'

'Very. Have you talked to anyone else about it?'

'No. Even if I'd wanted to, I wouldn't have before I'd talked to you, because I didn't like to think of other people knowing something about you that you didn't know yourself, if you see what I mean.'

'I do.'

'Do you ever want to see her again?'

'Nancy? I haven't thought of it – not for many years. I used to think I'd bump into her on the street, or look across a room and she'd be there. It didn't seem possible that she had simply disappeared and we would never meet again.' Gaby, listening to him, was struck by how they could talk now about something that had been tacitly forbidden for so many years. 'But bit by bit,' Stefan continued, 'that changed, until it didn't seem possible that we'd meet. She'd be a stranger now.' He hesitated, and then asked, 'What's she like?'

'Oh – well, in many ways she's just the same. Older, of course, and it's a shock to see someone after so many years. Like a jump-cut in time. You realize how much you've aged as well, how much time has gone by and you're no longer young. But she's still slim and classy and ironic and sharp, and she makes everyone around her seem a bit tawdry, if you know what I mean. Or me, at least.'

Stefan nodded.

'And she still has a way of being very stern and then all of a sudden smiling. It was so odd, I was furious with her, furious and hurt, yet in spite of that I found I wanted her approval. No, not approval exactly. Her recognition. She recognizes people. Do you know what I mean? When she looks at you, you feel she's really seeing you. You don't get that with many people. I used to think that when I was with her I was a better person. More me.'

'She loved you,' said Stefan. 'I used to get jealous of you two sometimes.'

'You used to be jealous of us, I used to be jealous of you, Connor was sometimes jealous of us and now sometimes I'm jealous of them, in retrospect at least. Aaaah, I don't know, Stefan. I don't even know if I care any more. I'm so tired of thinking about it. I used to think she loved me. And I loved her. Perhaps I still do. Can you love someone you no longer know?'

'Of course,' said Stefan. 'You can love someone who's dead, can't you? Or someone who's gone far away?' He poured more whisky into their tumblers, then chinked his glass against Gaby's.

'Or aren't you just loving a memory?'

'Well, you could say that love is always made up of lots of things – and memory's a large part of it. All the things you've been to each other in the past. You could say memory is what makes us who we are now, and without it we would be blank. That's what's so scary about losing your memory, because it's a bit like losing yourself.'

'Yes.'

'Are we going to go to bed this evening?'

'I don't know. I should check on Connor anyway.'

Gaby went up the stairs to their bedroom and pushed open the door. The room smelt faintly of sick, and she went across and opened the window to let in fresh air, then bent down and pulled the duvet further up over Connor, so that his shoulders were covered. He shifted and muttered something, and Gaby laid her hand on his dark hair for a moment before she left him.

'Let's play cards,' she said, coming back into the living room.

Stefan groaned.

'Come on, just a couple of games of racing demon or something.'

'You always beat me. Ever since you were about nine, you've beaten me.'

'That's because I'm so competitive. If you cared more, you'd do better.'

'Your nails are sharper than mine. And I've always suspected that you cheat.'

'I do not cheat!'

'We're drunk.'

'Talk for yourself. I'm not. I'm stone-cold sober.'

'One game, then.'

'I used to play quite a lot with Ethan.'

'You must miss him.'

'I always thought that when he left Connor and I would do something extraordinary – set off on an adventure, be carefree again, be foolish and irresponsible the way you never quite can when you've got children around. Instead I went running off in some demented search of my past and created pain and havoc.'

'Not created. Discovered.'

'I'm not sure, Stefan. Don't you think that the act of finding something out, changes it? Just like when you say something out loud it becomes more real, more concrete or unavoidable.'

'Hmm.'

'I can't believe I'm saying this – I'm such a believer in talking about what you feel and facing up to what you've done, but perhaps some things are better left locked away and never examined. The truth is brutal.'

'I agree with that, but I don't think you do.'

'Don't I?'

'Where are the cards?'

'I'll get them. Pour us some more whisky. However much I drink, I don't seem to be getting drunk.'

'Do you want to get drunk?'

'Not exactly. But I want something to break up inside me. I thought maybe whisky could do it, but I don't think it will.'

'Break up?'

'Break up, dissolve, be burnt away.'

Thirty-three

Ethan found the note two days later, when he was late for a lecture and rummaging futilely through his possessions for a pair of clean socks, all the while promising himself that he would go to the laundrette that afternoon. He pushed the pile of notes to one side and saw the signature without realizing he was seeing it. Then he did a double take and pulled it out to hold up to the light. '7.30 p.m.: I came to see you but you were out – if you want to see me, please call a.s.a.p. Lorna xxx', he read. He stumbled over to the window, opened the curtains and read it again, out loud.

When could she have come? He'd been here at seven thirty last night. And the night before, he was sure of it. Yes, he'd gone out later, at nine or something. That meant she must have come round when he had got lost on his bike and ended up at Reginald's house. She would think he didn't want to see her! She would think he'd read the note and simply not bothered to get in touch.

He didn't have her phone number, though: he'd never dared ask her. Before he had time to think, he called Harry, who answered almost at once.

'Hi, it's Ethan.'

'Ethan. Fancy a game of squash or something?'

'I can't. Sorry.'

'Another time, then,' Harry said carelessly.

'I just needed to ask you for Lorna's number.'

'You did, did you?'

'Yeah.'

'Why's that?'

'I just want to ask her something, that's all.'

'You just want to ask her something. I bet.'

'Look, Harry —'

'You know we're not going out any more, don't you?'

'No. I didn't know. I'm really — I mean. God. Are you OK?'

'Why shouldn't I be?'

'No reason. I only —'

'What?'

'I didn't know.'

'Yeah.'

'Can I have her number, then?'

'No.'

'No?'

'I don't have it any more. I erased it.'

'Oh.'

'For Christ's sake, Ethan. You know where she lives, don't you? Just go and ask her.'

'Ask her?'

'Whatever it is you want to ask her.'

'Right.'

'It's OK, you know.'

'What is?'

'Whatever happens. It's no big deal.'

'You mean —?'

'I mean,' said Harry, in a slow, sarcastically patient

voice, 'that it's fine by me if you go out with Lorna. It wasn't a great romance, and now it's over.'

Ethan mumbled something about there being nothing between them anyway and – but Harry interrupted: 'Whatever. I'm just saying it's OK. You're my friend.'

'Harry.'

'Yeah.'

'I – you know. Thanks. And ditto.'

'Ditto? *Ditto!*'

'You're my friend too.'

'That's better. Off you go, then.'

Ethan pulled on two unmatching dirty socks and a shirt that was clean but balled up at the end of his bag and creased. He pulled his fingers through his hair, then over the stubble on his cheeks. He grabbed his mobile, wallet and the key to his bike lock, then ran out on to the streets without even a jacket, not noticing how cold it was. He fumbled with the key, dropping it and cursing. It seemed to him that every second counted; that if he got to Lorna at once – a.s.a.p. – then it might turn out well, but that a few moments could tip the balance against him.

It did not take him long to arrive at the hall of residence where she lived. He skidded to a halt, locked his bike against a lamp-post and pelted indoors, taking the stairs two at a time. But when he got to a few feet from her door, he stopped with a thudding heart. What was he going to say? What if she hadn't meant anything by her note? And, now he came to think of it, of course she hadn't. Why on earth should he have assumed she had from the few casual words pushed under his door? It was only the agony of hope that had converted them into anything more than amiability. He took a step backwards, blushing at the mistake he had nearly made although there was no one to see him. For several seconds, he hovered in agonizing indecision, turning over the alternatives in his mind. He could leave now, and avoid humiliation and pain, or he could stay and find out what he already knew: that she didn't love him. But what if she did? What if she felt the same way? The memory of her kiss still tingled on his skin. It was just a kiss. A kiss on the cheek. How many people, men and women, did he kiss on the cheek to say hello, to say goodbye? Everyone. Why should be imagine that Lorna's kiss had meant more than goodbye? He didn't believe that Lorna felt about him the way he felt about her, but he wanted to cling to the uncertainty. Not to know for sure meant that there was room for doubt and for deluded dreams, which, however painful they were, seemed better than the dull, flat knowledge that would fall on him once she had turned him away.

He took another step backwards. Somewhere in the distance he heard a voice. Two voices. They were coming towards him, up the stairs. Oh, God, what if Lorna was to find him standing like this outside her door? What would he say? Hello, I was just passing . . .

Two young women turned on to the corridor. They looked at him as they approached and one smiled in a friendly, incurious manner. He tried to appear purposeful, pulling his mobile out of his pocket and pretending to press keys to call a number. He lifted the dead instrument to his ear and said, 'Yes? Yes, it's me. Yes.' They passed and turned the corner, out of sight. Ethan put the phone back into his pocket, grimaced at his foolishness and strode up to Lorna's door. He didn't pause to think, just knocked firmly, three times, and stood back. He pushed his hair out of his eyes, turned down the collar of his jacket and stood up straight, waiting.

It had never occurred to him that Lorna might not be there, though it was the middle of the morning in the middle of the week in term-time. He knocked once more, louder. No, the room was empty. He pressed an ear against the wood and listened. Nothing. He turned away, and as he did so a figure came along the corridor, swinging his bag and whistling. 'Looking for Lorna?'

'Yes. I was just passing . . .' Ethan dribbled to a pause.

'She's not here.'

'I know.'

'I mean she's gone away.'

'Gone away?' Ethan echoed.

'She went yesterday. She said it was something about her family. Her sister was ill or something.'

'When will she be back?'

'No idea.'

'Oh. Where do they live?'

'Her family?'

'Yes.'

'I haven't a clue. No, hang on a minute. She said it was somewhere near Bath, I think. Yeah, because we talked about the Roman baths and she said she'd never been even though she lived so close. Why?'

'No reason. Thanks.'

Ethan left and went back to his bike, cursing himself

for not taking Lorna's number before he left. He pedalled to the station and when he arrived there, phoned Directory Enquiries and asked the number for Vosper, he didn't know the initials, near Bath. There was only one Vosper in the area, Jonathan Vosper – did he want to be put straight through? No, he said in panic. No, but could he check the address to make sure it was the right person, after all? He repeated the words the operator said – Tye Cottage, End Road, Ofden, Bath – memorizing them, then disconnected, wheeled his bike into the station. He would have to change at Bristol, Temple Meads, but the journey would take less than an hour and a half. He bought a return ticket for a train leaving in thirty-five minutes, checking that he could take his bike with him, then went and bought himself a double espresso that burnt his lips and made his head buzz. He realized he was cold in his thin shirt, and slightly dazed with fatigue and hunger, but the thought of eating made him feel nauseous. He bought a paper and boarded the train for Bristol, settling back in his seat and looking at his mobile to check the time. His lecture would be over by now. The next would begin in an hour. A whistle went and the train pulled out of the station.

Ethan tried to read the paper but soon found he wasn't taking anything in. It might as well have been written in a foreign language. He looked out of the window and saw that the blue light was already softening to a silvery grey. It was mid-afternoon. His second lecture would be under way. He should be sitting scribbling notes while the hands ticked round the clock on the wall and the day faded outside. Instead – but he didn't want to think about what he was doing. He put his head on the seat back and felt the train's motion in his body. He had always loved travelling by train, gazing out of windows at unfamiliar landscapes speeding by, half thinking and half letting thoughts drift over his mind like early-morning mist in a valley.

He tilted his head and stared out at the unknown worlds he was passing. There was a canal, with a footpath running along it, going straight into the distance. A wood, half stripped of leaves and mysterious in the dusk. A single house with smoke coming out of its chimney and its downstairs windows already lit. A field of cows. A syncopated section of houses whose gardens led right up to the track: as a boy he had always thought it would be exciting to live by a railway and lie awake at night hearing the rumble of trains passing to who knew where. Something about the stream of lit-up carriages in the darkness still filled him with the longing to be off as well, travelling to a faraway destination with a single light bag and a few notes stuffed into his back pocket. The exhilarating loneliness of it, with its whiff of homesickness and longing. His mother loved to travel. She used to say that her idea of bliss was to get on to a train, any train, and see where it took her. He had asked her if she'd ever actually done it but she'd shaken her head and laughed, saying that she and his father would some day soon. 'You'll see,' she had said. 'We'll become vagabonds when you've left home. We'll do things back-to-front – stability and responsibility in our youth and recklessness in old age. Won't we, Connor?' His father had given his secretive smile, the one that meant he was saying nothing.

At Bristol, Ethan had only a few minutes to wait for a connection to Bath and contemplate bolting back to Exeter. He bought himself another cup of coffee and carried it carefully in one hand, wheeling his bike with the other, on to the second train, then sipped it slowly, trying to ignore his nervousness. Now the day had almost gone, and when he gazed out of the window he saw his face staring back, and for a while he let himself become lost in his reflected features through which he could discern the landscape outside.

At Bath, he bought a map of the city and outlying areas and soon found the small village of Ofden, and even End Road leading north from it. It wasn't many miles. He didn't have his bike lights with him, so when he left the city he was cycling in a gloomy half-light in which shapes became incomprehensible – a stooped figure became a small tree, what he took for a barn or tumbledown out-building turned out to be a copse, and a bulky horse or bull was just a haystack. He was shivering with cold now, and it was too dark to consult his map so he relied on memory to take him along the small road until he came to a sign pointing left to Ofden.

The village where Lorna lived was really a straggle of houses, a few larger and older than the rest, set back from the road and surrounded by lawns. He stopped at what he guessed was its centre, where there was a triangle of grass and a tiny post office, its metal shutters pulled down. Ethan had been planning to buy a bunch of flowers, a bottle of wine or a box of chocolates – he'd imagined himself standing at the door and holding out the gift for Lorna's ill sister, like a kind of entry into her family. But he clearly wasn't going to find anything here. End Road forked left off the road that led out of the village and he cycled along it for a few hundred yards until he came to a gravel driveway, full of potholes, that led up to a battered grey house with large windows and a porched door. The upstairs windows were dark, but downstairs the curtained windows were illuminated. He pushed his bike over to the open wooden gate and made out the name of the house: Tye Cottage.

Ethan took a deep breath, cleared his throat, as if he was about to make a formal announcement, and wheeled his bike slowly up the drive. He thought a shape passed in front of one of the windows and wondered if it might have been Lorna; the very idea made his forehead prickle with sweat. He leant his bike against the tree that stood to one side of the house and walked up to the front door. Taking hold of the brass knocker, he rapped it boldly, hearing it reverberate inside the house. Then he took a few paces backwards.

There was the sound of bare feet slapping across tiles and the door swung open to reveal a girl of eight or nine, glaring at him. She was small and skinny and her dark brown hair was in two tight plaits. Ethan took in the thin face, the fierce eyes and flushed cheeks, the knobbly knees under the short corduroy skirt.

'Hello,' he said.

'What?' Her voice was surprisingly loud for such a small body.

'Are you the one who's been ill?'

'That's Polly. Come with me,' she said, took his hand in hers and yanked him over the threshold into the house.

'But listen – sorry, I don't know your name.'

'Phoebe.'

'Listen, Phoebe.' He dug in his heels. 'I've come to see your sister –'

'I know.'

'You know?'

'Come on,' she said. Her fingers were hot and sticky in his and she hauled him through the dingy hall and to the carpeted staircase that led from it. Ethan could hear the sound of voices from the room to the left, but the child wasn't going to let him stop.

'This way,' she said, turning at the top of the stairs along a short corridor, and stopping in front of a door on which a sign written in large green letters read 'Keep Out. No Entry Without Knocking.'

Phoebe didn't knock. She kicked the door open and pushed Ethan inside. The curtains were closed and the lights off, and for a few seconds Ethan stood in the darkness, which smelt sour and close, trying to make out the shapes around him. There was a narrow bed to one side of the room, and a desk beside it, under the light grey rectangle that was the window. A wardrobe to the other side, and perhaps that was a chair or a stool.

'Phoebe?' he said.

Phoebe had disappeared. He took a step back and a shape rose up out of the bed.

'Who's that?' The voice was small and hoarse.

'Sorry,' Ethan stammered. 'You're ill?'

'Are you the doctor?'

'I'm Ethan.'

'Who's Ethan?'

'I came to visit –'

'I don't know Ethan. Where's the doctor?'

'I'll go now. Lie down. Go back to sleep. Sorry for waking you. I thought –'

'Daddy! Lorna!' The figure flung out an arm and caught the glass that was on the bedside table, sending it flying with an arc of spilt liquid across the room. 'Someone!'

The child wriggled back frantically in her bed until she was pressed against the wall.

'It's all right, Polly. I'm going. I'm not here to harm you. Aah, please don't cry.'

'What is it? Polly, I'm on my way.'

Ethan knew that soft, low voice. He gave a small moan and stood aside as Lorna hastened into the room and knelt at the side of her sister's bed. She didn't see him standing there, and he watched in silence as she laid her hand on Polly's forehead. 'It's just a dream,' she was saying. 'A feverish dream.'

'There was a man in my room, watching me.'

'I'm going to get a flannel for your head. You lie down again. Look, you've spilt your lemon barley. I'll get you some more. You have to keep on drinking.'

'I want Mummy.'

'I know. I know you do. But I'm here.'

'There was a man.'

'No, don't you worry.' She pulled the covers over the child and straightened them. 'You were dreaming.'

'No,' said Ethan. 'Not a dream. It's me, Lorna.'

Polly gave a rasping shriek, then broke into a spasm of coughing and clutched at Lorna, who was struggling to her feet.

388

'Ethan? Is that you?'

'I didn't mean to frighten her.'

'Ethan?' she repeated. She put a hand to her hair and pushed the stray locks back from her face, and with that one anxious, womanly gesture Ethan felt a moment of hope. 'But what on earth –?'

'I wanted to help.'

'I don't understand.'

'Who's that man? Why's he here?' Polly wailed from the bed.

'Hush, it's all right.'

'I said it wasn't a dream. I told you so.'

'Is it a dream?' asked Lorna.

'I didn't see your note.'

'What?'

'What's going on?' a voice asked from outside, and the door opened once more. Another girl – this time a teen-ager, as far as Ethan could tell – burst into the room, still in her coat, with a backpack slung over one shoulder, closely followed by Phoebe. 'Oh,' she said, when she saw Ethan. 'Hello.'

'Hello.'

'I'm Jo,' she said.

'I'm Ethan.'

'He was standing in my room,' said Polly, from the bed, 'looking at me.'

'I've just come in from school and Phoebe said the doctor was here and then I heard these terrible screams, as if someone was being murdered.'

'I think I confu –'

'Lorna said it was a dream. She didn't believe me.'

'But I didn't think we were expecting the doctor and, anyway, even in the dark I can tell you're not one. Are you?'

'No,' said Ethan.

'No,' repeated Lorna.

'Why did you lie to me?' asked Phoebe.

'It was a misunderstanding. I didn't mean –'

'Oh, well,' said Jo. 'Never mind. You OK today, Polly?'

'My throat hurts and my chest hurts and my glands hurt and my ears hurt and my mouth hurts and . . .'

'That'd be all the screaming. You should go to sleep.'

'I'm bored of sleeping and, anyway, when I close my eyes everything tilts and it's scary. I want to do something.'

'Shall I read to you?' asked Ethan, who was feeling quite light-headed by now.

'Why are you here in my room?'

'What? Oh, well, I was in the area so I thought I'd come and see – actually, I have no idea what I'm doing here. You might as well be dreaming me. Or I'm dreaming you.'

Lorna came and stood by his side, close enough so that if he reached out he could stroke the soft shine of her hair or take her slender hand in his. 'He's my friend,' she said to Polly.

'He still shouldn't just turn up in my room like that.'

'Sorry.'

'OK, then.'

'Thank you.'

'No. I mean OK, then, you can read to me.'

'Polly –'

'No, I'd like to,' said Ethan. 'Can we turn on the light?'

'Only the small one or it hurts my eyes.'

Ethan went to her bedside, feeling bulky and shy, and bent down to turn on the shaded lamp on the desk. The light dazzled him momentarily so that when he turned he only saw the other sisters as silhouettes. Then their shapes resolved and he found he was gazing at Lorna at last. She looked small – smaller than Jo, who seemed tall and strong and glowing with health – and almost plain. Her hair was pulled back in a crooked ponytail; she was wearing no makeup or jewellery and her face was tired, with purple smudges under her eyes. She was wearing old jeans and a grey man's sweater with the sleeves rolled up. Her feet were bare. Ethan thought he had never seen anyone so purely, simply lovely in his entire life and it was all he could do to prevent himself kneeling at her feet.

'Oi! What book are you going to read me?'

He sat carefully beside the girl in the bed, his back to the others. Her hair was greasy and her cheeks blotchy; her eyes glittered at him. 'What do you want me to read?'

'Dunno.'

'How old are you?'

'Ten.'

'Double figures.'

'How old are you?'

'Nearly twenty.'

'Well, then. That's twice me.'

'Exactly. How about this?' Ethan took a book from the top of a pile by the bed.

'OK.'

Ethan started to read, intensely conscious of Lorna standing by the door. The book was some kind of fantasy set in sinister marshes and peopled by all manner of strange beasts with complicated histories and long names, and very soon he lost track of it. He spoke the words, but his thoughts wandered. He heard when Jo and Phoebe, whispering to each other in piercing hisses, then Lorna left, pulling the door to with a muted click. He heard footsteps going down the stairs. He heard voices. Shortly after that a beam of light swept through the window and a car pulled up outside in a crunch of gravel. He read about poisoned berries and girls with the power to know people's thoughts, about babies with wings curled up at their shoulder-blades and dogs with red eyes and dripping tongues. A faint, rasping snore stopped him and he put down the book. Polly's mouth was slightly open and a tiny trickle of saliva had worked its way down her chin. With the hem of his shirt, he wiped it away, then stood up, pulling the duvet so that it covered her shoulders. He turned off the light and tiptoed from the room.

For a moment he stood on the landing. A man's voice was coming from directly below him, and, a bit further off, the sound of a TV: canned laughter. He went slowly down the stairs, into the tiled hallway, then hesitated outside the door where he could hear voices.

'Is he staying the night, then?' the man asked.

Ethan knocked and pushed open the door on to a large kitchen, festooned with wet sheets. Lorna was sitting at a wooden table, chopping onions and her father was opposite her, struggling to open a bottle of wine.

'Hello,' said Ethan. He saw that Lorna had changed into a white shirt and brushed her hair. There were earrings hanging from her lobes. She had put gloss on her lips. I hardly know her, thought Ethan. I've only talked to her a few times. What am I doing here? He hardly dared to look at her.

'You must be the mystery visitor who's created such confusion in the house.'

The man examined him with Lorna's eyes; Ethan tried to hold his gaze. He was solid and rumpled, wearing a shabby cardigan over an unironed shirt over a T-shirt ripped at the neck, and slippers on his feet. His hair, silvering at the temples, was past his collar.

'I'm Ethan.'

'Jonathan Vosper. We weren't expecting you.'

'No. Well, you see, I'm a friend of Lorna's from university and when I happened to find myself in the area I thought it would be nice to – you know – drop in and see how she – you, I mean, I don't mean to talk about you in the third person like that, Lorna – to see how you were . . . I didn't mean to intrude.'

'Don't worry. We're glad you just *happened* to find yourself in the area,' said Jonathan Vosper, with a snort of laughter.

Blushing furiously, Ethan stammered something incomprehensible.

'Do you like curry?'

'Curry? Yes. I love curry.'

'Hot?'

'Very,' said Ethan, bravely.

'Hot,' said the father to Lorna. 'We'll have it very hot. Suicide curry.'

'Am I staying?'

'Aren't you?'

393

'Lorna?' said Ethan, summoning up his courage. 'Am I staying?'

She looked gravely up at him and a surge of joy passed through him. Of course he knew her. He had known her from the moment he had first seen her.

'I don't know,' she said.

'It was under my clothes. My room's such a mess.'

'Do you like Monopoly?' asked Jonathan Vosper.

'No. I hate Monopoly. Lorna?'

'Pity. I thought we could all play a game before supper. It's been ages.'

'Will you come for a walk with me, Lorna?'

'It's dark outside and Lorna's making curry for us. We've been living on baked potatoes and pasta.'

'Lorna?'

'Yes,' she said. She stood up and rinsed her hands under the tap, dried them thoroughly, then put them on her father's shoulders. 'I'll play Monopoly after supper, Dad. All right?'

'You'll get cold.'

'You have a glass of wine,' she said.

'The curry.'

'I'll be back.'

'But . . .'

'Dad!'

He grimaced and rubbed his craggy face. 'Sorry.'

Ethan followed Lorna out of the kitchen and into the hall. She pulled a jacket off a hook and put it on, then handed him a thick moleskin one.

'Where are you two going?' Phoebe was standing at the top of the stairs.

'For a walk.'

'It's dark. You won't be able to see anything.'

'We know that.'

'Can I come too?'

'No, you can't,' said Ethan, opening the front door and feeling the cold air biting through him.

'You're not a doctor.'

'I know.'

'So you can't tell me what to do. I wasn't talking to you anyway. Lorna?'

'No,' said Lorna.

'But –'

They closed the door on her rising wail.

They walked side by side but not touching, until they could no longer see the house, where faces might be pressed to the windows. Now they were out of range of the light it threw, and on the narrow road they were in darkness. The sky was clear and pricked with silver, but there was no moon. Trees leant in from either side like shadows. Ethan listened to the sound their feet made. He listened to the wind in the trees, like waves breaking on the shore. He listened to his heart thudding. Soon, he would have to say or do something, and the hope that was making his knees weak and his stomach liquid and his breath shallow and ragged would turn into a more certain, solid emotion. But for now he walked dreamily beside Lorna, not looking at her but feeling her figure beside him, moving like a dancer's down the road.

'Lorna,' he said at last. 'I – Tell me if I'm a fool.'

'You're a fool,' she said.

'I found your note under my stuff by the door. I didn't

see it until a few hours ago. I didn't have your number and I called Harry and he said it was over between you and then I went to your room and someone said you were with your family and I just – I just had to – I had to find you, and I went to the station and I got the train and I came here, and I know your family probably thinks I'm mad and you probably think I'm mad too, and maybe I am a bit mad because I'm so much in love with you every bit of me hurts and aches and burns and if you don't put your arms round me soon I'm going to fall over or start to cry. Please.'

'You don't need to cry,' she said. 'Or fall.'

She put one hand on his shoulder and turned him towards her. In the gloom, they stared at each other. He could see her soft dark hair, her eyes, the pale column of her neck. He put out his hand and with one finger touched her cheek. 'You're not just a dream?'

'I don't think so.'

'Because if you turn out to be –'

'Ethan, do you always have to talk so much?'

'No,' he said. 'No.'

He ate prawn vindaloo until his eyes watered, drank red wine, told stories and jokes, teased Phoebe, begged for anecdotes about Lorna as a child, gabbled with happiness, ran up the stairs with lemon barley water for Polly, washed the dishes, helped Jo with her Spanish verbs, played Monopoly with Lorna's father and made him happy by going spectacularly bankrupt in record time.

Then he lay on the living-room sofa-bed, covered with a thin, lumpy duvet and looking at the ranks of framed family photographs on the windowsills. He saw Lorna as a baby, as a tiny girl with bobbed hair and gappy teeth; he saw her growing up. He saw her with her mother, her father, her sisters, her pet rabbit; then second to the right in some large family gathering but he would have recognized her anywhere. In shorts and sandals with an ice-cream; in wellington boots and braces; in tight jeans and a T-shirt that showed the curve of her new breasts. As a teenager, standing as straight as she did now, she had had the same luminous smile on her smooth oval face. Standing with her sisters round her mother, gaunt and old with illness.

He could hear lavatories flushing, taps running and doors shutting upstairs. He turned off the light, put his head on the pillow and waited, his eyes wide open in the darkness, until at last he heard her footsteps coming lightly down the stairs towards him.

Thirty-four

<u>1 December</u>

Alex finished with me yesterday. He said he wanted to be 'free' and he thought I did too. I wanted to say: 'Free to go off with Odette?' but I didn't really need to know. I've had my fill of knowing for the time being. Now I just want to get on with life and not have my head full of new, exciting, sad and hurtful things. And then I wanted to say that 'free' is just another word for 'lonely', but I didn't, of course – because, actually, I only thought of that after he'd gone and I couldn't really run after him and tell him, could I, just to have the last word? Anyway, he would have thought of something much cleverer in reply. I shrugged and said, 'OK.'

And it is OK and I think he was probably right and we don't really want to be tied to each other when our lives are opening up and there are whole new worlds in front of us. I mean, I'm not exactly over the moon at being dumped. I feel a bit low and drab and Sundayish – and it is Sunday, and it's grey outside, and the kind of cold that makes your bones ache. But it's my pride not my heart that's hurt. You fall in love with someone and you can't imagine not being with them – I mean, you don't go around thinking it's for ever, not when you're still at school, but you don't see there being any end. As soon as you do, it's really over, however long you struggle to convince yourself you can work it out. I had already seen there was an end with Alex, I just didn't think

398

we'd quite reached it. Or am I saying all this to make myself feel better?

I told Mum at once. Maybe before I would have hidden away with it for a while, but I thought I'd done enough of that with her to last us a good few years. I can always tell what's going through her head. I could see, in the split second before she gave me a firm but not prolonged hug, that she was working out how to be sympathetic without inflating it into a grand tragedy. She wanted to strike the right balance, not make me feel alone because she didn't understand or more miserable because she had overreacted. She said he was a blind idiot and he didn't know how lucky he was to have gone out with me in the first place. 'Fuck him,' she said, in her brisk voice. I was so surprised I almost passed out. My mother never swears. Then she reverted to type and made a pot of tea and brought out the chocolate Digestives. Chocolate's very good when you're feeling a bit down. Chocolate, baked potatoes with lots of butter, rice pudding, scrambled egg on brown toast, dunked biscuits, tea.

I've just noticed something. I'm not addressing this to you any more (except now I am, of course, but that doesn't count). Now that I've found you, it's as if you're fading away and losing your power. Or maybe it's just that you're no longer a ghost who's haunting me day and night. You're real and ordinary and about my size. A woman who made mistakes. I almost miss the you that you were because there's a kind of hole where you once were. You were like God, invisible and omnipotent, and I could pray to you and curse you and wonder if you really existed and think I wasn't responsible for my own life and mistakes – you were. Is this what growing up is? Not being able to blame it all on someone else?

Tomorrow I'm going to go round to Goldie's and we'll revise for our mocks together; they're the week after next and I'm really behind. Then I'm going to give in my notice at the café. Soon it'll be Christmas, but before then I'm going to try to meet my – what do I call him? My biological father: Connor; Dr Myers. And maybe my half-brother, Ethan, if he wants to meet me. The thought of having a half-brother makes me tingle. I wonder what he looks like and if he's at all like me. I wonder what he thinks. I wonder if he knows. I wonder if he hates me.

<u>Later</u>

I plucked up courage and Googled him. Dr Connor Myers. There were hundreds of entries and I only selected a few because most were specialist websites and talked about things I had never heard of, though I'm a scientist myself, or I want to be. Maybe I get that from him. Maybe I'm good at maths and physics because he is.

At least I know now that I look like him. Nancy said so, but I didn't pay much attention to that. I thought it was maybe her way of distancing herself from me – I look like him so I don't look much like her, apart from the colour of my eyes, of course. Then I saw his picture. He's thin and dark-haired, with high cheekbones and an intense stare: you can sense it even from a computer screen. And even I could see myself in his face. It was a very odd sensation – disquieting. This man whom I hadn't thought about (why haven't I? why have I thought incessantly about my real mother and hardly at all about my real father?) and now I discover he's got my face. Or I've got his, I guess.

He's got lots of letters after his name and lots of publications with titles like 'RSD: Nerves and Their Consequences', and 'Pain Neurotransmitters and Their Effects', which talked about things like 'neuroplasticity' and 'allodynia' (I looked that up – it's when even the smallest puff of air or a drop of water can cause agony). But some links led to more general articles. There was a piece about him opening a pain clinic and an interview with him in the Guardian about torture. There was a bit where he said that torture turns a human into an instrument and 'uncreates the self', and that it is 'pain made visible'. He said things like, pain becomes the world, the body has a memory, the self is split into subject and object. I couldn't grasp what he meant – it was like some of the things in physics that you have to hold on to with all the power of your mind because you know that as soon as you let them go you'll lose them, like you lose a dream on waking. I've kind of lost what he was trying to say already, though I feel it's some-where in my brain and when I'm feeling alert and clever I'll go back to it and try to grapple with it. He ended by quoting Primo Levi: 'Anyone who has been tortured, remains tortured.' And then Emily Dickinson: 'After great pain, a formal feeling comes.' I found myself thinking I'd really like to meet him – not as my biological father, but as a man who's done lots of interesting work and has a head full of ideas I'd never thought about before.

I found myself hoping I was like him. Is that a dangerous thought? And what would Mum and Dad feel if they knew I was thinking it? Maybe he'll turn out to be grim and dry, like creepy Mr Casaubon in *Middlemarch,* but he didn't sound like that.

There was nothing about his wife or Ethan.

His wife: Nancy's friend, Ethan's mother. I haven't thought

about her. Nancy didn't even tell me her name. I've been imagining myself as the centre of this story, but there's a whole other story going on that I haven't started to imagine and which I'm only on the margins of. My story's about finding out where I come from, but hers is a story of betrayal and I'm a symptom of that. Poor woman. I hope she's all right.

Thirty-five

At the end of the first week of December, when the trees were bare, the ground hard and days had shrunk into a few pinched hours, Gaby put her hands on Connor's shoulders, kissed him on both cheeks, then steered him in the direction of the front door.

'Gaby –' he started to say, but she shushed him.

'It's OK, you know. You're not going to your execution, you're going to meet your daughter.'

'You do know how much I –?'

'Go on. You don't want to be late, do you?'

'I suppose not.'

He looked so stricken that she relented. 'Don't torture yourself,' she said gently. 'You'll go mad like that. I want you to go. I want you to like her and her to like you. I want you to answer her questions and be honest with her. Otherwise there's no point, is there? She's on some kind of a search – for herself, who she really is – and you've got to help her.'

'I suppose so.'

'You know so. You've agreed to meet her, so you should meet her wholeheartedly.'

'I feel as if I'm betraying you all over again.'

'You're not. And I don't feel like that.'

'You're sure?'

'Sure.'

'But –'

'You really will be late.'

'I love you.'

'I know you do.'

'Will this always come between us?'

'It's not like that. It's more complicated than that and – oh, look, Connor, this isn't the right time. You're half-way out of the door to see Sonia.'

'Right. I'll go, then.'

'Yes.'

'So – goodbye.'

''Bye.'

'And, Gaby –'

'Go!'

'And you'll be around later?'

'Of course. I'm not about to run away.'

'Sometimes I'm scared I'll come home and you –'

'Connor! This is mad. *Go*.'

He bent his head forward to kiss her and she half turned her face so that he touched her cheek, not her lips. She wasn't angry, she wasn't jealous, she didn't feel she was a wronged woman, she didn't want to punish him, she didn't want what had happened so many years ago to lie like a shadow across their lives – yet she felt that their relationship had changed and she didn't know how to win back the frank and confident affection she used to take for granted. As for making love – she couldn't imagine how it would happen again. A terrible self-consciousness had gripped them both. For a couple of weeks, she had continued sleeping in Ethan's room. Connor had never tried to come in and she had never expected him to. He would wait for her to make any first move. Eventually she had returned to their bedroom, but she might as well have been in a separate space. They lay rigidly on their own sides of the bed, careful not to touch each other by mistake. Sometimes he would reach out and hold her hand; sometimes she would touch his shoulder or his warm, sinewy back when she said goodnight, or would lean over to kiss his cheek. But on most nights they went to bed at different times. The dark and silent spaces of the night, which in the past they had wrapped themselves up in together, had become lonely, empty ones. Sometimes when Gaby woke in the small hours, she would lie and listen to Connor's breathing and long to wrap her arms round his body and press her face into his neck. But she never did.

'Shall I get us something simple for sup –?' he was saying, as she closed the door, unable to bear his fretful hovering a moment longer.

She leant against it and heard his footsteps going down the path. Then she went into the kitchen and pulled open the fridge. It was clean and bare, just a carton of semi-skimmed milk and a bottle of white wine in the door, a slab of cheese, a carton of eggs and a few jars of condiments on the shelves. She pushed it shut and went slowly up the stairs to get ready for the day. She dressed in jeans and a bright red shirt, then piled her hair on top of her head and put on a long pair of earrings. Winter lay ahead of her – a time for a fire in the hearth, candles, puddings. Perhaps she should buy herself some new clothes, she thought. Something velvet, something cashmere, something sequined, something to put a spring in her step. Or gloves and buttons and scarves with stripes. She was trying not to think about Christmas, though she had always loved it, in spite of Connor's grumpiness and atheist's disgust. He liked to be austere and year after year suggested donating money to a charity of their choice and going walking in the Lake District; year after year she sent the money to charity, then got the largest tree that would fit into their living room and clogged its branches with tasteless baubles and tinsel that gradually spread across the carpet, made pomanders with oranges and cloves and hung them from the beam in the kitchen, bought advent calendars and crackers and too many presents, which she wrapped in lavish paper and tied with ribbons that she scraped into tightly sprung curls, filled up the cupboards with mince pies, dates and chocolates, organized drinks parties that overflowed up the house with drunken voices, invited any lonely friend over for the day itself, went round the house singing carols in an exuberant, out-of-tune voice, wore clothes that glittered and carried with her an air of festivity that made the smallest gathering into a celebration. This year, though, she wasn't filled with the same delight. Rather, she felt anxiety and anticipatory weariness. She didn't know, feeling as she did, how she would get through the whole charade yet again, and suddenly all the years of childish pleasure seemed shrill to her, and false.

But this wasn't the way to be thinking. Today she was resolved to work hard, make contact with friends, fill the hours with activity that would stop her brooding or imagining Connor's meeting with Sonia. It was cold outside. The glorious autumn had led into grey, chilly winter; experts were predicting a ferocious cold snap. She put on boots, coat, gloves, scarf, a hat that she pulled down over her ears, and marched out into the street. The sky was a milky white and the houses and trees bleached of colour. She pulled her phone out of her pocket and, during the walk to the Underground station, called her friend Sal and arranged to meet for lunch. Then she tried Ethan, but got his voicemail – he was probably in bed. She could picture him lying there, one arm thrown across his face, his mouth slightly open and his long lashes closed.

Gaby's resolve lasted until mid-afternoon. She worked hard all morning, doing the tedious, bureaucratic jobs like filing and working through her emails that she had been putting off, then spent an hour with Sal in a bistro, dodging all the questions she didn't want to answer and putting on a good show of cheerfulness. But at three o'clock, when she'd answered all the emails, made the urgent phone calls to theatres and reached the bottom of the in-tray, she was hit by a wave of dejection that left her startled and breathless. She gripped the edge of her desk, lowered her head and waited for it to ebb away, and it was at this moment that Gilbert, her boss and friend, walked in, whistling tunelessly. He was wearing a dark suit and a flamboyant dandy's tie; a hat was squashed on to his head and a coat hung on one arm. His belly bulged over the top of his trousers and his cheeks were red from the cold and perhaps from his long lunch. The whistle died on his lips when he saw Gaby. He slung his coat over the chair and tossed the hat on to his desk. 'What's up with you?'

'Nothing.'

'Do you expect me to believe that?'

'Really – nothing.'

Gilbert held up a hand in protest. 'Hey, Gaby. Tell me to mind my own business if you want, but don't try to tell me nothing's wrong. I'm not a complete idiot, you know. Nor am I blind. For weeks now you've been down in the mouth. I thought maybe it was woman's stuff at first – you know, mysterious things I don't understand. But it's more than that, isn't it? Something's upsetting you.'

'Gil, I –'

'You don't need to tell me. But if you want to, here I am.'

'I know you are.'

'You're not going to say anything, are you?'

Gaby opened her mouth to tell him once more that she was fine, nothing the matter, just winter dreariness – then changed her mind. 'Do you want to go for a walk?' she asked.

'Sure. We can go to the park if you'd like.'

'It's easier to say things if you're not looking at some-one when you say the words.'

'You're not dying, are you? You've not got cancer or anything?'

'No!'

'Or Connor?'

'No, Gil.'

'Ethan – it's something to do with Ethan. Drugs or –'

'Ethan's fine.'

'Thank God for that. Get your coat and we'll be out of here.'

Out on the street, he wrapped an arm round Gaby and

matched his steps to hers. It occurred to her that she hadn't been hugged for a long time and she leant gratefully into his solid warmth, breathing in the rich brew of cigarettes, wine, aftershave. 'So?' he said.

She swallowed. 'So . . .'

It didn't take her long; there was just enough of a story to get them round the park twice and back on to the street as the light was failing, although she started in her childhood, when she had had a best friend called Nancy, and continued steadily through the parallel accounts of her friendship and her marriage. Gilbert was a good listener. He didn't interrupt, occasionally made a sympathetic humming noise or tightened his grip on her shoulder to show her his attention wasn't flagging.

'And that's about it,' she finished. 'Here I am.'

'Here you are.'

'But where is that? I don't know where I am any more. I can't live like this. I'm distant from everything. From Connor especially. I mean, we've talked and cried and been incredibly honest with each other – but at the same time, I'm far away, looking at myself. And he's very aware of it. Even when I'm making a huge effort to be warm and generous, he can tell I'm not really there. And I don't know how I'll ever be there again.'

'What do you want?' Gilbert asked.

'Oh – want. I want to want things again. I want to want Connor. I want to want my life.'

They walked a few paces without saying anything.

'What do you think I should do?'

'You don't need anyone's advice, Gaby. It's too important for that. But perhaps you should go away for a bit.

I don't mean a separation or anything like that, I mean go away to get a fresh view on what's happened.'

'Do you think that might help?'

'I don't know. Maybe.'

'But Christmas is coming. Ethan'll be home soon. I can't just up and go.'

Gilbert chuckled. 'You can, you know.'

'And it's the busy time at work.'

'Oh – work,' he said dismissively. 'Don't worry about that.'

'Really? You wouldn't mind?'

'No one's indispensable.'

'I know.'

'Except in a marriage.'

'Perhaps.'

'I've got a cottage you could use.'

'You have? Why don't I know that?'

'I never go there, that's why. It was my brother's and he left it to me when he died. Sol and I used it a bit before we split up, but not much. We weren't very good at roughing it and it's a bit run-down, to be honest.'

'That doesn't matter.'

'And pretty remote – it doesn't have a phone line and it's heated by an old wood-burning stove, which isn't very efficient. I keep telling myself I have to do something with it – sell it or do it up, or both. But I've never got round to it, so it just stands there. It could be lovely, with some work.'

'Where is it?'

'On the Welsh borders.'

'Wet, then.'

'Oh, yes,' Gilbert said with relish. 'At this time of year, it's wet and cold and grey, with armies of nettles in the garden, the wind whistling down the chimney at night, slates falling off the roof, and the water comes out of the tap in spurts of rusty brown. Very authentic, if you like that kind of thing.'

'It sounds perfect.'

'Mice in the roof, I wouldn't be surprised.'

'Bats?'

'Probably. But views out of the windows to take your breath away, and nothing for miles around but fields and lanes and little woods.'

'Lovely.'

'Anyway, Gaby, it's there if you want it. On the other hand you might prefer a hotel in France for a few days instead.'

'No. If I go, I'd like to go there.'

'Just tell me when you've decided. I don't need any warning.'

When Gaby got home, Connor was at the kitchen table, still in his suit trousers but with his tie pulled loose and his shirtsleeves rolled up, hammering a piece of rump steak flat with both hands. A bunch of tight yellow roses, still in their paper, stood in a jug by the sink.

'Hello,' said Gaby, standing in the doorway. 'What are you cooking?'

He stopped what he was doing and rinsed his hands under the tap. The smile he gave her was tense and un-certain. 'Hello. I thought just steak and rocket in ciabatta and some good red wine. All right?'

'Fine.'

'And then we can talk, Gaby.'

'Yes.'

'I'm serious. We need to talk. I'll tell you about today, of course, I'll answer any questions. But it's more than that. This has come between us like a wedge. No, listen, you've been extraordinary. You couldn't have reacted with more generosity or honesty. Yet it feels to me that we're standing together in a cold shadow. That's the only way I can think to put it.'

'It's a good way to put it,' said Gaby, gently.

'It makes me understand how happy I've been with you.'

'And I with you.'

'This sounds horribly like an elegy for something lost. We mustn't lose it, Gaby. We have to get it back – oh, I know, of course, that nothing can be exactly the same. We can't swallow a forgetting-pill to erase the knowledge we both now have. Though to be absolutely honest, there have been times over the years when I did almost forget what I'd done. It seemed to have happened to a different person. Not me. I know that sounds like a way of forgiving myself. I don't mean it like that.'

'Sonia makes it impossible for that to happen again, doesn't it?'

'Yes. Of course. Sonia.'

'Shall we start with her?'

'Do you want a glass of wine?'

'Not yet.'

'Right.'

They sat opposite each other at the table. Connor

looked down at his hands as he talked. 'We didn't meet for very long. An hour or so. We went and had coffee in the café near the hospital. You know the one.'

'I know.'

'She was a bit late – or I was a bit early. She wanted first of all to know about –'

'No. What did she look like?'

'You met her. You know what she looks like.'

'I want to know what she looks like to *you*. What you felt like when you met her, your first thoughts and impressions.'

'Oh.' Connor paused, then said softly, 'She's lovely.'

Gaby felt as though someone had taken her heart and squeezed it brutally in their fist, but she kept her eyes steadily on Connor's averted face.

'Lovely to look at and just – well . . . lovely. Young and bright and full of curiosity about things. Half the time we talked about my work. She wants to study science. She's obviously very clever, but also she's got this real intellectual hunger, as if she's been half starved for years. In that way she reminded me of –' He stopped.

'Of you.'

'I was going to say that, yes.'

'You felt proud of her.'

Connor looked at his wife. His face twisted in pity. 'I suppose I did.'

'Of your daughter.'

'She's not my daughter. She was very clear about that. It was pretty much the first thing she said. She's not my daughter and I'm not her father. I'm her genetic donor.'

'Yes.'

'Gaby, you asked me and I told you.'

'Right. So – what did she ask you?'

'She had a list of questions written out. It was somewhat disconcerting. For example, she wanted to know about illnesses, genetic predispositions, things like that. I told her about my father's cancer, and the pre-cancerous growths in my intestine a few years ago, and about my mother's alcoholism. And I mentioned that I had a mild tendency to depression that I kept at bay by running. It was all remarkably dispassionate.'

'What else?'

'Um – she said did I realize how like each other we were.'

'And you did?'

'Yes. We even have the same way of –'

'I know.'

'Of course. And she asked about how it happened.'

'Between you and Nancy?'

'Yes.'

'And you told her.'

'But nothing I haven't already told you. She wanted to know if I'd ever suspected she existed. She was confirming Nancy's story for herself, I suppose.'

'Mm.'

'She asked about Ethan. She wants to meet him.'

'Of course she does.'

'She seems genuinely delighted at the idea that she has a half-brother.'

'What did you say?'

'And I said I'd talk to my family about it.'

'By your family you mean me and Ethan?'

414

'Yes.'

'Right. You've talked to me. I'm going to leave it to you to tell Ethan. I think that's best. You don't want me hovering round you.'

'Gaby –'

'It's fine. Maybe you could visit him, take him out for a meal or something.'

'I was thinking of waiting until he came home.'

'It's up to you. Shall we have that glass of wine now?'

'Of course.'

He got to his feet and opened the bottle he'd put out earlier, then poured them half a glass each, clinked his glass against hers. 'To us,' he said.

'Did she ask about me?'

'You?'

'There's no reason she should have. I've probably never crossed her mind. But I wondered if she mentioned me at all.'

'She said that she hoped this hadn't been destructive for me. That's a way of asking about you, after a fashion.'

'Hmm. And what did you ask her?'

'Oh. If she felt that this whole experience had helped her come to terms with her background, things like that,' said Connor, vaguely.

'What else?'

'Well, she wanted to know if we would meet again and I said I was sure that we would before long.'

'What does that mean, before long?'

'I don't know. Before next year.'

'That soon! I see.'

'Not that soon – a few weeks . . .'

'I see,' she repeated, and took another sip, frowning. 'She's in your life, isn't she?'

'I don't know, Gaby. Honestly, I don't know. But I won't do anything you don't want me to do, I promise you that.'

'You're asking my permission?'

'That's not how I would want to see it. I want to feel that we're in this strange situation together, making decisions as a partnership.'

'We're not in it together, though, are we? Of course we're not. How can we be?'

'Look, I know that's true in a way. What I'm saying now is that we have to find a way through this together.'

'I know.'

'So where do we begin?'

'We begin with me going away.'

Connor gave a start, so that some of his wine splashed on to the table.

'I need to step outside this hot little muddle we've made.'

'Of course,' he said drearily. 'When do you want to go?'

'I thought – tomorrow?'

'Tomorrow!'

'Gil turns out to have a cottage on the Welsh borders I can use for as long as I want.'

'But tomorrow?'

'Yes.'

'You're leaving me, aren't you?'

'I don't know what I'm doing. But I have to go.'

Thirty-six

It was one of those days when the darkness never lifts entirely, yet as she drove down the narrow lane under the tangled arch of bare trees, Gaby felt herself stirred with excitement. Snarling winds, a few vicious spits of rain, a grimly lowering sky: this was what she had come for, this heaving emptiness of green, sodden grey and churning brown, where she could be alone. She glanced down at the piece of paper containing Gilbert's precise directions, written in his beautiful italic hand. She had to turn left down a tarmacked track after a few miles on this road, so she did, over a hump-backed bridge, along a brackish stream, and as she rounded the corner and the tarmac turned to gravel and mud, she saw the cottage in front of her, half hidden by trees, half invisible in its slaty greyness.

Gilbert had not exaggerated. It was certainly remote. No other dwelling could be seen from here, unless you counted the ruined grey walls of what must once have been a sheep pen on the shallow hillside behind the cottage. And even from the outside, it looked run-down. The window-frames were rotting, the stonework in need of pointing; there was moss in the guttering and the windows were dirty and streaked with bird shit. Weeds grew high in the garden that ran down to the stream, so it was hard to make out the ancient rose bushes and shrubs. Yet it was a pretty house, low and grey, with asymmetrical windows. On one side, stone steps climbed to a square wooden door that Gaby knew opened into the junk room and wood store. The rickety porch had a bench inside it, and ivy spread over the walls. Gaby could imagine the cottage restored, tended and lit up, smoke rising from the chimney – a little grey haven among the wild beauty that surrounded it.

She pulled to a halt outside, climbed out of the car and opened the boot. She had packed an old leather case with a sketch-pad and paints, but apart from that she had only brought the essentials: loo paper, bed linen and a towel, two thick Victorian novels, and a few clothes – an extra pair of jeans, a couple of shirts, a warm jersey, long scarf, thick socks, walking-boots, night-things, slippers and a fluorescent yellow waterproof with a peaked hood that would have looked more appropriate on a fisherman out in the North Sea. But when she had left, Connor had insisted on loading her up with provisions. He'd produced two bottles of red wine and one of white, with a corkscrew in case the house didn't have one; several vacuum-packed half-baked baguettes that kept for days and she could simply pop into the oven a few minutes before eating; a packet of smoked bacon and half a dozen eggs; a third of a tub of spreadable butter; a jar of marmalade he had made last year; a bag of green apples; a mango, ready to eat at once; a slab of his favourite chocolate; a portion of frozen vegetable lasagne that he'd found at the back of the freezer; half a litre of milk; porridge oats for her breakfast, and golden sugar to sprinkle over it; ground coffee; Assam tea and green tea; and finally an old hot-water bottle in case the cottage was cold. She'd protested that there would be shops and cafés near enough, and that she was coming home soon anyway, but he had looked so eager, his arms full of food, that she had relented.

She picked up her case, bundled the sheet and duvet under her arm, then walked to the front door and fished out of her pocket the key Gilbert had given her. It took several goes to make it turn in the lock, and then the door stuck on the pile of envelopes and flyers that had been pushed through the letterbox. It was almost as cold inside as it was out, and the dank smell caught in her nostrils. She pushed her case indoors and went back to the car to collect the boxes of food. Then she looked around her. The front door opened directly into the sitting room, which had a couple of baggy, comfy sofas, a writing desk and a bookcase in it, as well as a wood-burning stove in the corner. It led directly into a kitchen of higgledy-piggledy cabinets and a tiny cooker; the window gave on to the patchworked hillside.

Gaby applied herself to Gilbert's instructions. She found the stopcock and turned it on, feeling absurdly proud when water gushed in orange-brown splashes out of the tap. She found the switch for electricity and turned that on too. Sure enough, light filled the rooms. She went out of the house and up the stone staircase at the side, unlocking and dragging open the warped wooden door and peering into a dark space, remembering only then that Gilbert had advised her to take a torch. But she could see logs piled along one wall, and she took as many as she could manage and brought them back into the house. She couldn't remember the last time she had made a fire;

Connor always did that. There was a pile of yellowing newspapers on the table and she scrunched several pages into tight balls and laid them at the bottom of the wood-burning stove. Now she needed kindling. The twigs and fallen branches outside were wet, but in a room leading off the kitchen – a kind of walk-in store room and larder, with two fishing rods leaning against the wall and whose shelves held a few mysterious tins and packets – she found a box of sticks clearly left there for the purpose. She arranged these in a neat roof across the paper.

There. Now she could light the fire – except she had no matches. None in her pockets, none in her bag, although she did have a packet of cigarettes bought at a petrol station on the way. There were none, it seemed, anywhere in the house – she opened drawers and ran up the steep, narrow staircase to see if a box might be hiding in one of the two bedrooms. Gaby cursed, blowing on her numbing fingers to warm them. Then she went back to the car, turned the key in the ignition and depressed the cigarette lighter. When it popped back up, she held it against a tight twist of paper until it caught light, and ran back to the house carrying it between cupped fingers. It went out as she reached the kitchen, so she returned to the car, and this time lit a cigarette, which she used to light one of the paper balls in the stove. Flames licked and caught; the sticks started to smoke. Gaby carefully laid three small logs in a wigwam round them. The flames dwindled and expired.

Twice more, she went through the whole process, watching the flames catch, then die. Surely it should be easier than this. If that stocky man on television could go into icy wildernesses and light a bonfire by rubbing sticks together and coaxing flames out of wood shavings, surely she could get a wood-burning stove designed for the purpose to work. At last, nearly an hour later, a small fire was burning, but giving out no heat. The smoke wasn't going upwards either, but outwards, seeping through the stove's glass doors and filling the room. Gaby twiddled the handles at the bottom of the contraption, which she assumed must have something to do with directing the air flow, and the smoke became thicker, so she returned them to their original position and opened the doors to let the smoke billow into the room.

At least the cooker was a basic electric one, and the kettle was one you plugged in and turned on. She filled it with water and rummaged in the box for the tea-bags. There was a teapot in one of the cupboards with a chipped spout, and an unexpectedly beautiful tea-set – delicate cups and saucers in bone china. She went into the chilly sitting room with her tea and sat on one of the sofas, sipping it. It was four o'clock. The grey day was ending and the long evening stretched in front of her. She wasn't sure what to do with it and, filled with a need to talk to someone, she pulled her mobile from her pocket to call Stefan. But there was no signal here; no signal and no landline. If she wanted to talk to someone she would have to get into the car and drive somewhere. Briefly, she was filled with foreboding, and the sound of the wind clattering seemed menacing. Then she heaved herself out of the sagging sofa, closed the curtains in the kitchen and the living room and unpacked the box of provisions into various cupboards. She found that Connor had put in two large boxes of matches and she thanked him silently, then went upstairs with her case and bed linen.

Of the bedrooms, one was large and carpeted, with a double bed, a tall wardrobe containing several blankets and pillows, a set of shelves lined with a motley collection of paperbacks. Its window overlooked the driveway. The other was much smaller and plainer, with whitewashed walls, unvarnished wooden floorboards, a threadbare rug. The chest, whose two drawers were empty except for a European plug and three ancient mothballs, was the only piece of furniture in the room, aside from the single bed. But the window gave Gaby a view of the hillside, and it was here that she decided to sleep. She made up the bed and put her books on top of the chest: *David Copperfield* and *Middlemarch*, the two longest novels she had been able to find that morning. Even if she did nothing but read for the whole time she was here, they would keep her going. She took off her shoes and jacket, put on her slippers and an extra jersey, put her toilet bag in the bathroom and went back downstairs, treading heavily on the stairs to break the silence.

It was very strange, she thought, being in a house where there were no other people, no phones, no radio or TV, no CD-player, not even anything like a dishwasher or washing-machine, whose sound would give the chugging reassurance of a domestic routine. She whistled, then said out loud, to break the silence: 'Right. This is what you asked for so you'd better make the most of it.'

What she wanted was a richly melancholy, nostalgic mood to settle on her so that she could brood on her life and find it full of meaning. She wanted to be done with the thin, faltering dejection of the past weeks and enter a time of full-hearted sorrow, anger, hope and love. She wandered into the sitting room, where the fire was now blazing steadily, giving out heat, and the smoke had dispersed. Crouching in front of it, she closed her eyes and felt the warmth on her cheeks. For several minutes she didn't move. Outside, she could hear the rain strengthening; it seemed to be beating on her skull and suddenly she leapt to her feet. Her walking-boots and waterproof still lay on the floor where she had left them. She put them on, then opened the door and stepped out into the weather.

There was no moon and no stars and it was icily cold. The rain stung her cheeks and bounced off the muddy drive like bullets. The wind whipped her hair against her skin. Almost immediately Gaby's hands felt raw and her chin, nose and ears burnt. She pulled up the hood of her jacket and set off towards the hillside, feeling her boots sink into claggy mud. She clambered over a slimy stile, disentangled herself from tenacious briars, stumbled at a rabbit hole, but on she tramped until she was far enough up the hill to turn round and look back at the cottage. From this distance, it seemed quite cosy: the lights were on in all the rooms and smoke was rising out of the chimney. She clambered higher and the cottage became smaller, a fuzz of soft light in the streaming darkness. She was wet through; the waterproof jacket seemed designed to funnel rain on to various parts of her body; it ran in a channel round the collar and spouted down her neck; it gushed off the gutter of its hem on to her jeans, which stuck to her thighs uncomfortably. Her boots were full of water and made a sucking noise with every step she took. Rain poured down her cheeks and dripped off her nose. Her ears were throbbing with cold and her eyes filled with tears, which were viscous in the low temperature. Several times she stumbled and fell, and with each fall into ice and mud her spirits rose. She was hungry, she was soaking, she was freezing, she was tired and alone and scared. But she was all right.

Gaby didn't get back to the cottage until past seven o'clock. She peeled off her sodden layers of clothing inside the door, then ran up the stairs to towel her hair and pull on her thick dressing-gown. A few minutes later she went into the sitting room, put more logs on the dying fire and blew on the embers to get it going again. Next, she went into the kitchen and considered what to eat that evening. She opened the fridge and studied the food Connor had given her. Tomorrow, she thought, she would have the lasagne, but tonight she would make herself bacon and eggs, mopped up with a baguette and swilled down with mugs of strong tea. She remembered seeing tins on the shelf in the larder and when she went to look, she found baked beans. Better and better – Connor hated baked beans and Gaby couldn't remember the last time she'd eaten them. Perhaps she'd even have the meal in bed, with blankets piled on top of the duvet, and *David Copperfield* open in front of her.

Which was what she ended up doing. She left the curtains in the bedroom open so she could see out of the window from where she lay propped up in bed, several pillows behind her back, the hot-water bottle at her feet and on her lap a plate of bacon covered with broken, oozing egg and sticky orange beans, that she pushed onto her fork with pieces of buttered baguette. The rain continued, and when she snuggled down under the duvet and closed her eyes, its steady patter against the pane comforted her. It was the last thing she heard as she sank into sleep.

She woke with a start, confused. Where was she? She gazed out of the window, wondering if a sound apart from the rain and the wind had woken her, then, just as she was about to slide back to unconsciousness, a thought snagged her and she groaned. She had left the car door open when she was trying to light the stove with its cigarette lighter. The interior lights had been on for hours, and now the battery would probably be flat. She knew she should go and shut it, but her bed was piled high with blankets and the place where she lay was so beautifully warm. She folded herself up more tightly in the duvet and laid her arm over her eyes to shut out any vestige of light.

But she couldn't just lie there and let the last of the battery be used up. In her imagination, she was getting out of bed, wrapping her dressing-gown round herself, hurrying down the stairs and sliding her feet into her boots. It would only take a minute, less, to get up and close the car door. She could have been back in bed by now if she had done it at once. She would count to ten and then she would force herself out of the lovely nest she had made. Now she would count another five. One, two, three ... Thick with sleep. Heavy limbs. Eyes deep in her skull. A forest of dreams just ahead. What a strange land sleep was. The wind tapped at the window and the rain made a staccato rhythm against the pane. Just a little longer. One deep breath, in, out, longer. Then she would go. If Connor were here he'd do it for her. But Connor wasn't here. Nobody was here. She wasn't here either, not really, she was billowing through the air, turning through the dark water. Too late now. Gone.

Thirty-seven

Her throat ached, her eyes ached, her glands, ears, sinuses, chest, head. Every bone in her body felt sore. Her skin prickled. She stumbled out of bed, down the stairs and outside into the drizzle to shut the car door, though she knew it wouldn't start now – even the light above the mirror had gone out. What was more, it occurred to her, as she went back to bed, she couldn't phone the AA to come and rescue her because her mobile didn't work here. Never mind. She'd think about all of that later. For now, she felt thick with illness, and all she wanted to do was roll herself up in her duvet and close her eyes once more. Connor had told her enough times that you couldn't catch a cold or flu by getting wet, they were airborne viruses, yet it seemed to Gaby that her march through the elements yesterday evening had brought this on.

She slept all morning, wrapped in thick, feverish images, then got up to go to the bathroom, refill the hot-water bottle and put a blanket over the duvet. She slept intermittently through the afternoon, surfacing every so often from fretful dreams of things going wrong. In one she was in the vast, hot, dimly lit Top Shop on Oxford Street where Connor seemed to have his office, but she couldn't find him. In another, she was at home, but a stream had burst outside the front door and was rushing in a torrent through the kitchen. Then there was something about a cupful of ants she was supposed to drink but every time she lifted the cup they crawled over her face and into her ears and nostrils. She woke up coughing and spluttering. Her throat was full of glass; her glands throbbed; jets of pain shot through her eardrums; when she sat up, pain sloshed through her skull.

She made herself a mug of green tea and crawled back to bed. Sometimes she was hot and clammy and sometimes she was cold and clammy. The duvet got twisted up and she found that she was lying under the scratchy blanket, which made her skin itch. She wished she was a child and that her mother was there with clean sheets, cool flannels, soft towels, mugs of broth. Connor was good at looking after her when she was ill. He didn't make a big fuss of her, the way she did of him, but he tended her. I'm married to a vigilant man, she thought, and hot tears started in her eyes. For a few minutes she cried, in a snuffly, wretched way, then blew her nose hard on the wadge of loo paper she'd fetched from the bathroom.

Now it was getting dark outside. The grey day had ended and night was beginning once more. She closed her eyes again and drifted into a half-sleep, where images surged through her mind. She saw Ethan, Connor, Stefan, Nancy. They were watching her, waiting for her. She saw herself, as if she was watching a film of her life. She let herself remember meeting Nancy – such a fierce, clever child with her jutting jaw and pale eyes. Like a lynx. They used to play a game, dividing people into cats and dogs. She and Ethan were definitely dogs – a bit undignified, unconditional, clumsy, emotional, vulnerable, trusting and foolish. But Connor and Nancy were more like cats, self-possessed, rational and remote, holding themselves back from the world, assessing it through narrowed gazes. Except, thought Gaby, turning over in bed and finding a cool spot on the pillow, the last few weeks seemed to have turned Connor into a dog, with spaniel eyes following her.

When she looked at her watch again it was ten o'clock. When she sat up her head pounded, and when she swallowed the glass still stuck in her throat. Her mouth was dry and tasted awful. She made her way into the dark, cold kitchen and drank three glasses of water, which was so full of iron it tasted like blood. The rain had stopped, but she could still hear water dripping from the trees outside. Apart from that, there was silence.

It was three o'clock when she woke again in her narrow bed. She lay very still, breathing softly, and could almost feel the darkness pressing on her. Her limbs ached and her chest hurt. Her skin crawled with an obscene discomfort. Nobody could get to her here, and the car was an inert lump of metal in front of the house. She turned over to face the dark square of window and went back to sleep.

At nine o'clock the next morning she swung her legs out of bed and stood up warily, feeling the iron ball swing inside her head and smash against her right temple. The light made her eyes ache. She took a few groggy steps to the bathroom and leant against the wash-basin, trying not to see her face in the mirror, but she couldn't avoid it.

Her hair was lank and her face was waxy and rearranged. One eye looked lower than the other, and there were huge circles round them as if she had just removed swimming goggles. Her lips were pale and cracked.

'Blimey,' she said – tried to say. Her voice was thick and hoarse; she didn't sound anything like herself. She started to cry again, but stopped because she didn't have the strength for tears.

She crept down the stairs. Her breath smoked in the kitchen, and there were flowers of frost inside the window-panes. The sight of the greasy plate from two nights ago made her feel nauseous. In the sitting room a dull pile of papery ash lay at the bottom of the wood-burning stove, but Gaby couldn't summon the energy to fetch Connor's matches and build a fire. She would do it later. For now, she boiled the kettle for another mug of green tea.

At four o'clock she made it downstairs again, and this time she got herself another hot-water bottle, and took a biscuit back to bed with her tea, although she only ate one bite.

At one in the morning, she woke hollow with hunger and thought about Connor's vegetable lasagne in the fridge. Eventually she went downstairs, turned on the oven, heated it, put a small amount on to a plate and took it back to bed. She sat against her pillows, wrapped in blankets and looked at it. The smell of melted cheese made her feel weak with desire. She ate only a few mouth-fuls, feeling them settle heavily in her stomach, but the simple act of swallowing good food made her contented. Out of the window she saw that the sky was clear; stars glittered and a gibbous moon hung low and large above the hill. Tomorrow would be a beautiful day.

The days that followed would seem later like a dream, separated from past and future. Gaby was as weak as a kitten from her illness, and she behaved as if she had been snowed in. She made no attempt to call the AA to fix her car. Indeed, she rarely left the house, and when she did it was only to go to the wood store or to stand in the garden, contemplating the landscape that spread out under the cold blue sky. She lived on baguettes and marmalade, porridge – made with water once the milk was finished – sprinkled with golden sugar, and green apples, all eaten at whatever time of day she felt hungry. She didn't open the wine but drank ferrous water and green tea. She spent her time either in the sitting room, where the stove burnt day and night, or in bed with a hot-water bottle. She stopped putting on clothes and took to wearing her dressing-gown over a T-shirt and knickers, with thick socks on her feet. The water never ran hot enough for a bath, so she washed in the basin every now and then. She rather liked the wild, gaunt face that confronted her in the mirror, denuded of all artifice. This was who she really was.

She started drawing and painting – something she hadn't done for years, even though she had recently enrolled at the evening art class. She did watercolours of the scene outside her window, with the pale sun and the hill that, once she looked at it properly, was violet and brown and blue and yellow as well as hues of green. And she sketched the winter birds that came to the windowsill to peck at the pieces of stale baguette she left there. There were long-tailed tits, blue-tits, chaffinches, robins, wrens and, once, a green woodpecker that stared at her beadily through the glass. At the end of each day, she burnt what she had done. Sometimes she read *David Copperfield*, although she often found that she hadn't taken in the words, and would have to go back and read them again; or poems from an anthology she found in the living room that contained many of her old favourites. She learnt one by heart, 'The Sunlight on the Garden' by Louis MacNeice, and recited it to herself as she stirred her porridge or tended the fire. And sometimes she wrote in her notebook, trying to work out what she really felt about the events that had turned her life upside down.

But for many hours of each unstructured day she simply sat and let thoughts come into her mind, then pass quietly out again. She could not remember a time in her adult life that she had been alone with herself like this. She had spent so many years trying to please and charm other people – her husband, her son, her friends, her boss, strangers she met in the street. A lot of her thoughts then were more like plans and strategies for the day. Now, she could wear a dressing-gown and socks all day long, get up at three in the afternoon, eat dinner at five in the morning, watch winter birds at the window, think.

What did she think?

She thought of all the reasons why she should stay with Connor: because she loved him, because she liked him, because she knew him so well that he had almost become invisible to her, because he knew her, and in spite of her recklessness, folly and greed, he liked her and loved her too, because Ethan was his son, because of all the memories they had together, because of the future they planned, because he was patient, because of the way he smiled at her, because of the way he frowned when he was working, because he was clever and dry and sardonic, because he had cried in her arms, because he danced so badly, because he put his tongue on his lip when he concentrated, because he knew old songs from musicals and sang them in the shower, because he was kind, because he got up early to make her tea in bed, because he accepted her for what she was and didn't try to change her, because he needed her, because the thought of being without him made her feel cold and lonely and scared.

Yet for all this, their old life together now seemed unreal to her, like a well-edited film that she was watching from a distance. She lay in her narrow bed, darkness outside, pictured scenes from their marriage and thought: Was that really me? Was that him? Was that us? Was that the life we led together for so many years?

And then she thought: Where have those years gone? She had always imagined she would escape the sadness of time passing, but it had mugged her all the same, thwacked her round the head and kicked her in the shins when she was least expecting it, like a hooligan charging out of a dark alleyway with a crowbar. Just a memory ago she had been young and vibrant, chockful of energy and hope. You're supposed to gain things as you grow older in return for the things that you lose. But what had she gained? Dignity? She hadn't got that. Peace? No. Wisdom? It seemed unlikely. And what had she lost?

Beauty, youth, innocence, possibility. Your past grows longer and your future shrinks. And you lose your parents and your children – often at the same time so that you go from being daughter and mother to being neither. What are you then? What was she then?

So she thought: How much of this whole brouhaha is to do with Ethan leaving home? A great deal. Perhaps almost everything. Of course, hadn't she known that all along? Goodbye is the hardest word.

Gaby threw off the blanket that was wrapped round her shoulders and stood up from the slovenly mess of her bed. How many days was it since she had spoken to anyone? Maybe she didn't have a voice any more. She picked up all the dirty plates and mugs from the floor and the windowsill and took them downstairs, dumping them in the sink. She put two more logs on to the fire, then opened the fridge. There was nothing inside it except three eggs, the bag of ground coffee and the mango, which was now overripe and oozing nastily out of its skin. She opened the cupboard and there was nothing there either, except tea, marmalade, golden sugar and porridge oats. In the larder there was a jar of stem ginger in syrup, half a bag of basmati rice, years past its sell-by date, a dented tin of octopus chunks and a packet of chicken stock cubes. She put on the kettle and, when it had boiled, poured the water over a stock cube. It would be better if she had bread to dunk into it, but she had put out the last of the baguette for the birds. She contemplated rescuing the pecked remains from the windowsill, but decided she wasn't that desperate. She sipped the stock thoughtfully, then ate two spoonfuls of marmalade. She looked at her watch. It was half past six and she was suddenly ravenous. She would be sad to leave this house, but she would have to quite soon, if only to find something to eat.

But she didn't know how she could return to her old life. She didn't know the way.

Thirty-eight

Exeter was a different city now. It was the landscape of his dazed, lovesick happiness. It was the place he walked through holding Lorna's hand, sometimes stopping to pull her roughly against him. In its little restaurants and bars, he sat opposite her and couldn't take his eyes off her. In crowded clubs where he talked and joked with friends and pretended he was there with them and not simply consumed with waiting, he could feel her come through the door even when his back was turned. When she spoke, though her voice was low and quiet, it pierced the air like a laser beam focused on him alone. In his room, which had previously been squalid and comfortless, he woke to see her soft hair spread on the pillow beside him and had to remember all over again that he wasn't dreaming.

'In a few days, term will be over,' he said one morning, drinking coffee in the café they'd first gone to after they'd met in the bookshop.

'Five.'

'I'll miss you.'

'Me you, too.'

'What will you do?'

'Oh, you know. The usual things. Buy last-minute presents, get things ready.'

'Is it hard?'

'Without Mum, you mean? It was pretty gloomy last year. Horrible. Dad moped and drank too much and tried to make up for that by getting everyone to play charades and board games. Phoebe got hysterically overexcited and then had a fit of crying that lasted for hours. Polly was really, really quiet. Dad's mother stayed in bed, and at the last minute Mum's father didn't come. Jo and I had our work cut out.'

'Let me guess. You did all the cooking and stuff.'

'We did it together. The turkey was dry and the sprouts were mushy and the potatoes were greasy. I'll do better this year. I didn't know what I was doing then.'

'But now you've had practice.'

'Lots of practice.'

'Do you ever mind?'

'What do you mean?'

'Being a surrogate mother.'

'But I'm not. Really. I'm nothing like her. They don't feel I'm their mother.'

'You are, though. I've been there, remember? You're the one they turn to now. They depend on you. And so does your father.'

'You mean surrogate mother, surrogate wife?'

'Kind of.' He picked up her hand and carried it to his lips. 'I don't mean it in a bad way.'

'You may be right, but what can I do? He's so lost and they're so young. We don't have many aunts and uncles or grandparents and sometimes I think they're hanging together as a proper family by a thread. It's my job, Ethan. I don't have a choice, do I? So I just have to get on with it.'

'But this should be the most carefree time of your life

yet every time one of them is ill or upset you go rushing back. It doesn't seem fair on you.'

'Fair? You mean I should get resentful and bitter? I don't see it like that. I don't want to.'

'No, you wouldn't. I can see it like that for you, though.'

'Well, thank you,' she said.

'I'm serious!'

'So am I – thank you.' She smiled up at him and pushed his unruly hair behind his ears.

'But anyway, here's the thing – I've had an idea. Come to us at Christmas.'

'To you!'

'Yes.'

'You mean leave them on their own?'

'No, of course not. I mean all of you come to us.'

'Everyone?'

'Yes, of course.'

'You're mad!'

'No. It'd be great.'

'Ethan, I've never met your family, never even set eyes on them, so it would be weird enough if it was just me. You're talking about my three sisters and Dad as well.'

'They'll love you. And you'll like them, I know. They're cool.'

'No, Ethan. What would the girls think, anyway, if they were grabbed out of their family home and taken to the house of strangers?'

'I'm not a stranger.'

'You've met them once.'

'We got on, didn't we?'

'Oh, they think you're on a par with Johnny Depp.'

'So . . .'

'We've been together for a week, Ethan.'

'What's that got to do with anything?'

'Do you know what I love about you?'

'What?'

'Your ability to –'

'No. I mean, do you realize what you just said?'

'Ssssh. Everyone's looking at us.'

'You said you loved me.'

'I said, do you know –'

'– what I *love* about you.'

'Ethan!'

'The L word! You've not said it. I've said it to you but you've never said it to me.'

'It's nearly time for my seminar.'

'Say it again, Lorna.'

'I'll pay for this, shall I?'

'Please.'

'What?'

'Say you love me.'

'If you insist.'

She leant across the table and took his face between her hands, studying him intently. She stared into his eyes and, for a dizzy moment, felt she was going to disappear inside him. 'I love you, Ethan Myers,' she said, loudly and emphatically enough for the neighbouring tables to hear her clearly. 'I love you very, very much. There. Will that do?'

She kissed him on the mouth, feeling his lips smile under hers, then become serious once more. Her hands tightened on his skull. His breath was hot in her throat.

'Oh,' he said, when she let him go and sat back. His face was wiped clean of any expression.

'I've got an idea,' she said.

'Mmm?'

'Do you want to hear?'

'Anything.'

'How about if I brought Polly, Phoebe and Jo up to London for the day to go Christmas shopping?'

'Yes,' he said dreamily. 'You can stay the night with us.'

'Maybe. You should talk to your parents, though. They might not fancy four strange girls descending on them out of the blue.'

'Mum would completely love it.'

'We can go on the London Eye or something. Or skating at Somerset House – that might be the best.'

'I'll arrange it. I'll arrange everything! A surprise day. Leave it with me. When, though? When will you come?'

'I'll let you know. Now I'm going. No, you don't need to come. Finish your coffee. What time are you meeting your father?'

'Midday. He's going to ring me before his train gets in and I'll be at the station. It's the oddest thing, him taking a day off. Positively unnatural.'

'Perhaps he misses you.'

'Yeah – I hope everything's OK at home.'

'Of course it is.'

'See you tonight?'

'Yes, tonight.'

'I can't wait,' he said.

She giggled, standing up and pulling on her coat. 'You have no choice.'

'Miss your seminar.'

'No! Anyway, your father's about to arrive.'

'We've got half an hour at least.'

'Ethan, I'll see you tonight.'

'Think of me.'

She bent towards him, her coat falling open. He saw the swell of her breasts and the delicate sharpness of her collarbone. He closed his eyes as her perfumed hair fell over his face and her lips brushed his.

'I'll think of you. Not a minute will go by that I'm not thinking of you. Enough?'

'Never enough.'

As soon as Connor saw Ethan walking towards him, thinner than he had been when he'd left and with a dreamy, vacant sweetness in his face, he knew he was in love. A pang passed through him; he understood Ethan's capacity to be hurt and wanted to warn him against caring too passionately. They embraced awkwardly on the station forecourt, passengers surging past them in both directions.

'Dad,' said Ethan. 'This is nice.'

'Well,' said Connor, 'I wasn't around when you left and we haven't seen each other – I thought it'd be good to catch you before . . .' He faltered under Ethan's candid gaze. 'The truth is,' he said, 'there's something I needed to talk to you about.'

'Oh, God. I knew it.'

Connor took his son by the forearm. 'It's all right,' he said, in his doctor's voice. 'Let's go and find somewhere to sit down and then we can talk.'

441

'It's Mum. She's ill. I knew there was something wrong when I last saw her. She's got cancer.'

'No. Gaby's fine.'

'Really?'

'Really.'

'And you're all right? You're not ill or anything? You look a bit peaky.'

'No, I'm perfectly all right. Where can we go? Do you want to eat?'

'You're having an affair. She's having an affair.'

'No!'

'I knew as soon as you said you wanted to come and see me in the middle of the week, a few days before I was coming home anyway, that something was going on.'

'Is this really the best place to talk about it?'

'I don't see why not.'

'Can't we at least find somewhere to sit down?'

'OK, if you want – there's a café over there with free tables. Will that do?'

'I suppose so,' said Connor, doubtfully.

'Come on, then. We can have lunch afterwards.'

'You might not want to have lunch with me afterwards,' said Connor, as they went into the café.

'For God's sake, Dad. Just tell me.'

'Shall I order coffee for both of us?'

'Whatever.'

'Just filter coffee?'

'I don't care. Mud and water would do. Just tell me.'

'Two coffees,' said Connor, to the woman behind the counter. 'One white and one black, please.' His knees were trembling and when he picked up the mugs his hands were shaking so much that coffee spilt over the rims and splashed his wrists. He walked over to the table Ethan had picked and put them down, then sat opposite his son.

'OK,' said Ethan. 'Tell me why you're here. What's up?'

Connor took a deep breath and made himself look his son in the eyes. 'It goes like this,' he said.

Thirty-nine

Gaby didn't hear a car, but as she sat in bed, draped in a blanket and drinking her first glass of wine since she'd arrived at the cottage, there was a loud knock at the door. She frowned and glanced at the time. A few minutes past nine – who could be here at this time of night? For a few seconds, she thought it might be Connor, but Connor would never arrive unannounced, just as he wouldn't ring her or write. She had often thought that in a relationship people tended to treat each other the way they wanted to be treated themselves. She had said she wanted to be left alone to think, and he would honour that to the letter. If it had been the other way round, she knew she would have been unable to resist contacting him. She would have sent him the postcards and left the messages on his voicemail that she would have liked to receive herself. She would have tried to get him back; she would never have let him leave.

So if it wasn't Connor, who was it? Who else knew she was here? Only Gilbert. Would Gilbert drive all the way out here to check on her? She scrambled out of bed, pulled the blanket round her and went into the bathroom to press her face against the window. There was a car outside, but she didn't recognize it. Maybe it was a burglar. Burglars didn't usually drive up to the front door and knock, though. She went downstairs slowly and stood by the door. 'Who is it?' she called.

'Me.'

'*Me.* That's no answer.'

'Come on, it's raining out here.'

'What if I don't want to see you just now?'

'Then tell me to go away.'

'Will you?'

'No, I'll sit in the car and wait. Come on, Gaby.'

'OK.' She opened the door and Nancy was standing there in her canvas jacket, with a neat holdall in one hand.

'Christ!' said Nancy. 'Are you all right?'

'Why?'

'You look – well, have you seen yourself?'

'I'm trying not to look in the mirror. I just haven't dressed today. Or washed or anything. Not for days, actually. It's quite nice sometimes, not making an effort. I wasn't expecting visitors.'

'Are you going to invite me in?'

'Do come in,' said Gaby, with exaggerated politeness. Nancy stepped over the threshold and put down her bag.

'How did you find me?'

'I spoke to Connor.'

'Oh.'

'He told me you'd gone away.'

'That's right.'

'And I persuaded him to tell me where you were. I needed to see you.'

'Shall we go into the kitchen?' Gaby took a pile of dirty

dishes off the table and dumped them in the sink, then gestured to a chair. 'Wine?'

'Thanks.'

'I can't offer you anything to eat. There's no food left in the house. My car won't start. Its battery went flat on the first day and I was ill anyway, and my phone doesn't work here so I've been housebound. It's been quite nice, really. Odd. I sometimes think I could easily go mad, you know. This wine's going straight to my head.'

'Drinking on an empty stomach – you look half starved.'

'You're the first person I've spoken to for – how long have I been here?'

'A week.'

'A week, then. Except to myself, a bit.'

'I've got jump-leads in my boot.'

'You would have. You probably have a first-aid kit, too, and a jack you know how to work.'

'I'll do it tomorrow morning.'

'Are you staying the night, then?'

'I've brought a sleeping-bag.'

'You can have the main room.'

'Shall I go and buy us some food?'

'No. It's not worth it. I'm probably leaving tomorrow, and I've no idea where a shop is that would be open at this time. You can have a stock cube, if you want.'

'A stock cube?'

'You have to dissolve it in boiling water, of course, but then it's like having soup. Or there's a tin of octopus chunks.'

'Hmm.'

'And some ancient rice, plus a few eggs in the fridge.'

'That's a bit more like it.'

'What?'

'Leave it to me.'

Gaby sat back, swaddled in her blanket and sipping wine, and watched Nancy busy herself, washing dishes, cooking rice in the chicken stock, wiping surfaces. The room was warm and she felt mellow and heavy-limbed. Nancy put two plates on the table, knives and forks, the bottle of wine. Then she set down a dish of steaming rice, over which she had arranged chunks of hard-boiled egg and octopus.

'Here we are,' she said.

'It's like nail stew,' said Gaby.

'What's nail stew?'

'It's a story my mother used to tell me. There was this old couple living in a hovel in a forest, and although they had worked hard all their lives, they were always poor and had to struggle to survive. There came a time when a great storm raged round their home, bringing trees crashing down, and they couldn't go out. Soon there was nothing left to eat. Then there was a knock at their door. When they opened it they found a weary traveller on the threshold, asking for shelter. They invited him in and said he was welcome to share their home, but they had nothing to offer him to eat. "Aha!" he said. "But I have a magic nail. I will make you nail stew." He set a cauldron of water to boil on the fire and then he searched the room. He found potato peelings in the sink and a bone, he found an old carrot on the floor and the end of a parsnip. There were some stale crusts in the cupboard, as well as

447

an onion and some grains of rice. He threw them all into the cauldron. Some dried herbs were hanging from the beams and he added them to the mixture. Then he pulled a rusty nail out of his pocket and threw that in too. After half an hour or so a delicious smell filled the hovel, and he ladled out three bowls of flavoursome stew. He said, "You can always make a meal, if you have a magic nail." Something like that anyway – my mother used to tell it better than that.'

'Eat up, Gaby.'

'This is all right, you know!' She shovelled hot forkfuls into her mouth, gulped red wine. 'God, I didn't know how hungry I was. Is there more?'

'Plenty.'

'Pity we don't have any pudding. We could eat the stem ginger.'

'Good idea.'

'So why are you here?' Gaby got up to fetch the jar from the cupboard.

'Two reasons. First, I was worried about you. I needed to make sure you were all right. Connor said you didn't want anyone to disturb you, but I thought – well, actually, I thought, What would Gaby do in my place? And the answer was that you would charge in.'

'So you charged in?'

'Yes.'

'And the other reason?'

'I thought – this might sound peculiar, given the circumstances. I thought that perhaps this was our second chance.'

'Second chance for what?'

'To be friends.'

'Oh. I see.'

'I was thinking. I never told anyone about what happened, not a soul; there was no one I could possibly tell. But if it hadn't been you I'd betrayed, I would have told you, if you see what I mean.'

'I think so.'

'I could have told you because you were the only person in the world who would understand me, understand what it felt like to me. Because you knew me so well.'

'Hmm,' said Gaby. She speared a piece of ginger and put it into her mouth, letting its sweetness dribble down her throat. A terrific happiness lurched in her stomach. She tried not to smile.

'What does "hmm" mean?'

'I've got a condition to lay down.'

'What condition?'

'That I don't forgive you.'

Nancy grimaced and opened her mouth to speak.

'Wait. We can't be friends if you're the sinner who's been forgiven and I'm the saint who's forgiven you. I'm not going to be the sweet, virtuous, noble one who's suffered and come through. I hate that.'

'I am the sinner, though.'

'Oh, fuck that,' said Gaby, with joyful gusto. 'You're just human like the rest of us. That's the trouble with you and Connor, you're so bloody principled. Rigid with principles – it's dangerous. You can't sway and bend, you have to resist or break.'

'I know you don't want to forgive me, but I want to be forgiven.'

449

'Forgive yourself, then. Shall I show you photos of Ethan? He's your non-godson after all.'

'I'd like that.'

'He's lovely, you know.' She drained the rest of her wine and felt her head spin. 'A humdinger. The very apple of my eye.'

'Gaby?'

'Yes.'

'You should go home to Connor.'

'Yes. I know I should, but nothing will ever be the same again.'

'Nothing ever is. It's called being alive.'

Later that night, Gaby woke and lay with her eyes wide open in the darkness, listening. She could hear no sound coming from Nancy's room. At last, she got out of bed and crept across the cold landing, dragging her duvet after her. She opened the door and moved into the room, just able to make out Nancy's shape on the far side of the double bed, like a caterpillar in the sleeping-bag. She climbed into the bed beside her, pulling her duvet over the two of them. She put her arms round her, laid her face against Nancy's back and closed her eyes.

There are compensations for the fact that the landscape darkens, she thought. There are mysteries in the shadows that the sunshine never shows. After a few minutes she fell asleep to the rise and fall of Nancy's breathing.

Forty

'I thought I'd find you in the kitchen.'

He dropped the wooden spoon with a clatter and spun round, taking one step towards her, then stopping. She could read the uncertainty on his face. 'Gaby! You're home. I didn't hear you come in.'

'What are you making?'

'What? Oh, custard.' He put out a hand and moved the pan off the hob. 'You know how Ethan loves it and he'll be home on Monday.'

'I know. And I know you cook for comfort too.'

'You look all in. And you've lost weight. Are you all right? Have you been eating properly? Sorry. That's not the way to welcome you back. I'm fussing because I don't know what to say. I'm so glad to see you, it's all I've been thinking about, yet now you're here I feel absurdly shy.'

'I feel shy too. How long have we been married?'

'Twenty years in February.'

'Wow! That sounds so respectable. We should have a party or something.'

'An anniversary party?' His eyes beseeched her.

'To celebrate making it this far and to toast the next twenty years.'

'I don't – are you telling me it's all right?'

'All right? We can do better than all right. I'm not

about to go anywhere else, Connor. If you want me, that is.'

'Want you!'

He crossed the room and made to put his arms round her, but she held him off. 'I tell you what, why don't we go out for a walk before it gets too dark? There are things we need to say to each other.'

'Right.'

'And when we come back we can go to bed.'

'Yes.'

'And then I'm going to take you out for a slap-up meal, with candlelight and champagne and all the other romantic clichés I can think of. A single red rose.'

'You know, Gaby, I was standing at the stove stirring the custard and feeling so wretched and empty inside, and now I feel so happy I want to weep. All this week I've been imagining what it would be like if you weren't here.'

'It'd be very quiet and tidy.'

'Quiet and tidy hell.'

'Come on. Walk.'

'Hug me first. Harder. So I know you're real.'

In the dusk, she held his hand. His fingers were warm in hers. She looked at him and he was smiling. 'Nancy came to get me,' she said.

'I know.'

'She told me I should come back to you.'

'Did she?'

'Yes. If I was her friend, would you mind? I mean, would it be too odd?'

'Nothing's too odd if it makes you happy. When Nancy first went away, I was relieved – yet every time you mentioned her name or talked about going to find her, this terrible shame and anxiety flushed through me, like poison in my veins. I'd feel nauseous for hours afterwards. Now I don't feel like that. Secrets can be terrible things.'

'And you don't feel anything for her?'

'Not the way you mean. You have nothing to fear, not from her or from anyone, I promise. But I like her. For years I couldn't feel that. She was abstract to me, in words that started with capital letters – the Terrible Mistake.'

'And before too long I want her to meet Ethan.'

'All right.' He hesitated. 'When you were away, I went to Exeter and told him.'

'Was he all right?'

'All right? Well, the first thing he did was sweep our cups of coffee on to the floor. Then he stood up and called me a tawdry wanker.'

'Tawdry wanker?'

'Yes. I thought he'd shatter into thousands of pieces, he was so angry. He looked at me as if I was the most contemptible creature on the face of the earth.'

'But then you talked?'

'He said I'd always acted so above everything, and I was just another hypocritical lecher after all. Then he marched off.'

'Oh. Did he come back, though?'

'Not for a long time. I didn't know what to do. After forty-five minutes or so, I called him on his mobile and left a message saying I'd go on waiting for him and I quite understood his reaction. He did come back, about

453

an hour after that. He was very stony with me. It's you. He's enormously protective of you. And after a bit he was allowing himself to be anxious about us and a bit hysterically humorous – you know the way he can get. By the end he was a bit calmer – for him this happened so long ago that it feels more like old history than a live issue.'

'But are you OK together?'

'I don't know about that. We will be, I hope. He feels I've let him down – that he had an idea of me that turned out to be false. He's right, of course.'

'Only a bit right. He's a creature of extremes. All one thing or all another. When you left him, did he seem all right?'

'I think so. Shaken, angry, rather emotional, but all right. You don't need to worry too much about him, Gaby. He's a resilient young man, in spite of his volatility. And he's in love. Stupid and awash with love. Head over heels.'

'With Lorna?'

'How did you know?'

'My maternal antennae. Is she in love back?'

'So it seems. He's talking of bringing her and her sisters to stay with us at Christmas. Why are we talking about Ethan instead of us?'

'Because that's what parents do.'

He stopped under a tree and took her hands in his.

'Sometimes it's important to talk about us, and say things out loud. I've been rehearsing this for a week but that doesn't make it less true. I've only ever loved you, Gabriella Graham. You were always the one, from the minute I saw you standing in the glare of my headlights, looking slightly mad. I know we've been together more than twenty years and we've got used to each other's ways and perhaps stopped seeing each other clearly or remembering what we feel. I know I did a terrible thing. But I never stopped loving you. You're standing there in your grubby clothes, with your peaky face and greasy hair –'

'Hey!'

'– and more lovely to me today than you were when we met. If you weren't here, the light in my life would go out.'

'Ooooh,' said Gaby, smiling at him. 'Here's my re-hearsed speech, then. You made mistakes but so did I – not a single big one like you, but lots and lots of silly, selfish ones and perhaps they add up to more in the end. I always knew I was lucky you chose me. But I chose you, too, and I choose you again now.' She giggled and dropped his hands. 'This is like getting married all over again, isn't it? I might break into song.'

'Maybe we needed to get married all over again.'

'Shall we go home now?'

'You're my home.'

'Time for bed.'

Forty-one

<u>16 December</u>

So anyway (Goldie says I begin all my sentences so anyway),
I'm not writing this to you any more because the you I was
writing to doesn't exist any longer, except inside me. I was
always writing to myself, but I think maybe I should give it to
Mum and Dad – not my ghost parents but my real ones, the
ones who've been with me all my life, in foul weather and fair.
I know I've been strange recently, and I know as well that they
might find some of the things in here a bit painful to read, but
I figure that most of it they know already. I think this is the last
entry. Maybe I'll give it to them at Christmas or New Year. Or
the winter solstice. My new beginning, which isn't really new or
a beginning. I used to think you could start again, be someone
different, find a key and open a door on to a whole other
world, but I don't really believe that. Not any more. The thing
that for most of my life I thought was a key wasn't, not really.
It was just another bit of the jigsaw puzzle – like that night-
mare jigsaw my grandmother gave me a few years ago, with
five hundred pieces and pictures on both sides. I found my
mother and she wasn't my mother; I found my father and he
wasn't my father. They were strangers. Nice strangers. Familiar
strangers. Like me and yet quite unlike as well. I hope Mum
and Dad won't mind that I visit them from time to time, get to
know them. There's no kind of threat there; I hope they know
that.

Or from Ethan. When I told them about meeting him, I could see it was hard. I hadn't expected that. But, then, I hadn't really thought about it, not from their point of view. Then Mum started talking about how she and Dad had always wanted to have a big family. When they got married, they started trying almost at once to have children. They assumed it would happen easily, and they had it all planned out, the way people do. They had names for girls and boys. Their future was crowded. They bought a house with spare rooms and a garden that was big enough for the swing and the climbing-frame. It just didn't happen. Every month, they went through a cycle of hope and despair. Mum got depressed. Dad drank too much. One by one their friends had children. Not them. They had godchildren and nephews and nieces and nice holidays and a neat house and plenty of time to go to films and the theatre. They were quite old by the time they managed to adopt me – old for first-time parents, I mean. They had waited for years and years. I don't know why we had never talked about it before. They had talked to me about how they met and fell in love, and they had often described my arrival, which, when I was younger, felt like a fairy-tale – the one thing they most wanted in all the world had been granted to them. But that space in between, of waiting and hoping, of absence, they hadn't discussed. I guess that's why hearing about Ethan was painful – I had the brother they hadn't been able to give me or something. Except he's not really a brother, is he? He's like a shadow brother, a might-have-been and what-if. Our childhoods, where we might have played together and squabbled, are over.

I liked him, though. That's not putting it right. I really liked him. I don't think it would be possible not to. He's totally

457

endearing. There's something unprotected about him, or uncensored or something. Maybe that was just the shock, though. He had only heard a few days ago and he still seemed a bit dazed. He kept looking at me and saying I was so like Connor and then he'd rub his face hard and smoke another cigarette. He smokes an awful lot and talks a lot too – in a random kind of way sometimes, as if the thoughts float into his head and he says them. At one point I discovered we were talking about something he'd read recently on how many heartbeats there are in a natural lifetime. I think that was because he was nervous. He seems clever – but not clever in the same way as his father. He's more jumbled up and poetic and romantic. Not precise and gloomy. He told me that when he was growing up he had always wanted a brother or sister and he used to try and persuade his parents to have another baby. But every time he said something like that he blinked and shook his head as if he was trying to clear it. I think he was remembering what it meant about his mother and father and Nancy. He said he's never met Nancy – or, at least, not since he was a baby. It must be weird for him. I grew up knowing I was adopted, but he grew up knowing he was a single child in a small, happy family and suddenly, bang!, right in the middle of his life this secret explodes. Me. I'm the secret. Like a little time-bomb that was always ticking away only no one heard me.

It's all about memories, isn't it? They say that blood is thicker than water. Memories are thicker than both. Memories are what binds you. I have no memories of Nancy, Connor or Ethan, only memories of their absence. But I remember Mum and Dad. Being there.

Forty-two

On the shortest day of the year – her favourite day because after that light returns – Gaby threw a party. It wasn't an ordinary Christmas party, though: she invited only a few people – Nancy and her lover, if she wanted to bring him, Stefan, Sonia and her parents, Ethan, of course.

'You're mad,' said Connor, when she told him, three days before it was due to happen. 'Completely, utterly mad. It's a truly terrible idea. Your worst ever.'

'Why?'

'It just is. I can't think of anything more awful than putting us all together in one room. It's like a psychological experiment about embarrassment and pain. You can't be serious. You've gone too far this time.'

'It might be lovely,' said Gaby, although she was beginning to feel anxious about it herself. 'Healing. Anyway, I've asked everyone already. I can't just cancel.'

'You certainly can. You're not telling me they said yes.'

'They're all coming, except I don't know about Nancy's bloke.'

Connor stared at her with an expression of absolute bemusement. 'What about Stefan?'

'Stefan says he's looking forward to meeting Sonia.'

'And is he looking forward to meeting Nancy?'

'Actually, they've already met.'

'What?'

'They've already met.'

'Why didn't you tell me this?'

'I only knew yesterday and you were away at your conference. I'm telling you now. He said it was interesting.'

'Interesting?'

'He really seemed fine. Quite cheerful. He said he might bring a friend to the party. I don't know what he meant by "friend", or even if it was a man or woman. I didn't want to ask.'

'That doesn't sound like you. Have you told Ethan?'

'No. Not yet.'

Ethan also thought it was a mad idea, but he seemed impressed rather than appalled by it. His only objection was that 21 December was the day that Lorna and her three sisters were spending in London.

'Then they'll have to come as well,' said Gaby, recklessly.

'Wow. It'll be a bit like experimental theatre.'

'Is that good?'

'You never know until it happens – that's one of the points.'

Gaby bought herself a long red dress with flared sleeves that cost far too much. She ordered a crate of sparkling wine and decorated the house with lights and streamers. The Christmas tree tilted under the weight of its gaudy baubles. On the evening, half an hour before everyone arrived, she lit candles and made a fire, then prowled round the house nervously, waiting for the guests.

Ethan arrived first, with Lorna and her three sisters, whom he introduced. Gaby bent down first to the two smaller girls, who hovered nervously on the threshold. Her heart was full of the knowledge that they had no mother. One had her plait in her mouth and was sucking it noisily and glaring. The other held Jo's hand tightly and jiggled as if she wanted the toilet. 'Come in,' she said. 'I'm Gaby. Put your things upstairs. Ethan will show you where everything is. OK?'

'Are you Ethan's mother?' asked Phoebe.

'That's right.'

'Did you know he pretended he was a doctor?'

'Oh! That was a very odd thing to do.'

She stood up and held out her hand to the third girl. 'You must be Jo. I'm really pleased to meet you. Come inside. Let me take your coat.'

At last, she allowed herself to look at Lorna, who was standing behind her sisters. Ethan had told her she was beautiful, but she wasn't, not really. Yet when she smiled, her smooth, oval face became radiant and you couldn't take your eyes off her, and when she moved inside the house Gaby saw that she carried herself like a ballet dancer. Ethan, following them all, clasping several bulky shopping-bags to his chest, was clumsy with eagerness. Love made him uncoordinated; happiness made him stumble helplessly on the stairs. Lorna, beside him, took his hand.

It seemed like a play to Gaby, taking place on the brightly lit stage she had prepared, everyone nervous but with their parts to play. Nancy came alone, brisk with anxiety and marching up to Ethan at once. Gaby knew how she steeled herself to be like this: apparently confident and assured. Sonia, white-faced, arrived with her parents and a friend she called Goldie, who guided her through the door and stood protectively close to her to make sure she was all right. Connor wore a black suit like an undertaker's and poured the wine. Phoebe and Polly sat under the Christmas tree and whispered in each other's ears, giggling. Stefan arrived late, carrying an enormous bunch of flowers, and tripped over the rug in the living room. His shirt was inside out.

The stage-fright took time to subside. Gaby managed them all into groups, steering people together, making introductions, easing them into conversation. So, now, Ethan was talking to Nancy, looking seriously into her face and nodding. There was Connor with Sonia, but every so often glancing her way as if he needed her permission; then with Ethan, anxious and eager; then with Sonia's mother, who seemed quite calm, and her father, who was stiff with nerves. Gaby couldn't hear what they were saying, but at one point she saw Sonia's mother lay a hand gently on Connor's arm as if to comfort him and she smiled to herself, satisfied. There was Lorna talking to Sonia, that transfiguring smile on her young face; Ethan talking to Goldie; Stefan showing Jo some magic trick with a pack of cards that he pulled out of his pocket, spilling slim lengths of rope over the carpet as he did so. Nobody looked unhappy. Perhaps it was working, she thought; on the darkest day of the year comes good cheer. She went round the room pouring wine into glasses, handing out little eats, murmuring pleasantries, moving on.

'Have we met?' asked Sonia's mother, narrowing her eyes and staring into her face, but Gaby shook her head and told her she must be very proud of her daughter.

'Oh, I am.' But she sounded sad.

'And,' added Gaby, suddenly, insistently, 'you should be very proud of yourselves, too, because you've done such a good job as parents.'

She watched the woman's face relax, smile.

'Thank you,' she said. 'That's a kind thing to say. Especially this evening. Especially coming from you.'

Now Stefan was in the corner with Sonia and her father. He was showing them his rope trick. Sonia threw back her head and laughed. Her father moved away, but Sonia stayed talking to Stefan. She was animated, intense, and he was bending towards her, with that shy, vague smile on his face. Connor was with Nancy, Sonia's parents with Ethan, Lorna and Jo. As on a carousel, people moved slowly round the golden room. Now all the teenagers were grouped together, laughing, swapping opinions. Stefan was sitting on the floor with Phoebe and Polly, showing them tricks; their faces were rapt with attention. Stefan's friend – very definitely a woman, with a laugh like a bell pealing – had arrived and was talking to Nancy. Gaby watched them all. Her heart was full. She didn't know if it was happiness or sorrow that made it so.

Now Nancy and Connor were standing together with Sonia's mother and father. The two sets of parents. Gaby stared at them, unable to tear away her eyes, then had to leave the room. She went into the downstairs cloakroom and washed her face in cold water, then sat on the closed lavatory seat, resting her head in her hands. She waited like that for several minutes, hearing through the door the hum of conversation, the lilts of laughter. When she returned to the living room, the smile was back on her face, and she picked up the wine bottle that could take her from group to group so that she didn't need to stop and talk.

Sonia's parents were making to leave. She saw Sonia talking to them as they pulled on their coats; the girl's face was tipped up towards them and she looked suddenly very young and vulnerable. Her mother put her arms round her daughter and they stayed like that, in a freeze-frame, while the party went on around them. Then they separated, tearful and smiling.

'Thank you,' said Sonia's father, coming up to Gaby and shaking her hand for a long time, returned to the awkwardness of his arrival. 'Thank you, and I have to say that you've been very unselfish. I don't think I could have done this, in your shoes.'

'Nonsense!' said Gaby, blushing. 'It's been a pleasure.'

She saw them out, then returned to the room. Polly was sitting on the sofa now, her head on Jo's shoulder, as though she was about to fall asleep. Stefan was talking to his new friend, who had her arm through his and looked entirely comfortable.

'Excuse me,' a tentative voice said behind her.

She turned. 'Sonia. Hello.'

'I met you, didn't I? I'm not dreaming. You were the woman in the café.'

'That's right. Forgive me.'

'Forgive you? What for?'

'I trampled over everything.'

464

'You made all this happen.'

'In a way.'

'I think you're brave and amazing.'

'That's a very generous thing to say.'

'It's true.'

For a moment, Gaby stared at the girl – Connor's daughter, Ethan's sister, the girl she had never had – and couldn't speak. Then she smiled. 'Thanks,' she said. 'I appreciate that.'

'Oh, well –'

'And, Sonia?'

'Mm?'

'I'm very glad you're here.'

There were tears in the girl's eyes. 'Really? You mean that?'

'Yes. I do.'

Nancy approached her as Sonia turned away.

'Thanks for coming,' Gaby said to her. 'I know you probably think it was an insane idea.'

'Of course it was. I expect no less. I think we were all very obedient, don't you?'

'Unexpectedly so.'

'And courageous.'

'Was it so awful?'

'No, not awful. It was – actually, it was almost unbearable.'

'Oh.'

'I mean that in a good way.'

'Good?'

'Because we all bore it, didn't we?'

'I guess we did. Yes, we all bore it.'

Now Ethan and Lorna were standing beside her. He put his arm round her shoulders. 'Are you OK?' he asked.

'Me? Fine.'

'Really OK? About everything?'

'Really OK about everything. I promise. How about you?'

'This must be the very weirdest evening of my entire life and I've known some weird ones. But I'm fine. We're fine. Aren't we?' He looked at Lorna.

'Yes, we are,' Lorna said. 'We're just fine.'

Gaby saw their hands touch; their fingers curled together. She smiled. 'How did you two meet, anyway?' she asked them.

'I saw her,' said Ethan, joyfully, ready to tell anyone. 'I saw her walking along a street at night and I fell in love with her on the spot. Long before I met her or knew her name, I was smitten.'

'How romantic.'

'What about you and your husband?' asked Lorna, shyly.

'How did we meet?' asked Gaby, smiling into the young face in front of her. 'Ah, well, it was all a bit dramatic. We met by an accident.'

'By accident?'

'By *an* accident. I remember it as clearly as if it happened yesterday.'

'Go on, then,' said Ethan, resignedly; he had heard it all many times before.

'It's a long story, for another place and time.'

Ethan and Lorna moved away, still holding hands, and Gaby stood on her own, sipping her wine. It was a long story and it had happened a long time ago, but she found herself thinking of it now and remembering the young woman she had been then, the future unfurling before her; the young man she had met in a sunken lane by the smoking wreckage of a car. Now Connor glanced up and gave the small smile, almost invisible, that he reserved for her. She looked around at the figures before her. Her life was in this room, the people she loved and who loved her. She pressed one hand against the bruise of her heart.

Behind her she heard a few notes from the piano and turned. Ethan was sitting on the stool, letting his hands drift across the keys while Lorna, Sonia and Goldie stood round him.

'Play a Christmas carol,' called Jo, boisterously.

'"We Three Kings",' said Phoebe. 'That's my favourite. I can play it on my recorder.'

Ethan started to play. Stefan, from the other side of the room, began to sing with the theatrical unselfcon-sciousness of the shy, and one by one everyone joined in, even Connor, or perhaps he was just mouthing the words – Gaby couldn't tell from where she stood. Soon they were in a circle round the piano, all singing 'Silent Night', 'Once in Royal David's City' and 'O Come, All Ye Faithful', while the candles threw a soft, guttering light over the scene. All except Gaby who stood back and watched them.

'"In the Bleak Midwinter",' said Nancy. 'That's beautiful.'

As Ethan played, Gaby slipped unseen from the room. Their ragged, lusty voices followed her down the hall and through the front door. Outside it was cold, dark, clear.

She gazed up at the sky and the brilliant stars. At the moon, which lay low and large on the horizon, shining down on her and bathing her in its mysterious light. She turned back to the house. Through the uncurtained window, she could see the Christmas tree and, beyond that, the group of people singing. Their mouths were open and their heads tipped back. Firelight and candlelight lit their faces. They were beautiful to her, timeless, and tears came to her eyes.

She didn't know how long she stood like that, watching them. A thought came into her mind and she held it there: she could leave now, simply walk down the road away from them all and never come back. Then she took a deep breath and made her way slowly towards her home. She pushed the front door quietly and went into the warm, crowded room. She opened her mouth to join in the singing, and nobody had even noticed that she had been gone, or saw that now she had returned, to be with them once more.

P.S.

This is the last time I'm going to write in here. For a while I needed to pour out my feelings – to the mother I had never met, to the parents I had always had, to myself above all – but I don't think I do any more. The urgency has died away, the frantic need to know and the fear of what I would discover. So what have I discovered? Not who I am. I don't think one ever fully does that. Maybe something about love: Mum and Dad have loved me without ever asking for anything in return; they loved me so much they were even willing to let me go. Perhaps one day I can be a parent like that. That's what you do with love, you hand it on. You receive love and you give it, and stronger than genes, thicker than blood, it binds us and it sets us free. That's what I believe, anyway.

So I guess this is the end. Although it's never really the end, is it? Just, the words stop.

Nicci Gerrard

ABOUT NICCI GERRARD

Ever since I can remember, I wanted to write and yet – like many people I know – I waited a long time before I actually began. I thought that there would be a perfect time (it's like having children, there is never a perfect time), and that I could somehow arrive at a place that was clear, free and still, far from the messy, incessant processes of life.

When I was a child growing up in Worcestershire, I gobbled up books, any books, whatever I could lay my hands on – and I wrote stories. I used to lie under my covers with a torch, scribbling with a blunt pencil onto loose pieces of lined paper, although in the morning the words never turned out to be quite so wonderful as they had seemed the night before. I wrote a diary intermittently which, when I came to re-read it years later, I found to be excruciatingly self-conscious, gushingly romantic and often anxious and self-pitying. And I went on long solitary walks and gushed out hundreds, even thousands, of poems, heavily influenced by W.B. Yeats and T.S. Eliot, full of alliteration and a sense of adolescent longing. But for some reason, as I became older, writing became less joyful and much harder; I lost all confidence in myself.

'I gobbled up books, any books, whatever I could lay my hands on'

I studied English at university; looked after emotionally deprived children in a home in Sheffiield; did a further degree; taught adult education courses; disappeared off to LA; returned with my tail between my legs; became a freelance journalist and reviewer; co-founded and edited a magazine devoted to women's books and arts, *Women's Review*; became the stand-in literary editor of the *New Statesman*; the deputy literary editor of the *Observer*. And all the time what I wanted to do – one day, somewhere round the corner and out of sight – was to write, and all the time, I wasn't writing.

'I had a demanding job, a large, young family, a chaotic house, an overdraft, a life that was full of nappies'

I married, had two children, got divorced, met Sean, married again and had two more children. By now I was a feature writer and excutive editor on the *Observer*. I had a demanding job, a large, young family, a chaotic house, an overdraft, a life that was full of nappies, dirty washing, odd socks, snotty noses, broken dreams, night terrors, finger painting, swings and slides, an incipient sense of panic – and it was at this point that I at last began to do what I had failed to do for so long: write anything that was longer than 2,000 words.

In the corners of days and in absolute secret, Sean and I wrote our first Nicci French thriller, *The Memory Game*, in 1995. Our writing day since then has followed more or less the same pattern, which is to say, no pattern at all, for we seem to live in a house where all compartments have broken down – work, marriage, children, everything seeping into everything else. I have always hated Cyril Connolly's famous dictum that the enemy of promise is 'the pram in the hall'. For me, the pram (or buggy, trike and skate board) in the hall brought a pell-mell creative happiness that neat single life never could. (I've always preferred the model of Mrs Gaskell, who apparently worked in a study next to the kitchen, a child under her desk and soup bubbling on the hob.)

Now we've just finished our tenth Nicci French thriller. *The Moment You Were Gone* is my third solo novel. But I try not to describe myself as 'a writer' – instead, I say that I write. Writing is not really a career, it's not even a choice; it's more like a compulsion, and there are times when it feels a bit mad: to sit alone in your study hour after hour and day after day, grappling with words, erasing them, beginning afresh. Each time that I finish a novel I am ripped by a terror that I'll never be able to manage it again – and then what will I do? And who will I be?

THE MOMENT YOU WERE GONE

In our family, there was a secret. Like many secrets, much of its power came from the fact that it was hidden and worked its effects surreptitiously. For many years I did not know about it, but looking back now I can see what a powerful impact if had on all of us. Discovering it sent a tremor through all our lives. I must have been about nine, and we were on holiday in the Scottish highlands – or at least, I think we were, although perhaps I've invented that – and sitting in our old white camper-van, whose registration number I still remember. Perhaps it was raining outside, and perhaps we were eating jam doughnuts and drinking hot chocolate. I don't know though – the memory crumbles when I try to catch hold of it. However, I am certain that one of us four siblings asked my mother exactly how old her brother, our uncle, was. When she told us, there was a baffled pause as we calculated that only five months separated them, and that wasn't possible. Was it?

'The tall, conscientious woman whom my mother called 'Mummy' until the day she died, was her biological aunt'

'It's because I was adopted.'

It's hard to explain why this announcement – which came out of the blue and cast a clarifying light over everything – felt so shocking then and even now, all these years later, feels painful. I can't really remember what happened next, whether the full story was told to us at once or we extracted the details bit by bit. But the bare bones went like this: my mother's biological mother, Nancy, died when my mother was a few months old. Her biological father, Nancy's husband Bob, did not – for reasons which remain mysterious – choose to keep his tiny daughter. Instead, she was brought up by Nancy's sister and her husband. The tall, conscientious woman whom my mother called 'Mummy' until the day she died, was her biological aunt; her quiet, endearing father was her uncle; her beloved brother was actually her cousin.

'She wasn't even supposed to talk to her parents about it, nor about Nancy'

When my grandmother eventually told my mother that she was adopted, she was six. My grandmother said to her, 'but we don't talk about it', a sentence that bound my mother to secrecy more closely than any oath; consequently, she felt unable to tell anyone at all. For this was over seventy years ago when adoption – even the kind like my mother's, when she was born to married parents and taken in after a tragic death by her own close family – was something not to be discussed. She wasn't even supposed to talk to her parents about it, nor about Nancy, her blood-mother, or Bob, her spectral biological father who was still alive somewhere, but had dropped soundlessly from her life and did not want to claim her. As a girl, my mother was hungry for affection and eager to win her parents' approval; she pledged herself to silence and pushed the secret underground.

Because my grandparents worked in Africa, she was sent away to boarding school in England at five, where she was ferociously and continually homesick – sometimes I think my mother was homesick for almost all of her childhood, not just at school, but at home as well, because for her the notion of home and belonging was so complicated and fraught with danger. Love could not be taken for granted: she had to win it.

'Only now, when she is in her seventies and her parents are long dead, is she beginning to speak about it'

As an adult, she told my always-steadfast father, of course, but she did not tell her four children until surprised into disclosure, nor her closest friends. Only now, when she is in her seventies and her parents are long dead, is she beginning to speak about it, and even then it is with a reluctance, as if she is breaking a promise she made all those decades ago. It is very hard for her to shake off the belief she was brought up with, that her adoption had to remain secret, unspoken. Nancy, her unmentionable blood mother, always haunted her, though she knew so little about her. She never found out what she looked like, except for the fact that she was vivaciously lovely and widely loved (as is my mother). Neither did she own anything that had belonged to her. It was as if Nancy had been erased, leaving behind her changeling daughter as the only evidence of her too-short life. And my mother believed – probably hoped and also maybe feared as well – that she resembled Nancy. She adored her adopted parents and her brother, but she certainly wasn't like them: they were tall while she was small; they were reserved, shy and dignified and she was full of a restless vitality and emotional intensity.

'Her unmentionable blood mother always haunted her'

My mother was always passionately loving and unconditional. After a childhood largely spent in dormitories and countries far from her own parents, she had to invent the idea of home and family for herself, from scratch, just as she had to teach herself how to cook. She welcomed other people into our house with a spontaneous, full-hearted generosity that I can see now partly came from knowing what it was like to feel acutely homesick. She cooked feasts for crowds of us, and food became a symbol of care and nurture. Perhaps she was being the mother she would have liked to have had herself, and in this way she was also rescuing herself from her anxious childhood. I think now that my mother, instead of looking for herself in her past, searched for herself in the future – in the family she created, the home she made, the children to whom she passed Nancy on.

We inherited her secret, and it took me a long time before I gave it to anyone else, thus repeating a pattern of denial and an odd kind of fear. Even now, I write this with difficulty; pushing against the grain, treading on shifting ground. We didn't talk about it very much as a family (although in our family we talked compulsively

about almost everything), and I only once mentioned it
to my grandmother, towards the end of her life, because

'There is something primal about this need to find our blood relatives'

I felt that the last vestiges of the 'truth', whatever that is,
would die with her and that somehow it was important
to be in possession of whatever information there was. I
think I felt then that there was a simple answer, which,
like a cure, could heal my mother's hurt. It was a friendly
but entirely unsuccessful conversation in which I learned
nothing new; the past was going to keep its secrets. But
like my mother, I became haunted by the idea of Nancy.
(Curiously, I never really thought about my biological
grandfather, Bob, nor about the other children he
apparently had in his second marriage.) I imagined what
Nancy looked like; I envisaged her as a link in the chain
that tied her, my mother, myself and then, later, my own
daughters together. There are certain physical traits that
I share with my mother (down to odd, precise details:
we both use flamboyant hand gestures when excited; we
both had trembling right legs when we went into labour),
and I wonder if Nancy had them too. If she hadn't died,
she would simply be my grandmother, ordinary and
taken for granted and fading over time. Because she
was snuffed out, and her memory forbidden, she has the
bright and constant allure of a myth.

Like a bubble winking its way to the surface, the idea of
writing a novel in which adoption plays a central role

came gradually. In *The Moment You Were Gone*, Sonia's situation is quite unlike my mother's of course (for a start, her adoption was never a secret; also, Sonia came from a messy betrayal, whilst my mother was born into a traditional family and in her alternative life might well have been the eldest of several children if Nancy had not died). But Sonia is consumed by the need to discover where she came from, feeling that her own identity will remain partly hidden from her until she finds out her origins. There is something primal about this need to find our blood relatives: Sonia wants to know if she has her mother's eyes and hair, her father's hands; she needs to source her genes and her DNA and feel that she is physically connected to the past – and this need often increases, rather than diminishes, as we grow older. When we're young, we like to think of ourselves as uniquely individual, not cut from the cloth of our parents; later, the sense of continuity is consoling, even rather miraculous.

'She found that she was at last able to stop simply blaming him for everything'

A year or so ago, I met a woman who, in her late twenties, had finally tracked down her biological father, after many years of obsessively agonising over him. She didn't actually want to meet him and have what she called 'the conversation' (why didn't you want me, why did you leave me, how could you...?); she simply wanted to see him and know what he looked like. She found out where he lived and watched him come and go. He wasn't charismatically beautiful (as she had sometimes imagined), nor a foul monster (as she had also imagined), but an ordinary, ageing man, a bit down-at-heel and drab, with a ratty leather jacket, thinning hair and the beginnings of a paunch. He made her feel sad. As soon as she had seen him, he stopped being the ghost that haunted her imagination, and became a flawed human being, and she found that she was at last able to stop simply blaming him for everything that had ever gone wrong for her, and to imagine instead what it must have been like for him.

But my mother's gift for creating a home and bestowing hospitality, I gave to Gaby – who is messy, impulsive, often foolish, but who is full of the kind of irrepressible, generous love that my mother has always had.

There's a Nancy in the book as well, of course. Cool, contained and upright, she has the name but not the imagined character of my biological grandmother, who died seventy-five years ago but I feel has not yet been laid to rest.

This book is about friendship, motherhood and love, but it is also about identity and belonging. It is dedicated to my father and mother: the rock and the flame.

NICCI GERRARD

THINGS WE KNEW WERE TRUE

At sixteen Edie knows things. She knows that her mother is charming and beautiful, that her older sister Stella is the golden girl of the family, and that her father – clumsy, quiet Vic – is loving, gentle, sometimes detached. And she knows she loves Ricky, even if her parents don't approve.

But one autumn evening when Vic fails to return home from work, Edie's world is suddenly turned upside down. Her life is changed forever, the certainties of her childhood destroyed in one terrible moment.

For twenty years Edie wonders about the truth. What really happened to her father? What became of her lost teenage love? When she reunites with her sisters in their mother's house to sift through their childhood belongings, not only is Edie forced to face her unresolved past, she makes a passionate and dangerous attempt to return to it. And, it looks as though the truth of what happened all those years ago will finally be revealed.

NICCI GERRARD

SOLACE

Irene's husband has chosen another lover.

And over time, Adrian nurtures his deceit and with his new lover, Frankie, he finds the courage to leave Irene and their three children.

Irene is, at first, hurt, angry, broken. If it wasn't for the children, she believes her life would come apart. Their agony, and hers, seems almost too much to bear. But as she battles through the daily routine, the promise of a new life gradually emerges.

She discovers a different Irene – not the endlessly selfless, chore-laden wife and mother – but a woman with the possibility of love. And a future that only she can dictate. Would she really want Adrian back, even if he were to leave Frankie and return to her?

'Beguiling, poignant, wonderful' *Sunday Express*

NICCI GERRARD

If you enjoyed this book, there are several ways you can read more by the same author and make sure you get the inside track on all Penguin books.

Order any of the following titles direct:

9780141017532 SOLACE   £6.99

'Gerrard brings tenderness and insight into a story of surviving everyday life'
Harpers and Queen

9780141012476 THINGS WE KNEW WERE TRUE   £7.99

'A moving and perceptive insight into deception and renewal' *Sunday Mirror*

Simply call Penguin c/o Bookpost on **01624 677237** and have your credit/debit card ready.
Alternatively e-mail your order to **bookshop@enterprise.net**. Postage and package is free
in mainland UK. Overseas customers must add £2 per book. Prices and availability subject
to change without notice.

*Visit www.penguin.com and find out first about forthcoming titles, read
exclusive material and author interviews, and enter exciting competitions.
You can also browse through thousands of Penguin books and buy online.*

IT'S NEVER BEEN EASIER TO READ MORE WITH PENGUIN

*Frustrated by the quality of books available at Exeter station for his journey back to
London one day in 1935, Allen Lane decided to do something about it. The Penguin
paperback was born that day, and with it first-class writing became available to a
mass audience for the very first time. This book is a direct descendant of those original
Penguins and Lane's momentous vision. What will you read next?*

He just wanted a decent book to read ...

Not too much to ask, is it? It was in 1935 when Allen Lane, Managing Director of Bodley Head Publishers, stood on a platform at Exeter railway station looking for something good to read on his journey back to London. His choice was limited to popular magazines and poor-quality paperbacks – the same choice faced every day by the vast majority of readers, few of whom could afford hardbacks. Lane's disappointment and subsequent anger at the range of books generally available led him to found a company – and change the world.

'We believed in the existence in this country of a vast reading public for intelligent books at a low price, and staked everything on it'
Sir Allen Lane, 1902–1970, founder of Penguin Books

The quality paperback had arrived – and not just in bookshops. Lane was adamant that his Penguins should appear in chain stores and tobacconists, and should cost no more than a packet of cigarettes.

Reading habits (and cigarette prices) have changed since 1935, but Penguin still believes in publishing the best books for everybody to enjoy. We still believe that good design costs no more than bad design, and we still believe that quality books published passionately and responsibly make the world a better place.

So wherever you see the little bird – whether it's on a piece of prize-winning literary fiction or a celebrity autobiography, political tour de force or historical masterpiece, a serial-killer thriller, reference book, world classic or a piece of pure escapism – you can bet that it represents the very best that the genre has to offer.

Whatever you like to read – trust Penguin.